MW01268360

REVIVING
POTUS 1

by
Gil Hudson

Copyright

Edited by Paula F. Howard, A Howard Activity, LLC

Interior design by Paula F. Howard

Cover design by Bob Hurley. Impressions.com

Aha! Press, an imprint of A Howard Activity, LLC

PRINTED IN THE UNITED STATES OF AMERICA

ISBN: 978-8-9852263-3-1

Available for purchase on Amazon.com and at TheWritersMall.com

Dedication

I dedicate this book to my devoted wife, Aletha Ann Hudson who has spent the last 52 years of her life supporting and encouraging me in every new adventure I have embarked upon. Without her understanding and encouragement, this work would not have been possible.

Acknowledgement

I wish to thank and acknowledge my niece, Jenny Hale, who provided me with the sound and steady advice I needed. To receive support from such a nationally-known and successful author gave me the confidence I needed to complete my work.

I would also like to thank those many friends and acquaintances who where willing to read the earlier versions of this book and provide me with honest assessments and suggestions that turned out to be invaluable insights.

Part 1

Chapter 1

April 2, 1798

The door to the clinic banged open and five disheveled men rushed in carrying a stretcher on which a bloody young boy was crying in agony, blood pouring from a wound in his left leg. "We need help! Get the doctor . . . he's been shot!" One of the men yelled as they placed the stretcher in the middle of the clinic floor. The other patients in the waiting area jumped back to make room as nurse Aletha White ran over to the boy. Dr. Palidore Montgomery came running from an examination room at the sound of the commotion.

"Sam, run back to room two and tell Kevin to get out, so we can get this boy in there. You men, help me move him." Four of the men grabbed the stretcher again and passed a shaken Kevin in the hallway as they rushed into the exam room placing the stretcher and the boy on a high table.

"Thank you, now please leave, so nurse White and I can work." As the men began leaving the room, one man remained.

"I am not leaving!"

"Who are you?" the doctor asked.

"I'm his father and the one who shot him."

"Then stay out of my way, and don't talk," Dr. Montgomery said. "Whoever put the tourniquet on, saved his life so far, but he is bleeding badly." He nodded to his nurse, "Aletha, cut his pant leg off, and let's clean this up."

Aletha moved swiftly as instructed and continued working rapidly on the wound without need for further instruction. The doctor noticed the boy about to nod off and yelled, "Hey! Not yet! Stay awake, Son . . . you need to stay awake!" Aletha put a cold washcloth on the boy's sweat and tear-stained face as his eyes opened again. Palidore pressed down on a specific spot below the tourniquet with his thumb. "Still bleeding too much. Aletha, run to my office, and get me the brown satchel near my desk, quickly please."

Nurse White did as requested; when she returned, she placed the bag on a small table next to the high one Palidore was working on. The boy's head was lying still; the father was standing anxiously to the side with pain in his eyes.

"Now, listen carefully to me. Take out the jar labeled 'A' and unscrew the top. Be careful not to spill any contents." Aletha carefully followed instructions. Palidore looked at the man. "Sir, come over here and keep your son awake, slap him, if necessary, but do not let him doze off." The man stepped next to his son on the opposite side of the table and began talking to him and touching him to keep him awake.

"Aletha, give me a scalpel; I need to open this wound up more to see where the bleeding is coming from. I am afraid the bullet may have hit his femoral artery, so this may be difficult to control." He inserted a retractor and enlarged the wound opening to see inside the leg as blood continued to seep out in with a slight pumping movement. Nurse White pressed against the edges of the wound with gauze attempting to keep the area free of new blood so the doctor could look.

"Now, listen to me, Aletha. Take a spoonful of that powder from Jar A and gently spread it out on the tray next to me." She did as instructed. Palidore took his finger and pressed against the powder, then placed his finger into the wound, repeating this several times. Each time his finger hit the wound, the blood would immediately congeal and appeared almost to freeze. Slowly, the bleeding stopped except for a small amount still leaking from the artery. Palidore examined it closely to see if his powder had taken effect, but when he touched it, blood spirted out hitting Aletha in the face. Quickly, Palidore applied the tiniest touch of the powder directly onto the artery. Almost instantly, the blood congealed and froze. He looked carefully. All bleeding had stopped.

"Quickly, now, sit him up!" Palidore commanded. Nurse White and the boy's father helped the boy into a sitting position on the table. "You have him? Hold him up. I've got to prepare something." Palidore took another small jar from the bag labeled "B" and put a small amount in a glass of water, mixed it, and handed it to his nurse.

"Make him drink all of this." She put the glass to the boy's lips and after multiple sips, he had drunk the entire contents. "Ease him back down on the table," Palidore said. "He can rest and sleep now if he likes." They laid him back down and Aletha washed his face with a wet cloth.

"You're okay now," Aletha said in a soft, calm voice. "You're going to be fine. Just relax and rest." When she looked up, she saw the father's tears streaming down his cheeks and watched as he began sobbing almost uncontrollably. She went to him and guided him to a chair along the wall.

"You will have to leave us for now, sir, we are not done here, yet, however, we must not disturb him with your upset. You can sit right outside the door." The father nodded and quietly left the room.

Aletha resumed her position next to the doctor who instructed her, "Please take some of that peroxide in the blue bottle and clean the wound. It's something new that should help prevent infection."

"I know what it is, Palidore, you told me all about it when you were able to acquire it."

"Right. Well, just pat some around the wound and wipe gently with some gauze." She followed his instructions while Palidore manipulated the wound opening again. He could now see the artery clearly and spoke in a whisper. "The bullet, indeed, nicked his femoral artery. I have put some of my special compound on it and sealed it, but I am uncertain about what might happen when we release the tourniquet. I am going to try and strengthen the artery, so please, open the jar that is labeled 'C' and take a small amount and place it in a small dish. Next, add a small amount of water, maybe only a teaspoon." Aletha stirred the mixture, creating a thick solution.

"Now take a small amount of gauze and soak it with the solution." Aletha followed his direction, but Palidore interrupted her. "A much smaller piece, please." When she had the new piece ready, Palidore held out his hand to receive it, and gently wrapped it around the artery. As they watched, the gauze began to slowly shrink and formed what appeared to be a perfect bandage around the artery. "Okay, let's hope this holds," he said while reaching to untie the tourniquet and holding his breath. A few seconds passed before Palidore was able to breathe normally again. He looked over at his faithful nurse and smiled.

"Good job, Aletha, I think, with God's help, we have saved this boy's life. Now, let us clean this up, sew up the wound, and apply a bandage around his leg."

"I can do that," Aletha smiled. "Why don't you go inform the boy's father." Palidore, nodded and walked out into the hallway where the father was leaning against the wall.

"It is a bit of a miracle, but I believe your son will recover. He has lost a lot of blood, so he will need rest and nourishment for the next several days. His artery was, indeed, nicked and had you not tied a tourniquet and brought him here so quickly, it would have been a different story. But we have stopped the bleeding and he will heal. However, he also needs to avoid any activity with that leg for at least a week."

"I don't know how to thank you enough," the father said overcome with emotion.

"None is necessary, but I am curious how it happened."

"It was entirely my fault. Steven found my handgun and was looking at it. Being afraid, I grabbed it out of his hand, not realizing he had already cocked the hammer back. It just went off like that, discharging a bullet right through his leg."

"I see, well, as I've said, you also helped to save him with your quick action. But if you don't mind, can you share with me how it is you wound up bringing him here?"

"My assistant, Jeffrey, a patient of yours who is in your waiting room, suggested we bring him here and you were closer than my own doctor." Palidore seemed to accept the explanation.

"Well, again, I am sorry, but in all the excitement I failed to get your name, I am Dr. Palidore Montgomery." He held out his hand to the man.

"Of course, and I am William Grayson."

"*Senator* William Grayson?"

"Yes, the same."

"Well, Senator, why not tell your friends in the waiting room that your son is going to recover thanks to their help." They proceeded into the small waiting area where Senator Grayson made the announcement. Aletha, who was finishing, could not help but smile as she heard the loud applause erupt from the waiting room. Arrangements were made for where the boy would stay to rest before being taken home, again.

Later when the last patient had gone, Aletha cornered Palidore. "Are you going to tell me about the ABC jars?" Palidore paused and looked at her, knowing he owed her some explanation, but not just yet.

"Aletha, the truth is, I had no right to use those medicines on that boy. They are not approved and never will be."

"But they worked so well, why not?"

"I want to tell you, but cannot, at least not now. All I can say is that they won't be approved because there is a finite quantity,

5

and they can't make anymore, so they will never be approved. Please never mention this to anyone or they may take my license away."

"You know you have nothing to worry about. I'll never tell another soul, but will you ever be able to tell me more? I mean, what did we give that boy to drink?"

"Aletha I just can't talk about it, but the solution he drank helped insure he would not get a blood clot caused by the other medicine I used on the wound. Now as much as I would like to, I just can't go into this in any more detail. I shouldn't have used them, but I was at my wits end, and I knew I had to try something. It worked this time, but without you, nothing would have worked. So that boy has you, and God, to thank."

"Palidore, what if Senator Grayson tells someone."

"He won't – he has no idea what we were doing. Besides, I think he will want to put the whole incident behind him as soon as possible."

"I suppose so, but I won't ever forget what we did here today, even if I am sworn to secrecy. "

Chapter 2

Washington, D.C. - July 2, 1798

The evening meal was Palidore and Anabel's special time together. Palidore's medical practice kept him so busy that he and Anabel had come to cherish their evenings sitting across the table from one another, always starting with a glass of their favorite wine. He had just begun to pour her first glass when there was an unexpected knock at the door. Palidore froze, the bottle of wine stayed midair in his hand. He glanced across the lonely candle flickering softly from the table's center. "So sorry, my dear," his voice showing apprehension, "I'll get it."

Anabel could read Palidore like a book and knew by the tone in his voice and the way his gaze released, he was concerned one of his patients was interrupting their dinner and special time together. That, once again, it would fall victim to his profession.

Reluctantly, Palidore put down the wine, rose from his seat and went to answer the door. It opened upon the face of a handsome young soldier who appeared too young to have fought in the war.

"Dr. Palidore Montgomery?" the soldier questioned.

"The same," Palidore responded, whereupon the messenger handed him an envelope with an attractive blue wax seal on back.

"Thank you, sir," he responded and gripped the door to shut it, however, the soldier quickly wedged his foot in the way.

"I am sorry, Sir, but my instructions are to return with a response to the letter. I will be pleased to wait out here while you read it and consider your reply."

Intrigued, Palidore immediately refocused his attention on the soldier and opened the door wider. "Why don't you come in. You can wait in my study. Can I get you something to drink?"

"No, thank you. I will need to be on my way as soon as I have your answer."

Palidore felt Anabel's arm slip around his waist. "What is it," she whispered in his ear while standing on her tiptoes at his side. Palidore rested his right arm on her shoulder, gave her a slight squeeze, and made a slight nod of his head toward the dining room.

"Please. Come in," he said to the visitor and showed the soldier where to sit, asking once again if he needed anything. The soldier, again, declined.

"I'll return shortly," Palidore replied, and escorted Anabel back to the dining room. Once out of ear shot, Palidore showed Anibel the letter with its waxed seal. "He won't leave until I send a response," he informed her.

"Well, don't just stand there - open it!" she said excitedly. Slowly, Palidore began opening the envelope, trying carefully not to break the decorative seal.

"Oh, for God's sake, give it to me!" Anabel said, snatching the letter from his hand and ripping it open, breaking the waxed seal in half. Seeing the inside address, she froze, immediately placing three fingers over her mouth. "Oh, I am so *sorry* Palidore. Here!" as she apologetically handed the letter and torn envelope back to him. With a questioning eye on Anabel, he carefully removed it from her shaking hand with a thumb and forefinger. Then took a deep breath and began reading it himself. After reading to the very end, he continued staring at the letter in disbelief until Anabel finally said.

"Well, what does it say?" Anabel asked whereupon Palidore read it out loud:

Dear Dr. Montgomery,

As you may have heard, I will be in Washington for the next few days to take part in the July 4th celebration. I would be honored if you would meet with me on Thursday, July 5th for a short visit. Should this be agreeable to you, please inform my messenger and I will send a carriage to pick you up on Thursday at 9:00 a.m. Our meeting may not take long, but you may plan on a meal here with me prior to your return home. I realize this is somewhat short notice, but should your schedule allow you to accept this invitation, I would be most appreciative.

G: Washington

"Why would the President want to see me?" he said, folding the letter along its lines again. Then slowly shifting his eyes from the letter to Anabel, he saw her staring intently at him.

"Well, of *course*, you are going to meet with him!" she said, excited at the prospect.

For the first time, Palidore tried to think what he might have planned for that day. "Well, after the holiday, my office will be full of patients" he quietly mumbled to himself as if he was thinking out loud. Anabel quickly retorted

"Well, they will simply have to reschedule. It is not every day you get an invitation from the President!"

"You mean *former* President. John Adams is our president now," he said.

"Palidore, you know *exactly* what I mean! George Washington was our *first* president and if he wants to meet with you, then you are most definitely going to meet with him! What else could you possibly do? Now go in there and tell that nice young man you will be honored to meet with the President."

As if in a fog, and still wondering what it was all about, Palidore turned and shuffled out of the room to see the messenger. Upon entering the study, he looked a little more carefully at the young soldier and noticed he was in a dress uniform carrying the rank of captain.

"So sorry I took so long. You may inform President Washington that I will be most honored to accept his invitation and look forward to meeting with him." The soldier stood, reached inside his tunic removing a piece of paper, and made a mark on it.

"I will inform the President of your response." He gave a slight bow and turned to leave. Palidore saw him to the door and let him out, quietly closing it behind him.

Returning to the dinner table, he sat down looking somewhat dumbfounded. Anabel was also sitting there lost in thought. Neither said anything for a while. The lone candle began leaking wax onto the table, still flickering between them. Finally, Palidore looked across to his wife and broke the silence.

"Can you believe this? I just don't know what the President could want with *me*." Anabel also at a loss for words, got up and removed the plates. Neither had eaten much at all.

"You are a good physician, Palidore. Perhaps he is interested in your medical advice." Palidore rolled his eyes, thinking of many other doctors he knew and respected.

"I am sure he has the best doctors available. I'll just have to wait and see what this is all about."

That night Palidore did not sleep well, so he rose early, dressed, and left for his office. Not living far from his clinic, he enjoyed the brisk walk. Normally, it allowed him time to clear his mind and prepare for the day. Today, however, his only thoughts were of his upcoming meeting with President George Washington. As he strolled along listening to birdsong and seeing the early morning sun give sparkle to dewdrops on several lawns, he hoped that tending to his patients would allow him to think of something else, if only for a short while.

Upon arriving at the one-story building, he saw several patients already waiting outside. It seemed no matter how early he traveled, there was always someone waiting to be seen upon his arrival. His father had experienced the same thing, therefore had set out two benches where anyone waiting would have a place to sit. Few people made appointments; they simply showed up when something was wrong. Only people he had already seen and had been instructed to return for a follow-up visit actually made an appointment.

"Good morning," Palidore greeted those waiting. "I'll be with you shortly after Nurse White arrives and opens the door. We must get things ready for the day." No one complained.

He unlocked the door of the one-story white clapboard clinic which had black shutters on either side of a single window facing the street. Once inside he opened the curtains, letting a little morning sun seep in. Nurse White always left a lantern on near the reception desk and another in his office.

"It does a man no good to enter a darkened room," she often said. Today, he was glad to have a cheery light welcome him as he stepped inside. Still preoccupied with thoughts of his upcoming visit with the President, he walked over to the wall displaying his medical diploma.

While staring at his diploma, Palidore let his mind reminisce a bit. He had grown up in northern Virginia and wanted to follow in his father's footsteps by becoming a doctor. His father, a British citizen, had been raised and educated in Egypt where his own parents had worked for the British government. The allure of the Americas had appealed to Palidore's father, and he migrated as soon as possible, settling in northern Virginia to practice medicine. His father had home-schooled Palidore and taught him as much as possible about medicine and special things he had learned in Egypt.

UNIVERSITY OF PENNSYLVANIA
To all before these presents shall come
Greetings
Let it be known that
Palidore Hugh Montgomery
Having completed the studies and fulfilled the requirements of
the faculty for the Degree of
Doctor of Medicine
Has accordingly been admitted to that Degree, with all the rights,
honors and privileges thereto appertaining
In Witness whereof, the Seal of the University, and the signatures
Of the Duly Authorized Officers are affixed to this Diploma

Done this 4th day of June 1768

But his father had also determined that Palidore should attend the University of Pennsylvania, School of Medicine. It was a new school with the best teachers. Consequently, his father's patients had raised the money to send Palidore to the university in exchange for his promise to return to them as their physician.

So as a young man, he went, studied, graduated, and as promised, returned to take over his father's practice.

Now Palidore's own handsome son was set to graduate soon from the University of Pennsylvania. He was looking forward to that occasion with much anticipation. Pondering the memories, he realized how far he and his family had come. He thought about his father and the mysterious medicines he had brought back with him from Egypt, and how proud his father would be to know that his son had now personally been invited to meet with President George Washington!

What a journey, he thought, wondering if this meeting with the president had something to do with his profession. *Probably,* he guessed *But, why me? I am well respected in the profession, but certainly, not considered a physician of great renown. Perhaps someone recommended me to serve on a medical committee? Or, perhaps, the president has some malady about which he doesn't want anyone to know. Perhaps, that is why he is seeking a meeting with a relatively unknown physician,* Palidore thought. *Either way, it seems I will soon know either the truth about President George Washington, or some secret.*

Chapter 3

Standing just four feet, ten inches in height, nurse Aletha White was an attractive brunette bordering somewhere between cute and beautiful. Although petite, she was an authoritative figure, well organized, and extremely competent.

Palidore had hired her right out of nursing school and put her in charge of running his office in addition to her normal nursing duties. It was one of the best decisions he ever made. He could trust her with anything and never had to worry about details associated with running a medical practice. That left him at liberty to devote his full attention to the actual practice of medicine. He considered himself lucky, actually blessed. Aletha always arrived at work dressed in her all-white starched nurse's uniform looking like a true professional from head to toe. Today, she entered Palidore's office looking particularly official and quickly brought him out of his trance.

"Time for daydreaming is over, Palidore; the waiting room is filling up. Things will be better once Hugh graduates, but we are several months away from that so, it's 'all hands-on deck' for now." Palidore looked up, focusing on her familiar face.

"Room Two is first. Joe Spence is back; his shoulder is out again. His brother is with him this time. I think you should teach him how to pop it back in for Joe. No need for him to come here every time it pops out. But don't *you* do it. Make his brother do it while you're in the room, so he learns how to do it himself! Then go to Room One. Sally is here for her six-month pregnancy check and she's all worried again that something is wrong, when it's not; so, give her a little pep talk when the exam is done." She spoke non-stop at him with all the instructions running together.

And, so it went all day, from one room to the next as nurse White directed him. It helped Palidore divert attention from his upcoming meeting with the President.

At 6:30 p.m. the last patient left.

"Well, that's it until after the Fourth. See you on Thursday," Althea said.

"About that, Aletha," Palidore said with a bit of hesitation in his voice. "I think we should take the Fifth off and reopen on Friday the Sixth."

"I don't think so, Doc," Aletha said quickly. "We're always busy after a holiday."

Unwilling to tell to her about his meeting with George Washington, Palidore remained silent not knowing what would come of it. All the questions she would have both now and after the meeting were almost too much to contemplate. Anabel and he had decided to keep it a secret until they knew more, so now was not the time to tell Aletha.

"Well, I've made the decision, so please post a note on the door before you leave," he said with authority. Aletha gave him a curious look and flapped her arms to her sides.

"Well yes, *Sir*!" emphasizing the "Sir." She was mighty, but she knew who was really in charge.

Palidore arrived home, and upon opening the door, was greeted with a kiss from Anabel. A wonderful aroma emanated from the kitchen.

"Now that's what I call a greeting!" he said. Since skipping most of his dinner the previous night and not having time to eat during the day, the aroma sparked his appetite. Anabel took him by the hand

15

with an amorous smile and led him to the dining room where two glasses of wine were waiting at their place settings. The solitary candle was already lit.

"What is that divine aroma?" Palidore asked as Anabel pulled the chair out for him.

"It's pot roast for my very important husband," she replied with a celebratory grin emanating from her happy face. Palidore, seated, raised his glass of wine in tribute to his wife.

"Well, I'm not sure I'm all *that* important, but I am beginning to feel a little more excited about the meeting."

"Me too. I've been thinking about it all day and I think I know what it might be about." With eyes raised, Palidore said, "Please, don't keep me in suspense any longer."

"Well, I think you might be up for receiving an award." Palidore shot her a questioning look as Anabel continued "Now hear me out! You remember Senator Grayson's son who was accidentally shot? Everyone knew he wouldn't survive, but you *saved* him! Everyone is still talking about it. So, maybe the president has heard about it, and wants to give you the recognition you deserve." Palidore smiled, looking down at his wine, and shook his head.

"That was a miracle. God saved that boy, not me. Even so, every doctor has had such cases."

"Maybe so, but how many doctors have saved a *senator's* son?"

"Well, if that is the case, I would not have gotten this curious type of notice. I suppose it's possible, however, that he just wants to thank me. He and Senator Grayson are close friends, I understand." Then he sniffed loudly through his nose. "The wine is fine, but I am starving, can we eat now?" Anabel took the plates and went to the kitchen, returning with their meals. Palidore was so hungry, not much talking took place during the main course. It wasn't until dessert when he was enjoying his favorite apple pie, did Palidore speak again.

"What do you think I should wear to this meeting?"

Anabel smiled. "I have it all cleaned and laid out for you. Your black suit with that gray tie and your father's pocket watch. You must look like the distinguished doctor you are."

"But it's a morning meeting," he said after a pause. "Isn't that a little formal?"

"Not at all for a meeting with the President. You know he dresses quite well, himself, and you don't know who else might be there." Palidore could see her mind was made up, so he let the subject go.

"Where is this meeting?" Anabel asked. Palidore looked up at the ceiling as if trying to recall, then looked at her with a smile.

"You know, I really don't know, only that the President is sending a carriage to pick me up at nine in the morning. But it can't be too far because we are supposed to get there, have the meeting, and be done in time to have something to eat before returning me here."

After dinner, Anabel began cleaning up; Palidore wandered into the living room which doubled as his study and sat in his favorite chair. It was a dark blood-red hammer-nailed leather piece with matching ottoman. Across from the chair was a matching love seat and between them an oval table. His small desk was toward the other end of the room by the fireplace on the opposite wall. On the table was his favorite pipe and smoking tobacco. He liked spending time in this room playing with his pipe more than smoking it. Often, he enjoyed a stiff drink of his favorite scotch whiskey. But tonight, still quite full from dinner, he decided to forgo the scotch. The weekly paper was on the table, so Palidore sat back with his pipe and began to read. When Anabel finished, she checked on him and accused him of nodding off which he promptly denied as he roused himself from his napping position. But both admitting to tiredness, so he put out the lamp and they followed each other upstairs to retire for the evening.

***

That night both Palidore and Anabel slept well. Waking first, Anabel let him sleep until she had gotten ready. Then she woke him with a little kiss on the forehead.

"Good morning, my dear, it's time to get ready," she said. "We need to leave in an hour." The Fourth of July day parade and picnic was an event everyone would attend. Anabel had packed a lunch of fried chicken, potato salad and her famous chocolate pie. Lemonade and tea would be provided at the site. They were going to be joined at the parade by Dr. Robinson and his wife, Sarah. Palidore had inherited his father's home which was centrally located. They were not far away from most things in the capital. Still, it would take about an hour to get to the parade site. The Robinsons would meet them there as they had in the past.

Palidore and Marshall Robinson had graduated from medical school together and had remained close friends. Ever since graduation, the two had met monthly for a long weekend. Anabel never knew what they did at these meetings. Palidore said they were involved in some private medical research, but Anabel thought they were just playing cards with other men.

This Fourth of July was a beautiful day with clear sky and a pleasant breeze. The buggy ride was uneventful. Still, Anabel was curious.

"Will you tell Marshall about your meeting tomorrow?"

"My intent is to keep the meeting under wraps until we know what it is about."

"I know that's what we decided, but Marshall and you are so close I didn't know if that would apply to him."

"Well, when we are alone, it is possible I might mention it, just to see his reaction," Palidore said. "On the other hand, I probably will say nothing."

They found Marshall and Sarah at their usual spot on the lawn of the Presbyterian Church. The hospitable Presbyterian women always had lemonade and tea ready for everyone. Comfortable outhouse facilities were behind the church. Anabel spread their blanket on the lawn. She and Sarah made sure they were well-situated before the parade. Children were running around; it was a festive atmosphere.

The long parade began with several groups marching, lots

of decorated wagons, some jugglers, and clowns, and of course the politicians waving to everyone. But it was the parade of soldiers everyone was anxious to see.

This year, soldiers from the fort at West Point were supposed to be marching. West Point had become a significant military training facility since the war, and there was a great deal of talk about turning the site into a school to train young men to become military officers.

The couples were enjoying the picnic when the soldiers came into view. There were so many men, considerably more than they had expected. The scene was eye-catching with all the soldiers marching past in dress blue uniforms and waving flags. The sounds of the drums and flutes matching the cadence of soldiers' feet, brought tears of pride to many an eye.

As the soldiers kept passing, the crowd began to cheer louder. Everyone began straining to see the reason why. Soon President George Washington came into view following the troops and riding a beautiful white stallion. Instantly everyone was on their feet, giving him a thunderous applause. Passing by the church, the President looked in Palidore's direction and waved to the crowd. People went crazy. For a moment Palidore thought the President was waving directly to him, but he then felt certain that was not the case as the President didn't even know what he looked like. Marshall also looked shell-shocked. The two men slowly turned and looked at each other.

"How about that?" Palidore said.

"Yeah, how about . . . that." Marshall quietly said.

Sarah and Anabel had tears in their eyes and were hugging each other. "What a way to end a parade!" someone called out. The little group turned and began picking up their belongings. On the journey home, Anabel asked Palidore if he had mentioned the meeting to Marshall. "No, there never seemed to be the perfect time to discuss such a thing," Palidore said.

"Well," Anabel replied, "after seeing the President, I am even more excited about your meeting, I just wish he had invited me too."

Arriving home, Palidore put the horse and buggy away as Anabel brought things into the house. When he finally came in Palidore told Anabel he was going to take a bath so he wouldn't have to wash in the morning. Anabel told him to go ahead, she would make a small meal before they went to bed. After dinner Palidore lit his pipe which he smoked while consuming a generous glass of his favorite whisky prior to retiring. He hoped the whiskey would help relax him enough to be able to sleep. He had some trouble drifting off but when he did, he slept well.

***

Early the next morning, Palidore woke, shaved, and came downstairs. Anabel had warm biscuits ready and a small bowl of fresh fruit. Palidore ate a little but said nothing. Anabel knew not to try and engage him in conversation when he was in a pensive mood. When he finished, she just gave him a big hug and whispered: "This is an honor, not something to fear; just try to relax and enjoy your day. Everything will be fine." Palidore took her face in his hands, gave her a kiss then returned upstairs to dress.

Once ready, he came down and walked into his study. Picking up this week's newspaper again, he started reading but soon realized he wasn't recalling anything he had just read.

It was a long hour before the knock came at the door. Palidore jumped up and answered it quickly. To his surprise, the same captain stood before him who had delivered the invitation a day earlier.

"Are you ready, Sir?" the soldier asked.

"I am," Palidore answered. He gave Anabel a quick kiss and turned to leave when Anabel pulled him back by his hand.

"I love you Palidore Montgomery."

He smiled, gave her another kiss before jogging down the steps to the carriage. The covered vehicle had its own driver. The captain opened its door and motioned for Palidore to enter before joining him. Once on their way, Palidore addressed the soldier.

"Captain, I must apologize, but I never asked your name."

"No problem doctor," he answered. "My name is Ronald Hudson. Please feel free to call me 'Ron' if you like."

"How long have you been President Washington's personal messenger, if that is the correct term?" Palidore asked.

"I am one of several personal assistants assigned to him. Since I am the youngest, I usually deliver the messages, but also have other duties as well. I have been assigned to the president since he left office in Washington."

"Does he frequently invite visitors to see him?"

"Well, he keeps a very active schedule, meeting with people all the time. You know he decided early on to found Washington, D. C., and he also planned and oversaw the construction of the White House. So, he is always meeting with people concerning his various pet projects."

"Then my meeting is in the normal course of business for the President?" Palidore asked.

"Well, I would not say that. He does meet often with many people, but he already knows most of them, or they are working on one of his projects. So, I would say this meeting may be a little different."

They remained silent for a while before Palidore asked, "Ron, how should I address the President? His majesty? His Excellency?"

"No sir, you should refer to him as 'Mr. President,'" Ron said. Palidore, wasn't sure he understood that correctly. "But the word 'President' is a title. You would not refer to a king as 'Mr. King' or a queen as 'Mrs. Queen' so why would I refer to a president as 'Mr. President?'"

"You are correct, but the president himself made that determination some time ago. He felt the emphasis should not be on the person, but the office the person holds. Therefore, he has directed that he should always be referred to as 'Mr. President' which is how President Adams is now also addressed. Once people got used to referring to President Washington as 'Mr. President' they kept doing so after he left office. I must admit, after a while, it just seems like the natural thing to do. So, I suspect once a person has become President, he will continue to be referred as 'Mr. President' for the rest of his life."

Chapter 4

The carriage stopped in front of a lovely, private stone residence with a large part covered in ivy. The door to the carriage was opened by another officer and Captain Hudson and Palidore both exited onto a pebbled walkway.

"Dr. Montgomery please follow me," Captain Hudson instructed. They went up several steps to the front door where another officer greeted them, opened the door, and invited the men to enter. Showing Palidore to a small study, Hudson invited him to have a seat, saying he would return later.

Palidore hardly had a chance to sit before President George Washington entered and greeted him in an upbeat manner. "Dr. Montgomery, thank you so much for coming!" he said in a jovial tone, reaching out to shake his hand. The president's casual, spontaneous manner, totally caught Palidore off guard.

"Mr. President, it's an honor to meet you," he said with a slight nod of his head. The president invited him to have a seat, however, instead of sitting himself behind the desk, as Palidore expected, the president chose to take a seat opposite him in a most unofficial way.

"How was your journey here?" the president asked.

"Quite pleasant," Palidore answered. "I enjoyed talking with Captain Hudson, a most remarkable young man." Then, unexpectedly, the president jumped up with exuberance.

"I'll be right back. I want to invite someone else to join us."

Just that quick, the president was gone, leaving Palidore alone in the room. He sat motionlessly and studied the walls, the floor, even the ceiling, noting they were all made of wood or wood paneling. A chair rail circled the room, meeting at the wood fireplace. The ceiling was a maze of inlaid woods of various tones set apart by large crisscrossing wood beams Only the dark green drapes next to the lone window and the circular rug on the floor gave color to the room. Palidore thought it all looked rich and quieting. He could envision himself smoking his pipe or having a drink in this same room.

Almost as abruptly as he had left, the president returned with none-other than Dr. Marshall Robinson. Both Palidore and Marshall looked stunned to see one another. "I think the two of you know each other," the president said.

"Of course!" Palidore could hardly contain his amazement. "We are very good friends."

"Yes, well, I apologize for the short notice I have given each of you," the president said. "I was not sure if either of you would be able to attend, so by issuing *two* invitations, I thought at least one of you would be available. I can't tell you how grateful I am to see you both."*There goes the "award" theory*, Palidore thought as Anabel came to his mind.

"Please, gentlemen, sit!" the president intoned. He was obviously excited about something. There were four chairs surrounding a table. Marshall and Palidore took two seats on the same side of the table with the president sitting across from them.

"Would you like some tea?" the president asked. Both men, still trying to collect themselves, mindlessly answered they would. He ordered tea brought in from a waiting figure by the doorway.

"Before we begin, I should explain the presence of so many officers surrounding me and why I was in the parade yesterday with so many young soldiers. While I can't tell you everything, I *can* say there is some concern over whether our previously good relationship with France may have deteriorated to the point where an attack against our country may be imminent. Because of this, President Adams has asked me to assume the position of Commander-in-Chief of the Armies, and I have accepted. While I will be very much involved, I will, nevertheless, be able to do a great deal of the work from my home and can delegate most of it to others." Palidore and Marshall shifted in their seats, nervously waiting to hear more.

"Now, please don't worry, I have not summoned you here to conscript you into the army. No, that is not it at all. So to the point, then," he nervously cleared his throat. "I know you are wondering what my true motives are in inviting you here, and, as I believe in being direct, so let me get to it. My purpose in inviting you here is to find out more about . . . your collection of bodies."

Palidore and Marshall immediately shot a fearful look at each other. Then Marshall looked down at the floor, sending a clear signal to Palidore that he needed to handle this topic. Palidore couldn't believe what he had just heard. *How did he know?*

Just then the doors opened and a handsome, stately black man with just a touch of gray at the temples of his closely cropped hair entered. He was perfectly attired as a butler and poured each man a cup of tea. "Is there anything else, sirs?" he inquired.

"Not now, Frank, thank you." Frank left, closing the doors behind him. The interruption had given Palidore time to think. He finally addressed the president.

"I am not sure we are at liberty to discuss this."

"Well," said the president, "let me assure you that you are in *no* trouble and my inquiry is not intended to cause you discomfort. I am aware of the physician-patient privilege, but I am not sure it applies beyond the patient's death. In any event, I am not inquiring about their health issues. I am specifically inquiring as to *why* they have not been interred." Palidore took a deep breath and slowly let it out before addressing the question.

"I can assure you, Mr. President, their remains are being preserved in very strict compliance with their wishes. But forgive me for asking . . . how was your attention drawn to this? We are speaking of people who were not interested in the public knowing about their decisions concerning the disposition of their own bodies."

"I was anticipating this question, and think you have a right to an honest answer. As you might expect, I am well-connected in this area, and quite frankly, privy to more information than I actually desire. But that is not how I came to know of your work. You may not be aware, but I have trouble attending funerals. The minute I arrive at someone's viewing, everyone's attention leaves the deceased and migrates to me. That is the last thing I want . . .to be the center of attention when full focus should be devoted entirely on the decedent. For that reason, I have, at times, gone quietly to the internment just to stand alone in back. To do this, I need to know what arrangements have been made ahead of time. So, I have people check for me and let me know what arrangements have been made.

"Not too long ago, I was shocked to hear that Richard Brockwell had passed away. I fought beside him at Valley Forge and wanted to pay my respects. My people reported that the service would be at Saint Paul's Anglican Church, but the family had not made plans regarding his internment. The Brockwells have *all* been buried in the church cemetery where they have a family plot. So, I could not understand why they would have trouble deciding what to do. However, I did not want to contact the family about it at such a time.

"I am a member of the Anglican Church and serve as church warden for both the Fairfax Parish in Alexandria, and the Truro Parish. In that capacity, I know most of the priests and so I contacted the Brockwell's priest. He was at a loss to understand this either and informed me the family had left the remains with

Richard's doctor and then confided to me that two other individuals had been handled in the same fashion.

"Sometime later, I was able to find out that Richard was Dr. Robinson's patient and the other two were your patients, Dr. Montgomery. Once I learned the two of you were close friends, it seemed a bit of a coincidence, to say the least. So, I felt the best course of action would be to just ask you directly. And *that* is why I summoned you both here today.

"Again, since these families have an absolute right to dispose of the remains of their loved ones in any manner of their choosing, I have concluded there is nothing wrong going on, just . . . *unusual.* So now that I have answered *your* question can you please answer mine? Where are the bodies, and why have they not been buried?"

An awkward, prolonged silence followed before Palidore finally spoke. "Please understand, I am not trying to avoid your question, Sir, I am just having a hard time formulating a proper response. I suppose the best way to start is by saying that each patient made his *own* decision regarding internment, or lack of same, ahead of time, so their families were not necessarily involved. Each decision was precisely what the deceased loved one wanted.

"You are correct to point out there are three such individuals, and they all attended Saint Paul's Anglican Church. That is not actually a coincidence. It all started with one individual from that congregation who had a serious physical problem and knew he was going to die. He was about sixty years of age. When I informed him that science was close to a cure, but it would not be in time to save *him,* he had a difficult time accepting his fate. He wanted me to preserve his remains the best I could, in the hopes that scientists in the future would be able to revive and cure him."

"And you agreed to that?" the president interrupted. Palidore hesitated, but then responded.

27

"Well, not at first, but he apparently convinced his elderly father to also beseech me. I did everything I could to dissuade him. I told them there would be considerable costs involved in just keeping the body preserved, but he was a man of considerable means. He wanted me to do what I could and promised he would put up enough money to keep the remains safe for several *decades*, if necessary. It was a parting gift to his only son, his inheritance, so to speak. In an abundance of caution, I reduced our agreement to writing which I have in safe keeping."

"What about the others?" the president asked.

I am getting to that," Palidore said. "For quite some time, Dr. Robinson and I have been conducting our own scientific experiments with an ancient preservative that my father brought with him when he migrated here from Egypt. We have been impressed at how well the remains of small animals were being preserved with no visual signs of decay, even after several years had passed. This is what we used on my patient, and what the patient and his father agreed to. I never had any intent to do this for anyone else, and, indeed, as part of my agreement with the patient and his father no one else was ever to know about this.

"But then Saint Paul's is a large church with a huge congregation, and in time, another patient of mine was in a similar situation. This patient was also in his sixties and had a considerable estate that he had already gifted to his children. The children of this patient somehow had learned about what had been done for my first patient. They would not disclose *how* they knew, but they also had significant resources and wanted a similar outcome.

"Without going into further details, this same preservation occurred once more with the patient of Dr. Robinson. Of course, both of us have many patients and friends who are also members of this congregation, so it has been difficult to say 'no.' Since what they were asking us to do would not actually harm any of the patients, and would make the relatives feel better, we ultimately relented," Palidore said. "However, there is surely a limit as to how many bodies we can store and monitor. We are very concerned and have privately discussed the possibility of having to change our church or move out of the area."

"I certainly hope that won't be necessary," President Washington said. "It seems you have stumbled onto something that may someday prove most useful or, at the very least, a significant area of new research. Your work raises more questions. I hope you will have time to answer them."

Chapter 5

Marshall and Palidore looked at each other. "We've probably already disclosed more than we should have," Marshall said. "However, the only thing you have learned from us today, that you did not know prior to this meeting, is *why* we did what we did, and the reasons for doing what we have done. If we go further, can you assure us that it will be kept in strictest confidence?"

"Most certainly," President Washington said. "You have my word." "Alright then, what is your first question?"

"Well, I suppose I would like to know if it is scientifically *possible* to revive a body, especially a well-preserved body."

Marshall took this question. "We believe so. Every physician has had a patient who was absolutely clinically dead. No heartbeat, no pulse, no breathing, eyes rolled back, then suddenly, the patient takes a big breath, opens his eyes wide, and just . . . comes back. We don't know *why* or *how* this occurs at this point, simply that it does. I, myself, have seen this happen twice, and I'm sure Dr. Montgomery has also." He looked over at Palidore who nodded his head.

"So, it becomes a timing issue. These patients were clinically gone for maybe a minute or two. No one has charted these occurrences conclusively as far as we know, but we would be interested in knowing just what the longest time span has been.

"In any event, assuming the body is maintained in the exact condition it was when it *became* unresponsive, then it would seem scientifically possible to revive it. Obviously, we do not presently have the ability to cause this, but Benjamin Franklin has shown us that it is possible to direct lightning, and even harness it; therefore, we believe in time, some form of shock can be brought to bear on the body to initiate a response from a corpse. Remarkable things are happening in medicine today, and we firmly believe that will continue to happen. That is the hope."

"How are you able to preserve these bodies?" the President asked.

"Palidore, I think you should take this one," Marshall said.

"Where to begin?" Palidore questioned. "Have you seen or read about the pyramids in Egypt?"

"Of course," the President responded.

"Well, as you may know, the pyramids were effectively tombs for ancient kings of the times. When a king died, his body was treated with chemicals, wrapped tight in chemically- treated clothing, and placed within the pyramid. A common belief is the pyramid was intended as a monument to the king. But others believe it was a further attempt to protect and preserve his body in that airless atmosphere. In short, we believe the king harbored the same hope as our currently deceased patients had. . . the desire to be reawakened in a future time. So, if they were to be revived, by some future physician, it would be necessary to keep the body safe. Hence these massive *protective* structures were created." Palidore stopped and waited for all this to sink in before continuing. He looked at Washington who was transfixed by his words.

"I hope I am not boring you. Perhaps you feel that Dr. Robinson and I have lost our minds."

"No, quite the contrary! I find this *most* intriguing. Please continue."

"Well, we have the same problem the ancient Egyptians had in preserving the bodies only we cannot afford to build a pyramid, and we have more than one body. So first, we have needed to treat the body, then we have needed to keep it safe. First, let's deal with how we have preserved the body, which brings us to the experiments that Dr. Robinson and I have been conducting. Are you interested in the background behind this?"

"I am fascinated, please don't leave anything out."

"As I believe I've mentioned before, my father's parents were British citizens who worked for the Crown and were stationed in Egypt. Actually, my grandfather was the British Ambassador to Egypt. Accordingly, my father was educated there. He received all his medical training in that country. Now, Egyptians take great pride in their ancient medical history. For instance, are you aware that the Egyptians were able to perform brain surgery? "

"I did not know this," the president responded.

"Well, we know this because we found various holes drilled into some craniums while examining the heads of some ancient bodies. The holes had apparently healed over time and were filled back in. This meant they had been operated on, and survived. The point is the Egyptians were quite advanced in the field of medicine. My father was an excellent student and became fascinated with Egypt's ancient medical remedies. He spent all his spare time experimenting with some of the ancient compounds. When he migrated to America, he brought significant quantities of three chemical compounds with him. During his years of medical practice here he continued to experiment with these compounds and, in time, included me in those experiments. I now possess those items and Dr. Robinson and I have been using them to conduct our own experiments.

"One compound which I will call 'Compound A,' turns any liquid into a gelatin substance. The second compound called 'Compound B,' seems to reverse the effect of Compound A, but *only* if the gelatin hasn't fully set yet. So, if you took a very small amount of Compound A and put it in a large quantity of water, it would seem to change the viscosity of the water, but since the solution is so weak, it would not turn it into a gelatin completely. At least not immediately.

"Now, if you add Compound B to this mixture, then the water would return to normal. However, if you have a fully-set gelatin created by Compound A and try putting some Compound B on top, nothing seems to happen. That is why we have concluded that it only works if the gelatin is still somewhat in a liquified state.

"As an interesting side note, each uncovered pyramid where a body was found had a small bottle next to it that once contained some liquid which we believe was a sample of that individual's blood. The contents had dried up, of course, but next to *that* jar was another small vessel which contained a small amount of what we now know as Compound B.

"We refer to the third compound as 'Compound C' and when mixed with water turns into a paste capable of totally sealing whatever it is covering from the atmosphere. We think this paste was used to cover the bodies in the pyramids including clothes that the bodies were wrapped in. All three compounds are initially found in a powdered state. We do not know *how* they were created or *what* they are composed of, but apparently, these elements were in abundant supply in ancient times.

"Because of the presence of the small quantity of Compound B found with each Egyptian mummy, we assume the ancients somehow believed it should be used to reverse whatever actions were done to initially preserve the body. Are you following this so far, Mr. President?" Palidore asked.

"Yes, completely. It is fascinating; please continue," Washington said while leaning forward and totally engaged in the conversation.

"So," Palidore continued, "we believe that *prior* to death, some of these individuals were orally administered a solution containing Compound A. This would enter their blood stream and circulate throughout the body eventually converting all liquid in the body into a gelatin-like state. Since the body is mostly water, the entire body would be effectively preserved. Compound C would cover the entire body to seal it from air. The combination almost certainly would protect the body for years, decades . . . even centuries."

"But, gentlemen," Washington interjected, "if a person consumed Compound A prior to his death, wouldn't it just kill him?"

"Well, once a body is placed in this vegetative state, it would no longer function, that is true. However, it is more like *pausing* a life, stopping everything, rather suspending its action, until such time as it could be revived later. So, I guess the answer to your question is 'yes' but with some qualifications," Palidore responded.

"Then, technically, your three patients were killed."

"We don't look at it that way. Please remember, all three were close to death. We simply prepared a cocktail containing strong pain medicine, a powerful sleep aid, and combined it with a mixture of Compound A. Then, we prepared the same cocktail without Compound A. Each patient was so close to death that it was unlikely they would ever wake up after consuming whichever cocktail they chose.

"Remember, each one was fully knowledgeable concerning the effects of these treatments and were advised by us that because of our Hippocratic Oath, 'to harm no one,' that as their doctors, we could not *recommend* they take the cocktail containing Compound A. It was by their own wishes we prepared the mixture, left it with the patients and exited the room. The patients, and their families, made their own decisions. Both of us were together outside the rooms so we could bear witness for each other that neither of us administered a lethal dose of anything."

They sat quietly for a moment as the President mulled over

the entire explanation. He rose, walked over to the window and stared outside for what seemed like minutes, then turned back.

"How long does it take for the mixture to work?"

"In each case, it took nearly an hour before someone came to fetch us." responded Palidore. "Of course, we couldn't know how long they waited before consuming the cocktail. But when we were summoned, the bodies had turned cold. We would then take the body, treat it with the paste made of Compound C, then wrap it in cloths permeated with that same compound. Then each body was placed in a casket and transported to Dr. Robinson's office, where he has an unused, windowless room. We are currently trying to determine a more secure and permanent location."

"When does Compound B come into play." "Because no significant amount of time has passed, we are still working on a theory and have been conducting experiments to verify it," Marshall said.

"Which is . . . ?" Washington's expression was neither incredulous nor doubting.

"Well, we believe over time, the effects of Compound A gradually begin to wear off and the body begins to return to its 'liquid state' as it was prior to consuming Compound A. That is, we believe the blood is restored to its liquid form. At that point, if nothing is done, the body will begin to lose its moisture and decay will set in. At that point, there would be no hope of doing anything further with the body to restore it. That is what we believe happened to the mummies.

"However, we think that if a mixture of Compound B could be administered as soon as possible *after* the blood begins to liquify, there would be no degradation of the body. It would be at *that* point in time when an attempt could be made to revive the body to its former state, assuming the science has progressed enough to make it possible." Marshall explained.

"What kind of experiments have you conducted to verify

your theory?" asked the President. Marshall explained they had experimented on small animals to date and had taken several small containers of each animals' blood and treated each with a different strength mixture of Compound A. Compound B had very little effect on blood in jars where the blood had congealed.

"However, jars where the solution containing Compound A was the weakest, and the blood had not totally congealed, then Compound B immediately returned it to its prior fully liquid state. Based on this," Marshall said strongly, "we believe as the effects of Compound A wear off, there will come a time when Compound B can be successfully used. In anticipation of this, we have drawn off a sufficient sample of each patient's blood before they consumed Compound A. We treat that sample with the same ratio of Compound A that was consumed, and we begin watching the blood in the jars. When it begins to liquify again, we, or whoever will be watching in the future, will know to administer Compound B. It is timing that is important as we have previously indicated.""One interesting note," Palidore interjected, "we aren't completely sure who was to monitor the small jars of blood left beside the mummies in the pyramids, or how they were planning to do that. They might simply have run out of time, or not instructed someone correctly. Perhaps, they hoped that future physicians would know more when the time came."

"Obviously, this did not work out so well for the Egyptians," Washington said. "None of them were revived, I assume."

"Well," Palidore said "that would appear to be correct. However, in one pyramid the two jars were found, but the mummy was gone. Marshall and I have read everything available and even examined the remains of one of the pharaohs. What we want to determine is *how long* it took before the effects of Compound A wore off. Based on my father's experiments, we know it is likely more than one hundred years. We still retain a sample of blood from a dog that he administered Compound A and it's sample blood is still congealed. That has been more than sixty years since he commenced that experiment.

"The body of the pharaoh we examined was more than three *thousand* years old. It is quite clear that Compound A wore off without further care since his body had deteriorated to the point we found almost no muscular tissue at all, however, his skin was still intact. Since Compound C is placed directly *on* the skin, we think it can preserve the skin almost indefinitely. We also believe that Compound A will last at least a hundred years, perhaps longer, and Compound C will last longer still."

"How do you remove Compound C?" asked the President.

"Good question," Marshall spoke. "We attempted to remove it with a solution of Compound B which had no effect. This is another reason we know that Compound B is intended only for use with Compound A. But to answer your question, we have been able to remove Compound C with alcohol. There are some things we *have* become successful at solving."

Chapter 6

"IF you don't mind, gentlemen, shall we continue our conversation while we dine?" Realizing their hunger for the first time, both Palidore and Marshall answered in the affirmative.

"Then, please, follow me." Washington rose and showed them to an adjoining dining room where a large selection of breads, cheeses, and fruits were laid on platters along with slices of beef and ham. "In an effort to keep our conversation private, I have asked the help to prepare the table and leave us to assemble our own plate. I apologize, if that is not to your liking. You will notice new cups of tea have already been poured for you."

"This is more than generous," Marshall said, helping himself to generous portions of everything.

"Quite perfect," Palidore said, looking over the buffet-style spread. As they refreshed themselves, the three men enjoyed small banter and repartee. Then the president brought the conversation around to the prime subject again.

"Is now an agreeable time to resume our conversation?"

"Absolutely," Palidore said.

"It was a delightful luncheon," Marshall said in agreement.

"Now then, you indicated you had received large sums of money from the relatives of each of the decedents. I would like to inquire what that would be, and what are you doing with the money?"

Palidore fielded the question.

"We have created a trust fund for each individual and have invested the money. We are the named trustees of the funds but we have the right to appoint successors. At present, only my son, Palidore Hugh Montgomery, Jr., has been named a successor. He will graduate from the School of Medicine at the University of Pennsylvania in a few months' time and will help us on this project."

"What is the money used for at present?" the president asked.

"Nothing right now," responded Marshall, "but we see expenses coming in years ahead for which we need to be prepared.""What kind of expenses?"

"Well, we think ultimately there will be need to move the bodies to a new location. One that is intended for our purposes, a location that will be fireproof and secure," Palidore said. "We believe that will be the largest expense. We must also continue our experiments and keep records to be passed along to future caretakers. Ultimately, people may need to be added for security and to help with our experimental findings. We are also developing a plan on how a revived person will be cared for in the future. One can only guess when that might occur, but we know there will be expenses.

"That is precisely why most of the money must be invested," Marshall said, "so that sufficient funds will be available in the future to maintain the bodies, and eventually help pay the costs of medical procedures should they be needed if a revival attempt does succeed. We can only speculate on what the future may hold, or how high those expenses might be.

"Well-trained personnel, a surgical center, and medical supplies will also be needed. We do not anticipate doing much of this during *our* lifetimes as we do not believe anything further can be done for the present patients in our control. Their dreams lie in the unforeseeable future.

"However," Marshall continued, "if the hope of our present families is to be taken into consideration, then the money will be needed to be properly invested and kept, so there will be sufficient funds, if and when the time for revival arrives."

"How can you guarantee the bodies will stay preserved for such a long time, and there will be trained personnel to assist them in the future?" Washington was showing increased interest.

"Well, to be perfectly honest," Marshall said, "we cannot guarantee *anything* more than our best efforts to establish a proper system to be handed down from one generation of medical caretakers to the next. Hugh, Palidore's son, is already aware of this, and completely on board with our efforts. But no one can read the future with any degree of certainty."

"However, who is man if not a dreamer of possibilities?" Palidore said. "Look how far we have come with only ideas of those who have gone before us? We can only promise to have the plan, records, medical facilities, and a system in place for as long as we live. From that point on, we hope those who follow after us will take their responsibilities as seriously as we have taken ours, and that they will be as dedicated to the possibilities as we now envision them."

"One last question, gentlemen: Do either of you intend to have *your* bodies so treated?" Washington asked. Palidore and Marshall looked at each other and paused briefly.

"As you can imagine," Marshall said, "we have speculated about this for some time. After much discussion, we have pretty much concluded that we are not sure we would welcome being brought back into this life since we both believe in an afterlife."

Washington sat silent in thought before he spoke again.

"Gentlemen, this has been most enlightening, to say the least. I commend you on your efforts and only wish for your success. It is admirable to put such effort into a project knowing in advance you will never know if your endeavors will be successful.

You are not unlike the brave soldiers who gave their lives never knowing whether this country would survive, but did so, without complaint, and look at us now. Our country will always be in debt to people of vision who seek the greater good without expectation of personal reward. Please rest assured that if your success depends on my silence, then you have nothing to fear."

"Thank you," Palidore and Marshall said in unison,

"Before I summon your carriages, is there anything else I can do for you, gentlemen?"

"Well," Marshall said, "you can tell us what we are supposed to say to our wives when we get home. They will be curious, and since we have not confided about our project to them, they will wonder about this meeting with you."

"I see. That does seem to present a problem, now, doesn't it?" the president responded with a telling smile. "Why not tell them that you have been invited by me to be founding members of the Medical Society of the Potomac?"

"I wasn't aware there *was* such an organization forming," Palidore said, totally surprised.

"Well, it is something I have been mulling over for some time now," Washington said, "and though I must admit I did not have anyone specifically in mind to help me with this, I would like to enlist your help. You have sparked my curiosity about your work and, perhaps, you will keep me up to date as we work together on our new project."

Palidore looked at Marshall, and both smiled in agreement.

"That is perfect," Marshall replied.

"So then, if you like, you may tell your lovely wives that you will each receive a special invitation from Martha and myself to our initial meeting which will be held at Mount Vernon. I think, perhaps, the organization should consist of physicians with small independent practices. Doctors who practice on the front lines of society, so to speak. The educational men and big groups already have established societies. So, what do you think? That should give you some plausible cover. Besides, it's probably a worthwhile effort to start anyway."

"Once I tell Anabel that she will be invited to Mount Vernon," Palidore said, "that should solve *everything*, and yes, it is a good idea."

"I agree," Marshal said, smiling with a nod of his head.

"Then, it's settled, " the president concluded. "Oh, one more thing before you leave. Why don't the two of you put together the criteria and articles for the Society. I will gather a list of doctors to be invited."

"Is that a little presumptuous for us to do?" Marshall asked. "I mean, won't other doctors wonder why we were 'anointed' to this task?"

"Well, Dr. Montgomery is an independent physician who has some notoriety in that he saved Senator Grayson's son, so that will be my motivation. I will indicate he was empowered to pick another qualified physician to assist him. By the way, I can't thank you enough for what you did for the boy. I should have mentioned it earlier."

"Well, that wasn't necessary," Palidore said. "I think God had more to do with it than I. In all truthfulness, I must confess I put a small amount of Compound A directly on the wound to stop the bleeding. Once that was done, he had a chance. I was later able deal with his blood situation. Perhaps I was lucky."

The president looked at him. "I am glad you said that. It has given me something to think about. I've certainly enjoyed this meeting immensely. I will look forward to meeting with you again."

Palidore and Marshall both stood and gathered their hats and canes from a small table.

"Gentlemen, once again, it has been a great pleasure! I will send Captain Hudson to pick up your criteria and articles regarding the Medical Society which I will need before I can set a date for the meeting. How much time will you need?"

"Not much time. We will pretty much copy the set we have for our local society, then add some unique information. Perhaps, a week."

"Fine, then Captain Hudson will pick them up a week from tomorrow. Where should he I send him?"

"To my home," Marshall answered. "Palidore and I have a small office there. Now, given this new incentive, we will have even more to discuss. It is becoming a very important little office."

"Until we meet, again," the president said.

Chapter 7

It was nearly dinner time when the carriage stopped in front of his home. The meeting had taken much longer than Palidore, or any of them, had expected. As he exited the carriage, he thanked Captain Hudson, then bounded up the stairs to see Anabel who had been watching out the window, and was now waiting for him at the open door. "Well, what happened?" she couldn't wait any longer to hear. Palidore wrapped his arms around her small frame, picked her up, and gave her a good kiss on the mouth.

"Well, I assume everything went well!" she laughed, relieved at his good mood. Palidore put her down and motioned to the house. "Let's go inside and when I am equipped with a good drink and my pipe, I'll tell you all about it!"

Anabel took his hand and led him inside. Palidore went directly to his Baptist bar, opened the doors, and poured himself a goodly glass of his favorite scotch whisky, taking a stiff drink. Then, he started for his pipe.

"Fix me one of those, too," Anabel said. "I may need to mellow out a little before I hear your story. Do you know how anxious I have been waiting for your return?" Palidore gave her a curious look. He could not remember the last time Anabel had consumed whisky but proceeded to pour her a drink. Not quite as much as he had measured for himself, however, since he felt certain she would not finish it all, and he did not want to waste any of the precious liquor.

The glasses contained Edradour Scotch Whisky which came from a small distillery in Scotland and was hard to come by since it was only produced for members of the Royal Family and House of Parliament. His grandfather, by virtue of being the British Ambassador to Egypt, had the right to order the whisky as one of his perks in office. Palidore had kept ordering it in his father's name long after his death, just continuing the tradition. Apparently no one ever bothered to question it. Palidore felt the government owed his family that much. Though, truthfully, he was always afraid someday someone would figure it out and cut him off. But just in case, he had an ample supply stored in their home.

Now sitting on the soft leather covered chairs, they placed the drinks on a small, round wooden table. Anabel lit two candles and replaced the glass globes. Palidore put some of his favorite cherry-flavored tobacco in his pipe and lit up.

Anabel took a sip of her drink. Immediately, she gasped and said, "For the life of me, Palidore, I don't know how you can drink this stuff!" "Well, you asked for it. Do you want me to fetch you some wine?"

"Not just now. I have waited long enough for you to return. Please, tell me what happened; I can't hardly wait!" she said.

"Well, the carriage left me off in front of a very interesting home. The entire outside of the house was made of large stones partially covered in ivy."

"Oh, I've heard of that house," Anabel interrupted. "It's called the 'Stone House' and was on display last Christmas."

"The President said it was owned by a friend of his, and was always available to him when he was in the area." Palidore continued. "Supposedly, the owner picked out all the stones himself. It was quite nice, but not too spectacular. Actually, it is somewhat similar to our home inside, but just a bit larger."

"Enough about the house, what happened?" Anabel said.

"I am getting there, just setting the stage a bit," Palidore said, knowing he was stalling somewhat, trying to figure what to say or not. "But first you need to know something else."

"What?" she said

"I wasn't the only doctor there," he responded.

"How many doctors were there?" she asked.

"Counting myself, there were two, but you will never guess who the other doctor was."

"Please don't play games, just tell me."

"Marshall Robinson was the other doctor."

"I can't believe it!" Anabel gasped. "Sarah didn't say anything about Marshall being invited to see the president at the picnic on the Fourth! As close as we are, you certainly would have thought, she would have confided in me. I just can't believe it."

"Well, if you recall, we didn't mention my invitation to them either. Perhaps they decided to do the same thing."

"Oh, I suppose that's a fair way to see things," she said, catching her breath. "I suppose you are right. So now, I am *really* curious how the two of you men, out of all the doctors, were selected to meet with President George Washington."

At this point, Palidore felt a little guilty about the forthcoming deception by omission he was about to commit. He drew a large breath of air and began. "Well . . . the President is forming a group called the 'Medical Society of the Potomac.' It is to be comprised of local independent physicians who have small practices, or as he said 'doctors on the front lines.' Since Marshall and I both fit that criteria, and both our fathers practiced in the area prior to us, we have been invited to be founding members."

"Oh, how wonderful!" Anabel said. "When will this come about?"

"This is the part I think you are going to like the best. We, and by 'we' I mean you and I, will be getting a special invitation from the president and his wife, Martha, to the founding event which will be held at Mount Vernon." Anabel jumped up and screamed, dancing around the room, bumping into the table, almost turning over both drinks and the lamp. Palidore rose and grabbed her, holding her tightly to calm her down and prevent any real damage. "I thought you might like that part," Palidore said. In the back of his mind, he felt the guilt take hold. His mind wouldn't let him think on it. His only solace was knowing the invitation part was real, even though it hadn't been the true purpose of the meeting; nevertheless, this part was not a lie. He felt good the joyous news made his wife so happy, and noticed her eyes were wet with joy.

"Oh, my goodness!" she exclaimed, "I know this will be a most formal event and I have nothing to wear! How many people do you think will be there? How will we get there? Where will we stay? It certainly will be an evening event and too late to return home once it is over. I need to get in touch with Sarah. She will know what to do. She is so good at these things. Remember the Veterans Ball? Wasn't that lovely? Do you think we can travel together?"

Anabel never gave Palidore a chance to answer any of her questions. He reached for her hands, then stood and circled her around, brought her close and took her head in his hands to give her a kiss in an effort to calm her a little.

"We will have plenty of time to figure this out, but those are good problems to have, don't you think?" She smiled, laid her head against his chest, then gave him a big hug.

"Now," Palidore said, this time placing his hands on her shoulders and putting her at arms length. "Marshall and I have agreed to meet this weekend to discuss issues involving the new medical society, so maybe that would be a good time for you and Sarah to get together and do some planning of your own. We are invited for the weekend."

"Yes, yes, yes! This just keeps getting better! But today is Thursday, so that's just the day after tomorrow. I'll need to pack." She started for the stairs. "How about a little something to eat?"

Palidore said to her retreating figure. Anabel yelled back as she ascended the stairs.

"I am not hungry, but there's plenty for you in the kitchen. Help yourself!"

Palidore smiled, deciding to sit for a while to finish his drink as well as Anabel's and enjoy his pipe. He, too, needed to come back down to earth; he thought briefly about the mad house facing him tomorrow at the office.

I really hope Nurse White isn't still upset about taking the day off right after the holiday. Things were always unpleasant when she was in a bad mood. God knew he needed her though. He would almost have to stop practicing medicine if she would ever quit. *That is another woman I need to keep happy.*

Chapter 8

The next morning Palidore left for his walk to the office at about 7:00 a.m. The morning horizon had a red tint to it; he could already feel the humidity rising and knew it was going to be a sweltering day. Along the way, he tried assessing his feelings about the conversation Marshall and he had yesterday with President Washington. On balance, he was pleased it had occurred.

In a way, perhaps it seems that Marshall and I are doing something worthwhile after all, he thought, *almost like an official stamp of approval, if I may go so far as to think so.*

The president's promise to keep their conversation in strictest confidence was reassuring, but it occurred to Palidore that if the president had questions about the bodies they had preserved, then someone else might also be having questions. *The fact the president even knows about them is something for us to discuss very soon. Who else might be talking about our work?* For sure the pastor had some grave concerns for the bodies not buried in the ground but, hopefully, their pastor-parishioner privilege would prevent him from mentioning it to others. *Especially since the pastor must know the bodies had been cared for in a manner in accordance with the wishes of the deceased men's own families.* In any event, it seemed clear to Palidore that Marshall and he had all the bodies they would ever need for their future work.

As he approached the clinic, he greeted the "early birds" already lining up and advised them the office would open when nurse White arrived. He entered the office to find Aletha already inside getting things ready for the day. "You're here early," he said.

"Well, with our taking yesterday off, I thought I had better be here as early as I could. I am surprised we don't have more patients waiting," she said. "How was your day off? Was it worth it?"

"Yes, very nice and most definitely worth it. Did you see the parade? The soldiers from the fort at West Point were amazing, and to be followed by President George Washington was a real treat," Palidore said.

"Actually, I missed it," Alethea said. "We had friends over and I spent the day cooking and tending to our guests. As it turned out, the extra day off *was* a welcomed relief. It allowed me to get things cleaned and put up. So, I thank you for that. But we only have today before the weekend. Having another day off so quickly seems strange," Alethea said, "almost unnatural."

Well, she seems in a good mood, for the most part, Palidore thought. He had been a little nervous about it. "Okay, who do I see first?" he asked, wanting to change the subject. He would tell her about the formation of the new Medical Society of the Potomac in due course. *Probably the later the better,* he thought.

"That would be Herbert Miles in Room One. He is complaining about his back. No wonder, as big as he is, I'm surprised he can get out of the bed. You better hold your nose. I don't think he's had a bath in a month!" she advised. The day progressed reasonably well, and they even had time for a small lunch break. Finishing around 4:00 p.m., Aletha said, "Well, I guess I was wrong about taking the day off after the holiday."

"Maybe it's just a timing thing with the Fourth being on a Wednesday. Perhaps, people have decided to wait until Monday. That may turn out to be the hectic day."

Late afternoon, Palidore enjoyed his walk home despite the heat which had developed earlier. His street was lined on both sides with massive trees and large branches stretching over the road almost forming a tunnel of cool, welcomed shade. At home, he surprised Anabel with his early arrival. She had just finished making fresh lemonade, so they each took a glass and headed to the porch where they sat in their favorite rocking chairs.

"This is how I like us to spend an early evening," Anabel said. "Just watching people walking by." Occasionally, they engaged in conversation with a few of their neighbors. After sitting a while, Anabel spoke while she collected their glasses.

"I'm packed for our overnight trip to spend with Marshall and Sarah, Palidore, dear. I've laid out some things for you also."

"Why does that not surprise me?" he said.

"Now don't get started with me, I have every reason to be excited. You've had your time with President Washington, and now, this is my opportunity. I am just as excited about meeting Martha. She comes from quite a well-known family of her own, you know? Then there is the whole thing about seeing Mount Vernon." She seemed absorbed in her own thoughts, almost as if carrying on a conversation with herself, before becoming aware of him sitting there.

"What time do you want to leave tomorrow?"

"It's about a two-hour ride to the Robinson's home, so I'd like to leave by eight tomorrow morning. That way, we should arrive by ten. Then, Marshall and I can get a few things done before lunchtime." Palidore said.

"That suits me just fine. I've packed some food and thought you might want to take some of that dried beef to cook for dinner."

"That sounds good. I'm also taking a bottle of my Edradour Scotch along. Marshall really likes it and cannot acquire any of his own."

***

The following morning was another beautiful day, and the trip to the Robinsons was uneventful, arriving as planned just before ten. Marshall and Sarah were on the porch waiting and obviously pleased to see them arrive. In short order, everything was unloaded and the horse put up in Marshall's barn. They exchanged pleasantries after which Marshall and Palidore headed for their work in his study as the ladies settled in the parlor.

Once they settled, Marshall said, "Do you have any regrets about what we've disclosed to the president so far?"

"Actually, I was thinking about it yesterday and really feel it was a good thing. In a way, it's almost a validation of what we've been doing."

"Precisely my thoughts. What an amazing day, beginning with seeing you there!" Marshall said. They both laughed. "I guess we had better do our homework for the Medical Society of the Potomac." There was a pause, and then Marshall asked, "Do you think he just came up with that on the spur of the moment?"

"At first, I thought so, but as our conversation went on, it seemed like it was something he had been mulling over for a while like he said," Palidore said. "I mean you don't just *invent* something like that as quickly as he did. I'm not saying it was part of a grand plan, but it just seemed too quick to have been invented on the spot."

"I agree. He is clearly a quick thinker, but it was almost as if he was searching for another reason to meet with us again." Changing the subject Marshall added, "Okay, so we need some criteria for membership in our new Medical Society. Have you given this any more thought?"

"I have," Palidore said. The men entered into a long discussion that took a few hours.

Chapter 9

Anabel looked to Sarah. "I was shocked when Palidore said both he and Marshall had been invited to see President Washington at the same time. I need to apologize for not mentioning Palidore's invitation to you on the Fourth, but we really didn't know what the meeting was about. We thought it best not to say anything to anyone. Palidore said if the opportunity had presented itself, he was going to tell Marshall that day, but then he told me on the way home, they were never alone long enough to discuss it."

"That's funny, because we went through the exact same discussion," Sarah said. "When Marshall told me about Palidore being present, I was amazed. I just can't understand why only our two husbands received invitations and on such short notice," Sarah replied. "Somehow I just have a funny feeling that something else is afoot. I just can't put my finger on it."

"Palidore didn't mention anything else about the meeting, and I can't see how it took all day for them to talk about forming a new medical society. But then Palidore only tells me about half of what he hears about anything," Anabel said. Sarah laughed and confirmed that Marshall wasn't overly verbose either.

"Funny, I had similar thoughts, but finally decided to give up trying to speculate about it," Sarah said. "I suppose we should be content to focus on the fact we've been invited to Mount Vernon and are going to meet President and Mrs. Washington."

"Palidore and I were thinking this will likely be an evening event," Anabel said. "If it is, then we will not be able to make it home for the night. We'll need a place to stay. Mount Vernon is large, but I don't think it has enough bedrooms for every couple likely to attend."

"Marshall told me he knows some people who live nearby," Sarah mentioned. "We will likely be able to stay with them, so it is unlikely we will have to find an inn."

"How fortunate," Anabel smiled at her friend. "I suspect we will just have to wait until the invitations are sent before we will know much more. Surely we will need to plan on packing for two days. I certainly hope we have a little more advance notice than our husbands got for their meeting with the president. Besides, I will need a new dress, and you know how long that can take," Anabel said."Perhaps, we should plan on going shopping next week."

***

Marshall and Palidore finished writing their draft of the criteria for membership and initial articles to be sent to the president. Captain Hudson would be coming to get them on Monday.

"Let's add a cover letter suggesting to the president that we welcome his adding or correcting anything we've written," Palidore suggested. "I don't wish for us to seem overly aggressive. What do you think?"

"Yes, that way we can thank him for the many kindnesses he showed us during our visit," Marshall said.

"You know, Marshall, perhaps it is time for us to taste the Edradour Scotch that I have brought," Palidore said. "After all this headwork, I have worked up a thirst. What about you?"

"You brought some?" Marshall's eyes brightened.

"You bet your sweet arse I did, buddy," Palidore smiled back.

"Wonderful! We should probably also season the beef that

has been soaking since we've arrived," he said, showing the way toward the kitchen.

After socializing over dinner with the ladies present, they had little time for a private discussion which they intended to have regarding their experiments. So, after dinner, the two men headed back to the study with their pipes. Marshall shut the door, and they took opposing seats in front of a small table sinking down into oversized black leather chairs.

"Palidore, we need to find a more permanent place for our bodies," Marshall said, beginning a long overdue conversation. He paused, "I would also feel better if we started referring to them as 'the inventory' from now on. I think it sounds better should anyone overhear our conversation."

"I know we've discussed the fact that we probably needed a more secure and permanent facility, but I somehow sense from the tone of your voice that storing the inventory has suddenly become an acute problem." Palidore said .

"Actually, it is because my practice is in need of expanding our waiting room. It is not nearly as large as yours since it only holds eight people comfortably," Marshall said. "It would be simple to remove the wall between our waiting room and the room housing our 'inventory.' My nurse suggested this change a while back and keeps wanting to have access to the adjoining room so she can prove to me how correct she is. I keep putting her off, but I think she has become curious about what we are keeping in there and I can't keep putting her off. Quite frankly I have run out of excuses. Besides, we have all this money from the families now, and part of that is to be used for safekeeping the bodies . . . I mean, 'the inventory.'"

"I know you are absolutely right. I understand completely, but it has always been convenient having them, uh 'the inventory' so nearby. We never need an excuse to go in there since it makes sense for us to be in there," Palidore made his point. "Once we move 'the inventory,' we will have to invent a rational reason for acquiring the premises, as no one can know of our intended purpose."

"I understand. So, what now? Any suggestions? I mean we need to think of something," Then Marshall chuckled. "Maybe the Medical Society of the Potomac will need an office."

"You know, that is really not too bad of an idea. Oh, I know normally these groups operate out of someone's office, but Sarah and Anabel don't *know* that, and they are the only people who would question why we would be going to the building," Palidore said. "We could simply find a place and rent or buy it and put a sign on it for the society."

"Well, for that to work, we probably will need to hold some office in the Society. How certain are that we can make that happen?" Marshall asked. "There are potentially dozens of physicians who might belong."

"It probably won't be difficult. President Washington tasked us with setting it up and he will likely introduce us. Usually, no one is very anxious to hold such an office and we are likely to be tapped for it anyway."

"Right. Well, in the meantime, I will look for a place, and you can keep looking, too," Marshall said. "One more thing, I think we should somehow put all the information we have about each person in our 'inventory' on their bodies. It seems likely nothing will change during our lifetimes, but someday, someone will want to know as much information as possible about each person: What was wrong with them; time placed in their current state; and most importantly, why the families agreed. The hardest thing will be to keep such information in reasonably good condition over such a prolonged period of time. What do you think? Any ideas on how to accomplish this?" Marshall asked

"Why not put the information into a bottle and wrap it in a cloth treated with Compound C and paste it on their bodies? That should preserve it," Palidore answered.

"That's brilliant! You do the write-up for your two patients and sign the documents, and I will do the same for my patient. We can then get the bottles ready and figure how to attach them to the bodies," Marshall said. The men sat for a moment thinking over all that was before them.

"Do you think we might have one more touch of Edradour before retiring," Marshall asked.

Palidore smiled. "Sounds like you have had another stellar idea." He was in a more relaxed mode as he looked at his friend and picked up the bottle to pour.

Chapter 10

On Monday, Captain Hudson picked up the documents for President Washington from Marshall. He and Palidore had speculated that, in all likelihood, the earliest possible response they could expect from Washington would be the following Friday. However, it took over two weeks before they heard anything. Finally, Captain Hudson delivered a reply at Palidore's home on a Saturday morning.

"Do you need to wait for a response?" Palidore asked."No, not this time," Captain Hudson smiled, handing him the letter. Palidore thanked him, and the captain left. Walking back inside, Palidore opened the envelope and read.

Dear Dr. Montgomery:

Thank you for preparing the proposed

Criteria for Membership and Articles for the Medical Society of the Potomac. I have no additions or corrections to suggest. It looks like you have covered everything. My staff indicates the potential membership of independent doctors practicing in the defined geographical area with at least ten years of service could number around forty-three.

I realize that such events are normally evening functions, but I want to conclude everything by late afternoon on Saturday, September 22nd. This will allow guests time to travel home, or wherever they want to spend the night, and still be able to attend church on Sunday. I believe we should gather here around 10:00 a.m. This will afford us a chance to give everyone an abbreviated

tour of Mount Vernon and end up having a luncheon meeting
around 1:00 p.m. I think we would likely adjourn around 3:00p.m.

I have sent a similar letter to Dr. Robinson. Hopefully
the two of you can get together soon and let me know if this is
agreeable, or if you have any suggested changes. I will look
forward to hearing from you soon. I am

> *Yr. Most Humble Servt*
> *G: Washington*

On Sunday, Palidore saw Marshall at church and both felt
it would be impossible to do anything but agree with plans the
President had made.

"Let me send a reply on Monday," Marshall said. "That
should allow the president time to prepare and send invitations as
soon as possible.

"Good," Palidore agreed. "That will also give our wives time
to make plans, but we must admonish them not to reveal anything
to anyone prior to actually receiving the formal invitations, don't
you agree?"

"Yes, indeed," Marshall said.

***

Sarah and Anabel were excited all over again and glad they
had already ordered their dresses, but now felt they needed to
purchase matching umbrellas for the sun.

On Saturday the 11th of August, Captain Hudson once
again knocked on Dr. Montgomery's door, and hand-delivered the
personalized invitation.

"You are being kept quite busy, Captain," Palidore said.
"Are you hand-delivering all the invitations?"

"Exactly that, sire," Captain Hudson answered. "Fortunately,
I have help. There are ten messengers delivering four invitations
each, so none of us mind. That is the president's way of knowing
how many exactly are receiving them." The captain then advised

there was a reply card and addressed envelope included for a return answer when ready.

Palidore thanked the captain who returned to his horse. He then handed the envelope to Anabel. "I think you had been look at this." She opened it and read with inflection.

President and Mrs. George Washington request the honor of your presence at the inaugural meeting of the Medical Society of the Potomac to be held at Mount Vernon on Saturday, September 22, 1798.

Enclosed you will find the membership criteria which our information indicates your medical practice does meet. If you are interested in belonging to this prestigious group of physicians, and your schedule allows, please respond as soon as possible. If you are interested in belonging, but cannot attend, please also provide that information.

Enclosed you will find a schedule of events planned for the day as well as a response card to advise us of your intentions. Martha and I look forward to your participation.

President and Mrs. G: Washington

Inside the envelope was a separate hand-written note which Anabel held up and waved in the air. "We have a separate note." She, then, proceeded to read it aloud with much fanfare.

"Palidore, since you and Marshall have been so helpful in organizing this event, Martha and I are inviting you and your spouses to come a day early to go over the agenda, and plan for the formal part of the event.

Of course, you will spend the night as our guests here at Mount Vernon. Assuming this is agreeable to you, we will send a covered carriage to pick you up around 10:00 a.m. on Friday and ultimately return you home on Saturday night. Martha and I are looking forward to meeting your wife, as I am looking forward to visiting with you, again.

Go: Washington

"I can hardly believe this!" exclaimed Anabel. "You are on a first name basis with President George Washington! How can this be happening?"

Palidore quickly said,

"I would not go that far, my dear. Certainly, we will only refer to him in the most formal manner. I think he just wanted to personalize the invitation and make us feel welcomed. This, however, is not a two-way street. We are by no means on their level of society and will, most assuredly, handle our interchanges in a most respectful manner.

"Really, Palidore, now do you think I was going to walk up to him and say: 'Good to meet you, George!'?" she looked at him with a blush of anger to her cheeks. "I know how to act, but we did get a 'first name' personal note, you can't deny, and I am most excited." Anabel responded.

***

Well in advance of the carriage arrival on Friday, September 21st, Palidore and Anabel were packed and ready. Almost like clockwork at 10:00 a.m., Captain Hudson once again arrived with the covered carriage. He strapped their luggage onto the back, then opened the door inviting them to enter the handsome vehicle. As before, there was a separate driver and Captain Hudson joined the Montgomerys in the carriage sitting next to Palidore.

"The trip will take us about two hours," Captain Hudson said. "We'll stop halfway for a break and to use the facilities." He opened a wooden box that sat on the floor between them. "We have water, tea, and lemonade right here in the carriage," He said, displaying the items. "If you need anything, or have any questions, please let me know."

"Thank you," Anabel simply said, sitting quite still as if in a trance. "That's wonderful; we are fine for now," Palidore said.

The ride was as comfortable as possible with the move and sway of a four-wheeled carriage pulled by two handsome black horses. They made small talk until arriving at Mount Vernon by noon. The Robinsons were nowhere to be seen.

"Perhaps, Dr. and Mrs. Robinson have not yet arrived. We must have had the faster horses," Palidore attempted to joke.

President Washington and his wife, Martha, were standing at the front door. After exchanging greetings, everyone proceeded into the house.

"Dr. Robinson and his wife are expected after 2:00 p.m.," President Washington said. He asked Captain Hudson to take their luggage to the Lafayette bedchamber before inviting Palidore and Anabel to follow Martha and himself into the small dining room. It was painted Kelly green with a white ceiling uniquely decorated. There was a window letting in just the right amount of sunlight next to the table which had been set for four places. The president then invited everyone to take a seat.

They were served a salad with smoked fish, tomatoes, and cheese lightly touched with dill sauce. Tea was provided, and the luncheon was finished with a moist slice of frosted chocolate cake. After lunch, Martha showed them to their bedchamber to freshen up after their busy morning.

"We call this the 'Lafayette' bedchamber because the Marquis Lafayette stayed here." She pointed to the likeness of the Marquis on display. "George and the Marquis are best of friends. They fought together during the war. I think George always wondered why a French nobleman would be so willing to take such risks for another man's country," Martha said. "In any case, we hope you will find this bedchamber most comfortable." She showed them the small lever on the wall next to the door.

"Should you need anything at all, just pull down on it

and a servant will come and attend to you." Anabel looked on in amazement. "When Mrs. Robinson arrives, I will return and show you ladies around while the men talk together," Martha told her.

"That would be wonderful," Anabel said.

A little after 2:00 p.m., President and Mrs. Washington greeted the Robinsons and Martha showed them to the Blue Bedchamber adjacent to the Lafayette Bedchamber.

"Please make yourself at home. I will return shortly to show you the rest of the house."

Some thirty minutes later, Martha returned with Captain Hudson and knocked on both doors. While the ladies joined her to begin their anticipated tour of Mount Vernon, Captain Hudson greeted the men and took them downstairs to the president's personal study. There was a table with four chairs set comfortably apart. The Captain indicated they should have a seat and the president would join them shortly. After Captain Hudson left, Palidore turned to Marshall with eyebrows raised.

"Well, Marshall, what surprises do you think we have in store for us today? "

Chapter 11

W hile waiting for President Washington to join them in his study, the two doctors looked around the room, noticing how the sunlight was pouring in. There were two windows on the same wall looking out over lovely grounds. Natural light was warming the room with sunbeams illuminating small dust particles floating in the air.

On the adjacent wall to the left of the windows were a significant number of books on shelves enclosed behind beautifully beveled glass doors. A large circular blue rug in the center of the room displayed a spread-winged eagle in its middle. The president's desk seemed a bit small for such an important man, but it was neat and the chair behind it seemed appropriate for the size of the desk. A number of certificates and paintings adorned the walls. The sideboards appeared to house personal mementos and keepsakes.

"I wonder how many great stories are represented by all these items," Palidore remarked to Marshall.

"Exactly," Marshall said. "I wish I had time to hear each one of them."At that moment, President Washington bounded into the room.

"Gentlemen, welcome to my innermost sanctum." With a sweep of his hand, he continued speaking. "This is actually my favorite room. I spend most of my time here, even getting dressed in this room each morning so as not to bother Martha since I rise so early. I've taken up the habit of having my clothes brought down the night before by Frank. I think you have already met him."

The doctors nodded affirmatively as the President continued.

"You'll notice the high ceilings; that helps keep the temperature reasonable. But before I waste any more time, let's sit and go over our plans for tomorrow."

He went behind his desk and took out papers from its top drawer, then handed each doctor a copy, keeping another for himself. "As you can see, I will call the meeting together and welcome everyone. Then, I'll call on Father John to say a prayer. After that, I will introduce Vice-President Jefferson.

"Thomas somehow learned of this event and sent a messenger to ask if he could become involved. He thinks he is going to build a great university out west of here in his town of Charlottesville and wants there to be a school of medicine. He has already designed the whole damn thing! It is absolutely amazing; and you know, I have no doubt he will convince the commonwealth to fund it. If I know anything about the man, it will probably be in operation within the next decade, if not sooner.

"In any case, he wants to put in a pitch for his school at this event. I am sure he will bring his drawings and I have no doubt this is all part of his campaign to move his pet project forward. That is how he operates from the ground up. He also heads a group of politicians which we now refer to as 'The Jeffersonians' who have banded together in an effort to control not only his pet projects, but an agenda for the whole country going forward." Palidore and Marshall simply sat transfixed by this one-sided conversation.

"While I agree with most of what they want to do, I fear it is the beginning of a political party which I very much oppose. I understand that banding together to acquire political strength may seem *logical*, but I worry that over time, one's allegiance to a political party may become greater than one's allegiance to our country, and *that* could become a very bad thing.

"Thomas and I have not always been on the best of terms. As you may recall, he was my Secretary of State until I had to ask for his resignation due to disagreements we had concerning policy matters. Notwithstanding this, his thinking on many things is well-placed and we maintain a deep respect for each other. He is, in my opinion, actually a *brilliant* man and will likely succeed John Adams as president.

But I am boring you with this talk. I just wanted you to know why he is attending, and let you be aware that any conflict you may have heard concerning Thomas and myself has more to do with a political difference of opinion than any ill feelings we may harbor towards each other as individuals."

"Well, thank you for sharing that with us," Palidore said, rather stunned by the frankness of the conversation. "I must confess I have not always followed the political news and was unaware of any issues between you and Vice-President Jefferson. I think most of the country holds both of you in the highest esteem." Marshall sat nodding his agreement as Palidore spoke.

The President then continued. "Thank you, but shall we move on? So, rather than have me get up again, I have asked Thomas to introduce you to explain the purpose of the new society. Hopefully, this will save time. It seems the vice-president is a close friend of Senator Grayson whose son you saved. So, he wants to publicly 'thank you' for that before turning the meeting over to you. You can then briefly tell the audience about the society and go over the proposed Articles and By-Laws. Which of you gentlemen will do that part?"

"Marshall did most of the work on them, so it is only fitting he should handle it," Palidore said.

The president immediately turned his attention to Marshall.

"Please, take my advice, then, and do *not* start reading this stuff to them. No one needs to sit through that. Just tell them they each have a copy and how certain you are that they have studied it. I've already talked to a couple of them who are set to jump up and move the adoption of the Articles and Bylaws. That motion will be immediately seconded. At that point, you should ask if there are any objections to the motion. There will be a few seconds of silence while everyone is pondering what you've just said. Whereupon you should quickly say 'hearing no objections to the motion, it is so ordered.' Believe me, this works every time . . . really speeds things up. The poor brassards will never even know it was adopted without there ever being an actual vote.

"After that, quickly move to the next item which is the election of initial officers. Someone will stand and nominate Dr. Montgomery for President, and Dr. Robinson for Secretary-Treasurer. Another will then move to request the nominations be closed and it will be seconded. Again, simply ask 'Any objection to closing the nominations?' After a brief period of silence you declare: 'There being no objections, the nominations are closed.' You can then look over to Palidore and say something like: 'Well, Palidore, I guess we have been elected.' Then, turn it over to Palidore for a few remarks before lunch is served."

The men sat in silence; actually, breathless with the speed of all they had heard. Washington looked from one to the other.

"Palidore, why not then take a few minutes to go over the vision for the society and give them a deadline for sending in nominations to serve on the Board of Directors. Let them know that once the deadline is met, you will send out ballots to each member so a board can be formed to begin planning functions of the society. You can then ask if there are any questions before we eat. Usually, the promise of good food will act as a sufficient deterrent to any lengthy questions.

"If it looks like someone wants to get talkative, act like you didn't see them, and sit down. The staff has been instructed to immediately begin serving food as soon as you sit down."

Palidore and Marshall, again, looked at each other.

"With all due respect, Mr. President, I mean 'George,' it seems you are advocating a rather expedited meeting. Do you think that is wise? I mean we might offend someone."

"Knowing a great deal about how things are *usually* done, and the way things *must* be done to get anything accomplished, I *absolutely* think this is how it needs to be handled. If not, we will be wasting at least three good hours at which end, half the people will be upset over some small item or language in the by-laws that is otherwise meaningless. I once sat in a meeting where people almost came to blows over what color the napkins should be at the next dinner! Believe me, with all that's in these documents, people would have no problem getting heated up. I've seen it too many times. Everyone will be much happier to just move on to the meal."

"Well, certainly, we will defer to your greater understanding of politics," Palidore said. "I assume this falls in the arena of a political kind of gathering?"

"I believe it does. Actually I am convinced that any significant meeting of intelligent men has a political undercurrent." the president said. "After the meal, I will thank everyone for coming. Martha will already be positioned near the door, and I will then move to join her. That will be the cue for you and your wives to join us so we can individually acknowledge each couple as they exit the building."

Chapter 12

The president stood and said, "Now that we have the meeting planned for tomorrow, perhaps, gentlemen, if you are interested, I will show you a little of Mount Vernon that most people never see."

Palidore and Marshall indicated interest in seeing anything the president wanted to show them. Washington walked over to the left of the bookcase and a door the men had not noticed until then. He opened it and they saw a small landing in an alcove with a doorway directly in front of them and two sets of stairs on either side. As they faced the door, one set of stairs to the right was ascending upwards, the second set of stairs to the left of the door descended downwards.

"The ascending staircase goes to our bedroom," Washington said. "The stairs leading down are the interesting ones." He motioned them to follow. The two men glanced at each other and began trailing the president as he descended the narrow steps into what appeared to be a makeshift kitchen where two lanterns were already lit.

"During my last renovations to Mount Vernon," the president said, "this was where the food was prepared. We still keep supplies and food here. I also have a nice supply of wine and whisky as well. I had the stairs built so I could come down without being noticed, and help myself to stored provisions. For some reason, I still enjoy coming down here. Most of the time I am by myself, but sometimes I ask my servant, Frank, to join me for a drink. Frank serves me in much the same way a butler would, and while it may not be socially acceptable to drink with one's staff, I find this the perfect place to break that ridiculous rule. Frank is special to me, and I consider him a friend with whom I enjoy talking from time to time.

"He offers a different perspective of where our country should be headed, and I think he helps keep me grounded. In any event, Frank has certainly lived a different life than I, but no less valued."

"Do you own him?" Marshal asked abruptly. Palidore couldn't believe he had asked such a question, but the president didn't seem bothered at all, and quickly responded.

"I do, but Frank knows he is free to leave whenever he wants. He likes it here, and I don't think he will ever choose to leave, even after I am gone. But here is what I want to show you. From down here you can easily see how each addition was added to the house."

He led them out of the small kitchen to a wide-open expanse. There were a series of lit torches perfectly spaced, lining both sides of the corridor The entire area was an off-color white painted brick beneath a curved roof. Washington walked over to a roped-off area.

"Now, look at this," he said pointing to a large dry well made of brick that descended into darkness. "This is where we are able to keep ice. We make it in the winter by forming large blocks to freeze outside, then put it in these leather bags with hoops attached and lower them into this dry well. The supply can last all summer. When we need ice, we send down a hook and pull up a bag and crush the block into small pieces. I am very proud of this."

Palidore and Marshall looked around without a word and nodded. What could they say? It was ingenious.

Washington proceeded to walk ahead a bit and pointed to limestone footings of what was once the original house and original cornerstone

"Do you see the initials 'L.W.' here? These are the initials of my older brother, Lawrence Washington. I acquired this property from him in 1754 before any of the additions. In 1758, I made the first addition by adding a full second level to the house; the second and final addition was the north and south wings which were completed in 1774."They continued walking a considerable way before the president took a left turn into another small room that looked like a supply closet. There was a table set in the middle with four chairs. He motioned for them to have a seat. He then went over to one of the shelves, moved some items, reached back and came out with three small glasses and a bottle of whisky.

"This is pretty good stuff, if I do say so myself. We make it here." He then proceeded to pour each of them a drink and joined them at the table. "I am not sure where we are right now, but it seems the hallway is longer than the house. At least it seems we have walked a good distance," Marshall said.

"A very good observation, Marshall. You are correct. We have crossed under the piazza and are currently under the lawn. There is another tunnel leading off this one which will take me to the Potomac River. I cannot show that to you, but it is an escape route for Martha and myself should the need arise. The door opening is disguised very well at the river. As you may imagine this is not something that is generally known. Captain Hudson would be upset with me for letting you know of its existence. Among his many duties, Captain Hudson is in charge of my security and takes it very seriously. So please, do not repeat what you have just learned."

Both Palidore and Marshall indicated they would never repeat it. But at this point, they independently began wondering why President Washington was taking them into his confidence to such a degree. It was becoming a little unnerving. There had to be a reason.

"As you can see, this is about as secret and secure a place as you could find anywhere. And, of course, gentlemen, you must realize that anything we talk about here must stay here."

There was moment of silent among the three. Palidore and Marshall shifted in their chairs. "Sir, we are honored at the trust you have placed in us," Palidore said, "which begs the question as to 'why,' since you have known us for so short a time?"

"Yes, well, let's get to it then. I have thought a great deal about our prior discussion concerning the treatment of your 'special bodies.'"

"We have decided to refer to them as 'the inventory,'" Marshall said looking directly at Wasington.

"Excellent idea," responded the president, "I was wondering if you have established criteria for selecting future individuals to be treated by you at their death?"

"We have not given it much thought as the individuals involved were all dying. It was hoped their maladies could possibly be curable in the future. So I guess such would be the primary consideration," Palidore said.

"An individual who died in an accident or was killed violently would not be a good candidate," Marshall added. "It is imperative that in order for the chemicals to work, the patient's heart would need to be functioning so the compounds would circulate throughout their bodies.""And I suspect it would need to be someone with a small family, or not well known, to stop speculation over what happened to their remains. As you know, with our prior patients that eventually became an issue," Palidore said.

"Any other criteria?" asked the president.

"Well, they would have to have money. We really cannot adequately calculate costs to maintain the inventory over future years, so we do need a financial commitment," Palidore said.

"But we have pretty much decided not to do any more at this time," Marshall said. "It could become too controversial, and we are not certain that society is ready for our experiment yet. But, sir, why do you ask? Have you someone in mind?"

"I do indeed and you are looking at him," Washington said.

"*You*, sir!"

"The very same," the president answered.

There was a long period of silence as Palidore and Marshall tried to comprehend what they had just heard.

"Before you respond," Washington continued, "please let me give you my thoughts on the subject, and the reasons for my request: First, I am not afraid of dying. I have seen more death and held more dying men than any one person should ever have to do. Secondly, I am a religious man and do believe in an afterlife. Thirdly, I realize in all probability, this may not work.

"Not withstanding this knowledge, I must confess that since our last discussion, I have been *consumed* by the thought of how this wonderful country of ours might look in a century or two. As a new nation, we have begun a grand social experiment to see if good men can truly govern themselves. I remain so hopeful that what we have begun will work, and that this great nation will shine as a beacon of hope to people the world over who hunger for freedom and just the chance to succeed on their own, free from dictates of an all-powerful government, king, or dictator.

"Therefore, knowing there is almost no chance that I will ever get to see how all this will work out, it nevertheless seems to me that there is nothing to lose by trying. When we declared our independence from England, our chances of success were almost zero, yet here we are today, a free and independent nation.

"Since death is a certainty, there does not seem to be anything to lose by trying to cheat it in this way. At least when that time comes, I will know that I did try; *and* there remains a slight possibility this experiment could succeed! That God might use it as a means of granting me a peak into the future."

Palidore and Marshall sat dumbfounded. How much did they truly believe in their own experiment? This was the moment of decision. This was the man to challenge them into believing in themselves. Would they be able to do it?

Just as Palidore started to say something, Washington interrupted him before he could get any words out of his mouth.

"I know, or at least I *think* I know, what all your concerns might be, and the questions you might have about what responsibility you will bear, but I believe you should have a chance to take in this request, talk together without my presence before you give me your answer. With that in mind, I propose we finish our drinks, take a break, and make our way back upstairs to find our wives. We can reconvene after dinner when we will have more time to consider any concerns you might have about how this would work. I believe I have thought through the issues well enough to answer any questions or concerns you might have at that time.

"But for now, I think I owe you the opportunity to put your thoughts together and formulate your questions. Now if you will allow me, I would like to propose a simple toast."

Palidore and Marshall raised their glasses in agreement, grateful for the opportunity to ponder this incredible request and formulate an appropriate response. They stood as the President rose and with his drink raised, simply said: "To the Future!"

"Here, Here," Marshall and Palidore answered in unison. The men all downed their drinks together in one motion.

Chapter 13

The president told them to leave their glasses on the table as Frank would be along later to gather them. Leaving the small room together, the men heading down the passageway to the main house. Upon their return upstairs, the president pointed out a few other items about the house, but there was an uneasy feel to the conversation. Both Palidore and Marshall were clearly deep in thought. They had just entered back into the study when they heard Martha in the hallway.

"There they are. We are about finished with our tour; have you gentlemen finished making the rounds?"

"Well, we have made some rounds, but not likely the same tour you ladies have taken," Washington said, giving a sideways glance at the two men.

"It seems we have taken up most of the afternoon," Martha said. "We plan to have our dinner at 6:00 p.m. so perhaps we should let everyone freshen up a bit and plan on meeting in the small dining room. If that is all right with everyone?" They all agreed and smiled at the thought of having a few moments to relax from the rigors of such a visit.

"Before you go to your rooms," the president said, "if you don't mind, I would like to introduce you to a special guest I have invited. He has set up something for us on the piazza,"

With that, they all walked outside where they were introduced to Nicephore Niepce. After formal introductions were made, the president continued. "Nicephore is a friend of Marquis Lafayette who became most interested in his work. He has been working on a method to capture and preserve images of people and landscapes. Nicephore has developed a process allowing for such images. He calls it 'photography' and he is about to formally introduce it back in his country. He is going to show us two images he has just finished."

Nicephore then removed two flat, metal objects from his bag and displayed them. They showed a reproduction of Mount Vernon from two different perspectives.

"Why that is simply amazing!" Palidore remarked. "I certainly would welcome an opportunity to discuss the science behind your process. I find it revolutionary."

"I would be most honored to discuss it with you, monsieur, but my work is far from finished. It seems the images fade away after a month or two so to preserve these you would need an artist to retrace the image. " Nicephore said. Everyone praised the images."Well, Nicephore has agreed to try and capture an image of all of us," Washington said, "if you are willing to give it a try." Everyone quickly agreed, and Nicephore instructed them where to stand. President Washington and Martha were in the middle with the doctors and wives on either side of the hosts.

"For this to work, I need everyone to remain perfectly still for several minutes while the images are burned into this box I have here," Nicephore instructed. "That is why photographs of people do not usually turn out well. Scenery, on the contrary, does quite well given the fact that it doesn't move. So, the quality of the image is dependent upon you keeping perfectly still until I tell you to move again. Will you be able to do that?"

Everyone agreed to try. He then advised they should look as relaxed as possible. The entire process took only a few moments, but when Nicephore told them they could move again, they all breathed a sigh of relief. They were about to leave when he suggested they repeat the process just in case the first attempt did not turn out well. Somewhat hesitantly, they returned to their various positions and went through the process a second time.

"I will process these images and expect to have them available before you depart tomorrow," Nicephore said. Everyone thanked him and began walking toward their rooms discussing how amazing the afternoon had been.

"Well, if this photography gets much more perfected it will put a lot of portrait painters out of business," Anabel said.

"I wouldn't worry too much about that," Sarah responded. "Most everyone would want something in color, besides it is really hard to stand still that long. Surely there will never be any photographs of children!" They all laughed at the thought.

Before reaching the stairs, Palidore asked the president if he and Marshall could use the study for a few moments.

"Of course," the President said. "I will look forward to dining with you later, and to our next conversation."

***

The ladies returned to their bedrooms while the men moved back into the study and sat down at the table once again.

"This can't happen," Marshall said.

"I know, but *how* do we say 'no' to George Washington?" Palidore responded. "He must know we would be opposed to it. Yet he felt very confident that he could convince us because he has even provided us with *this* time to prepare our objections."

"So, again, I ask: How do we say 'no' to the president?" Marshall asked.

"Well, he wanted to know about our criteria for the perfect candidate, and we clearly said that person should *not* be well known. He surely does not fit *that* criteria. He is probably the most famous person in the country, if not the entire world!" Palidore said.

"Okay, then, *that* will be our first objection," Marshall responded, "and I think we need to let him know we could surely face serious criminal liability if we were found to be in possession of the body of our country's first president," he continued. "Surely, he wouldn't want to visit such a predicament upon us."

77

"And how are we going to deal with Martha? She certainly would not be in favor of this idea at all, unless he is intent on not telling her," Marshall said, "but how could *that* happen?"

"You know," Palidore said, "there is a compelling argument that it is not even physically *possible* to do this. Think about it: We are not his doctors, so how, and when would we be able to administer the first compound? And even if we *were* able to administer Compound A, how much time would elapse before we had access to the body so it could be treated with Compound C? Certainly, there would be an elaborate funeral with dignitaries from all over the world coming to see his body lie in state. That, alone, would mean a delay of *weeks*. Too much time would have passed by then, and too much damage done to the body, to make him a viable candidate. Surely he will see that it is clearly impossible!"

"How much time do we need between applications of each compound," Marshall asked.

"I think a week is the very longest we could wait," Palidore responded.

"*That* is our best argument, I think," Marshall said. "He will certainly understand the science, and will need to understand this simply cannot be done."

"I agree, but I am not looking forward to our next conversation with him," Palidore said.

"Nor, I," said Marshall. "Well, I just hope our objections will be convincing enough to dissuade him." The men stood up, firmly convinced the logic of their objections would solve their dilemma. They headed upstairs to their bedrooms, somewhat pleased with their plan.

"Well, really, Palidore! It's about time," Anabel said as he entered their room. She and Mrs. Robinson had been ready and waiting for what seemed an outrageous length of time."I thought you were never going to get back here. Please wash up and change your clothes quickly so we are not too late."

"Of course, my dear, but I think we have plenty of time, we are just going downstairs," Palidore remarked, "and it will not take me long to be ready."

"Just get going, *please!*" said Anabel, clearly anxious.

The couples met outside their rooms almost simultaneously and descended the stairs together. The ladies led the men to the small green ornate dining room. A table was set for six this time, with two tabor candles already lit. A very stately, black gentleman dressed in a tuxedo greeted them and showed them to their seats. Both Palidore and Marshall immediately recognized Frank from their previous meeting with the president but did not let on, as they did not want their wives to start with questions. No more had they been seated when Martha and George Washington came in. Everyone immediately rose up from their seats.

"Please remain seated," Washington intoned in his deep, bass voice, pulling a chair out for Martha. Once she was seated, everyone else sat, again.

"I see you have met Frank," the president said. Then turning to Frank, he continued, "Frank, this is Doctor and Mrs. Montgomery, and Doctor and Mrs. Robinson."

"It is my pleasure to formally meet you," Frank responded. "I look forward to serving you. Mrs. Washington has selected one of the president's favorite wines. It is a French wine, but it derives its unique flavor from Syrah grapes. It has a bold taste, but is not as dry as a Merlot."

"We will have to yield to your knowledge," Anabel acknowledged. "I am afraid we do not qualify as connoisseurs of fine wines."

"Well, actually neither do we," Martha responded. "Frank finds the wines, we try them, and then just buy more of the ones we like." Everyone politely laughed. Frank proceeded to pour a small amount of wine for each of the ladies and asked if they would like to taste it to see if was acceptable.

"Oh, this is lovely," Sarah said, sampling a taste."Yes, I do like it, too," Anabel echoed her approval. A broad smile appeared on Frank's face revealing even, white teeth as he continued pouring a full glass for everyone.

"It is recommended that this wine be served at room temperature," Frank said, "but the president prefers all his wines to have a slight chill to them. So, your first sips will be as the president prefers, and your last sips will be as the winemakers prefer. Please enjoy."

Frank set out a plate containing a variety of cheeses and crackers, left the room, and returned shortly with an assortment of olives and pickles. Before leaving, again, he said. "I will leave for a while to prepare for the next course. Is there anything I can get anyone before I exit?"

The president looked around checking everyone's expressions. "I believe we are all content for the moment. Thank you, Frank."

Martha looking at the president. "George, can you offer the blessing?" The president folded his hands, lowered his head to pray.

"Our heavenly father, we have gathered here together, at this singular moment in the history of your kingdom and ask that you may bless those at this table with your love; thank you for allowing our new association with one another to enrich our lives so we may indeed do your will. In the name of your son, Jesus Christ, our Lord and Savior, we pray. Amen."

There was a moment of silence as everyone kept their heads bowed in respectful silence.

Then Martha commented, "Well, George, that was a *very* unique prayer," not looking at him.

"I don't know, it just came out that way," the president said while taking a cracker and some cheese before passing the plate to his right.

"I can't tell you enough how much I've enjoyed the tour of your home," Anabel said. "It is just so wonderful! Each addition seems to have added so much to your home. I must confess, I can't imagine there ever being anything else that could be needed."

"Well, thank you," Martha said. "We do love it here, but to be honest, I am a little tired of all the construction and sincerely hope it is over. However, there always seems something more that needs attention. Right now, George is busy in the basement, but at least that is out of sight."

"Did Mrs. Washington tell you ladies about the ice well?" Palidore asked the ladies.

Anabel and Sarah seemed perplexed, so he continued. "In the basement, if that is what you can call it, they have a brick-lined dry well. During the winter, they freeze blocks of ice, place them in leather bags and lower them into the dry well where they can last all summer. So, when they need ice, they take a block and crush it up. Pretty amazing, isn't it?" "Is that how this water is iced?" Sarah asked.

"Precisely," Marshall answered. Just then Frank reappeared and set out a small cup of soup in front of each place setting.

"French Onion soup for your enjoyment," he announced before leaving again.

The soup was followed by a course of lamb lollipops and asparagus. For a brief moment, everyone looked lost as to how to eat the lamb, but when they saw the president pick one up with his hand and eat it off the bone, they followed his lead. By their expressions, it seemed everyone enjoyed its unique flavor. Dessert, consisting of banana pudding with a piece of mint chocolate on top, was delightful. Frank removed the last plates and returned with a small after dinner drink which tasted a lot like coffee with a hint of butterscotch.

Sarah whispered to Anabel, "Do you suppose it would be improper to ask for another one?"Anabel shot her a curious look when Palidore spoke.

"Well, this has been a wonderful delight. Thank you so much, Mr. President, Mrs. Washington." He nodded to each of their hosts as he said their names. Anabel, Marshall, and Sarah also chimed in with compliments.

"I usually enjoy spending the evening in the chairs on the piazza," Martha said. "The view is wonderful at this time of evening and there is usually a delightful breeze."

"That sounds wonderful," Anabel added.

"I think the men will remain here for a while longer," the president said. "We have a few more items of business to attend to right now. We can join you a little later when we are done."

"Very well," Martha said as she and the ladies rose and left the room. Frank came back and inquired if there was anything else needed before he retired.

The president thanked him again for the meal. "There will be nothing else this evening, Frank, enjoy your night. Please close the door as you leave." Frank smiled, bowed, and backed out of the room closing the door.

Palidore Montgomery, Marshall Robinson, and President George Washington were left alone to begin a conversation that was about to change the course of history.

Chapter 14

Washington offered the men a glass of brandy before settling into the topic uppermost on his mind. "Gentlemen, before we begin, may I say something? If you would feel comfortable doing so, I would appreciate you calling me by my first name when we are alone. Of course, while in the presence of others, you should continue referring to me by my title. It's just that I would feel more comfortable, if we were privately on a first name basis. It would put me more at ease."

"Certainly, if that is your preference," Palidore said.

"Fine, then," the president smiled. "I assume you've had time to talk about my request? Naturally, you will have concerns. I am ready to discuss them now."

"Yes," said Marshall, "we do have some rather grave concerns."

"Mr. President, I mean, *George*," Palidore said. "We have taken your request *very* seriously, but we do not see *how* this could be possible, given who you are. As you know, we are not your doctors, so we do not see how or *when* we would be able to administer the first, and most necessary Compound A to you before raising red flags from your doctors and, even if we could administer it, we would, most assuredly, be blamed for your death. And that is the *least* of our concerns. Given your position, you would lie in state for a length of time, which would then prevent us from applying the second Compound C at the appropriate time. It would be a disaster." The president nodded his head as if to say he understood.

"Certainly, there will be an elaborate funeral," Marshall

continued, "Your body will lie in state while dignitaries from all over the world need time to arrive and pay their respects. This could last for weeks. We believe too much time will necessarily pass before we would be able to apply Compound C to your body and too much natural damage will be done by that time for the second compound to succeed. In short, we do not believe you are a viable candidate."

The president nodded his head again.

"Are those all of your concerns?"

"Well, we have others, but if we can't get past these objections first, we see no reason to discuss anything further." The President looked at both men silently for a moment.

"I understand what you are saying, however, I have thought this over for some time since I first heard of your work. I can assure you that none of your concerns will be a problem. First, I do not intend on making you my doctors, and you would not need to be present at the time of my demise."

Marshall and Palidore stared at each other with questioning looks on their faces. "But sir . . . *George*," Marshall said, "haven't you just heard what we said?"

"Yes, you have already explained to me how it all works," George said. "While we were in the basement, you spoke in detail. You said there are two solutions to be administered at the beginning: One with just pain killers, and the other with pain killers and compound A. You then leave it to the patient to decide which to take. Isn't that what you said?"

"Well, yes that is what we told you," Palidore answered.

"So, that is all I ask of you. You can provide me with those two items. At the appropriate time, I will make my decision as to which of the two I shall take. The only difference is that you will provide these items to me well in advance of my demise."

"But, George, you cannot mix these items together too far in advance. Compound A has a certain time frame in which to be effective. The solutions need to be mixed near the time of death."

"I understand this, but it seems to me that you could put the dry compounds in their correct measure into two envelopes, properly labeled along with instructions on how much liquid should be added. Then, at the correct time, I could prepare them myself, and make my decision."

"Say we do that," Marshall spoke, "and you choose to take the solution containing compound A, we *still* have the problem of delayed access to your body so that Compound C can be applied at the appropriate time."

"Actually, that is not a problem at all. We really have no immediate family. I have no children, and Martha's children have already passed. So, Martha is the only person who will have a say. I have for years told her that I want to be buried immediately without treatment, and without fanfare," Washington said. "I, of course, will find a time to review this with her and will leave written instructions.

"Our mausoleum is built over the emergency tunnel I told you about. Actually, access to the mausoleum is up a short staircase from the tunnel for security reasons. So, once my body is placed in the mausoleum and people have left, Captain Hudson will remove it and bring me straight to you at which time you will be able to apply Compound C," the president explained.

"Well, then, Captain Hudson will also need to know."

"Of course, but he will only know that I have requested my body be donated to science and because of my position, it *must* be kept a secret," the president said. "He is totally trustworthy and would not doubt my orders. I, of course, will go over this with him well ahead of time."

"So, *if* we do this," Marshall said, "we are concerned that at some point, notwithstanding the precautions, if it is somehow found out that we have your body, how are we not prosecuted as grave robbers or the like? If we are not prosecuted, then at the very least, we would certainly lose our reputations and become the most disliked doctors in the country." Marshall looked deeply concerned.

The President took an envelope out of his left side tunic and handed it to him. "In this envelope, you will find a letter from me confirming that I have requested my body be kept by you for scientific reasons. It notes how much I appreciated your willingness to do this and basically makes it very clear that you are in possession of my body at my own request. This would certainly prevent you from being charged for any crime, and quite frankly, I believe the public would hold you in rather high esteem. However, I do not actually think you will ever have to use the letter." Palidore and Marshall had dealt with many types of men in their careers, but they would later agree that none had the drive and determination that President George Washington seemed to have, especially at this moment. He was set on this course of action, and they could not seem to dissuade him.

"Well, you have apparently thought of everything, George, but I hope you know this still gives us a great deal of concern," Palidore said. "It is a huge responsibility for us, and presumably our heirs will need to keep your remains safe for decades, perhaps centuries. We just don't know if it can be done."

"I for one, am pretty sure, it cannot," Marshall said.

"While I am aware of some of your burdens this path will entail, I am also in a position to make it worth your while," George continued. "You indicated to me that you were looking for a place to keep 'your inventory' safe going forward. Well, I have a building in the city which will suit that purpose. In the envelope you now have in your possession is a deed to that building. It is yours, even if my body is never delivered to you. You may use it to house your inventory and, perhaps, someday I will be a part of that inventory.

"In addition, I am prepared to pay *twice* the amount of the combined total which your other patients have paid to date. That payment will be made in gold coin as soon as possible after you agree to accept my proposal. I am not trying to buy my way in, although it may seem so, but I also want to help ensure your success. Furthermore, I am not requiring anything back from you other than your word that you will do your best. So, now that I have expressed my sincere wishes, what do you say?"

"Mr. President . . . sorry, I mean George," Marshall said. "I guess we should have known we would not be able to turn down your request."

Palidore looked at both men and let out a resigned sigh. "I hope we are doing the right thing. But, regardless, sir, it will be an honor for us to be of service to you. However, you should know that you can change your mind at any time. We will gladly return your money . . . and the building."

Washington stood and walked over to the brandy snifter to refresh their glasses. "No, I am the one who is honored that you have agreed to my request. I know it is a mental and emotional burden on you, if nothing else. But I am convinced in my heart that I am no better a person in God's eyes than your other patients, and you should have no more regard for my body than the others you have in your inventory. As you have said, this will probably never work, and if it doesn't, I believe my remains will be just as content to lie wherever they wind up as they would be in an old mausoleum."

Palidore was grateful for another glass of brandy. After this conversation, he needed another strong belt of liquor. "You should know that I am not completely comfortable just leaving you with drugs and some written instructions on how to use them. I would much prefer delivering them to you personally and showing you how to prepare the solutions myself. You can provide us with money at the same time I can present the compounds to you. Is that agreeable?"

"Fine, however, please record the deed to the building now so you can get it ready for your inventory. And provide me with the figures the others have paid so I can get my funds ready."

"When and where do you suggest we meet again?"

"Why not met at your new building, so I can show you around. We could complete our transaction there," Washington said.

Palidore suggested they meet the following Friday

afternoon. Marshall agreed to take the deed and have it recorded prior to that meeting.

"Well, gentlemen," Washington said, raising his glass. "I propose another toast: Here's to the success of the Medical Society of the Potomac!"

Chapter 15

Anabel rose early and prepared herself for the day. Palidore had not been able to sleep well and was beginning to stir in bed. She looked at him as she patted her upswept hair. "How do I look?"

"Most amazing, my dear, I like your dress." Anabel smiled at his compliment.

"Sarah and I are going to help Martha place name tags on the table. She has it all planned so cleverly! There will be a small empty flower vase in the center of each table with a stick showing the table number. As we greet the guests, we will hand each lady a flower from one of three vases on our reception table: Either a red, blue, or white lace. Sarah and I will inform them of their table number and ask each lady to place their flower in the center vase on their table. That will end up creating a red, white, and blue table decoration. Isn't that just the loveliest way of involving everyone?"

"I am sorry, what did you say?" he responded, still waking from what little sleep he had managed during the night.

"Oh, never mind. Sometimes I feel I am talking to myself," Anabel said. "Time for you to get up and get ready! Frank will have fruits and light breakfast items out for us in the small dining room. We are to help ourselves. Now, Palidore, it is getting late; almost 9:00 am. The guests will be arriving in less than an hour. Sarah and I are going to help set up the reception area in the new room. I have no idea what you and Marshall are doing, but I am sure you have a plan," Anabel said.

"We haven't discussed it," Palidore said, "so I believe we will start with a little breakfast, then move to the piazza to greet guests and sample the orange juice with champagne. There is a name for that drink, I just can't, for the life of me, think of it."

"It's called a 'Mimosa,' dear. If you had paid attention when they first offered it, you might have remembered," Anabel lightly chided him."Actually, when the president mentioned it, he didn't call it a specific name at the time, so he must have forgotten its name, too," Palidore retorted.

"Now, don't be ill-humored, my dear. Honestly, for such a smart man, I am amazed at the small things you don't remember."

There was a light knock on the door. Anabel answered and found Sarah standing in the hallway.

"Are you ready?"

"Yes," Anabel answered. She turned to Palidore and said sweetly, "See you downstairs when you are ready, dear." The two women headed off to the small dining room.

Thirty minutes later, Palidore met Marshall where they ate a light breakfast together. Frank offered tea, but they declined, wanting to head to the piazza. Passing through the foyer, President Washington was by the door, talking with another tall man.

"Thomas, let me introduce you to Dr. Palidore Montgomery and Dr. Marshall Robinson. Gentlemen, let me present our vice-president, Mr. Thomas Jefferson." The men extended their hands in turn and bowed slightly forward in respectful recognition.

"It is an honor," Palidore said. "Very pleased to meet you."

"Sir, it is an honor for *me*. I believe you are the same Dr. Montgomery who saved the son of my good friend, Senator Grayson."

"Surely, that was more God's doing than mine," Palidore replied humbly.

"Well, then you were his instrument. In any event, the Graysons are forever grateful, as am I," Jefferson said.

"I see you are heading toward the piazza," Washington said,

"Let's go there together." Along the way, Washington kept talking to Jefferson. "So, you are aware, there will not be a head table for the meeting. We will simply approach the podium from our own designated tables when it is time to address the assembly. I find a head table causes people to focus more on the speakers than the purpose of the meeting."

"Well, George," Jefferson said, "that is so like you. But consider this: Perhaps the site of a head table full of important people would demonstrate the significance of the event."

"Ah, and that is so like *you*, Thomas," the President responded. "You feel the importance of each gathering as an opportunity to command their attention. Of course, please don't take my comment personally; it is simply an observation."

"Gentlemen, I believe all physicians attending this function are already committed to the cause," Marshall said. "Of course, that is simply my observation."

"Well spoken," responded the president.

They walked onto the piazza and saw Frank behind a table supplied with glasses, pitchers of orange juice, and bottles of champagne. There were also several baskets arranged with delicious looking cookies. Washington led them over to the dark-skinned man."Thomas, I would like you to meet Frank, one of my most trusted helpers," the president said.

"It is a pleasure to meet you, Frank," Jefferson said. Frank smiled, made a partial bow toward the vice president, said nothing, and handed each a drink. They all thanked him and turned to begin mingling with the growing crowd.

"Walk with me a moment," Jefferson said to both Palidore and Marshall, "So I can show you the model I brought with me of the University I have envisioned for Virginia." Palidore and Marshall briefly looked at the president.

"Go ahead without me; I have already seen it. I think you will find it interesting."

They proceeded into the meeting room now set up with a number of round tables, each with six chairs to accommodate three couples to a table. The room was quite large with several windows overlooking the outdoor piazza; ample sunlight was pouring into the room.

Sarah and Anabel had already placed name cards on the tables; they were now by the reception table greeting guests as they arrived. The men proceeded to a large rectangular table displaying a miniature view of several buildings, complete with sidewalks, roads, grass, and trees. It was really well done. Jefferson pointed out the proposed purpose of each building and was clearly very proud of his creation.

"I am looking for someone to serve on my planning committee for the medical school," Jefferson said, "and was hopeful one of you might consider serving. At present, the position would not be funded, but all travel and other expenses would be covered."

"What is there to do," Marshall asked.

"There is quite a lot of work needed beyond just constructing the campus. A proper curriculum must be developed, as well as a staffing plan. We would not have to employ all faculty at the outset. For example, I figure, we could hire only those professors needed for the first year's courses, then we could continue hiring the following year for the next year of classes, and so on. Equipment, supplies, and other items would have to be ordered, and so forth. Of course, the process is complicated and may take years to finish, but initially a medical clinic would have to be established to handle the medical needs of students and staff."

"I never gave a thought to such details," Marshall said. "You must be thinking constantly to be aware of all the needs you have ahead."

"Well, that is where I envision the planning committee would help. They could help run things while also attending to other duties," Jefferson said. "It would take a sincere commitment, but in all likelihood, the person taking on such responsibility would become the first dean of the school as no one else would know more about the school by the time it opens."

"I am not sure either of us would be qualified," Palidore said. "Neither of us has any teaching experience, and most of our knowledge has come from treating patients medically."

"You're too modest," Jefferson said. "First of all, you've *both* attended the University of Pennsylvania School of Medicine, so you've attended formal classes. Why, many of our doctors today, have had very little formal training; several have even learned their trade on battlefields. Besides, I am not interested in an intellectual. This school will need to teach what medicine is *really* about, not just theories and speculation." He looked at both men and seemed pleased they were still attentive to his words.

"In addition, I have it on good authority that you both devote a significant amount of time to medical research. While I am unaware of the *nature* of your research, this is exactly what we need. Someone who can teach from a 'hands-on' experience while, at the same time, maintaining their vision for the future and searching for new medical miracles.

"That's what I want this medical school to be about. Besides, after today's event, each of you will certainly be better known in the medical community, and your stature will improve at once. Either of you would likely be well-received on our board."

"Well, it is certainly an honor to be considered," Marshall said, "but I for one, would have to do an analysis of time it would involve. At present, I find it financially necessary to continue with my own medical practice."

Jefferson quickly added:"I don't believe much time would be required at first. That will come when we move forward. I remain hopeful that the state of Virginia will soon fund all start-up costs. That would allow us to at least partially pay for your time for committee planning. Initially, I need a plan I can sell to the General Assembly." He watched the expressions of both men before saying, "I didn't expect you to provide me with an immediate answer. I just wanted to see your reaction and plant the seed for you to mull over for now. Let me send you a timeline with a proposed schedule for the first few meetings. Please look the schedules over and give my request your careful consideration. I would be indebted to you."

Both Palidore and Marshall promised they would look forward to his paperwork. More guests approached the display table and were looking at the model. Jefferson was pleased begin explaining it to them as Palidore and Marshall walked on.

"Not my cup of tea," Palidore said.

"I think it would be fantastic," Marsgakk said. "I am really interested if I can make the numbers work."

"Then you should go for it. You deserve the position and would do a fine job. I hope it works out for you."

"I would miss our continued research together, Marshall, but as we have always considered, it probably won't work out anyway, although it is still an intriguing idea, and we will always need to stay in contact concerning our inventory," Palidore moved closer to Marshall and cupped his hand to whisper into Marshall's ear: "Besides, as you recall, we have agreed not to add any more inventory beyond our newest commitment to George."

Chapter 16

At the first meeting of the Society of the Potomac, people continued to gather, mingle and circulate at Mount Vernon. The mood was festive, and everyone had a chance to tour the stately home guided by one of the staff.

At his planned time, President Washington commenced to ring a bell several times. Staff members asked everyone to proceed to their designated seat at the dining tables. The ladies took great pleasure putting their flowers in the table vases and carefully arranging them. The president then asked Father John to say a Grace so the meal could be served immediately following the meeting, which the distinguished pastor was glad to do.

He then introduced Vice-President Thomas Jefferson who jumped right into his explanation and vision for the new University of Virginia. In great detail, he described the campus, the nature, and purpose of each building, and the reason this new university was completely necessary. Then he focused on the desire for a medical school, before taking a short detour to acknowledge Dr. Palidore Montgomery's saving of Senator Grayson's son. His talk took much longer than anyone expected, which he concluded by inviting those who had not seen the model set up in another room to please view it before they left later that day.

Because of the length of the vice president's speech, the plan for expediting the meeting, as previously outlined by President Washington, went exactly as planned. The Articles and Bylaws were quickly adopted, and Palidore and Marshall were elected to their posts.

"Does anyone have any questions before dinner is served?" Palidore asked. The hungry crown had no questions, whereupon Palidore raised his wine glass and proposed a toast.

"On behalf of the Medical Society of the Potomac, let us please stand and raise our glasses to our wonderful hosts, President and Mrs. George Washington."

Everyone stood at their seats in unison and a chorus of "Here, here," went up. Sarah and Anabel beamed with pride at their now-famous husbands as dinner was served. The conversations at the various tables were light and respectful. The third couple seated with Palidore, Marshall, and their wives, had grown up in Deltaville, Virginia, but had moved to D.C. after the husband had attended medical school in New York.

"Sarah and I have been to Deltaville," Marshall said. The couples conversed about the wonderful view from Deltaville, and the Rappahannock River where there was almost always an endless number of sailboats decorating the river.

As people were nearly finished with dessert, Palidore noticed President Washington moving toward the door where Martha was already stationed.. He told Marshall and the others it was their cue to join them. The two couples excused themselves from their table and moved to the door to join the hosts just as a bell rang. Everyone's attention turned toward the Washingtons.

"Martha and I want to thank you all for taking time to join us here today," President Washington said to the guests. "More importantly, thank you for helping with the formation of this very important organization."

People then began rising and filing forward to shake hands and bid them goodbye. Palidore and Marshall knew the people were lining up for a chance to speak to the president, but would speak to him and Marshall in the receiving line out of courtesy. Knowing he was not likely to remember all the names, nevertheless, he good-naturedly tried. His favorite trick was to immediately use the name of the person introduced to him again. So, if he was introduced to "James" he would immediately say something like: "Nice meeting you, James." It helped him put a face with a name.

Anabel and Sarah were star-struck and appeared to be soaking-up every moment of it.

As the last of the guests went out the door, the president addressed Palidore and Marshall. "I think that went well. Thank you, again, for all you have done to help make this a successful event. Captain Hudson will help you with your luggage since your carriages have already been brought around."

Before Palidore or Marshall could say anything, Anabel and Sarah jumped right in with their appreciative responses. Anabel and Sarah nearly swooned when the president gave each a slight bow and kiss on the back of their hands.

"Oh, I have something for you," Washington said almost as an afterthought. "Please give me a moment." He went to his study and returned with two folders handing them to each couple. Upon opening the envelopes, they were amazed to find the "photograph" that Nicephore had taken. Each copy was actually quite good, even though everyone looked a little stiff.

"This item will be one of our most valued possessions," Palidore said. Sarah could not contain her emotions and threw her arms around the president, giving him a peck on the check. Marshall looked as if he would scold her, when the President gave a sheepish smile.

"And that, young lady, may be one of *my* most valued memories of this event."

Sarah blushed as they started upstairs to their rooms to collect their luggage for Captain Hudson to pick up.

The ride home was warm and humid in the damp air. Palidore and Anabel were too caught up in reflections of Mount Vernon to say much to each other at all.

"Do you know what I think was most amazing?" Anabel asked. Before Palidore could respond, she answered her own question. "How normal, if that is the right word, that both George and Martha were. Perhaps, 'down-to-earth' is better. They just made you feel like you were old friends and quite comfortable in their presence. Not just to us, but everyone. There were no 'airs' about them at all. I guess that is why we are talking about them. I even feel comfortable using their first names."

"You are right, Anabel, they do attempt to make every effort to make you feel you are on their level, when you know that is far from the truth. I think the most amazing thing was this photograph." He held it up in his left hand before continuing. "Who would ever have thought it would be possible to capture a moment in time. Such a wonderful invention. I intend to get an artist to retrace the image as soon as possible then get it properly framed. We are truly living in amazing times."

Before he could say anything further, he noticed Anabel had nodded off and was leaning against him. He put his right arm around her and smiled. It was a good feeling to have her asleep upon his shoulder.

***

The following week was hectic. Palidore had to bring nurse White up to date. He had previously told her about the formation of the Medical Society of the Potomac, and the fact the meeting was at Mount Vernon, but she wanted to know all details including what everyone wore. She was disappointed he could not recall much of those details. But he was able to describe the house in detail, and his meeting with Vice President Jefferson and the plans for building the University of Virginia.

The patient load during the following days was so heavy, they didn't have time for lunch, nor was there any let up in sight. So Aletha was shocked when Palidore informed her on Thursday they would be closed on Friday. "

"But there is no way of contacting people in advance," she complained.

"We will have to post a notice on the door," he answered. Palidore tried to explain it was necessary to work for the new medical society, but Aletha couldn't resist contributing a bit of her own practical advice.

"I am pleased for you, Palidore, that you have gotten this important post. You deserve the recognition, but the society, itself, will not save any lives or make anyone feel better. I just hope our patients won't suffer. We personally know almost every one of our patients, and it's hard for me to tell them to wait when they are suffering."

"I know you are right," Palidore said, "and you have such a caring heart. I worry, too, but feel certain I will be able to absorb these new duties. In just a few weeks, things will be back to normal," he said.

Aletha raised her right eyebrow. "Would it be alright if *I* came in on Friday? I am not a doctor, but I can help some people, and at least schedule those I cannot."

"You don't have to do that, but if it makes you feel better, you certainly may do so. And don't sell yourself short, after all these years working together, I feel certain you know everything I know. Just make sure the patients understand that I am away, and it is their choice to allow you to see them or come back." Aletha smiled, feeling good about the confidence Palidore had in her.

***

Life at home was also hectic. With long days at work, suppers had been pushed back, and household duties had been neglected. Anabel was talking non-stop about their visit to Mount Vernon. She had taken to rearranging things in their home until Palidore finally inquired as to why. She confessed wanting to paint the dining room green to match the small dining room at Mount Vernon.

"It's probably silly," she acknowledged, "but I have so many fond memories of our trip that I feel the change will be a reminder of our visit there."

Palidore could see hope in her eyes and relented.

"That's a wonderful idea," he said, and was instantly showered with kisses and hugs. But he followed by saying: "Please don't think it can happen overnight."

Retiring to his study with a glass of his favorite scotch whisky and pipe, he sat at his desk looking at the photograph which had now been treated and properly framed. It was at that moment when Palidore realized their trip to Mount Vernon may well have changed his life . . . their life, in a profound way. He could only hope it was for the better.

Chapter 17

Marshall recorded the deed the president had given them and was now waiting in front of the property. Palidore arrived carrying a small valise and shortly thereafter, Captain Hudson arrived with President Washington who was also carrying a case, this one slightly larger. Hopping out of the carriage, the president shook hands all around.

"Well, what do you think?" he asked, gesturing at the building before them.

"It's amazing," Palidore said, "much larger than I expected." He was looking at a three-story brick building painted a light tan with black shutters on all windows. The top two stories had four evenly spaced tall, narrow windows. The first floor had three similar windows and a black door far to the right. There was a small fence on the ground level directly under the three first-floor windows with steps leading down to a basement area. At the bottom of the steps was a double black door with a small window next to it.

"The building has three floors, plus a finished attic and full basement. It was last used to warehouse building materials while we worked on the Masonic Temple," Washington explained. "I really have little use for it now, but it seemed ideal for your purposes . . . well, actually, I guess it will *still* store items – just a slightly different inventory," he said while smiling. He handed the keys to Marshall. "Let's go in."

Entering the first-floor door, they found themselves in one large open room. At the far wall, they saw one set of stairs going up to the second floor, and another set leading down to the basement.

"Please note how the tall windows let in enough sun to brighten the entire room," the president continued. "On sunny days, you won't need a candle or lamp to see inside this large area. Upstairs, all windows are separated by partitions making them into individual rooms all connecting to a common hallway. The third floor is identical to the second floor, except it is not partitioned off at this time. So, it is another large space like this first floor and can be easily renovated to suit your needs. I will let you explore the upper rooms at your leisure; but for now, let us go downstairs."

They headed toward the stairs down. Entering a door at the bottom, they were in a large living room-type area with a fireplace at the far end. The president informed them it had served as an apartment for the caretaker of the Masonic Temple until he passed away some time ago. He showed them two bedrooms and a dining room. The president lit a candle and placed it on the table. "This looks like a good place to conduct our business. Please have a seat."

They each chose a straight-backed chair and sat around a slightly dusty wooden oval table. The president put the suitcase he had been carrying on the table, opened it, and took out two large heavy bags. He proceeded to open each one, revealing a large supply of gold coins. "The exact amount we agreed upon. Would you like to count it?" he asked.

"No need, sir," Palidore answered quickly, "We certainly take your word for it."

The president took a deep breath. "Well, then, that should take care of my part of the bargain. But I have a few more questions to ask you about the process."

"Of course," Palidore said. "Please ask anything you like."

"What is *in* the medicine, and how will it make me feel?" the president began. Marshall fielded the question before Palidore could answer.

"First, the medicinal mixture contains a very strong pain

reliever," he said. "Palidore and I have actually tried the pain killer portion to judge its effects and experience it for ourselves. We can say it is quite interesting. The main ingredient is something called 'opium' which not only addresses any pain you might be feeling but gives you a euphoric experience that is difficult to describe. Then, of course, it also contains Compound A which would make you feel somewhat uncomfortable as it begins circulating through your bloodstream if it wasn't for the opium to relax you. There is also a mixture that will cause you to go to the bathroom several times in a short period of time. The effect of that is to cleanse your colon. Then, you will become very thirsty, so have plenty of water available and drink as much as you can. Those are the items you will consume . . . if you choose to proceed with Compound A. Remember, you will have a choice to take either the Compound A mixture to start the process, or if you decide *not* to go ahead with it, just take the pain killers by themselves," Marshall waited for the president to absorb the information. "Is there another question?"

"Well, yes. What will people *around* me think is happening if they don't know what I have taken?"

"A very good question! They, of course, will notice your need to relieve yourself often," Marshall said. "Because the liquid in your body is slowly changing into a gelatin state, it will make the flow of your blood begin to slow, and your heart will begin having trouble keeping a beat. The most pronounced symptom will be labored breathing because your lungs will not be able to inject enough oxygen into the bloodstream. An attending physician will likely try to address this issue first. But because he will not be aware of the cause, he will be unsuccessful."

"What then, will actually cause my death?" Washington asked.

"Well, it will seem most likely the symptoms leading you to consume the mixture in the first place have caused your death. However, the *actual* cause will be the mixture creating a lack of oxygen. You may possibly experience a heart attack. Then again, the gelatinized liquid may cause your body to react as if you were having a stroke. We cannot be entirely sure because it might also depend upon the very reason you made the decision to take the mixture in the first place. Does that help?"

"Somewhat," the president paused. "Will the process that Compound A has begun in my body continue to work after I am pronounced dead?"

"Yes, it will," Marshall said, "but our *real* goal is to make the solution so diluted that it A will have thoroughly circulated throughout your body *before* it begins to cause reactions with the other fluids naturally found in the body. When *that* happens, then your breathing and heart will stop, while the process in the blood will continue working until all your bodily liquid has turned to gelatin. Over the next three days, your body temperature will continue to cool to the point of almost freezing. Before this action is completed, we will need to finish processing your body with Compound C." The president sat quietly, pondering the information, forming a mental picture of his own death, and what it would seem like.

"One more thing," he added, "should this actually work, and I am revived, will I remember anything about the process at all?"

"Ah!" Palidore said. "*That* is the question we cannot answer for you. We really don't *know* since no one, to our knowledge, has ever been revived using this process. But what we have learned from our ancient Egyptian teachers leads us to believe this is possible. It is our best guess that you might have a brief period of amnesia followed by a time of some confusion before things begin to fall into place. But we are simply not certain."

"Well," the president said, "if I am at the point of deciding to take the mixture, it would most likely be as a last resort. I would only do so if there was nothing else to face but certain death, itself," he said. "Therefore, let us proceed with how best to prepare the solution."

Palidore took out a large glass beaker from his valise and sat it on the table. Then he removed some smaller jars, each containing what appeared to be dry granular chemicals of different colors. He placed them on the table. Lastly, he took out a small bottle of white wine and sat it next to the mixtures. When he had everyone's attention, he began to explain the procedure.

"We will prepare the mixture in the large beaker." He held up the first small bottle containing a light blue substance. "This substance will cause your body to expel any waste and you will have to relieve yourself more than once." Next, he held up a bottle with a brown substance. "This is a powerful pain killer, and it will ultimately put you to sleep prior to receiving the full effect of compound A." Finally, he held up a bottle containing a yellow substance. "*This* is Compound A, and I think by now, you know what *this* does."

Then he picked up the small bottle of white wine. "We could use water, but the alcohol seems to delay the effects of Compound A for a short while which helps buy you enough time for the mixture to thoroughly circulate throughout your body. I have measured everything based on your weight. However, before we proceed, I want to perform a small demonstration showing you what will happen, if you fail to do things in their proper order."

Palidore removed another beaker and a small pouch from the valise. "If I take some of this Compound A and place it in the beaker first, *then* add liquid . . . " he hesitated, "we will use *water* for *this* demonstration." He put a small amount of Compound A into the bottom of the beaker and began adding water.

"Watch as the first drops of water contact Compound A. See? Do you see the lumps of gelatin forming? It is immediately turned into a gelatin mass. Nothing will circulate. Now, why do you think that happened?"

Before anyone could venture a guess, he answered his own question. "Because at the *instant* the water hits Compound A, there is more A than there is water, that's why it needs to be diluted first. Now let us try doing it in reverse."

This time he took the third beaker and filled it half full of water. "This time, we begin with a *large* quantity of water." He began swirling the water as he slowly sprinkled a small amount of Compound A into it.

"As you can see, by doing it *this* way you start with a *large* amount of liquid which allows Compound A to be slowly absorbed until the entire amount is in the container. You will keep swirling the beaker, similar to how blood circulates in your body. Now keep the solution swirling as you add the other compounds until your mixture is complete. The only difference is that you will be using wine instead of water."

The president seemed to comprehend everything being explained and watching with rapt attention.

When he finished, Palidore took away the demonstration materials, leaving the initial bottles. "Now before we proceed, there is another important step that is not too pleasant. You will need to fill this small jar with your blood up to the line I put on it. Then, you will add this tiny amount of Compound A into it, preparing it just as I have just demonstrated. This jar will be kept near you at all times so future physicians will be able to see if the chemicals in your body are wearing off. If the blood in this little jar starts to liquefy then it can be assumed the blood in your body is doing the same thing. Do you know how to let blood from your body?"

"I do," the president answered.

"Fine." Palidore continued, "Since this is just a trial run, we will not collect a blood sample now, but it would be a *fatal* omission if you didn't save your blood treated with A in this jar at the time of the real event." Palidore began moving the beakers and mixtures around until they were in front of George.

"Now, I want you to prepare the mixture as if you were going to need it right at this time."

The president began rolling up his sleeves to keep his shirt clean. There was a bit of perspiration on his forehead, and he started to ask a question.

"No more questions," Palidore said, holding up his hand. "Remember, I won't be there to answer you, so try to do it now from memory. If you make a mistake, we can simply begin again." Slowly, George collected himself and began moving through the entire process using the wine first and adding compound A, then, one by one, the other substances as previously directed.

When he finished, and with his eyes still focused on the beaker, he sat it down at the table and smiled. "And there you have it! Or should I say: 'There *I* have it?'"

Marshall and Palidore congratulated him. "Well, done, Mr. President. Well, done!"

"Time will be of the essence," Palidore cautioned, "so you cannot let this mixture just sit around once it is prepared. Your blood must already be drawn, and you must be prepared to digest the concoction without hesitation. Do you understand? By that time, remember, you probably should be ready to lay down."

The men took a moment to look around the table at each other. The room was heavy with conviction. They understood this process was an undertaking by which the life of the country's first president would end, with the hope it would later be revived. No one seriously thought it would actually work, but they each enjoyed speculating what it could mean for the president, or the nation if it did work.

"Once again," Palidore spoke, "I need to remind you that despite the fact Marshall and I have shown you *how* to do this, it does not change our opinion. As medical doctors, we *cannot* recommend that you pursue this. However, if you do, we will live up to our agreement to keep you safe, and prepare a future generation on how to watch, preserve and hopefully, revive you at the right time."

After a pause, Palidore took out another package containing the same items they had just used and presented it to George Washington. Following an awkward pause, Marshall picked up the experimental beaker and handed it to the president.

"If you wish, you can time the process on this small sample of blood to see how long it takes before it is totally congealed. However, it will take longer in your body since the volume of blood in your veins will have diluted it."

"How long before Compound C needs to be applied?" Palidore replied

"As we've said, your body will continue to cool over the next few days until almost at a frozen temperature. We would like to treat you with C *before* your body temperature starts to warm to that of a normal corpse. So, the sooner Major Hudson brings you to us, the better our chance of success will be. But after a week, our chance of success will fall to zero," Marshall said.

They all sat in silence for several moments.

"Do you have any additional questions?" Palidore asked. The president seemed to come back from his inner thoughts and looked up.

"No, I think I fully understand the process now. I suspect we should take our leave as I am sure your schedules are as full as mine."

"We will do our best to fulfill our obligations to you," Marshall said. "But we cannot thank you enough for your generosity. This building will certainly fulfill our needs for decades to come."

"It is *I* who need to thank you," Washington said. "Your work is truly amazing, and should it succeed, I will join Lazarus as being one of the few beings in all of history to return from death. Who could imagine such a thing? I am most appreciative to have a chance to participate. And from now on my thoughts of the future will take on an entirely different meaning. I cannot *imagine* what it will hold."

Chapter 18

March 12, 1799 – Mount Vernon

Captain Hudson knocked on the door to President Washington's study. The president opened it and invited the younger man to enter his office.

"Captain, thank you for coming so soon. Please follow me downstairs." They crossed the study to the door leading down to the cellar. Once there, the president picked up a glowing lantern and instructed Hudson to do the same. "Quickly now, follow me." Briskly they walked the narrow main corridor, passing the ice well and entering a small room located on the right.

The walls of the room were built with a variety of unevenly spaced gray blocks in varying sizes. He walked to a specific stone and pushed hard against it. It moved inward, causing a hidden door in the wall to open. The door's opening was just large enough to allow entry for a single person. Once each had passed through, the men found themselves in a long tunnel intended as a secret exit leading to the river in case the president needed to leave Mount Vernon undetected.

They continued down the tunnel passageway to another small room where emergency supplies were kept. Entering, the president again opened a secret door in the same manner, by pushing a certain stone on the wall. Now, they proceed through that opening into a shorter tunnel and continued walking until they came to what looked like a large carved wooden piece of art attached to the wall.

Placing his left hand on a bird carved into the wood, and his right hand on the head of a snake hanging from a tree branch also carved in the wood, he turned the bird to the left and simultaneously turned the snake to the right. The artwork swung open revealing the entrance to a slowly elevating ramp. Hudson held his lantern high enough to see the short set of stairs at the end."Do you see these stairs?" Washington asked. "Do you know where they go?"

"Of course," the captain responded, "I managed this project. The steps proceed upward to the floor of your mausoleum. It allows someone secret access by using the trap door at the top of the stairs."

"Precisely," the president responded. "I am satisfied with the clever entrance to my mausoleum," he said. "Well done."

"Thank you, sir," the captain acknowledged.

"Now I would like you to install a few more pieces of art on both sides of the corridor walls similar in size and dimension to the piece that secretly opens the entry," Washington said. "That way, if someone attempts to find the doorway, they may try each piece, but never find the correct one. Perhaps, after a few attempts, they won't try any further."

"Yes, sir; and as you know, the correct piece of art will only grant access if the person knows exactly which two separate pieces of the design to turn simultaneously,".

"I understand. That is why several pieces of hanging art will serve our purpose. Having only one item of art hanging against this long wall invites curiosity. If I were to discover it, I might try figuring out its purpose."

"Of course, Mr. President; I will take care of it although, hopefully, no one will ever know about this entire tunnel except you, Mrs. Washington, and myself. The men who helped me build it were blindfolded coming and going to this work site. All they know is they were building an escape tunnel to the river. Even *they* do not know about this final doorway going upward into the mausoleum. I took the utmost care in having it finished by the most secure of means. And your suggestion will add another level of protection."

The president smiled at his faithful captain before asking, "And what of the first step? Have you had a chance to modify it as I requested?"

"Yes, of course, sir. Let me show you," the captain quickly responded beaming with pride. They walked to the short set of steps. "As you can see," Hudson pointed, "the steps are made of black granite, but only the first step can be moved. I'll demonstrate." Both men knelt and Hudson continued explaining. "You can remove the top of the first step by moving it about an inch to the right. It is heavy, so it may need a pretty good shove." Hudson moved the step and continued, "Now, once that is accomplished, you simply pull the entire step up like this. However, I suggest you only pull it halfway because it may be difficult to put back in place if you take it completely off. See? This area under the step provides a nice area to store something you want to keep hidden.

"That is exactly what I wanted. Thank you so much," he said. "Now, let us go back and stop by the whisky room."

They retraced their path, carefully closing each passage as they went. Arriving at the whisky room, they entered; the president retrieved two glasses and poured each of them a stiff drink. "Have a seat, Captain, I wish to discuss something with you."

Hudson sat and looked up expectantly. The president continued. "Do you know *why* we built the stairs up to the mausoleum?" "You indicated it would allow Mrs. Washington to visit from time to time as she wished, perhaps to place flowers without going outside or being seen."

"Yes, that was certainly my original intent, and what I said, but I have since decided upon another more important use for this access which I am about to disclose to you. However, you are *never* to divulge what you are about to learn *to anyone*. Do you understand?" Washington's face held a serious, determined look.

Captain Hudson's demeanor immediately took on a more serious nature. "Yes sir, certainly, it will be as you wish."

The president took a sip of his whiskey and lowered his voice. "Do you recall the doctors Montgomery and Robinson who were here last summer for the inaugural meeting of the Medical Society of the Potomac?"

"I do," Hudson said.

"Well, the doctors and I have reached an agreement concerning how my body is to be cared for immediately after my death. No one else other than the two of us, and the two doctors, are to know about this, *especially not* Mrs. Washington." He looked at the young man to see how this last remark stood with him. The look of surprise was in the young captain's eyes, however, there was also a look of agreement. Clearing his throat, Washington stood with his drink, and slowly walked around the room. He looked as if he was trying to figure the best to continue his conversation. He appeared a bit tense before he spoke. "The doctors are doing some very interesting scientific work and I am most interested in assisting them any way I can." He paused to let his words sink in. The captain was listening closely, as Washington continued. "Part of that assistance will be by donating my body to them for their experiments." A horrified look crossed Captain Hudson's face.

"Sir! I'm not sure I understand exactly what you are saying."

Washington had a look of exasperation on his face and threw up his arms. "I am not at liberty to reveal everything to you, so let me try once more: To participate in this. . . experiment. . . my body must be turned over to the doctors immediately upon my death. They will be fully in charge of it forever. But no one else must ever know of this. This is what I want. Do you understand now?"

The captain's face turned white and he nearly dropped his drink. After a long pause, he poke again in a pleading tone, "Surely, there are other, less notable individuals, who could be used for this experiment! *You* are the first President of the United States, the founder of our country! It just seems obvious that your remains should be revered, and remain here as part of the history of our country."

The president waved his hand to cut him off. "There *will* be a body placed here in the mausoleum, it just won't be *mine*. And the nation must *never* know the difference. Captain, I desire wholeheartedly to be a part of this experiment for reasons far deeper than I can ever relay to you, but I *will* need your help. If you have ever wanted to serve me, I am asking you for this now. Are you willing?"

Captain Hudson looked somewhat dazed as he stared into his drink. He stood and paced the floor mulling over the words of the man to whom he had pledged his life and loyalty. But this was different. He wasn't sure if the president had fully thought through the ramifications of what would happen if the plan failed. How it might taint his place in history. *Still, I have faithfully served this man who is a just and good man,* he reflected. *Who am I to question his decisions?* He paused only a moment before resigning himself to the situation. "But, of course, you knew my answer before you asked the question, sir. However, if I may be so bold to ask, wouldn't Colonel Lear, your personal assistant for so many years, be a better choice to handle these duties?"

"That is precisely why he cannot," Washington said, looking at him with relief. "Because of that very fact is the reason I must choose you. He has been too close to me for so many years and this would be too emotional for him to accept. You, however, have served me faithfully and I know without a doubt, that you have my best interests at heart. Only *you* will accept my command for something so personal. It is *you* I turn to in my hour of need. So, then, are you willing to do what I have asked?"

"Your will is my will, sir, even if I were to disagree or fail to understand," Captain Hudson replied.

"Very well, then," the president said, "I am most pleased. Thank you. Now, here are your orders: Martha and I will pick out my burial clothes, which will be my dress uniform. You know the one. I have more than one identical set and will provide you with a duplicate set of the uniform which you will keep safe until the proper time to put on my replacement. I have instructed Martha that upon my death, my body is *not* to be treated by any mortician. Instead, I am to be quickly dressed in my burial uniform and placed in a casket. It will be a closed casket, and after a small service, I am to be moved into the mausoleum as soon as possible. Martha has agreed to this, and will tend to those arrangements." He handed the captain a sealed envelope and continued "I have written those instructions down for you in case any problems may arise, or Martha is persuaded to postpone my burial. This will give you complete proof and authority of my intentions which you would need to present to her."

Hudson took the envelope from Washington and placed it inside his vest pocket. Then in an almost hesitant tone, he asked: "Since both you and Mrs. Washington look to be in good health who would make arrangements for you in the event that *she* would predecease you?"

"Well, if that happens, I will still be here, and can let you know the answer to your question at that time," Washington said. "Now, Captain, here is the most crucial step of all: After I am in the mausoleum, you are to retrieve my body and a small bottle containing a sample of my blood, that will be placed in a special box near my body. I have told Martha about placing the box with me, but she is unaware of what it will contain, only that it is special to me. She thinks it has something to do with my being a mason. In any event, it will be there, so be sure to look for it. Replace my body with the body of any other poor soul you can find, but hopefully a veteran. If necessary, the casket can remain empty until you find someone. Unfortunately, it will be necessary to keep all of this from Martha. She is a very proper person, to say the least, and I am convinced she would not approve of any of it. However, these are my explicit wishes and what I want to happen above all, do you understand?"

He looked directly at the captain. "Indeed, if she were to know, she may very well countermand my directions. Yet, you must not waiver in your determination knowing this is *exactly* what I want you to do. In any event you are to take my remains *immediately* to Dr. Palidore Montgomery. He and Dr. Robinson have moved their experimental assets to new facilities in the city. They are now in the building I used to own. But neither doctor is there much, so you will likely need to take me to wherever Palidore is working at the time, then on to the place where he directs you to go.

"Obviously to accomplish this, you will need to access the mausoleum via the special door and the stairs we just visited. You should be able to remove my remains through the emergency tunnel which leads to the river. Please prepare proper plans for this so I can review them with you as soon as possible."

Captain Hudson finished his drink. "I do not believe I will be able to accomplish this totally by myself. I will need at least one or maybe two additional persons."

The president took a moment to ponder the situation. "Do you think you can safely arrange for that?"

Hudson thought before responding. "If I can get a small cart or wagon in here, I probably can. I will position a cart at the tunnel exit and use it to bring in your replacement if I have one available at the time. In any event, I can then take you out the same way. I will have to wrap you in something to hide your identity."

"Well, if you can get that done then whoever helps you will not know it's me."

"Except that we are at Mount Vernon. Even so, at that point I will need a trusted man or two. No one knows about the tunnel and if I can get you far enough away from the entrance no one needs to learn of its existence.

"Still, I will be with a body in the middle of the night by the river which, to say the least, will look a bit suspicious."

The President reflected a moment. "I know you are right, but if you pick honorable men, they will know to hold their tongues."

The captain motioned to the whisky bottle for a refill, then appeared to have an epiphany.

"There is one soldier I know who can no longer speak due to his war injuries," Hudson said. "I also know him to be extremely loyal and trustworthy. Those who suffer the most seem to have another dimension of humanness in them to understand the situations of others. Perhaps just the two of us can manage to put your remains on a small boat, navigate the river and place your body in a wagon for the journey to Dr. Montgomery.

Washington's face brightened. "Then it appears we have the making of a plan!" He withdrew a small, rolled paper from his vest pocket and handed it to Hudson. "One more thing, sir, this is your new commission to the rank of Major. You have certainly earned it."

Hudson's eyes widened in surprise. He did not know what to say or how to react. Slowly, he took the scrolled paper from the president's hand, glanced into the president's face, unrolled it, and looked at it while his eyes moistened. Then he cleared his throat.

"This means a great deal to me, sir, and more for the fact that you personally presented it to me. I am very grateful."

"You are most welcome." the president replied with a smile. "I know I am asking a great deal of you, Major, but perhaps we will both feel better about things once you've had an opportunity to draw up detailed plans we can review. How much time will you need?"

"Well, I will need to look at the tunnel entrance, the shoreline on both sides of the river, assess the probable rate of flow of the current, find a place to safely leave a horse and wagon and determine how long it will take for me to set everything up. I should have details for you in a week."

"Excellent! I will look forward to reviewing the plan with you next week then, Major."

Lifting his glass, Washington presented it toward the officer in a toast. Hudson rose from his seat to touch Washington's glass in salute to their new understanding. An agreement that might very well affect the future of the nation.

Chapter 19

The following week, President Washington and the newly-promoted Major Hudson reunited at the president's study to review the major's proposed plan. Hudson had worked diligently during the week planning details and procuring necessary resources. He was anxious to share his plan with Washington and hoped his efforts would meet the the president's approval. He brought a sketch and began explaining it.

"As you can see from my sketch, the doctors are on the south side of the river which means to reach the tunnel entrance at Mount Vernon we will need to cross the river. I have located a livery stable somewhat downriver close to the water, which is here," he marked the spot. "It's ideal for keeping a horse and wagon for our purposes. Between now and the eventful day, I will occasion the place and use the horse and wagon to keep up appearances.

"This will develop into a routine so the manager will not become suspicious when the real day arrives. I have told him that I will need to use the facilities occasionally at night, and he voiced no objections. We made arrangements for me to pay him monthly."

"Tell me how much it is before you leave," the president said. "I will give you a year's rent today for you to have on hand." It pleased Washington that the major had taken his assignment so seriously. Major Hudson was the only person, besides the doctors, who knew his body would be entrusted to them after his passing. Of course, Hudson didn't know everything, such as the *real* reason they would receive him. Hudson only thought it was for scientific purposes. Washington now listened as the major continued narrating his plan.

"Of course, finding a replacement body is the most delicate task as it cannot be located in advance. The body must be found after your death, then moved. I have, however, discovered a cemetery used to bury veterans whose bodies are not claimed by anyone which is a rather frequent occurrence these days. As you can see this cemetery is also south of the river. My plan is to unearth one of the bodies that has been most recently placed there. With some luck, no one will suspect anything because the dirt will have already been disturbed.

And with the horse and wagon in place," Hudson said, "we will save a great deal of time on the day in question. I won't have to worry about timing my return with anyone. I've also located a second small wagon and positioned it inside the tunnel. So plans are falling into place.

"Now, do you remember the sergeant who I mentioned to you, the one who has no ability to speak?" Hudson asked. Washington nodded. "Well, I have spoken briefly to him without informing him of our *exact* plans. He only knows that I am occasionally asked to perform delicate tasks for you and there may come a time when one of those tasks will require the help of a loyal soldier who is able to follow orders without question. He seemed please that he would be selected to serve in such a capacity. I stressed that all matters concerning any project must always remain secret. Naturally, He indicated he would be honored to serve."

"Sounds like you have the right man."

"I certainly agree. Now, I have also placed a row boat in the woods near the river upstream from the stable. Upon the day in question, I will have the sergeant meet me at the cemetery where we will dig up a newly buried body, wrap him in a tarp and put it him the wagon. I will then have the sergeant rebury his empty casket to disguise the removal. While he is doing this, I will take the body back to the stable and change him into your uniform. The sergeant will be instructed to get the boat and meet me at our predetermined place of embarkation along the river's edge. Once the body is ready, I'll wrap him in the tarp again and transport him to the river in the wagon. We will then take the body across the river.

"As you know, the end of the tunnel, though nicely hidden, is fairly near the water's edge so it should not be too much of a problem for me to move the body on my own. The sergeant will be instructed to remain with the boat as I move the body to the tunnel entrance, just out of his sight. I will proceed into the tunnel, and using the wagon positioned there, will be able to transfer the two bodies before making my way back up to the tunnel entrance with you. I'll have to carry you from the tunnel to the boat where my sergeant will be waiting. He will, of course, think it is the same body I originally took in."

"I am a pretty stout fella," Washington said. "Are you sure you can handle carrying me on your own?"

"I believe so. It won't be far, however if need be, I will summon the sergeant for help. He is most reliable and trustworthy, although I would prefer he not learn the exact location of the tunnel entrance. We will then take you over the river and place you in the wagon. I will tell the sergeant to put the boat up while I pretend to take your body back to the original grave for reburial. He will certainly want to help me, but I'll inform him that only I may complete the task, as only I would be able to respond to someone questioning what I was doing at the cemetery. Of course, I will not need to go to the cemetery and will proceed, instead, to the doctors' office building. I will not leave you with anyone other than one of the doctors. The only thing I am uncertain about is whether the sergeant will wonder why it was necessary to move the body across the river in the first place."

"You will not owe him an explanation," Washington said, "but if you feel compelled, you can say the body was someone who had known a female friend of Martha's a little better than he should have, if you get my drift. Tell him Martha's friend became aware that he was gravely ill and wanted to place a locket on him, that he had given her because of their 'special' secret relationship. It simply couldn't be done before he was buried. It should not seem strange this woman would ask Martha for such a special favor since her paramour served under me. Because of the sensitive nature of this request, you were commissioned to fetch him to afford her friend the opportunity to pay her respects and place the locket on his body."

"I must say, sir, you certainly have a vivid imagination and an answer for everything," Major Hudson said.

"You give me too much credit. I do not sit around dreaming these things up. This actually did happen. But in the real-life version, Martha's friend. thought her husband had been killed in the war and began a quiet relationship with a soldier whom she cared for very much. When her husband unexpectedly returned, of course, she needed to immediately terminate her relationship with the soldier. When she learned her paramour had become gravely ill, she beseeched Martha to have me place the locket on the body when I paid my own respects. But I do not like being seen at funeral services since I draw too much attention away from the deceased, so I arranged to arrive just before they were going to take the body to the cemetery. I asked to see the soldier privately, and at that time did, in fact, place the locket on his body. So, when you raised your own issue of how to explain this secret mission, this event came to mind. Because I know it actually happened, I thought it might be a plausible explanation."

"Indeed, it will suffice for our situation very well," Hudson said with a smile.

Chapter 20

Palidore was tired and ached all over when he arrived home. It had rained nearly all day, and since he had walked to work, he had to walk home in the rain. November weather was cold and windy and today was a typical November day. Although he wore an overcoat, he hadn't walked far before becoming uncomfortably cold and wet.

Since his last meeting with George Washington, he had put in long hours working with his patients, or with Marshall at the new office in D.C. They had hired a contractor to make changes, had beefed up security, and had finally moved all inventory into the lower level of the new building. However, the more he worked with Marshall, the farther behind he got with his own patients, so late nights had become common for him.

"Thank God for nurse White who is willing to put up with my same hours, to say nothing of having to deal with Anabel," he thought. Sometimes Althea White simply stayed and slept at the clinic rather than going home and returning early the following morning.

When he finally arrived home, Anabel had started a warm fire in his study. She knew him so well; knew he would need it. Now, he entered the house quietly but cringed as the door squeaked upon opening. Still, no one stirred, so he continued inside quietly taking off his coat at the door and hanging it on the coat tree.

As tired as he was, he wasn't ready for bed. He couldn't sleep after a day like today. Walking through the dining room on his way to the kitchen, he paused for a moment and smiled at the new green and white paint now decorating their dining room walls. It had made Anabel happy to have something similar to the beauty of Mount Vernon's small dining room. She had even started decorating for Thanksgiving even though it was more than a week away.

He fetched a glass from the cupboard and returned to his study. Anabel had left the paper on his desk. He went over and poured a glass of his Edendour Scotch, picked up his favorite pipe and grabbed some cherry tobacco. Finally, after hours on his feet, he settled into his favorite blood red leather hammer-nail chair with its matching ottoman. He took a sip of his scotch and started fixing his pipe. Many times, he just played with the pipe rather than actually smoking it. Hand-carved out of dark wood, it had a funny little face on the front of the bowl. He put the cherry tobacco in and packed it down with his little packing tool, smelled the bowl, then took a straw from the tray on the adjacent table. Putting the straw into the lantern, it lit and he proceeded to use the straw to light the pipe. It took several puffs before the tobacco started to glow, then he sat back and relaxed.With his right hand, he felt the stubble on his chin. He hadn't shaved in two days, unusual for him. Then he picked up his glasses, put them on, took another sip of his scotch, and turned to read the paper. *These moments are to be cherished,* he thought and prayed tonight there would be no knock at his door with someone beseeching him to tend to a loved one. *Just one good night of rest*, he thought.

Despite the fire, he still felt cold and began to shiver. Looking at his feet resting on the ottoman, he decided the boots had to come off. Using his left foot, he managed to get his right boot off. As he tried to push his left boot off, a severe cramp pinched his inner thigh on the right leg. He bolted out of the chair trying to stretch it out. Grabbing the affected part of his leg with both hands, he violently massaged the muscle to stop the pain. But it stayed tight a long while before beginning to loosen. He hobbled to the kitchen and mixed a tablespoon of mustard before quickly taking it.

Hope this old remedy will work once more, he thought.

Unfortunately, this was not an unusual event for him. He had a history of severe leg cramps after being on his feet for extended periods of time. Then, as the pain subsided, he hobbled back to the study. His muscle still ached as he slowly walked around with one boot on and one boot off. Finally, after sitting on the ottoman for a few moments, he was able to remove the second boot. He grabbed the small blanket from the back of the chair and covered himself for warmth.

Easing back into the chair, he took another sip of scotch, put his glasses back on, and tried to read the paper. But only minutes later, he realized he was not comprehending anything. So putting the paper back down, he picked up his pipe again. After a couple of puffs, he laid the pipe down on its stand, closed his eyes and drifted off to sleep.

A rap on the door jolted Palidore awake. *Oh, no,* he thought, *What now?* Hoping his leg wouldn't seize up again, he tried getting to the door before the noise woke Anabel. Opening the door, there stood Major Hudson. Not noticing his new rank, Palidore greeted him. "Captain Hudson! What brings you here on a night like this?" The rain had begun weeping from the sky again and it was now pitch-black outside. Palidore could barely make out the silhouette of a covered carriage in the roadway with a wagon hooked behind. Something inside the wagon was completely covered and strapped down. Major Hudson looked solemn and was nearly breathless.

"Please come, sir, I have the president with me, and my orders are to get the body to you as soon as possible." Palidore could hardly believe what he was hearing.

Could the president have died? Unless he died only today, I would surely have heard something before now, Palidore thought. A thousand possibilities raced through his head as he looked at his boots again with dread in his eyes. "Of course," he said. "Let me get my boots on." He took enough time to slowly slip the boots back on so as not to spark another spasm. Fortunately, they went on easier than they had come off. He grabbed his coat, joined the major in the dark night and quietly closed the door behind him. His heart was pounding by now.*How could this day get any worse?* he wondered.

As they moved toward the carriage, he told Major Hudson they would need to swiftly proceed downtown to his office. As Major Hudson climbed up onto the driver's seat, he asked Palidore to get inside the covered carriage.

Palidore opened the door, put one foot on the low step and tried entering with his backside first, attempting to avoid another cramp. His right leg still ached from the earlier episode.

"Sorry to get you out on a night like this," a voice inside the carriage said, causing Palidore to scream and jump hitting his head on the topside of the carriage roof. Just then his cramp flared again and he screeched out in pain, grabbing his right leg as the carriage started off throwing him back into the seat. Feverishly, he grabbed at the leg again trying to stop the pain. "Palidore, are you alright? Is there anything I can do?"

The pain was so intense the afflicted man could not respond but kept working on the cramp until it finally began to loosen again. With emotions running high on this dark, wet, and gloomy night, he tried seeing who was sitting before him in the dark cabin."I am sorry, who are you?" "It's me . . . George."

Palidore could not comprehend the meaning."George, who?"

"George Washington"

Not being able to see well enough to recognize him, Palidore buried his face in his hands, forcing back tears that had started to flow. "I thought from what Captain Hudson told me at my front door, that you had died, and he was bringing your body to me to process."

"No, I am so sorry for the misunderstanding, but besides a slight cold, I am quite well." Palidore sat speechless and tried to regain his faculties before speaking again.

"So, if you don't mind my asking, just why are you here, and whose body was Captain Hudson referring to?"

"It's *Major* Hudson now, Palidore, but to answer your question, the body belongs to my dear friend, Frank."

Palidore was completely overwhelmed by now and trying to figure out what was going on. "I am so sorry about Frank, but why are you bringing Frank to me? For that matter, I do not know why we are proceeding downtown, if it is Frank covered up with the wagon trailing behind us. Please tell Captain . . . I mean *Major* Hudson to turn around. There is nothing I can do for Frank."

"My dear Palidore, we are headed in the right direction for now. I will explain everything to you, but I need to know if you are alright now."

Palidore felt the top of his head, still aching from hitting the top of the carriage. He proceeded to explain the cramping incident and all that had occurred. "However, I am beginning to feel better by the minute, thank you. Please tell me what is going on."

"Well, as you know, Frank and I are close, and recently, he wasn't feeling well. Very recently, he began complaining of a pain in his abdomen, so we finally had Dr. Smith attend to him. He was given medicine, but it did not seem to help. In fact, Frank's pain progressed to what I would call an *extreme* pain. It was so bad that he *begged* me to end his life. However, I just could not do it. Then I remembered the mixtures you left with me. I told him that if he took them, he would go to sleep, although he might never wake up, and if he ever *did* wake up, it might not be for an exceptionally long time. Frank did not care, he just wanted help. So, I mixed everything just as you told me and gave it to him. He drank it down right away, then everything proceeded exactly as you indicated it would. So, Frank's body is now in a condition to be preserved in the same fashion you had intended for me. I know he needs be treated with that last compound immediately and then be placed in your inventory, so I told Major Hudson to drive Frank's body and me to see you right away. I needed to be here to explain what happened, and I know I still need to make some financial arrangements for him, but please, Palidore, agree to take him."

Palidore could hardly believe what he was hearing. It was unbelievable. Everything seemed to be spiraling out of control. He had not bargained for this, but he could not figure out a way to refuse the president's request. He was cold, tired, his head hurt, and he ached all over. *I wish this night would go away*, he thought.

He sat in silence a long while before placing his head in his hands. *This could all be a bad dream,* he thought. *Maybe I'll wake soon in my nice warm bed next to Anabel.* But he wasn't that lucky. So, without changing the blank stare on his face, Palidore slowly lifted his head and asked if anyone had contacted Marshall. "No," the president said, "he has not been contacted."

Finally, they arrived at the office in the black night. Rain continued pouring down. After discussion, they decided to take the body downstairs through the double doors to the room below.

Major Hudson took a lantern off the carriage and used it to light the lantern next to the downstairs door. Palidore opened the door and brought in a candle from the lantern to light the other lanterns in the room. Major Hudson and Palidore moved Frank's body down the stairs, placing it in the center of the table in the room.

"Without Marshall here, I am going to need help preparing Frank," Palidore said to Washington. "If we allow Major Hudson to help, he will figure out what is going to happen to you. If *you* help, you might develop second thoughts about going through this yourself. So, which shall it be?"

"I'll do it," Washington said without hesitation. He then ordered Major Hudson to tend to the horses and carriage before taking a seat in the adjoining room. When the Major had exited, Palidore spoke. "Okay, we need to get all his clothes off." He then took scissors and began cutting the clothes away from the body. Palidore prepared a strong cleanser and handed the president a sponge. "You, start washing him down from his head to his feet. Once he is clean, we will need to remove all the hair from his body."

With a questioning look on his face, the president stood there. Palidore knew what he was thinking. He wanted an explanation.

"We will need compound C to be adjacent to the skin, so all

body hair must be removed. I have shaving cream and a couple of razors. I will start from the head; you can start with his legs."

It took nearly an hour for them to proceeded with the hair removal from the ice-cold body. When finished, Palidore took the cleanser and washed him, again. Then, he went into a closet and brought out a large bucket and a bag of dry compound C. He added water and began mixing it until it consisted of a watery paste.

"Now we will apply this to every square inch of his body." He handed the president another small sponge and they began applying the paste to the entire front and back of Frank's body, turning him when necessary. Finally, the task was done."We can take a small break and wait for the compound to dry. Then, we will turn him so he can dry on the other side. While we are waiting, I'll get the wraps ready." Palidore brought out several rolls of white cloth wraps some six inches wide. He began unrolling a wrap and placed it into the bucket of compound C making sure it was totally soaked. Once the liquid compound on Frank's body had dried, they began wrapping his body in the wet strips of cloth now laced with the compound. Finally, they finished and sat to rest.

"We will let the cloths dry some more." An hour later, Palidore spoke again. "Okay, I am now going to add drier compound C to the mixture until it becomes a thicker paste." After this paste was prepared, Palidore said "Now we need to apply this over all the cloths with our hands. We will have to turn him several times." They continued until he was totally encased in white cloths and looking like a mummy. "How old is Frank . . .was Frank?" Palidore asked.

"I believe he was around seventy," Washington answered."Does he have a last name?" "When he was purchased, he was just referred to as 'Frank.' I don't know of a last name."

Palidore wrote something on a piece of paper, put it into a small bottle and corked it. Then, he placed the bottle on Frank's chest and covered it with more of the paste.

"What does that do?" the president asked."I have written down

Frank's name, age, date of his death, also his medical complaints prior to his death. It will help whoever attempts to deal with him in the future," Palidore said. "Now where is his blood sample?" For a moment, it occurred to him that he hadn't asked if the president had remembered this vital step. But the president went over to his coat and retrieved a small bottle, handing it to Palidore.

"Oh, I see you have already added the small amount of compound A to the sample as it has already gelled." "Yes, wasn't I supposed to?" Washington asked.

"Yes, you were. I am just glad you remembered." Palidore then marked the bottle. "We will leave him here to totally dry out. Marshall and I will place him in inventory in a day or two. For tonight, there is nothing more we can do except, perhaps, return home. However, I need to stop by my clinic a few moments to let them know I will be late coming to the clinic in the morning."

"Of course," the president said. "I can only say thank you, Palidore. I will see that you are handsomely compensated for all you have done. It means a great deal to me that you have agreed to accept him."

"And you, sir, are most welcome. It is not every day I can serve my president in a meaningful way," Palidore said, then as if he remembered something, he gestured to Washington. "Wait here a moment." He went to the other room and shortly came back with a package, handing it to the president. "This is another package of chemicals for you. You can have them, but *only* if you promise to never use them on anyone other than yourself again."

"Never, again," George smiled. "I promise."

The men entered the next room to find Major Hudson asleep. The President touched his shoulder and Hudson woke with a start, jumping up and apologizing for falling asleep. The president waved it off. "Please take Dr. Montgomery home, but first stop at his medical clinic. He apparently has something he must do."

Chapter 21

M ajor Hudson brought the horse and carriage to a stop in front of Dr. Montgomery's clinic. It was early morning and still dark out, but the rain had stopped. Palidore went into the clinic to leave a message, and was startled when Nurse White greeted him.

"Well, you certainly are here early," he said to her. "Unless you spent the night again. Did you?"

"Well, there is plenty to do," she replied, "and I did not feel like going home last night in the rain."

"You are too devoted, Aletha," he said. He had only planned staying long enough to write her a note.

"The bad news is that I am not here early at all. I have been up all night and just stopped to leave you a note that I will in around noontime. I need a little rest, or I will not be of any use to anyone. I'll fill you in later, but right now I just need to get home."

"That's fine," Palidore. "I will handle things here until you arrive and will try to reschedule as many patients as I can. I hope you can get a little rest. You definitely look like you need some."

Seeing her in person had helped, otherwise, he would have worried about her response had she just seen a note. With that, Palidore turned again and walked out the door. Climbing into the carriage, he noticed the president now asleep. Palidore saw no reason to wake him and finished climbing in as quietly as possible. The president was still asleep when Major Hudson dropped Palidore off at his home.

Palidore quietly opened the door and went in so as not to

wake Anabel. But when he turned around after fastening the latch, she entered from the kitchen doorway."Where have you been? I have been so worried. You normally leave me a note if you are called out at night."

"I am sorry, my dear, you are right. Things were hectic and I simply forgot."

"Well, then, what happened?" she asked.

"Really, Anabel, I want to tell you everything, but I am so tired, I need to catch a couple hours of sleep before I can even go to the clinic. Would it be all right if I explain later?"

"Fine," she said. "While you are sleeping, I will draw a bath for you. That should refresh you when you wake up."

"That would be wonderful. I can tell you that I was tending to Frank, the president's servant, but it was too late, and there was nothing I could do for him. Naturally, the president had been hoping I could help, but it wasn't possible. Needless to say, he was quite upset."

"I can't believe it," Anabel gasped. "He was such a gentleman," she said. "Well, why don't you go upstairs, Palidore, dear. I'll begin preparing for your bath."

"Anabel, please wake me by ten-thirty. I will need time to get ready and be there by noon."

"Of course, dear," she said, and left the room. Palidore looked down at his boots and hoped he could get them off without another cramp this time. Then, making his way to their bedroom, he succeeded in removing the rest of his clothes. Grabbing a nightshirt, he slowly laid back on the bed, closed his eyes, and was asleep almost before his head hit the pillow.

It seemed like only minutes before he felt Anabel giving him a little kiss on the forehead to wake him from his sleep. Opening his eyes, he smiled into the kind face he loved. She told him the bath was ready, and his clothes were laid out.

Not long afterward, he was ready to leave. *Amazing what just a few hours of sleep, a bath and some clean clothes can do to make a person feel better,* he thought grabbing his coat and the lunch Anabel had packed for him before heading out the door.

That evening, Anabel told him about plans she had for Thanksgiving and how excited she was to show off her newly decorated dining room. Hugh was coming home from medical school and bringing the woman he was seeing and who was studying to be a nurse. It would be the first chance they had to meet Rebecca, and they were both looking forward to her visit. Marshall and Sarah Robinson would also be present as they had no local family and usually spent the holidays with the Montgomerys.

Palidore was also looking forward to time alone with his son. Hugh knew about the experiments and the inventory, but Palidore had not informed him about Frank, or the fact that at some point in time President George Washington wished to be part of their inventory. Hugh was next in line to preserve all their clients, therefore he needed to know everything. Palidore planned to take him to the new office and show him around. He would catch him up then.

That is going to be quite a conversation, he thought to himself as he began mulling over exactly how he was going to explain it all.

"So, what do you think, dear?" Anabel was saying.

"Ah, well, yes, it sounds fine," Palidore said, realizing he had been so engrossed in his own thoughts he had not heard a word

"Oh, Palidore! That's makes me so happy!" Palidore enjoyed making Anabel happy. He just wasn't sure what he had agreed to that made her so happy now. He would soon find out.

Chapter 22

Thanksgiving Day, 1799

A light snow covered the ground the evening prior to Thanksgiving; Anabel had the house well-prepared. Everything that could be done in advance had been completed. She had found a green tablecloth, now spread on top of their dining room table, and covered it with a second cloth, this one white, which she turned so the green one showed only at the corners. Several pies, cookies, and cakes were covered under glass domes, but not before the delicious aromas of her baking had filled the house, adding to holiday cheer.

She had also made a couple of vegetable salads and dressed a large turkey so it would be ready for the oven early tomorrow morning. *Good thing it's so cold out,* she thought. *I'll be able to keep many things out on the porch table to cool them.*

Palidore, for his part, made sure there was a good supply of Edendour Scotch on hand. He had already moved his best drinking glasses to the study along with tobacco for his pipe. His prized photograph with President George Washington and the others, taken at Mount Vernon, was well-positioned. This memory had become a wonderful moment caught forever and he wanted to see how long it would take Hugh to notice it and say something. *I wonder if Hugh has even heard of photography before?* Palidore wondered.

He had checked all lanterns making sure there was an ample

supply of oil and that all candles were lit. He had also arranged for the livestock to have plenty of provisions so he would not have to do anything for the animals while his guests were present. *I want to enjoy the entire time*, he thought. Despite all the cooking and preparations, Anabel had not had time to make supper for themselves this evening. She began cutting some cheese into bite-size portions which she placed on a large plate, surrounding the small pile with crackers, some freshly prepared bread, several small slices of salty country ham, pickles, and olives. *There,* she thought, *that will just have to do us for tonight. We'll be feasting on so much more tomorrow.*

However, Palidore was starving, and kept snitching from the plate until Anabel finally slapped his hand away.

"Hugh and Rebecca should be here anytime now, dear, so you will just have to wait. Why not go start a fire; it's getting a little cold in here." Palidore followed her orders and before long, had a nice fire going in the hearth.

"Anyone home?" a voice called from the doorway.

Anabel rushed into the main room to greet their son and collect her mandatory hug from Hugh, while Palidore tried to get up from his chair as fast as he could. Grabbing Hugh by the shoulders, he also embraced him with a hug. Almost simultaneously, they turned to greet Rebecca as Hugh introduced them. "Mom and Dad, I want you to meet my fiancée, Rebecca Johnson." Anabel and Palidore were so engrossed in meeting her, they had glossed over the fact that Hugh had referred to her as "his fiancée." Then Anabel noticed the ring on her third finger, left hand, and squealed with delight.

"Well, what a wonderful surprise! I thought we were going to meet our son's 'girlfriend' and are instead, meeting his 'bride to be.'" She reached to shake her hand but Rebecca surprised Anabel by wrapping her in a warm hug. She then hugged Palidore who had not yet been able to say anything.

"I think this calls for a toast!" he called out. "As it turns out, I already have everything set up in the study. And now, there is an even grander reason to celebrate." He headed toward the study and waved for everyone to follow. Anabel collected the coats and hung them on the coat tree before happily following behind them. Palidore began pouring scotch into four glasses.

"Please make mine small. I want to celebrate, but not *too* much," she cautioned him.

Palidore handed the first glass to Rebecca who was wearing a bright red dress accented by a white collar and white lace cuffs. She took the glass with her right hand, daintily leaving her baby finger away from the glass for effect. Once they all had a glass in hand, Palidore held his high in the air. "To my son, and his bride to be: May your future be as wonderful as this day is for us."

Everyone hoisted their glasses a bit higher. Palidore, Hugh and Anabel each took a nice sip, but to everyone's surprise, Rebecca drained her glass completely. "That's really *good!*" she said and handed her glass back to Palidore who couldn't believe what he had just seen.

"Another?" he asked.

"That would be nice," Rebecca replied. Palidore refilled her glass while shooting a glance over at Hugh. Anabel didn't know what to say, so she fetched a plate of goodies and brought it into the study. Then everyone settled into an evening of light conversation finding out more about Rebecca and getting an update on Hugh and Rebecca's studies. Hugh was two years older than Rebecca, but since his medical degree took longer, they would both be graduating in June.

"Well, tell me about your wedding plans. Are you going to wait until graduation?" Anabel asked.

"Oh yes. Hugh has made it clear to me that he intends to practice with his father, so we are planning a marriage as soon as possible after graduation. Do you think you will need another nurse?" she looked directly at Palidore who was caught a bit off guard by the question.

"Oh, I'm sure we will. Each doctor needs his own nurse, and

my nurse, Aletha, is just superb. I feel certain you will find her a great mentor. Maybe you will meet her before you return to school."

"That would be wonderful," she said.

To his relief, he noticed Rebecca was now just sipping her drink. He put another log on the fire as Rebecca stood and walked over to the photo.

"Wait a minute, what's this?" she said. "I have never seen anything like it before." She picked up the photograph to look closer and Hugh also came over to look. The appearance was a piece of shiny silver metal with a group of people in black ink on it. "This looks like you," she said, pointing to one figure, and looking up at Palidore. "And this looks like Anabel, but I don't know the others, well except that one kinda' looks like President Washington."

Palidore was pleased she had noticed."You are correct," he said with pride in his voice. "That is myself and Anabel. You are also correct about the gentleman in the middle. It *is* President Washington." Rebecca and Hugh both gasped, and stared more intently at the image.

"We were at a meeting at Mount Vernon," Palidore continued, "and the president introduced us to Nicephore Niepce who has invented a way of capturing a scene on metal. He calls it 'photography.' Everyone must stand still for a long time while his device works. Then, he does something to it and, ultimately, he is able to produce the photograph. We had it painted over to preserve the image at his suggestion."

"I don't know what is more amazing - you at Mount Vernon with President Washington, or the fact that it has all been recorded in this 'photograph.' This is absolutely amazing!" Hugh said.

Little does he know, Palidore thought, *this is just the beginning.* "Well, I will be happy to explain it all to you tomorrow in detail," he said aloud. "but it is getting late now, and I know you have had a long day of travel." "You are right," Hugh responded. "Where do you want us to stay?"

"You will be in *your* bedroom," Anabel said properly, "and

Rebecca will stay in the blue room. Palidore has already put your bags in the correct rooms. But before we go upstairs, I have something I want to show you both." She headed off to the dining room.

Rebecca finished her second drink, putting the glass down next to the exhausted plate of hor d'oeuvres and followed the procession into the dining room. "Well, Mother, I love it," Hugh said seeing the decorated room. "It is so cheerful! What in the world inspired you to do this?"

"While it is not *exactly* the same, I find it looks similar to the dining room at Mount Vernon," Anabel said.

"She fell in love with Mount Vernon," Palidore explained, "and beseeched me to allow this as a reminder of our visit. Actually, I am quite fond of it myself. Anabel has done a wonderful job of redecorating, don't you think?"

"Indeed, Mother, it's top notch," Hugh said, smiling and putting an arm around Rebecca.

"Well, I can't wait to hear more about your trip, but I think some rest would be in order." Anabel replied.

"Yes, of course, you are right," Hugh said, "Let me show Rebecca to her room." Everyone proceeded up the stairs. Soon a quiet fell over the entire house for the rest of the night.

Early the next morning, Anabel and Palidore were up early. Palidore built a fire in the wood-fired oven and helped Anabel with the turkey. She also had made hot oatmeal and placed small bowls at four places on the table. Cinnamon bread, butter, and maple syrup were placed on the table along with fresh fruit which she had just finished cutting up.

One by one, the guests came down to the wonderful smells emanating from the kitchen and found their places at the table. Anabel had a pot of hot tea ready along with a pitcher of milk.

Breakfast was over quickly as Anabel had hoped and now she could turn her full attention to the Thanksgiving meal. It would take all morning just to finish her preparations.

Marshall and Sarah arrived near noontime and were introduced to Rebecca. Sarah and Rebecca helped Anabel put the final touches on the feast as the men gathered in the study.

Palidore took the opportunity to suggest the three of them meet the following day at the new office downtown, so they could show Hugh the building and explain everything that had happened. Hugh immediately started with questions about how they could afford the building and its purpose, but both Marshall and Palidore held off answering him.

"We'll explain everything tomorrow," Marshall said. "Even though there is nothing secretive about it, the discussion would simply take too long today."

"Truly, it will be better for us to discuss it all tomorrow," Palidore said. "Let us enjoy Thanksgiving and each other's company." They agreed to leave in the morning and return in time for a dinner of leftovers.

By one o'clock the table was ready and looked glorious. Anabel was so proud of it all, she secretly wished Nicephore Niepce was there with his photograph machine to make a memory of it. The turkey was golden brown and sitting in the middle of the table illuminated by two tabor candles and surrounded by large bowls containing dressing, mashed potatoes, green beans, and cranberry sauce.

Everyone took their seats and Palidore said grace, then rose so he could better carve the turkey. Anabel passed out rolls, butter, and the vegetable salad. In addition to tea, each person had a wine glass filled with a delightful rosé wine. Anabel had wanted a white wine served, but Palidore never liked white wines much; the rosé was a compromise. Talk was lively with most of it focused on Hugh and Rebecca, their upcoming marriage, and their inclusion into Palidore's practice.

Marshall talked about his work with Thomas Jefferson and the new university to be built in Charlottesville. Of course, Anabel opted for the long version of their surprise meeting with President Washington culminating in the event at Mount Vernon.

After dinner, everyone decided to wait a while before eating the sweets for dessert. After the meal, as was their custom, the men retired to the study to smoke their pipes. Marshall and Palidore wanted to know what was new at the Medical School and Hugh, who was now up-to-date, thanks to Anabel's recitation of all events leading up to the meeting at Mount Vernon, still had lingering questions.

While the men were stoking their pipes, Rebecca surprised them by bringing in three small glasses containing some sort of liquor which she referred to as an "Irish Cream." It was something she had been able to bring back from Ireland when she had visited the past summer. They each took a little sip before grandly consuming it with ease. It brought approving smiles to all their faces.

"Thank you, Rebecca," Hugh spoke for everyone. "That was certainly a pleasant surprise, I must try and acquire some of this." Rebecca displayed a sheepish smile but remained subdued. Palidore put a couple more logs on the fire before moving back to the dining room where everyone had gathered again for the sumptuous cakes and pies. It had been a wonderful meal and the men, especially, took caution to thank Anabel and the ladies for all their efforts.

After dessert, Marshall and Sarah said they needed to leave for home as it looked as if it might begin snowing again. Hugh and Palidore helped lead the Robinson's horse from the stable and attach it to their carriage. Then everyone said their goodbyes, and the Robinsons left leaving wheel marks in the snow that had already fallen.

Though I am very glad to hear praise from the others, it is a lot of effort, Anabel thought, *Truly, I am glad this holiday comes but once a year.* Then, she gladly followed the others upstairs for the night.

Chapter 23

The next morning, Palidore and Marshall took Hugh to tour the new building. Palidore was anxious to bring him up to date and upon arrival, Hugh was impressed by the size and stature of the structure even as they went in the basement doors. Abundant light streamed through the adjacent window, but a lantern was lit to see better as they went deeper into the rooms. The entire lower level was made of brick painted white including the high arched ceiling. In one room was a bed and in another was a table as if someone had once lived there.

"Well, what do you think?" Palidore asked. "*We* think this is perfect for housing our inventory," he prattled on somewhat nervously. "Look here, we have moved them into this room." He opened a nondescript door to a room and displayed four wooden caskets neatly lined in a row. Each had a name attached along with a small bottle of blood topped with a cork sealed in wax.

Hugh looked around silently and seemed to be counting. Then he stopped in front of the last casket and stared. "Who is 'Frank' and why doesn't he have a last name?" But before Palidore could answer, Hugh swirled around with his arms out wide. "And, how much did all this cost?" he said loudly. Before Palidore could say anything, Marshall interrupted walking toward Hugh.

"Let's move here to the table and have a seat," he looked pointedly at Palidore. "Hugh has some questions that need answering."

They sat for well over another hour as Palidore and Marshall brought Hugh up to date on everything. Throughout the entire presentation, Hugh sat dumbfounded and said nothing, but his expression said enough. When Palidore and Marshall were finished, there was a pregnant silence before Hugh finally spoke.

"No! Hell, no! I won't do it. . . I *can't* do it! I can't be responsible for the body of our nation's first president. It is just not do-able. Someone will find out; someone will look to *me* and it will be all over.! I just can't *believe* you have agreed to this. It is so unlike you, Father. What were you *thinking*?"

Palidore waited until he was certain Hugh was finished before answering him. "I believe, if you had been with us, you would have done as we have done. George Washington is not someone you say 'no' to easily. But I have left out something very important which hopefully will change your mind, or at least make you feel better. President Washington has given us a closed letter with his personal seal which explains that each of us is acting on his own behest, and his personal direction; therefore, no one should bother or interfere with us as this is his *own* predetermination and final wishes. In addition, he believes he can have his body *secretly* delivered to us for treatment without anyone, including Martha, ever knowing. But just in case it *is* discovered, he has covered us with his letter. Of course, if for some reason his body is never delivered to us, we have no further responsibility or obligation."

Hugh simply sat and said nothing. It was an awkward silence, so Palidore asked if he would like to see the remainder of the building.

Hugh stood. "Sure, why not," he said rather reluctantly.

They proceeded to tour the remainder of the building with Palidore and Marshall explaining plans for each floor. It was late in the day when they finally exited the building, locked it up, and proceeded to their carriages. Marshall bid them goodbye, but his expression left a clear message that Palidore needed to bring Hugh in-line with their thinking.

As Palidore and Hugh headed toward home, nothing much was

said until they were nearly home. Then Palidore stopped the carriage and turned to Hugh. "I can't undo this, Hugh, and I need you to be on board with us. It is not what *any* of us could have imagined we would be doing but . . . well . . . it is, now, no longer a choice, it has become an obligation. Everything we have worked for will unravel if one generation opts out. What we have begun will take decades to complete. We must all work toward this end together."

Hugh could see the torment in his father's face, but could not continue to look at him. Slowly, he looked down, placing his head in his hands and elbows on both knees. After a moment, he said: "For *you* dad . . . I will do this, but *just* for you. There is no other compelling reason except that I love my father." He looked up into his father's face again and could see tears forming in Palidore's eyes. He reached over and embraced his father. When they parted there was a pause before Palidore started the carriage moving again.

"Thank you, son," he said quietly .

Chapter 24

December 12, 1799, was a frigid day at Mount Vernon, alternating between snow, hail and rain, but George Washington spent most of that day on horseback supervising activities on his estate. Unfortunately, he had not worn a coat heavy enough for the weather. Later that evening, when he sat down for a late dinner, he was still damp, and began having a slight cough and runny nose.

Throughout the night and into the following morning, Washington's condition did not improve, and Dr. Craik, the president's doctor, was summoned. Dr. Craik let blood, and gave him a concoction of sage, tea, and vinegar for the president to gargle. But all attempts were unsuccessful. The president, however, was still able to rise from bed and walk about his bedroom, even sit upright in a chair, but only for a few moments at a time before tiring again. On the morning of December 13, 1799, at 11:30 a.m., Colonel Lear prepared a tonic of molasses, butter, and vinegar for the president and said he should consume it.

"I will as soon as I can catch my breath," Washington said. The mixture did seem to help his cough some and he retired for the night. Around two in the morning, he awoke in terrible discomfort. Martha sent for Tobias Lear who rushed to the room and found Washington having difficulty breathing. He sent for George Rawlins, an overseer at Mount Vernon, who at Washington's request bled him. The blood was collected in a small metal bowl and left on the dresser. The president then asked for them to fetch Major Hudson and advised them that he was tired and wanted to be left alone for a while.

When Hudson arrived by late that afternoon, he entered the president's bedroom along with Martha and Dr. Craik. Washington asked everyone but Major Hudson to leave. Reluctantly, the doctor and Martha left. She took a long glance back at her husband with a worried look on her face as she shut the door."Major," Washington spoke softly in a hoarse voice, "this doesn't look good for me, and I want to be sure that you recall all the plans we have made."

"Yes sir, I remember," the young major answered. "How could I forget? However, it would seem to me that your passing is still a long way off. What does the doctor say?"

"Well, all of this developed rather suddenly, and the doctor really doesn't know exactly what is wrong. As you may surmise, it is never good news when your doctor must confess to his lack of knowledge." He took a moment to cough and found himself gasping for breath. "At first, I thought it was a cold, but now my throat is very sore, and I am having trouble breathing." He coughed again, this time there was a terrible deep rattle that made Hudson more concerned.

"I am convinced that when a person's time is near, most of them know it, and I feel that my time is nearing soon. In any event, Major, I need your absolute assurance the plans we made will be followed exactly."

"Yes, sir," Hudson said with a bit of emotion. "They will be followed *exactly* as you have ordered."

The president shifted his head on the pillow and seemed relieved. Then, he motioned the major to come nearer. In a low voice, the great man said, "You know the new access we built from the tunnel to enter the mausoleum from below?"

"Of course,"

"Well, I've never actually shown that to Martha, and have decided that she should *not* know about it. She can enter the mausoleum above ground, in a normal fashion. I want to be sure the side tunnel that leads to my mausoleum is also sealed off."

"That has already been done, sir," the major replied. "As you know, the escape tunnel is already sealed from view and this tunnel is off the main tunnel. In addition, I can report the other wooden panels you wanted on the walls have been erected and put in place. Should anyone find the tunnel to the mausoleum, they will only see four wooden panels on the wall and could not possibly know what they were for or that one is hiding a staircase. If by chance, they should decide to tamper with the panels it would be nearly impossible for them to know what parts on the correct panel to turn in order to gain access. Accordingly, I feel the world will forever remain ignorant concerning these tunnels. Even if they *should* be discovered, they will never know how access is gained to the crypt."

"Major, do you recall what I said about the small box that Martha will place near my body? It has a Masonic emblem on it. Its right over there. Take a good look at it. It will contain a small jar of my blood which must arrive with my body when you deliver me to Dr. Montgomery and no one else is to know. Do you understand everything you are to do Major?"

"Of course, sir, Mr. President," Major Hudson said. "Your wishes will be followed precisely, sir!"

"Thank you, Major," the president said, now clearly tired. "You have brought me much comfort. I am counting on you now."

Major Hudson stood at attention and saluted his commander-in-chief. The president raised a shaky hand to his forehead and returned the salute."You are dismissed, Major."

Turning away from the dying man, Hudson opened the door and stepped out acknowledging the others without a word as they filed in. Leaving the house, he mounted his horse and began reviewing what lay ahead and decided to check the cemetery for fresh graves.

I must also put my sergeant on notice as soon as possible, he thought. *I'll retrieve the small boat and check on the wagon. I can't believe the time has come.*.Major Hudson decided he would do another dry run across the river to locate the emergency exit. *Perhaps the foliage is overgrown by now. I must be certain I can locate the doorway and gain access to the tunnel. The last thing I need would be to discover I am locked out. No, if, or when, I hear the bad news, I will be ready to act,* he thought. The plan must be put into motion within two to three days, depending on how long it took to place the president's body inside the mausoleum.

When Hudson left the sick man's room and the others came back in, Washington motioned to the lovely woman who had been such an important part of his life. She approached his bed, and he took her hand. "Martha, I want you to know that I have enjoyed every moment of our life together."

"Oh, George, please don't sound like you are leaving," she choked back tears. "You will get strong again." He looked at her with a loving expression.

"If you say so, my dear," he responded. Then he looked at the attending medical doctors around his bed. "Thank you for your devoted service. But I am tired now. Can you leave me for a while?"

Reluctantly, everyone began filing out of the room once again. When the door closed this time, the president slowly rose from his bed and reached for a sack hidden on the bookshelf. He prepared the mixture Dr. Montgomery had given him. He treated the small jar of blood in the box with the mixture before putting the beaker back into the sack and depositing it deep inside a trash container.

Then, he sat on the edge of his bed and slowly consumed the mixture. Laying back on the pillows, he almost immediately felt a wonderful euphoric, calm numbness begin to spread throughout his entire body. In a matter of minutes, a rare, but discernable small smile appeared on the great man's face, and he lay still. President George Washington was gone.

***

Shortly after leaving the president, Major Hudson, had gone to the forgotten soldiers' cemetery and noticed a new grave had been dug, but which did not yet contain a body. *This may be perfect,* he thought. *The dirt should be easy to dig because it will still be loose.* From there, he proceeded to the riverbank, got into the boat, and traversed the river to the bank near Mount Vernon and the hidden tunnel.

It was cold and overcast, and fortunately, there was no one else on the river. He tied off the boat and worked his way up the hill to where he thought he would find the tunnel entrance. As he had suspected, the entire area was overgrown. Had it not been for the piece of cloth he had previously placed in a tree near the entrance, it would have taken him longer to find it.

Pushing back brush, he finally found the door, actually more of a hatch than a door. Trying to open it, he found it would not budge. Picking up a rock, he hit it several times, then tried again and found it loosen. After much effort, the latch lock moved, but there was so much dirt in the way that the door barely opened. Carefully, he began digging around the edge of the door and removed as much as he could. Then, he found a stick and after lifting the hatch a couple of inches, was able to probe the stick into the crack of the doorway. After looking and finding a larger, stronger limb, he levered the small stick in the opening to widen the crack enough to get the larger limb into the opening as well.

Now placing his shoulder under the large limb, standing and using his legs, he slowly pried the hatch open. Hudson crawled down into the tunnel. The oil-filled lamp was right inside where he had left it, but there was nothing to light it with right now. Feeling his way along the wall a few feet, he felt the small wagon previously left near the opening. Happy with this progress, he crawled back out and made a note to bring a lit lantern with him when he returned. Then, putting the hatch back into place, he concealed it with new brush, loose this time.

As he was leaving, he noticed activity near the main house. Taking out his monocular scope, he was able to see several horsemen leaving Mount Vernon at a full gallop. *Hmm perhaps something has happened*, he thought, not really wanting more news to handle. He was hoping this was a false call. Looking in the scope again, he saw Dr. James Craik leaving with his medical bag in hand, followed by George Rawlins, now being helped with his horse.

This could be momentous, he thought. *I don't think the doctor would leave the president until he was better, and there was no way he could have recovered so fast. So, this could mean the time has come!* There was too much happening. The Major knew in his heart this was no false call. He had to move fast. He hurried back in the boat and made it back across the river, fetched his horse, and headed out to find the mute sergeant.

Chapter 25

More than an hour passed after the departure of Major Hudson before Dr. Craik decided to check on his patient. He gently knocked on the door. Hearing nothing, he slowly turned the handle and peeked in. The president appeared to be resting peacefully, and he nearly turned back, but then decided to check closer. A small light coming from the bedside candle illumined the president's body but Dr. Craik could not tell precisely if the sick man was sleeping, so he entered and put an ear close to the president's mouth. Nothing. Immediately, he grabbed Washington's wrist to find a pulse. There was none and his wrist was ice cold.

Desperately, he called out: "Tobias! Come quickly!" Colonel Lear was there within a moment.

"He's not breathing, and there is no pulse," Dr. Craik said. "Help me get him upright." The two men sat the president up, hoping to revive him. The doctor pounded on his back while Colonel Lear balanced him from the front. Then they laid him back down. Sweat was now pouring down the doctor's face.

"This can't be happening, this can't be happening," Colonel Lear mumbled again. Dr. Craik lifted each of the president's eyelids with his thumb and noticed both pupils were fully dilated. "Do something!" Colonel Lear said half frantically, "Just do something!" But Dr. Craik slowly slumped to the floor. He wiped his watering eyes with a shirt sleeve, his head down in defeat.

"I'm afraid there is nothing anyone can do now," the doctor said in barely a whisper. Not believing what he had just heard, Colonel Lear went to the side of the bed himself and tried to wake the president by lifting him to a sitting position, again, and shaking him. The full realization began to sink in and Colonel Lear's efforts turned into a prolonged hug. Tears flowed from his eyes. Then the proud and proper Colonel, regained his composure, cleared his throat, and gently laid back down the lifeless body of his beloved general.

"We need to get Martha," Lear said softly. To his surprise, without notice, she was already at the bedside, and moved past both men.

"I am here. You can leave now . . . all of you can leave."

Neither man moved; they just remained as if frozen in place, until she finally, slowly turned from the president and said in a firm voice: "Did you not hear me? I want to be alone with my husband. Please leave now!" At that, both men turned and left Martha alone with her dear one.

The two men remained outside the bedroom door for what seemed an unsuitable amount of time. George Rawlins, who had remained outside the bedroom the entire past several hours, could read their faces, and did not have to be told what had happened.

After some time, they moved to the president's study where Colonel Lear began drawing up a list of who should be notified, and how the announcement must be made. They decided President Adams was the first person to be notified and that he should be the one to release the statement.

Until that could be accomplished, everyone was under strict orders not to say anything to anyone. A while later, George Rawlins asked the doctor: "Do you think she is okay? It has been almost two hours now."

"Perhaps, we should look in on her," Colonel Lear responded

"You heard her, she wants to be left alone," Dr. Craik said. "I am not going to be the one to poke my head in."

"Me neither," Rawlins said.

Changing the subject, Colonel Lear suggested a mortician

should be summoned. "There are many people here at Mount Vernon, so he does not have to know exactly who he is coming to see." Just as he finished saying that he heard a voice."There will be no mortician. His body will not be treated."

Looking toward the door to the study, the men saw Martha standing there.

Dr. Craik moved toward her now. "Mrs. Washington, I cannot imagine how you are holding up so well," he said in a compassionate voice. "But certainly, you must know that a mortician can be most beneficial at a time like this."

"His body will not be treated by a mortician or anyone," she said. "He is ready now." and as she turned to go back to the bedroom, the men followed, but stopped abruptly at the door when they saw the president lying on his bed dressed in his finest uniform. She had cleaned him, dressed him, combed his hair, and somehow even made the bed he was now laying on. The men turned their heads and looked at one another in disbelief.

"I will summon the mortician solely for the purpose of obtaining a suitable casket to put him in," Martha said calmly. "He will not leave Mount Vernon. He may lie in state in the new room, but his body will be placed in the mausoleum on or before this coming Tuesday which will give us less than four days to make all the arrangements. George, you are to fetch Reverend James Muir at the Presbyterian Church in Alexandria. Have him come here immediately," Martha said, fully in command. "He and George are very close, and I want *him* to take charge of services. Colonel Lear, you can inform President Adams what has happened, but you must let him know that I am firm about not moving him, or prolonging his internment. If need be, there can be a memorial service and a proper public service, but his body will *never* leave Mount Vernon, is that clear? Dr. Craik, thank you for coming, and for all you have tried to do, but your services are no longer needed here."

***

Martha was now in total command, and no one dared make even a suggestion or hint at not following her every wish. At least to the public, she appeared to have her emotions in check, shielding everyone from the true sorrow and grief that enveloped her very being. However, late at night, when she was alone and in the solitude of her bed, she broke down and cried endlessly. This type of suffering was not new to her, having outlived two of her four children, numerous relatives, and now both of her husbands. Even now, the pain of this loss was almost too much to bear, yet she knew what was expected of her.

She closed up the second-floor bedroom which she had shared with George, and moved to a room on the third floor, where she spent most of her time now, planning details of his service. She was determined to be as strong in death, as her husband was in life. She was intent on carrying out her husband's every wish concerning his burial as he had discussed with her, even if she did not understand or agree with all of it.

President Adams, Thomas Jefferson, and many other notable people matriculated to Mount Vernon in the following days. The staff jumped into action and performed admirable jobs of tending to the needs of guests and well-wishers as they had been trained to do for all previous events at Mount Vernon, but their faces, nevertheless, held sadness and were sometimes somber, many finding it hard to hold back tears.

Frequently, Martha was the one consoling them with a soft touch or a slight hug and often said: "This too shall pass." She met with Reverend James Muir and Reverend Thomas Davis of Christ Church, Reverend William Moffatt, and Reverend Addison. She listened to each of them intently, but then would let each one know what *she* wanted them to read from their intended remarks.

In her meeting with President Adams, she insisted that George's body not be moved from Mount Vernon but agreed to hold a national memorial service in Philadelphia at a later date.

On the evening before the Mount Vernon service, when

all preparations were finally ready, Martha decided to review her husband's last Will and Testament. Sitting in her bed by the light of a lone flickering candle, she read that she was sole heir to his vast land holdings, and all his wealth. But then she noticed, with amazement, that he had decreed all his slaves be set free. Upon reading this, she sat a little straighter in bed, blinked her eyes, and read it again. Slowly lowering to the bed, her hand still holding the will, she gazed off in disbelief. *How am I going to manage everything if I am to lose so many slaves?* she wondered. Then she raised the will again and continued reading. With great relief, she discovered he had not freed those slaves whom he had received as a dower gift from the estate of her first husband, Daniel Custis. She also noted those slaves of his who had married among her slaves would not be set free until her own death.

Exhausted, she put the will down at last and sat a few moments wondering how all this was going to work out. She had previously considered freeing a few of her slaves each year over the next several years, but now felt that would be impossible. Finally, she sighed, took a sip from the glass of water she kept on her nightstand, blew out the candle, and decided it was time to sleep.

Tomorrow I will lay my husband and the father of this country to rest, she thought. It would be a National Day of Mourning, and one remembered for all of history.

Chapter 26

Word of President George Washington's death spread fast, but neither Palidore nor Marshall received the news until two days later on Sunday at church. Palidore suddenly found himself in a state of panic. Anabel was in tears, but totally unaware of the concerns that Palidore was enduring.

All I know is that somehow, someway, Major Hudson needs to bring me the president's body as quickly as possible, Palidore thought. He would have to treat the body and place it in inventory without delay. He wanted to talk to the major and try to coordinate the handoff, but for the first time, it occurred to him that he really did not know how to contact Hudson. Nor did he know where the body would be brought. *Will he bring it to my home, my office, or the Medical Society's building downtown?* He chided himself for having failed to think this inevitable moment through better.

After the church service, he and Anabel found Marshall and Sarah and decided to convene at the Montgomery's home which was closest to church. Once home, Palidore had the horses put in the stable and Anabel and Sarah went to the kitchen to put together something for lunch. Marshall and Palidore went to the study and started a fire. Rather than eat in the kitchen or the dining room, the ladies brought lunch to the study where it was warm. They all sat before the fire and, for an awkward moment, said nothing. Palidore broke the silence. "All right, I know this is difficult for all of us because we have gotten to know President Washington and Martha personally, but we just do not have a proper social or political standing to do anything special. No matter how much we want to, we certainly cannot just show up at Mount Vernon. It can't be done."

"You could not be more correct," Marshall chimed in. "We must put aside our personal feelings and behave in the same fashion as the rest of the nation."

"If the body were to lie in state somewhere," Palidore said, "we could go together and pay our respects that way. "

Anabel, now near tears, again tried to say something but could not get words out. Sarah leaned in, put an arm around her, and tried consoling her."I don't know what we could possibly say to Martha, or how we would be able to hold our emotions in check, should we see her personally," Sarah said. "The men are right, the last thing we should do is give the impression that our grief is greater than anyone else's, or that we were uniquely close to the first family."

"I know you are all correct," Anabel responded with her head still down, "but I can't just *sit* here and pretend we weren't close to them, because I feel we *were*, even if we really weren't." A few moments passed as everyone sat alone in their thoughts."But don't worry, I will do the right thing," Anabel continued. "I'll hold my tongue and play it the way you think I should." Sarah gave her a squeeze.

"Well, then," Sarah said. "let's let the men talk while we clean the dishes. Nothing is better than to keep busy when one doesn't know what else to do." The ladies rose and took a few empty cups with them as they left the room and walked to the kitchen.

"What have you heard? Anything?" Marshall asked when they were out of earshot.

"Nothing," Palidore answered. "All I know is that it looks like he passed on the 14th which was Friday, two days ago. I believe he planned to be moved here quickly so I feel certain we are talking about tomorrow or sometime Tuesday, Wednesday at the very latest.""How long of a delay do you think his body can stand without being treated with compound C?" Marshall asked.

"I'm not really sure," Palidore said. "But I don't believe too much harm will come to him if we treat him no later than Thursday. However, I suspect that we are contractually required to treat him and put him into inventory regardless of his condition. That is, if we *actually* get him. I suppose there is always a chance that Major Hudson would be unable to deliver him to us. In any event, I just wish we had made more concrete plans with Hudson. I can't believe we have no idea how or where this is all going to happen."Marshall nodded and mulled this idea over a moment.

"I think we should tell Anabel and Sarah that we will be working at the Society building the next couple of days. What do you think?"

"Well, that is certainly where we are going to treat him, but I am not certain that is where he will be delivered," Palidore said. "It is highly likely that since I am closer to Mount Vernon than you are, perhaps he will be brought to my home, if it is at night, or to my clinic, if it is during the daytime. Therefore, it makes some sense that I should stay here. However, in the off-chance Hudson chooses to deliver the remains to the Society building, it seems appropriate that you should be there." Marshall nodded his agreement.

"I will tell Nurse White that we are close to finishing up some work at the Society building, and it is possible I will need to make an abrupt trip there should I get word from you that requires my attention," Palidore said. "We should both tell our nurses not to accept any new appointments for the next several days. What do you think?"

Marshall looked as if he had a question, but shook his head and replied,

"Well, that's it then. We have thought this through as much as we can under the circumstances."

Chapter 27

On Monday, Major Hudson learned about funeral arrangements from Colonel Lear. There would be a private service in the New Room at Mount Vernon on Tuesday, the 17th of December, after which the president's body would be moved to the mausoleum around 2:00 p.m. the same day. Later there would be a national funeral in Philadelphia, but his body would not be moved after being laid to rest at Mount Vernon. Colonel Lear was of the opinion the president's body should be brought to Philadelphia for the service, but Mrs. Washington wouldn't hear of it.

That was all Major Hudson needed to know to commence his plan. He decided not to strike too soon after the body had been placed in the mausoleum. Besides he would need additional time to prepare. So, he would wait until well into the night of the 17th before attempting the body swap.

He gathered the uniform the president had given him, a few food provisions, a canteen with water, some lamp oil, a lantern, an extra wick, and flint. Then, placing these items into a saddlebag, he fetched a hoe, rake, two shovels, a machete, some rope, and a large tarp. He placed the additional items into a horse-drawn wagon he had been keeping at the stable near the river. Then, he proceeded back to the stable with all supplies and left the wagon and goods covered with the tarp behind the wooden structure.

Next, he rode to the cemetery and was pleased to see there was a fresh grave not long covered over. Footprints indicated some brief service had already taken place. The dirt was fresh and loose.

Since the grave is in somewhat of a remote area of the cemetery, Hudson thought, *perhaps it will be safe for the sergeant and me to retrieve the body at dusk. We should go unnoticed, and still have time to transport the body before dark of night.* After leaving the cemetery, he headed out in search of his faithful sergeant.

The day was cold, windy, and overcast for the service, but those conditions made it perfect for Hudson's plans. It was just dusk when he met the sergeant at the cemetery with the wagon and tools. They checked for any signs of possible onlookers but were only greeted by sounds of the wind and rustling trees as remaining colorful leaves meandered to the ground. The men's feet squished into soft, wet grass as they made their way across the lonely graveyard toward their goal. Then setting down the tools, they proceeded to unearth the unknown soldier's grave.

Digging was easy since the dirt had not fully settled into place. When they struck the casket, Hudson indicated to the sergeant they would not be moving the casket for to do so would leave too big a void with not enough dirt to fill the hole back in. The sergeant did not question his instructions but simply followed orders.

The evening weather had deteriorated; it was now misting, and dirt was quickly converting into a muddy mixture. They began working faster. Once the top of the casket was opened, they placed the tarp upon the ground, and the sergeant jumped down into the open grave. He struggled to grab the body by its shoulders and tried maneuvering it up to Hudson on the ground above. On their first attempt, the major slipped and nearly fell forward into the grave with the body which had fallen back onto the sergeant. In their second attempt, the sergeant set the torso upright and lifted each of its hands up to Hudson so he could grab them. Hudson pulled the dead man out, and as he did so, he, himself, fell back into the mud. After getting back up, he helped the sergeant climb out of the grave. Both men were now covered in mud."Remind me to bring better digging clothes," Hudson remarked as they took a moment to rest. He saw the sergeant's eyes grow wide as if to say: "Will there will be another time?" But being mute, the sergeant said nothing.

Next, they moved the body onto half of the tarp and covered him with its remainder. Then, securing the body with rope, they lifted it into the wagon, ready for the journey to the stable where the major would perform another task. Hudson had taken a careful look at the soldier before they wrapped him up and was pleased to see that he appeared smaller in stature than the president. *I don't think I'll have too difficult a time getting the president's uniform on him,* he thought.

They quickly filled the muddy dirt back over the now empty casket and arranged the top dirt as best they could. "Please go get the boat and meet me at the embarkation spot. I'll take the wagon, but I'm stopping off at the stable first, so just wait for me by the boat." Hudson said.

As uncomfortable as the weather was, it provided a good cover. No one bothered being out in such inclement conditions, especially at that time of day. Once Major Hudson arrived at the stable, he jumped down and unlatched the large door before leading the horse and wagon inside. After shutting the doors, he took a moment to catch his breath, along with a swig of water from his canteen. Wiping his brow with one sleeve, he took a deep breath and began pulling the soldier nearly off the wagon by his feet. Grabbing the cadaver by the waist, he loaded him over his left shoulder, then went to his knees as he lowered the body to the ground. Next, he proceeded to untie the rope and remove the tarp. With that done, he took the knife and began cutting away the dead soldier's clothing. It was a tiring process, but finally all the muddy outer clothing was off him.

Exhausted, the major rolled over on the ground, laying on his back next to the fallen soldier. *I have to keep moving,* he thought. So after a couple of breaths, he stood again and poured water in a bowl, took a rag and soap and proceed to clean the face of the unearthed fallen soldier. Then, he carefully dressed him in the president's uniform. Once finished, he sat the soldier up, brushed a little dust off his shoulder, stepped back and looked carefully at him. "You are hereby promoted to Commander-in-Chief of the military forces of this great nation," he said aloud. He took another step back, came to attention, and saluted the corpse.

The hardest part of this night was nearing its mid-point. Now, he wrapped the soldier in the tarp again, and with great effort, placed him back in the wagon.

After reopening the stable door, he led the horse out by its harness, reclosed the door and climbed into the driver's seat. Once onboard, he prodded the horse and the wagon started off toward the river to meet his sergeant. It was well after midnight when they moved the soldier into the boat.Due to the wind, the water was choppy; a cold mist lay in the air. The moon peaked through a slight break in the clouds allowing just enough light to leave a slight reflection on the river. Aside from water noises, all was quiet. Climbing into the boat, they powered through the water with a quiet cadence of oars.

I am fortunate my sergeant is mute, the major thought. *I would not want to carry on a conversation at a time like this.* Just prior to reaching the shoreline an eagle circled above them between the moon and the water. Simultaneously, both men stopped rowing and stared up at the large bird soaring in the air until he lit in a tree on the nearby shore. Without comment, they began rowing again until finally arriving at a landing in the spot Hudson had previously designated with a white rag on a bush.

They secured the boat to a tree with a rope, then the major unloaded his bag and took out the lantern, put oil in it and watched as the wick absorbed the liquid. He used a spark from his flint to light a straw previously soaked with oil to light the lantern.

"Wait here for me, no matter how long I take," Hudson told his companion. "If I do not return by daybreak, leave this place and tell no one about anything we have done. Do you understand?" The sergeant gave his major a salute and helped him balance the heavy tarp-wrapped body over his shoulder. Then Hudson headed off through the brush and trees until he found the hatch to the secret tunnel where he placed the body as gently as he could upon the ground.

This time the tunnel door opened with much less effort. He proceeded down a few steps to the bottom where he lit the wall lantern and quickly located the tunnel wagon, moving it into position. Ascending the steps, again, he began pulling the soldier downward. The soldier's heels thumped upon on all three of the steps as they descended to the bottom. With effort, he placed the soldier into the wagon and secured the lantern to its front. That done, he took a moment to catch his breath.

So far so good, he thought, grabbing the rope handle of the wagon secured to each side of the front, and began pulling it down the pathway. He knew this tunnel well, better than anyone, and it did not take him long to reach the room where he could access the secret passage leading to the mausoleum.

When he reached the hidden stone, he pushed it to access the next passageway. He knew the opening was not large enough to allow for the wagon to pass through, so he maneuvered the replacement president over his shoulder and squeezed into the tunnel where he found the wheelbarrow he had previously placed there, and put the body in it. Now he made his way down the corridor until he stopped at the wooden panel that would yield access to the mausoleum.

Reaching the wall art, he let the wheelbarrow handles down and turned the two designated points on the carving to open the secret door leading to the area directly below the mausoleum. Once inside, the major left the soldier and walked up the inclined ramp to three steps. From there, he could put his hands on the tunnel ceiling. By pushing upward, the hatch would open and give access to the floor on the other side. The hatch was heavy since it was covered with stones of the upper flooring. But giving it a heavy shove, he was able to slip the left edge over the adjacent stones. Hudson then pushed it clear to the left achieving full access to the mausoleum vault and the president's casket..

He was surprised to hear muffled voices. This was unexpected and he stopped completely to listen. Backing down the steps, he chided himself for having failed to consider there would be guards stationed at the entrance outside. But consoled himself by reasoning that had he known, he would not likely have changed his plans. He had to be extra quiet now as he returned for his cargo and carried the man to the ramp, laying him down and unwrapping the tarp. He listened again. It was quiet now. *I am so glad there are no windows,* he thought. *If I'm extremely quiet, all should proceed as planned.* Then he hoisted himself upwards into the mausoleum and stood by the stone coffin, President George Washington's sarcophagus. Then, carefully, he slide the heavy top to one side revealing the body inside. He stood for a moment looking at his beloved commander-in-chief. It took his breath away to see the quiet repose of the great man's face, and the sight brought tears to his eyes.

No time for tears, he told himself. *I must check my emotions as I am completing his last command to me, and must succeed.* With that, he placed one arm under the president's neck and another under his knees, picked him up and descended the stairs to the tunnel where he placed his president gently onto the tarp next to the soldier he had brought. Then, he picked up the soldier and ascended the stairs back into the mausoleum, placing him into the president's casket and slide the top closed again.

Now descending back into the hole in the floor, he slowly moved the brick-covered floor access door back into place. One edge was a little out of line and gave him difficulty. His arms were tired, and he began sweating, as he strained to set it into place. Finally, with a loud thud, the hatch floor closed properly, but the noise had been loud, and he froze in place. Voices sounded and he heard the jangle of keys. The guards entered the mausoleum directly over him. He remained crouched on the steps below, afraid to move. He could hear them talking, but not distinct words as they moved about.

After what seemed an eternity, he heard the soldiers shuffle out; keys rattling again as they locked the door behind them. Major Hudson held his head in hands a moment to re-gather his composure before continuing his duty.

As he touched the president while wrapping the tarp, he couldn't help notice how extremely cold he was to touch. At first, he placed his hands on the president's face, trying to understand what was happening, but decided to keep moving. Securing the tarp with ropes, he hoisted the body over his shoulder, and carried it out the door, placing him in the wheelbarrow. *The hardest part is done,* he told himself. *We are almost at the end of this nightmare.*

Managing to roll the president out of the tunnel, he re-secured the lid to the entrance and concealed it with dirt and brushwood. Then, with the president over his shoulder, Hudson worked his way back toward the boat. After a short while, he simply could not go further without resting, so he gently laid his president on the ground, and decided he was far enough away from the tunnel entrance to safely fetch his sergeant whom he found waiting by the river.

Going forward, he caught the sergeant's attention and motioned him to follow as they headed back toward the body. As they reached the area, they could hear dogs, and were surprised to see two strays working at tearing off the tarp. Waving his arms and with a low yell, Hudson scared them off. Then he and the sergeant took the president back to the boat placing him inside. Once on the river, they rowed away with their precious cargo. As they rowed, the major decided to revisit the story he had given the soldier about the reason for moving the body. "As you will recall, I told you we needed to move the soldier's body to allow the president to place a keepsake on it for Mrs. Washington's friend.

I am sure you may have wondered if the president's passing might have made this mission a moot point. I wondered that myself but was informed by Mrs. Washington that, if possible, *she* would like the task completed. So here we are following an order from our fallen leader on a river, at night, in the cold. But at least, now it is accomplished."

The sergeant gave a shrug as if to say: "It doesn't matter." But the major continued his discourse. "Well, the President told me where I might find the item that was to be placed on the soldier's body in the event he was not able to be present. And even though I have no idea whether anyone will know that he kept his promise, I had to keep my mine." The sergeant just grunted and nodded his acceptance. His facial expression however, revealed an appreciation for the explanation even if none was necessary.

As they continued to row, the Major smiled to himself and shook his head. If his sergeant ever tried communicating about this night, it certainly would not be the truth as the truth had been kept from him. Even if he had *known* the truth, absolutely no one would believe such a fantastical story. They might even declare him a lunatic and try to put him away.

Reaching the shore, they loaded the tarp-covered corpse onto the wagon along with other items. The sergeant then retrieved his horse which he had tied nearby as the major climbed onto the wagon.

"Thank you for all your service tonight, my good man, but I can handle it from here," Major Hudson said. The sergeant looked perplexed and made a shoveling motion, pointing to himself and trying to communicate he would help re-bury the soldier. Hudson shook his head.

"This part I must do by myself, and the shoveling will be easy. Please do as I say and leave the rest to me. That is an order, Sergeant. Your services have been most helpful." Not totally happy with this last exchange, Hudson knew he would not be putting anyone back into a grave. He needed to dismiss the sergeant no matter how awkward it had become.

The sergeant seemed to understand his work was done. With a sharp lift of his hand to his head, he saluted his superior officer and rode off. Hudson headed back in the direction of the stable.

Now the final journey to meet Dr. Montgomery before dawn this very morning, he thought. *I will have kept a promise to my commander-in-chief so he may rest in the peace he has chosen.*

Chapter 28

Palidore rose early and left the house for his daily walk to the office. It was a cold, overcast day and he had instructed Nurse White to limit his patients to a minimum. He would be meeting Dr. Robinson as soon as he was able to get away. Of course, she had no idea why he needed to go to the Society building but had grown accustomed to these interruptions in his schedule. Palidore was convinced that if the president's body was not treated soon it would become an exercise in futility.

There had been no word from Major Hudson, but Palidore felt that if he had not been able to collect the body, he would have heard something by now. Since he had not, he assumed their plan was still in play. Now walking over the cobblestone street, his attention was drawn to a small whirlwind of curled, brown leaves swirling a few feet in front of him as he proceeded toward his clinic. He failed to notice a wagon by the side street he was getting ready to cross.

"Dr. Montgomery!"a loud whisper called out from the wagon's direction. Palidore stopped, looked around and heard it again: "Psst Dr. Montgomery!"

This time he saw Major Hudson sitting on the wagon drawn by a single horse. His heart jumped as he looked around furtively to see if anyone was present, then quickly jogged over to the wagon.

As he neared, Major Hudson called out quietly, "Where do you want him?"

"Please take him to the Society building," Palidore said with relief. "Dr. Robinson should be there. He will take charge for now. I will get there as soon as I can."

"Yes sir," replied the major and turned the horse to head down the street.

***

Palidore tried hurrying to attend the few patients who could not be rescheduled to another date. Eager now to get to the Society building, he needed to see what condition the president's body was in. As soon as he could leave the office, he advised nurse White not to expect him to return for the remainder of the day. Leaving by the back door of the office where he kept a horse and carriage, he headed off.

Upon arrival at the Society building, he quickly tethered the horse and rushed down the outside stairs to the double doors where he found Major Hudson standing guard. "Major, I don't think it is necessary for you to remain out here," Palidore said.

"Well, after I helped Dr. Robinson move him inside, I was not sure if I would be needed again, so I decided to wait here. Besides, my president told me that I was to deliver this package directly to you." He pulled a small box containing the president's blood from his inner coat pocket and handed it to Palidore who realized exactly what was inside.

"Thank you for this, and for all your help, but I believe Dr. Robinson and I can take care of everything from here so you are free to leave." As Major Hudson turned to go, Palidore abruptly asked, "Major, did you have any problems with him during the trip? Or to put it another way: Did his body sustain any damages postmortem?"

Hudson had his foot on the first step, but stopped, turned, and looked directly at the doctor before replying.

"I don't know what you are going to do with my president, but you can rest assured that nothing ill happened to him while he was in my charge. And before you ask, the answer to your next question is 'no,' no one other than myself knows that he has been moved here. He is safely in your care now. Please treat him with the respect to which he is entitled." Then Major Hudson turned to ascend the steps to his horse and wagon without looking back. He was relieved he had successfully

166

completed his mission but was physically and emotionally drained.

Palidore entered the building and locked the door behind him. Marshall had the president's body in a state of undress with everything they needed for the next step neatly set out. They started shaving all his hair and washing the body with disinfectant. Palidore stopped for a moment and held a lock of the president's hair in his hand. "What are you doing?" Marshall asked.

"I'm not sure," Palidore answered. "For a moment, I thought I might want a memento."

"You're kidding!" Marshall scoffed. "Put that down and let's get this done."

Palidore grabbed a nearby book and tucked the locket of hair inside a page with the idea he could retrieve it later if he wanted. Then they proceeded with the remainder of the process which took the next few hours. When the president's body was fully encased in Compound C and completely swathed in bandages, they moved him into the room with the other four bodies in their inventory. The bottle of Washington's blood was secured and placed next to the body as they had done with each of the others."Marshall, do we dare put his name on his person as we have done for the others?"

Marshall reflected on the question. "If we have done nothing wrong, we should treat his remains no different than we have the others. Besides we are the only ones with access to any of these bodies. We're the only ones who know who they are."

"I think you are right."

With that decision made, they put a small card matching the others in front of the casket. It simply read: "George Washington, December 14, 1799" As it lay against the container, the two men glanced at the card, and then at each other. They both felt a sense of relief that it was over, at least for now. In silence, they began cleaning up and putting things away. Finally, Palidore broke the uneasy silence.

"Are you going directly home?"

"Well, it seems a bit too late to return to work," Marshall said, "yet too early to head home. I may just ride around a while to let it all sink in."

"That sounds like an excellent idea; I may do the same thing."

Finishing their tasks, the two doctors left the building. Palidore took the scenic route home. The air was brisk and cold, but during the ride, clouds began to break apart allowing brief interludes of sun to peak through. *It's all going to be better now,* he thought.

***

That evening, Palidore couldn't help but admire once again the green and white dining room Anabel had fashioned after the small dining room at Mount Vernon. So much had transpired since their visit, but at last it was over, at least for now. He was looking forward to the resumption of his intimate evening dinners with his beloved Anabel. As he began to open a bottle of red wine similar to the one President Washington had served at Mount Vernon, he felt the tension at the back of his neck subside for the first time in a long time. *Tonight's toast is going to celebrate the resumption of our former life,* he thought, despite a small pull of guilt tugging at him for keeping such a significant secret from his wife. He had never held anything back from her before, but he was certain this time it was for the best.

As he was pouring the wine, an unexpected knock came at the door. Once again, Palidore stopped with his hand mid-air wrapped around the bottle of wine. However, this time, Anabel jumped up.

"Just finish pouring the wine, Palidore, dear. I will get it."

He followed her instructions and filled each glass generously to the brim as she left the room. Shortly, she reappeared with an envelope in her hand.

What now? he thought as Anabel handed him the envelope addressed to: "Dr. and Mrs. Palidore Montgomery." The return address simply said: "Mount Vernon." Palidore opened the envelope without ceremony and removed a card that looked to be an invitation. A small piece of paper floated to the floor escaping his notice. Palidore first read the card to himself, then looked at Anabel.

"We have been invited to the President's official funeral in Philadelphia."

Anabel heard what he said, but was already reading the small note which had fallen to the floor that she had picked up. "This note is from Martha, addressed to me," she said.

"Well, what does it say?"

She cleared her voice and held the paper out a bit further from her face, then proceeded to read it out loud:

Dear Anabel,

I realize we have not met often, but I rather sense a special bond between us and know that George had developed a fondness for your Palidore over the last few months. I have included this note in the hopes that you might understand more fully the nature of the invitation you have just received.

George's body will not lie in state at this public funeral. It shall remain here at Mount Vernon in keeping with his wishes, and I shall remain with him and, accordingly, not be in attendance. While I understand the need for this public funeral, I have taken it upon myself to see that there are at least a few in attendance who knew him in a more private atmosphere, outside his role as President. With that in mind, I would be honored if you and Palidore would be willing to attend the service in Philadelphia in that capacity. Should you be able to accept this invitation, please know that I will include your names on the list of dignitaries to be afforded special seating.

With kind regards, I respectfully remain your friend,

Martha

When Anabel finished reading the note, she wiped tears forming in her eyes with the back of her hand before noticing the surprised look on Palidore's face. He was standing there, motionless, mouth slightly open, without knowing what to say. She smiled, and looked once more at the handwritten note before saying in a whisper, but loud enough for Palidore to hear:

"And you said we weren't on a first name basis."

Part II

Gil Hudson

Chapter 29

April, 2025 - Washington D.C.

The Uber driver turned right off 31st street into an alley and stopped in front of a large brick building. Turning around to look at the man and woman in his back seat, he acknowledged them without smiling. "We've arrived," he said.

Stanley Vaughan, a distinguished-looking man in his mid-sixties, looked extremely fit for his age with silver-gray hair that was clearly an asset to his naturally handsome face. His wife, Martha Vaughan, an attractive, petite woman, looked about fifteen or twenty years his junior. She appeared reluctant to leave the car. "So, this is *it*?" she said somewhat sarcastically.

"Yes ma'am," the driver responded. Mr. and Mrs. Vaughan exited the vehicle in front of an attractive cream-colored brick building standing three stories tall. The top two floors were adorned with four long narrow windows and black shutters. The main floor had three similar windows and a door. In the sunlight, it was clear none of the windows were original as they had a mirrored effect. A set of stairs led down to double doors and what appeared to be a basement apartment. Another set of steps led up to the front door.

They ascended the steps to the front door where a small brass plate with black letters displayed the words "Montgomery

Cryogenic Services, LLC." Stopping at the top of the stairs, Martha looked around and noticed a large old warehouse across the alley being converted into flats. A large yellow banner with black lettering draped across the entire warehouse read: 'New Luxury Flats Coming Soon - Call 202-222-2222." Stanley rang the doorbell and waited.

"We're buzzing you in now," a voice said through the intercom. "Please push on the door when you hear the sound." They heard the noise, pushed open the door, and entered. Inside was a comfortably-warm waiting room painted an eye-pleasing green-yellow hue. Indirect lighting highlighted the ornate plaster ceiling. A small lighted waterfall in the corner trickled water while quiet music played in the background. The floor was highly polished walnut overlayed with a large circular rug. Built into the front of the reception counter was a large glass plate displaying the name "Montgomery Cryogenic Services, LLC." A soft purple backlight nicely profiled the name.

A pleasant-looking receptionist sat behind the counter.

"Mr. & Mrs. Vaughan, welcome," the woman said handing them each an electronic visitor's badge.

"Please put these on; you can wait over there." She indicated an area with comfortable-looking leather chairs. "Dr. Montgomery will be with you soon. In the meantime, can I get you something to drink?" They both declined and took their seats, getting comfortable just when a man bounced into the room with his hand extended."Mr. and Mrs. Vaughan, I'm Dr. Palidore Montgomery. I hope you didn't have much trouble finding us." The question was implied.

"No, not at all," Stanley informed him. "We took an Uber."

"Well then, let's move into my office."

The doctor led them into a short hallway and opened another door. Inside, the comfortably-large room was set with an ornate oval wooden-carved desk and black granite top. It was matched by a black granite-topped table in the center of the room surrounded by four hammer-nail blue leather chairs on casters. Immediately behind the desk, the back wall was covered with numerous large and impressively framed diplomas. There was also a wall to their right with a recessed illuminated case containing a single diploma behind glass.

UNIVERSITY OF PENNSYLVANIA

To all before these presents shall come

Greetings

Let it be known that

Palidore Hugh Montgomery

Having completed the studies and fulfilled the requirements of

the faculty for the Degree of

Doctor of Medicine

Has accordingly been admitted to that Degree, with all the rights,

honors and privileges thereto appertaining

In Witness whereof, the Seal of the University, and the signatures

Of the Duly Authorized Officers are affixed to this Diploma

Done this 4th day of June, 1768

(SEAL)

Stanley noticed the date and name and was about to say something when Dr. Montgomery spoke first.

"I see you've noticed the diploma of my ancestor. As you can see, we share the same name and profession. Actually, his father was also a physician by trade but did not, at that time, have formal training, so he did not have a diploma. I'm actually the sixth 'Palidore Hugh Montgomery,' but have decided to drop the Roman numerals from my name, as it seemed a bit too formal for my liking. The rest of the diplomas on this wall over here are also family members. Most of them are 'Montgomerys' as well.

"There have been at least one, sometimes two, Montgomerys who have become physicians in each generation following the first Palidore Montogomery. You'll notice a couple of them do not bear the 'Montgomery' last name. Those are females who chose to take their husbands' last names prior to receiving diplomas. There are also two diplomas bearing the last name of 'Robinson.' The Robinsons and the Montgomerys have historically maintained very close ties both professionally and socially even to this day."

Stanley Vaughan was still looking at the single diploma on the wall to the right. "But this one graduated in 1768. I didn't know they even had medical schools back then."

"Yes, the University of Pennsylvania had a medical school back then, and most of our family doctors went there early on. But as you can see, for more than a century, almost everyone else graduated from the University of Virginia," Dr. Montgomery said. "But enough about my family history for now. Let's have a seat and discuss how we may be of service to you."

They followed the doctor's lead, both taking a seat at the table. Then Dr. Montgomery continued. "Let me begin by telling you a little about our firm. I understand that you have our brochure, but I would like to review a few things before we deal with the specifics of your wishes.

"Montgomery Cryogenic Services, LLC, which we can just refer to as 'MCS,' is licensed in the field of Mortuary Science. In short, we are licensed to handle the remains of human beings. What sets us apart from a *regular* funeral home is *how* we treat the remains and expectations of our clients. The difference being that their remains will be so perfectly preserved, we anticipate one day it being possible to revive them once a cure has been found for whatever illness caused their demise.

"While we cannot promise they will ultimately be revived, we do guarantee that an individual's remains will be perfectly preserved.

"MCS is not the only firm offering this service, but we are the only firm that does not advertise, and all our clients must be referred to us by one of our member physicians.

"Lastly, all of us here are medical doctors and actively engaged in the practice of medicine. Our goal, therefore, is to maintain and preserve life. Cryogenics is a natural extension of that goal. When all medical efforts have failed, we can offer our patients one last chance of survival through cryogenics. Because it is an expensive option, we feel ethically bound to only accept clients who might have a reasonable chance to benefit from the process - hence the referral system. The physicians who participate in our referral system belong to a group known as 'The Medical Society of the Potomac.' This organization was originally started by my ancestor, the original Palidore Montgomery whose diploma you were looking at earlier," Dr. Montgomery looked between the husband and wife and waited for any questions. Not seeing any, he continued. "In truth, the original group was formed with a different purpose in mind back in 1798, but the group fell apart during the Civil War. When we decided to form the current network of physicians, we thought it would be unique to revive the name.

"Dr. Beyer, your physician, belongs to this society and referred you to us. You have consented to his forwarding us your medical records which I have reviewed." Dr. Montgomery stopped again, giving Stanley a chance to comment.

"Yes, well, I know why I am here, Dr. Montgomery. Dr. Beyer was very thorough and went over all my options and, yes, . . . we know, that I don't have much longer to go on," he said, looking over at his wife, he took her hand.

Dr. Montgomery noted the gesture before continuing his speech. "I concur with Dr. Beyer's opinion that you are a good candidate. He has already made you aware that you're suffering from a rare form of cancer for which there is no known cure. Existing treatments have not been successful. However, the cancer has not affected your brain or thought processes or your vital organs, for the time being. They are still functioning properly. Notwithstanding this, it is true, you are not likely to live much longer. I think you are very brave to be facing this truth so straight on.

"Also, I am not telling you anything you have not already discussed with Dr. Beyer. At some point, there will likely be a cure for your kind of cancer, but presently, it does not exist. Your diagnoses combined with the likelihood that your condition may be cured in the future makes you a perfect candidate for our services, if you are interested."

Mr. Vaughan looked ready to respond, but before he could speak, Dr. Montgomery spoke again.

"I don't mean to interrupt, but before you answer, for full disclosure, we need to discuss the cost. The fee for our services is $250,000 payable completely in advance. $100,000.00 of that sum goes directly into our operating budget; the remainder is invested by us to help fund the costs associated with continued preserving and maintaining of your remains. It will also pay the costs associated with any future revival attempts. Now, with this in mind . . .are you still interested?"

"Fortunately, money is not one of the things I need to worry about," Vaughn said. "I would, therefore, like to proceed. Before doing so, however, I want to know if it is possible to also pre-pay for my wife?"

Palidore looked over at Martha Vaughan and saw some confusion in her eyes. There was an expression of disbelief at his words. Her questioning look was piercingly directed at her husband. Then she looked away and down from his gaze. Palidore displayed a kind and understanding smile.

"Unfortunately, we're not able to guarantee that she can be received. It would not be proper to accept your money without knowing whether she will die of natural causes, or when. So, for example, if she were to die in an automobile accident, there would be nothing we could do for her. Having said that, we do allow people to pre-pay for a cylinder spot *next* to you. The cost is $50,000 to hold the place. If it turns out later that she is admitted, it will assure her a place right next to you and a credit would be given in the same amount against future costs in effect at that time. If she dies, and is not received by us, the money would be forfeited."

Stanley looked at his wife who still had not uttered a word. "I think I would feel much better about doing this if I knew she might someday join me. So, please, add that option to our contract."

Palidore took out a leather folder with gold lettering on the cover stating: "Montogomery Cryogenic Services, LLC." He opened it and took out a prepared contract. Then turned to the last page and checked a box indicating an addendum was attached after which he rose and went to a cabinet, opened a drawer, and fetched an additional page. He brought it back to the table and added it to the contract. Then he presented the contract to Mr. Vaughan for his approval."No need, just let me sign it - I've made up my mind."

"As you wish," Palidore said. "Please sign the last page, and initial the addendum. You will notice the last paragraph before your signature provides in part that 'a photostatic, emailed, pdf or digitally reproduced copy, shall be deemed as effective as the original, and the parties waive any right to require a production of the original.' This is important because we will email you a digital version and store the document that way. The contract you are actually signing will be destroyed in five years for privacy concerns."

Mr. Vaughan nodded, indicating he understood, and proceeded to sign as directed before taking out his checkbook. Palidore advised him that he only needed the bank's name, the account number, and bank routing numbers. Stanley pushed the checkbook over to him and Palidore wrote the bank numbers on another form, filling in the amount of $300,000.00 in the space provided before placing the paper in front of Stanley. "If you will sign this paper, we will be able to have the amount shown wired to our account from your account."

Stanley complied without a word."Now that our business part is over, would you and Mrs. Vaughn care to tour the facility?"

"We would," said Mr. Vaughan. Martha looked as if she were fighting back tears as they all rose from their seats.

"Is there a restroom I can use?"

"Certainly; right down this hallway," Palidore said, showing her the way. A short while later, Martha returned, and Palidore noticed a somber look on her face. "Do you still wish to tour our facility at this time?" he asked. Martha said nothing, but Stanley appeared relieved, and somewhat eager now that formalities were over.

"Yes, of course," he said, not looking at his wife. She looked up at the doctor and gave the slightest nod of her head.

"Very well then, let's proceed though this door." Palidore led them down the hallway and into a large room which seemed set up for some sort of instruction. It was divided into several seating areas with conference tables. There were several computers in various locations with a few people working at them.

"This is our educational room where staff and physicians frequently meet to discuss our clients, and monitor what progress has been made in various areas of medicine," Palidore said. "These people are doing what we call 'pairing'. Each of our clients are assigned to a study group that focuses on unique medical conditions which caused their demise. They constantly monitor medical progress being made and pair results of their research with the proper patient. This goes on here constantly. Most of the students are from the University of Virginia (UVA), but there are others from various other medical schools, too. They work for room and board on an internship basis.

"Our physicians are also assigned to groups and meet monthly to review the clients and check information that has been paired with their charts. They discuss possibilities and decide if additional attention should be given to a particular client."

The Vaughans scanned the room. In the middle was a sunken carpeted area with four steps down. It looked perfect as an area for up-close presentations. Indirect lighting was soft, but adequate for such purposes. All-in-all the environment was a pleasant one in which to read or study.

Palidore suggested they return to the hallway and directed them to an elevator. As soon as they reached it, he pushed the button. "We'll now proceed to the basement." When the doors opened, they entered, and Palidore pushed the "B" button. In short order, the elevator stopped with a slight bump and the doors opened to reveal a pleasant room with light lavender walls. However, over-time the colors seemed to change. It soon became clear the walls were actually white with a light source around the edge of the ceiling slowly changing the color of the walls inperceptibly.Sitting at a desk behind a circular counter was a young, pleasant-looking brunette woman whom the doctor addressed. "Jennifer, this is Mr. and Mrs. Vaughan, I'm taking them on a brief tour of the facilities." Jennifer looking up from a bank of four monitors and smiled.

"So pleased to meet you," she said in a lovely, low voice. "Enjoy your tour and have a pleasant day." Palidore motioned for them to follow. He opened a door off the large room which caused the lighting in a new hallway to illuminate. Not far down that hall, he opened a door to the first room they approached. "As you can see, this is a complete surgical suite equipped with the latest medical equipment. We refer to this as a 'processing room.' We have two such rooms and envision that one day we will be able to use the rooms to revive some of our clients. Right now, they are used solely to prepare our clients for preservation."

They all stood and looked around. The lighting in the room was, again, indirect, except for a rather large moveable light fixture over the operating table."Shall we move on?" Palidore inquired. As he returned to the door, the Vaughans followed him back into the hall where they re-entered the elevator and proceeded upward to the second floor. The elevator opened on a long hallway down which Palidore pointed to a room at the far end.

"The end room is a chapel," he said. Opening a nearby door, they entered an extremely large room which contained numerous rows of cylinders. There looked to be hundreds of them. The only light in the room came from the top twelve inches of each tube glowing with blue hues. Along the floor and down each row were strips of tiny white lights."Here is where our clients remain preserved," Palidore explained. "Each cylinder houses one person until their time to be revived arrives. The cylinders are filled with a liquid keeping each client perfectly preserved in a frozen state." He indicated that each cylinder was also capable of being lit up, revealing the person inside, simply by touching it.

"If the blue area is touched," he explained, "only the head will be revealed. If anywhere below the blue light is touched, the entire body will be revealed. But we never display a client to anyone other than appropriate staff or relatives of the client."He mentioned that should a problem develop with any cylinders, the blue light would change to red and begin beeping. "Jennifer would notice and immediately contact our technicians," he said. They exited the room and proceeded to the end of the hall. "Only some twenty-five percent of our clients elect to take the tour; I assume those are people who have a real interest in our science," he said, hesitating by another doorway. "This next room is not advertised in any of our brochures. We are not trying to hide anything, but those contained in this room were not treated in the same way we are now treating clients. However, they did receive the very best possible care available at the time each one passed and we are continuing to maintain them. Do you have any interest in viewing this room?"

"Most certainly," Stanley said immediately. Mrs. Vaughn simply looked ahead. Palidore opened the door. In front of them were twelve stainless steel vaults that anyone would expect to see in any morgue. They were numbered one through twelve. "The first five were clients of my ancestor, the first Dr. Palidore Hugh Montgomery whose diploma you were previously admiring. The others were treated in a similar fashion throughout the years by other members of my family bringing the total number to twelve."

"That means the first five are over two hundred years old. Is that possible?" Stanley asked.

"Yes, they are." "Do you know who they were. . . are?"

"No, but their original caskets appeared to have had names attached to them. Someone made the decision years ago to remove those names at some time. In any event even if we knew their names, the current Health Insurance Portability and Accountability Act, known as HIPAA would preclude the disclosure of their names now. So, someone was ahead of the game in removing their name plates. These are the first twelve numbers, and so out of respect, we started our current client numbering from there."

"How was their treatment done?"

"Well, the short version is that they were treated with ancient chemicals from Egypt that were brought to this country by the father of my ancestor. The same compounds used by the ancient Egyptians to mummify the great pharaohs," Palidore explained.

"So, in the last two hundred years, has science figured out how to cure what these clients died of?" Stanley Vaughn asked, becoming increasingly interested.

"Actually, we believe so. We could likely revive them, now, but we have to wait for the mummification compounds to wear off. So, unlike what we are doing now, we cannot control the timing of when we can try to revive these particular clients."

"How will you know when the time is right?" Stanley inquired.

"At the time the first twelve were treated, a small amount of their blood was also treated and placed in small jars. When the effects of mummification begin to wear off, the blood kept in the small jars will also begin to liquify from the gelatin state the bodies are in now. We have transferred the blood into better containers and have moisture sensors placed on them, so we don't have to manually monitor each jar as in the past. An alarm will go off when the blood begins to change."

"Have you any idea how much longer it will take?"

"Not precisely, but the father of my ancestor once treated a dog in a similar fashion some sixty years before the first five individuals were treated, and the mummification chemicals finally wore off the dog only several years ago. So even though humans may react slightly different, we feel the time may be getting close."

Before Stanley could ask another question, the power went off and an alarm began ringing. .

"Please, don't be alarmed, our generators will begin shortly, but we do need to cut our tour short and proceed back to the first floor. We will have to use the stairs. Will that be all right?"

"Of course."

Once back on the first floor, Palidore showed them to his office where they could look at the diplomas. He then excused himself for a moment. When they were alone, Martha turned to Stanley.

"Stanley, are you sure you want to do this?"

"Absolutely. It's my only hope!"

Martha sat silent for a long moment, then spoke sternly. "Stanley, you think you can conquer anything, beat anyone or anything no matter what the odds are, which is probably what has made you so successful. But you can't beat death! Our bodies are simply containers that house our souls until they are called back to God. If you want to be saved, you need to spend more time with the bible and a priest. Honestly, this looks like an elaborate scheme to scam scared, dying people out of their hard earned money. If you think I believe for one moment that those last twelve people are over two hundred years old, then you are crazy and . . . and that fifty grand you spent reserving a spot for me is the biggest waste of money you have ever made!" Tears were freely flowing down her face now.

"I will never . . . *never* be placed in one of those tubes or cylinders or whatever the hell they are. You can be sure of that! If this is what you want, then I'll honor *your* wishes and be certain you wind up here, after which I will *never* return. I will, however, return to my former job of being an investigative reporter, and you can *believe* this will be the first place I will investigate!"

Martha took a hanky from her handbag and wiped her eyes. Stanley sat motionless and said nothing. During the silence, Martha caught sight of what appeared to be an old photograph on the desk. Walking over, she took a closer look. One individual among several in the group resembled President George Washington. She was straining her eyes to see the other people when Palidore walked back into the room with a smile on his face. "Well, I am sorry for that, just a stuck back door. Now, do you have any more questions I can I answer before we resume the tour?"

"Actually, I believe we're ready to leave now," Stanley said as his wife moved to his side. "Can Jennifer call an Uber to pick us up?"

"Of course! Why not return to the reception area where you can wait for your ride. Please return your visitor badges to the receptionist before leaving. It has been my pleasure to meet you. Should you have any further questions, please don't hesitate to contact me." He held out his hand and shook both Stanley and Martha's hands in succession. However, he noticed that Martha would not look up to meet his gaze. *She, clearly, doesn't support this idea*, he thought.

Chapter 30

All directors moved to their seats at the conference table on the top floor of the Montgomery Cryogenic Services building. Portraits of former MCS directors were hanging in various sizes and frames on the genuine mahogany walls. The entire room was carpeted in a deep, rich plaid with a dominant forest green color except for the floor beneath the conference table. Everything resembled furnishings from a clubhouse at the Pinehurst Country Club.

Other than antique brass-illuminated wall sconces, lighting in the room emanated primarily from the large glass table in the middle of the room. The table consisted of a huge piece in the shape of a large oval. The surface of the table was five inches thick and rested on a series of cylinders that looked to be smaller versions of cylinders used to house their cryogenic clients. The top portion of each cylinder was illuminated blue, the bottom portion was black. The entire surface of the tabletop was illuminated white with built-in screens so each participant could receive and review documents sent directly to their seats. No electronic devices were allowed in the room other than the electronics built into the table.

Once seated, each director logged in by placing his or her hand on the diagram that appeared on the surface of the table in front of them as they took a seat. Once signed in, a series of thumbnails appeared on their screens with the first one enlarged to a legible size.

Each director could enlarge or shrink a page by putting his or her finger on the page they wanted to enlarge or shrink. By default, the enlarged document now displayed at each seat was today's agenda. Chairs around the table were an eclectic lot as each director was entitled to select and install a chair of one's own choosing. No two chairs were the same. Immediately above the table hung three large antique chandeliers. Oddly enough, the combination of ultra-modern and old colonial somehow seemed to work well in the room.

The Chairman's seat was at one end of the room where a large screen was displayed on the wall behind him. A small desk was positioned near him where the secretary sat. As people spoke, their words automatically appeared on the large wall screen which created an ongoing transcript of everything being said. From time to time, they were able make revisions or amend their comments, and the secretary would update the transcript.

Once the meeting was over, the official transcript document could not be amended. On rare occasions, the directors would go off the record, and the secretary would have to leave her seat and enter a door to a small soundproof room located immediately next to her chair.

As Palidore entered the conference room, everyone began to stand, but he waived them to keep their seats. Following behind him was an attractive brunette in her mid to late forties who looked younger than her actual age. A chair was set for her next to the chairman's seat where a low-profile, glass table-top podium was pre-set on the table in front of her seat. Everyone quietly sat and focused on their leader."I am calling together a special meeting of the Board of Directors to discuss unique issues facing the company," Palidore said. "I see from the electronic sign-in that all twenty directors are present, hence, we clearly have a quorum.

"Because of the delicate nature of the issues before us, I am asking that we go immediately off record. Are there any objections to going off record?" He waited half a minute. "Hearing none, then we are officially off the record, and I will ask the secretary to secure herself inside the soundproof room." The secretary got up and entered the small adjacent room, shutting the door behind her.Then, Palidore continued. "As you are aware, we are and have been, the faithful caretakers of twelve ancient bodies which can best be described as mankind's first attempt at cryogenics. Unlike services we now offer our clients, it is not possible to turn their cryogenic state on or off. Instead, the chemicals that were used to treat their bodies need to run their course and wear off on their own timetable. When this occurs, we will have an obligation to act immediately to try and resuscitate them, whether or not we are able to cure the underlying cause of their demise at that time.

"As you are also aware, samples of these individuals' blood have been monitored over the years since their treatment, and our sensors now indicate more than one of the subjects are showing signs of 'thawing' for want of a better word.

"We have known and have reasonably planned for the day this would happen, but now our planning must become more intense. Since we are all physicians, we are keenly aware of our medical options, and a sub-committee has planned for this day for a long time. At present the most crucial issue is to determine *when* exactly to jump into action.

"The body's circulation system must return to a liquid state so we can deal with it, but waiting *too* long could also render the body unrecoverable. We have five bodies that may soon be ready for our intervention. The subcommittee has this under control for the moment and has divided itself into two groups, which we have labeled the Alpha and Beta teams. You will, of course, be kept up to date, and there will likely be the need for more 'called meetings' in the near future.

"Now, if you will look at your agenda in front of you, please go to the second item labeled 'confidential.' As you are aware, we have never tried to hide the fact that we are in possession of these ancient bodies, or the fact that at some time we may want to try and revive them. We have even shown them to prospective clients. However, quite frankly, no one has ever seemed to care.

"As you may also know, the American Medical Association was not interested in printing my article concerning the possibility of reviving an ancient body. It seems clear the established medical community views us as some sort of radical fringe group of doctors. We, of course, would like nothing better than to prove them wrong. Successfully resuscitating one of these individuals would not only be history-making but would cause the value of our current enterprise to skyrocket.

"A public offering of MCS at such a time would instantly make each of us extremely wealthy, to say the least. Accordingly, it is more than exciting to speculate about the ramifications of our success and the impact it would have not only on us, but on the medical community as a whole, not to speak of the world, itself.

"However, before we get too excited, we need to factor in one overriding concern, and that would be . . . the patient. In other words, in the event we are successful in reviving one of the individuals in our inventory, we must ask: Can we expose him to the media without his permission? We need to think for a moment just what it would be like for him to face this modern world right out of the box, so to speak. No pun intended. How will he adjust to our world when he is suddenly brought back? That alone could be overwhelming.

"Now consider what it would be like if everywhere he goes there is a crowd of people yelling questions at him, and hundreds of people shoving cameras in his face."

The directors started whispering and talking amongst themselves as they began pondering the significance of the issue the chairman had raised. Palidore let them converse a few minutes before calling them back to order.

"Well, I see I've hit the bee's nest here, but please hear me out a little longer. I do not think we can develop an appropriate policy at this meeting. We will certainly need more time to reflect on our obligations and the significance of any decision we make.

"I think you may now understand why I have decided to take this meeting 'off the record.' Perhaps you may also understand, while the items listed on the agenda may be poignant, they were also made a bit vague as a precaution. It seems wise that we keep these developments *strictly* confidential at least until we decide what our policy will be. Is there anyone who disagrees with this?" The room fell silent. "Okay, then, there will be no further discussion on this topic today. Please think about all I have said and have suggestions ready for our next meeting.

"Now, let's move on to our next item on the agenda."

Chapter 31

The next item on the agenda simply listed a name: Lynn Radford. Palidore spoke from the lecturn: "I'm sure many of you have noticed this attractive young lady seated next to me. You may even have been a bit concerned that she was privy to the conversation we just had. However, as usual, there is a method to my madness. Ms. Radford has been fully brought up to date concerning our work, the ancient bodies, and the issue we have just addressed. I had planned on introducing her to you at some point *after* today. However, given the changing condition of our ancient inventory I've decided to speed up her introduction.

"Her expertise and knowledge could not be more timely or useful. You will find her resumé in front of you. Here, let me bring it up for you." Palidore highlighted his copy on the table and everyone's monitors simultaneously enlarged words into a more legible size.

"As you can see," Palidore continued, "it is quite extensive, so I will not go through it all at this time; you can do that on your own. I would like, however, for each of you to swipe over three pages and focus on the portion entitled 'Project Experience.'" Once everyone was focused on the proper page he proceeded.

"I have been searching for someone who might help us determine how to psychologically help an ancient patient adjust to the new world when brought into our time which is the future for the patient. When I began my search, I truly felt we had at least a

191

couple of years to work on this. I even wondered if I weren't being a bit foolish starting such research so soon. Well, I guess if anything, I wish I had begun my research earlier. In any event, I was fortunate enough to find Lynn." He looked over at the young lady and gave a smile of acknowledgment. "Do you mind if we address you by your first name?"

She smiled at him and nodded. "As I was saying," Palidore went on, "Lynn did her doctoral thesis studying people who had been removed from society in various ways, then reintroduced back into that society. You can see from her 'Project Experience' that she has studied foreign prisoners who, unlike our prisoners, were kept totally isolated for years. She also studied people recovering from prolonged comas. There was an orphaned child who raised himself in the wild. She even helped one person who survived a small boating accident to be left abandoned for years on a remote island.

"Well, as you can see, she possesses a unique perspective on how we should go about reintroducing such people back into our society. So, without further ado, please let me introduce Dr. Lynn Radford."

There was a polite round of applause as Lynn rose from her seat and stood behind the glass podium waiting for the applause to subside and begin speaking."Thank you, Dr. Montgomery . . . 'Palidore,' for inviting me here today." Redirecting her focus on the directors, she continued.

"Words cannot express my excitement about being involved in your project. I can feel the excitement in this room and can see it in your eyes.

"Imagine being able to reconnect with our past in such a way no one could have dreamed possible. Think of all the questions you would like to ask one of our forefathers. Imagine the questions you will have concerning where his soul has resided during the past couple of hundred years, whether he remembers anything or not.

"Now imagine yourself thrust two hundred years into the

future. Consider all the questions you would have about what has happened since you last walked on this planet. Imagine further how you would feel knowing that no one you knew, or loved, was still alive, not your wife, not your children, nor even your grandchildren! No friends, no relatives, no one! They're all gone, and you are here, in the future, totally alone. Oh yes, there certainly will be a lot of people roaming around, but none that you will know or recognize. You will almost certainly be overwhelmed by an intense feeling of loneliness and fear.

"So, you see, there is a conflict of interests here. We will certainly want answers to our questions from this lonely man, but he will most assuredly want answers to his questions as well. So how shall we determine which questions get answered first?

"To me the answer is simple . . . we must answer *his* questions first. This whole adventure *has* to be all about him. No matter how intense our itch is to extract from him what we want to know, we must put that aside, and totally tend to his needs. He is not, and cannot, become a lab rat. He is, and must continue to be seen, by us, as a patient in need of our help. Only when we have carefully brought him up-to-date and assimilated him back into our culture, will it be possible for us to fully seek the answers to *our* questions.

"Having said that, I believe he will, over time, inadvertently answer many of our questions while we are helping him. And . . . they will be answered in the correct context and in a manner that will be uncoerced and unbiased, thereby giving us a much clearer peek at the truth.

"Please understand this is a different issue than the one posed to you earlier by Dr. Montgomery. As I see it, it would be easier to work with our patients if the world was kept, at least for the moment, totally in the dark. However, if people are not given access to him or them, it will be possible to work with him even if the world is 'watching,' so to speak.

"I understand many of you may have a different opinion or,

perhaps, would like to take a different approach, but assuming there is ultimately an agreement to proceed as I have indicated, then I have developed a broad outline of what may need to be done in preparation for dealing with our first revived patient.

"If each of you would thumb to the next page of my presentation, I will continue from there." The directors each touched the next thumbnail document appearing on their screens. Palidore seemed intensely interested in everything Lynn had to say. When he hit his thumbnail document, it also appeared on the wall behind him. After ascertaining everyone was ready to proceed, Dr. Radford continued.

"Initially the patient will need to awake in a familiar environment. If he were to awake under the glare of intense lights in the presence of a hoard of people standing around in scrubs with masks on while also being connected to numerous wires and tubes and surrounded by monitors emitting strange sounds, it might be mentally too much for him to process.

"On the contrary, the patient should awaken in an environment that would seem familiar to him, an environment decorated in his time period. So, we will need to create a room in the decor common to the late 1700s. The people tending to him should be dressed in clothes of that era as well. Colors, lights, and artifacts should be what he would expect to see as much as possible, or at least *not* something that would alarm him. And to that end, even though I hesitate to say this, at least initially – and I apologize if I offend anyone - it may be necessary to avoid having persons of color tending to him. I know this is controversial, but in his time. people of color were mostly slaves and did not hold such positions. I am afraid that if they participated at his first point of awakening, the patient might resist their efforts to assist him with his healthcare and cause him to become unnecessarily agitated. It would also cause us to deal with that portion of his education immediately rather than a more normal sequence of things.

"So that brings us to the question: How do we go about determining the 'natural or normal' sequence of things? Well, stop for a moment and pretend to be him. Try to determine if you were him, what would you want to know first. This is not as easy as you might think, so I have developed a little quiz for you. Please flip to the next page of my outline and you will see ten items listed. Please use your finger to hit each item.

"The first one you hit will be what you think is the first thing our patient would want to know, and so forth. Go ahead and put them in the order you think best; the computer will tally the results and display them for us. Please proceed, you have one minute. It should not take any longer."

The directors immediately began hitting the screen in a variety of movements. When time was up, a list appeared on the wall behind Palidore.

"Well, let's look at the results. No surprises here, all twenty of you said the number one question would be 'Where am I?' Sure, everyone wants to know the answer to that question first. Even if he finds himself surrounded by familiar things, but the place doesn't look familiar to him, he will not know where he is and, therefore, want an answer to that question first. There is also a unanimous agreement the second question would be 'What is the date?" Of course, the patient will want to be orientated as to both time and space. The only other question to gain a unanimous response is the one which came in last at number ten. That question concerned the status of racial relations. In truth, that question might never have occurred to him at all since it wasn't a talked-about issue in his time. I included it to place in perspective my previous comments concerning the racial makeup of his initial nursing team. So, the questions concerning 'History,' 'Technology,' 'Communications,' 'Transportation,' 'Agriculture,' 'Social Norms' and 'Politics' also need to be addressed.

"However, despite the order we want to list them, they will actually need to be addressed as a natural outcome of our interactions with the patient. In preparation for this we will need to prepare what I call 'Information Modules' covering each subject. Some modules such as 'Technology' will have to have sub-modules. The subject matter is so vast it could not be dealt with in a single session. We have already started developing modules and sub-modules so we can easily focus on a subject that seems important to the patient now."

Palidore felt his smart watch vibrate and glanced down. After reading the message, he quietly rose from his seat which caused all directors to focus on him. This in turn caused Dr., Radford to glance to her left. Palidore stepped forward and whispered in her ear.

"Please continue. We have received a new client and I am obligated to meet his widow.

Lynn nodded, turned, and resumed her place at the glass table-top podium. "Dr. Montgomery has asked that I continue while he tends to a new client."

When Palidore entered his office, he found Martha Vaughan standing in front of his desk with her back to him holding the ancient photo of his ancestor and President Washington. He quietly approached to greet her.

"Mrs. Vaughan, I'm sorry we must meet again so soon. I think it was only a couple of months ago that Mr. Vaughan made his arrangements with us." His voice caused her to turn toward him still holding the framed photo. Palidore calmly approached and took the photo from her hand, gently placing it back on his desk and positioned it just so, as if there was only one specific spot where it could sit. Then, without looking up, he said, "You seem to have a fascination with this photo."

She ignored his comment. "Yes, this is a most difficult time for me. We knew Stanley's time was near, but it just happened so suddenly. It's still hard to believe I found him this morning on the floor and now he's here. The hospital personnel saw the band on his arm and called you. How very efficient of you, in any event, what happens now?" Palidore turned to look at her.

"Well, we are already processing him and will shortly place

him in his cylinder. Once he is in position, you will be notified of his cylinder number and may, of course, see him at any time." Palidore felt his smart watch vibrate again. He checked the message. "Oh good, it appears we have your paperwork ready, so if you will follow me, we will give you acknowledgement of receiving Mr. Vaughan."

Martha turned and followed him out of the office. She proceeded to the reception desk, took the papers, and returned her visitor's badge before speaking in a slightly sarcastic tone. "Lots of cars here today; your business must be *booming*."

"Well, we are having a board meeting upstairs that I actually need to return to, so that accounts for the excess number of vehicles in our lot. Again, I am so sorry for your loss. I know it is a difficult time for you, but you can rest assured that we will take good care of your husband. Should you have any questions, please don't hesitate to contact me."

Martha gathered the papers in her hand and slowly moved toward the front door. She stopped with her left hand still on the doorknob, turned, and gave Palidore a cold look."Questions . . . yes, I am sure I will have lots of questions." With that, she exited the building, proceeded down the steps, across the alley and into the warehouse condo complex to her flat, from where she intended to keep close tabs on Montgomery Cryogenic Services, LLC. Entering the building, she thought: *'Yes, Dr. Montgomery, just give me a little time and I will have plenty of questions for you."*

***

Returning to the board room, Palidore wasn't sure what to make of his meeting with Martha Vaughan. Lynn was still talking and glanced over to acknowledge his return.

"Ok, so we've discussed the patient's initial need for information. However, we've not discussed the timing, or should I say, the amount of time this instruction will take, not only to present the information he will need, but for him to process it. Initially, we can assume he will be eager to receive this information, however, it won't be long before he will grow tired of the process and just want to be left alone. In short, he will want to take a shot at his own version of resuming life on his own. You can be sure whenever that occurs, we will not feel that he is actually ready, and we will be confronted with the ethical issue of how best to keep some sort of control over him for as long as we can.

"Certainly, the quality of his life upon re-emergence into society will depend in large part on whether or not the public is made aware of the truth surrounding his identity. Should you decide on being up front with the public about your success in reviving this ancient individual, then it seems to me you will need, at the very least, to prepare him for the media onslaught that will surely follow his every step. However, if the decision is made to let the patient decide when, if ever, to reveal his secret, then he certainly will need an additional support system.

"I am suggesting that he will need a new identity. One that will allow him to function again on his own. A name, social security number, a more realistic certificate of birth, the whole ten yards. He may also need some vocational training, or perhaps, a pre-arranged job.

"As you can see, either way, we have much work to do to be prepared and properly treat our patient for the resumption of his life. I have been given a modest budget, so have assembled a small team to continue work on the learning modules. However, no one other than myself, knows who the modules are intended to help.

"Dr. Montgomery has also authorized the fabrication of a couple of mock bedrooms, which I believe are to be located on this very floor. However, deciding the issue Dr. Montgomery initially brought to your attention about disclosing his origin to the world or not, would be most helpful to my team in allocating our limited resources." Lynn then paused, looked down at her notes and took a shallow breath.

"I am afraid I have not adequately, nor completely, covered the subject of my presentation. To the contrary, this brief talk has, at best, only scratched the surface of the enormous task ahead of us, yet, I feel confident that you now have a better understanding of the responsibilities we may face should we revive one or more of these ancient individuals.

"As you leave you here today, it is my hope that you will do so with the knowledge that our preparations cannot be contingent upon a revival taking place. We must have a plan in place *when* a revival occurs. So we must continue to plan, as failing to plan is planning to fail. I want to thank Dr. Montgomery for including me in this project, and you, for your patience." The directors all rose to their feet and gave her a standing ovation.

Chapter 32

Martha Vaughan poured herself **a** generous glass of Chardonnay and sat in her stressless chair. "Alexa, play my favorite music," she commanded looking out her large multi-paned warehouse windows from her top floor flat. She had a perfect view of the Montgomery Cryogenics office building. She could see the front and the right side of the building and the driveway on the right side which led back to a moderate-sized parking lot enclosed by a white vinyl fence.

She had taken an interest in the luxury flats when she and Stanley had first visited MCS six months ago. That was after she had done research on cryogenics at the behest of her failing husband who believed such a process was his last hope after receiving his final medical prognosis, and because he was beside himself with grief and fear. She had done the research to appease him; it had never been something she had wanted. In fact, what she saw and heard on the day of their visit had been extremely upsetting to her.

She had come away from that meeting with a strong feeling that MCS had authored a high-tech scam to take advantage of chronically ill people by selling them false hope in a future cure. It was particularly upsetting they had claimed to possess well-preserved ancient bodies they would someday revive.

What a joke, she thought and remembered the hope in her

husband's eyes that day as he eagerly transferred three hundred thousand dollars on the spot as if money was always the answer. She vowed to find a way to expose the company for its fraudulent activity. Money wasn't the issue for her, it was because Martha believed her husband was given false hope and had been taken advantage of.

Others had tried taking advantage of her husband's generosity, and it had always been her job to protect him from them. This time, however, she hadn't succeeded. She just couldn't find it in her heart to crush his last hope. *Dr. Montgomery and his cronies at MCS know full well how no one can stand in the way of such hope in the mind of a dying loved one. What a scam. It's the perfect scam!* she thought.

It was during their visit six months ago when she took notice of the sign on the warehouse building. The phone number had been easy to remember. Later, she had acquired an option to purchase a unit. Because she was one of the first to buy, she had been able to reserve the exact unit she wanted and time to make a few changes. The most notable one was to move the wall separating the two bedrooms by five feet. That allowed her to enlarge her closet and bathroom space in the master. Then, the second bedroom, now smaller, became her office. Placing a hidden murphy bed behind a bookshelf allowed the room to accommodate an overnight guest if needed. She completed the transaction without ever telling Stanley.

Furnishing her flat with items she ordered online from Wayfair and Ikea had offered her a welcome escape from the gloom and doom surrounding her husband's failing health. Occasionally, when nurses were attending him, she would steal a day away to receive deliveries or do a bit of decorating. Her condo flat was the exact opposite of her palatial home in Georgetown. The initial goal had been to do it as inexpensively as possible since she intended to sell it once her investigation was over.

Now, however, she wasn't so sure she could easily part with it. In some strange way, she actually preferred her 1,100 square foot flat to the luxury and elegance of their home. This time, she wasn't trying to impress anyone, just please herself. She did indulge in a high-quality, adjustable bed, however, and a special 70" television with up-to-date electronics. She liked being able to control everything with her cell phone, computer, or audio command. With the touch of a button or a voice command, she could see who was at the door, change the temperature, lower the blinds, turn the lights on and off, even start a pot of coffee. She also liked the fact that each unit had its own enclosed garage and elevator. She was learning more about the area and discovering a multitude of things to do.

Before Stanley passed, she had completed preliminary work on her investigation. She had hired a title company to run the title on the MCS building and was surprised to discover it had once belonged to George Washington. He had, indeed, transferred the building by a deed of gift to Drs. Palidore H. Montgomery and Marshall Robinson.

The title exam also revealed some transfers over the years but always from one Montgomery to another Montgomery. Robinson had been bought out a long time ago. Combining that fact with the photograph she noticed on the desk in Palidore's office and the original Dr. Montgomery's diploma hanging on the wall, she concluded the original Palidore was either remotely related to the first president, or they had been close friends. In any event, she could not see how that changed the fact the current Palidore was running a scam out of the place now.

Public records revealed the real name of the business to be "The Medical Society of the Potomac, LLC," but that entity had acquired the right to operate the business under the assumed name of "Montgomery Cryogenic Services, LLC." There were twenty directors associated with the company, but their addresses were not available for review online. She had run a criminal background check on Dr. Montgomery's name as well as on all directors' names. She found nothing against any of them and assumed none of them had a criminal record.

Her attorney had reviewed the contract Stanley had signed

with MCS and found it to be binding. He had indicated that, as the surviving spouse, she might be able to avoid delivering him to MCS as there would be no one to sue on behalf of Stanley to enforce his wishes. However, if she chose to do that, she would not be entitled to a refund, so she decided having Stanley there might actually help her investigation. By having access to Stanley, she had access to the premises of MCS.

She had also begun doing Internet searches on each of the directors and Dr. Montgomery. Her searches revealed so much information, it was overwhelming, plus she needed to make sure each hit was properly associated with the correct person and did not regard someone else with a similar name. As she opened an electronic file on each director, and one on Dr. Montgomery, she moved various bits of information into the correct electronic files for later study and reflection.

The sun was setting now, and she sat with her computer on her lap, sipping wine. A guilty feeling began creeping into her awareness that on this very day Stanley was being "buried." *Or preserved, or whatever you can call it,* she thought. *Surely, I should feel some grief by now. Or maybe it just hasn't hit me, yet.*

The chair felt so comfortable. And even though it wasn't time to turn in, she felt the mental and physical exhaustion of today beckoning her eyes to close.

"Alexa, turn out the lights."

Chapter 33

Palidore's eyes were fixed on Lynn Radford, searching for her reaction. "What do you think?" They stood inside one of two bedrooms decorated in antique furnishings.

"If I didn't know better, I'd think I was actually back in time," she said. "They certainly do look authentic. Both rooms are beautiful, just warm and really comfortable. I can't believe you were able to complete them so quickly."

Palidore's watch and cell phone beeped simultaneously as a quiet announcement came over the intercom: "All members of Alpha team please report immediately to processing room one. This is not a drill. Repeat: This is not a drill.""This is it . . . I can't believe it's really happening," he said, turning and hurrying toward the elevator. 'Come quickly! Follow me," he said. Lynn tried catching up to him, not understanding what to expect. As the elevator doors opened, they both jumped in."What is it? What's happening?" Lynn asked.

Palidore looked straight ahead as they descended toward the basement. "Subject One needs our attention immediately." Lynn tried comprehending what that meant. She had planned and trained for this moment, but now, she was suddenly overcome with a real sense of apprehension. Elevator doors opened, and they exited, quickly moving toward Processing Room One.

Palidore never wanted his work viewed or equated with what occurred in hospitals. He felt this moment was more about restarting a life than saving one. In order for his clients to have their lives restarted, they would have to be processed perfectly, hence he had named the area a "processing room" not an "operating room," even though there was no difference; they looked essentially the same.

Bringing Lynn into an adjacent viewing room, he pointed to the Alpha Team. The three physicians, Drs. Samuel Robinson, Edward Beyer, and Richard Cotton, were now surrounding Client One who was lying on the processing table. Dr. Robinson was the attending physician.

"His blood sample has fully resumed its prior liquid state," Dr. Robinson said. "We must assume the client's blood has done the same. We will begin by removing the body wrap from the patient." The doctors carefully began cutting off all wrappings.

Then, Dr. Robinson's scissors hit something hard. "Hold on a minute, I've found something here." He carefully cut around the object. "It's a small bottle with a note inside." Palidore and Lynn were wide-eyed and moved closer to watch through the glass. Excitement was palpable as they watched Dr. Robinson reach inside the bottle and remove the note.

He opened the folded paper and read: "This man is Kevin Washburn. His age at the time of our treatment is sixty years old. His cause of death is likely from a blood disorder of some hematologic nature which we are unable to determine at this time.' The note is signed 'Palidore H. Montgomery, MD,'" Dr. Robinson said, then laid the paper on a nearby stand.Palidore felt a cascade of emotions consume him and was suddenly proud of what his ancestor had accomplished. He could almost sense the presence of the ancestor whose name he carried, being alongside him now, somehow reaching out to him.

We've got him; we won't let you down, Palidore thought. He'd never experienced an emotion quite like this before. Standing mute, he looked through the glass, nearly paralyzed, yet trying to regain his composure as the doctors proceeded to remove the remainder of the wrappings from the patient's body. When everything was off, they began washing the body with an antibacterial soap. "He really looks good," Dr. Beyer said. "Skin color is excellent. What did that note say his age was - sixty? I don't believe it. He doesn't look more than thirty-five at best."

Doctor Beyer attached electrodes for an EEG to be run. An IV was put into a vein to administer drugs. Then they put a virtual reality visor on him, inserting earphones in his ears.

"What are they doing? What are they putting over his eyes and in his ears?" Lynn asked.

"It's a virtual reality device in case he wakes. The hope is that he will think he is in a lovely room of his own era and the ear plugs will simply be playing very low, soothing music. The idea came from your own suggestion. To quote you: *'The patient should not wake up under the glare of intense lights to a hoard of people standing around in scrubs with masks on'* or something like that. We do need these people over him with the tubes, lights, and monitors, so it's our attempt to hide the surgical setting from him."

Lynn's smile revealed how pleasantly surprised she was they had taken her comments seriously. "That is absolutely amazing. What a unique way to address the problem."

A ventilator was hooked up to the patient and oxygen flow established. A crash cart was brought in, and the AED machine was initiated; then paddles were applied to his chest. Dr. Robinson called "All Clear" and hands were removed from touching the patient. Then the machine delivered a jolt of electric shock to the body. It caused the body to bounce once, but nothing more happened.

"Again," Robinson commanded. The body bounced a second time, but monitors indicated a heartbeat. Elation took hold among the staff. Dr. Robinson administered a mixture of the ancient compound B into through the IV as they watched carefully. The only sound was the ventilator forcing oxygen into his lungs. A warming copper infused blanket was placed over Client One. Now all eyes were on the EEG monitor.

"There it is. We've got it . . . look! We've got brain activity," Dr. Cotton said excitedly. In the observation room, Palidore and Lynn hugged each other delightedly.

Without warning, the patient began shaking violently and cried out: "No!" before abruptly sitting up, tearing the visor off his face, and falling back onto the table. The vital sign displays stopped pulsing. The heart monitor revealed a flat line.

"Is he smiling?" someone asked. Everyone could see that Client One lay on the table with a small but notably pleasant smile on his face. Then the doctors began working feverishly again to revive him. But nothing happened to change the results.

Finally Palidore used the intercom for everyone in the room to hear: "It's time to call it, Dr. Robinson. We had him back, even if it didn't hold. That is a victory . . . truly historic!" Dr. Robinson's eyes were downcast. "You did a fine job, Sam," Palidore continued. "Let's get an autopsy done, then put his remains in a cylinder for the time being."

Turning to Lynn, he saw she was trying to hold back her own emotions. "We were so close! I just can't believe it. He was back . . . he was back," she said.

Palidore put his arm around her and gave her a hug.

"I know, I know . . . but we *are* going to succeed, I promise - just keep doing what you do, and be ready for when it happens." Lynn broke away from his arm and turned to face him.

"But didn't you hear him? He said 'no.' Did you hear that? Why did he say 'No'?"

Palidore reached over and put two fingers on her lips momentarily stopping the flow of questions before responding.

"I think that's what he said, too. At least I *thought* I heard him say it. Let's look at the video to be certain, but if that's what he said, then I'm afraid none of us will ever really know why he uttered that single word."

Lynn regained control of her emotions before speaking again.

"If he said 'no,' then . . . then that could only mean one thing. He did not want to come back. You have to wonder if we are doing these people any favors," she said.

"You may be right," Palidore said, "but I'm not so certain. Perhaps the word 'no' was the last word on his mind when he initially passed away. Or perhaps he was saying 'no' to the force keeping him from returning to his body. Nobody knows, and no one will ever know. Let's not lose our focus here. If we are successful in bringing back even one of these individuals, they can ultimately tell us what, if any reservations, they had." He looked at her still concerned.

"Are you ok now? Are you willing to continue playing a role in all this?"

Lynn nodded her head. "I'm okay now. I guess this was just a little overwhelming for me. You're going to pursue it no matter what. So, if it's going to happen, with or without me, then I still want in." She forced a smile and wiped her cheek with her sleeve. Palidore gave her a quick reassuring hug as they left the observation room. On the first floor, he told his secretary to call an emergency meeting of the board as soon as schedules could be accommodated, but certainly within the week. He then wondered who else in the building beyond Lynn and the Alpha Team had any knowledge of what just transpired. He decided to send a text to his entire staff.

"There has been a significant development that will be addressed soon by the board. I am uncertain whether anyone other than the Alpha Team of doctors has any knowledge of today's development, but you are cautioned not to speculate or communicate, in any manner, anything you may have witnessed or heard here today regarding our activities. If you have any questions, please feel free to communicate directly only with me. Unfortunately, because of today's developments, I am left with no choice but to cancel any time off anyone may have scheduled until the board can meet and deal with these developments. Thank you for your patience and understanding." Not everyone was happy to receive his message.

Chapter 34

Martha peered out her loft window across the alley from the MCS building and noticed an unusually high volume of traffic pulling into the parking lot, one car after another. She went to her pre-mounted telescope by the window and took a closer look through its high-powered lens.

"From the looks of all the pricey vehicles, something big must be going down. Maybe it's time to go pay Stanley a visit," she said out loud to herself.

Martha quickly checked her appearance, grabbed her purse and cell phone then headed down the elevator to her private garage below. Climbing into her Audi S8, she hit the garage door button, and slowly backed out. She then proceeded to drive around the block before turning into the parking lot of the same MCS building she had been watching. It would have been faster if she had just walked across the alley separating her new modern warehouse condo from the MCS building, but she figured it wasn't time to reveal she had purchased a flat across from them.

No one needs to know about my little hideout at this time. The fewer who know, the easier it will be for me to servile their little activities.

She drove in and stopped at the gate sentry. "I'm here to visit my dearly departed husband," she said. The guard asked her name, checked a sheet, and politely tipped his hat.

"Of course, Mrs. Vaughan, please take one of the spaces identified for visitors." As the gate went up, she thought, *Gee, that went well, now they have a record of me arriving by car.* The visitor's spots were just beyond those reserved for directors, each of whom had a sign with their name on it designating a private space.

I wonder if there's a pecking order to determine which special director gets the closest spot and makes the lesser ones huff it a few more yards to the building? She was in a prickly mood. After picking a place closest to the last director, she turned the car and backed into the spot. Checking her lipstick and hair in the visor mirror, she slipped her sunglasses on and exited the vehicle which quietly locked itself as she proceeded past the private back entrance and back out toward the street. Walking up the front steps, she had to identify herself again before being buzzed in.

Then, she proceeded to the reception desk. "Hello, I'm Martha Vaughan. My husband is a client here and this is the first time I've come to visit. What is the procedure?" The receptionist typed a few keys on her computer and looked up at her in a friendly manner.

"It's really very simple, Mrs. Vaughn. I've activated your husband's cylinder so you can touch it to light it up. Here is your visitor's badge; please wear it at all times. If you will have a seat, a guide will escort you to your husband." Martha put the plastic badge on and took a seat as directed. In less than a minute a young woman approached.

"Mrs. Vaughan, are you ready?" Martha who had been looking in the opposite direction, snapped her head around to look at a pleasant-looking woman in her mid-thirties.

"Yes. . . yes of course, I'm ready."

"Please follow me."

They moved to the elevator, entered and proceeded to the second floor. It was a short walk down the hall before the guide stopped in front of a door.

"Mr. Stanley is in the seventh row, cylinder # 357. I will let you in, but first, let me explain. He is suspended in a cryogenic solution. If you want to see his face, simply touch the upper blue portion of the cylinder and it will light up. If you want to see his whole person, simply touch the lower portion of the cylinder twice in quick succession and the entire cylinder will light up. You will not need to turn the lights off as they will automatically go off after sixty seconds. You may stay as long as you wish and relight the cylinder as often as you want.

"Down this hall is a small chapel. Many visitors like to spend some time in there after their viewings. When you are ready to leave, please return to the first floor and turn in your badge prior to leaving." She waited for Martha Vaughn to ask questions, but she said nothing. Being well-trained, the guide pointedly asked, "Do you have any questions?"

"No, I don't think so," Martha answered. The woman opened the door to the cylinder room for Martha to enter. "There are a lot of cars here today; is something special going on?"

"Not really," the woman said. "The only thing happening is a special meeting of the board of directors," she explained before taking Martha inside the room and showing her the procedure, she had just described about lighting the cylinder. Then, she reminded Martha to turn her badge in at the desk on her way out, before leaving her alone.

Martha glanced around the room. She didn't know how many cylinders were there but it seemed to be an endless number of rows all with the top ten inches lit up, creating a bath of eerie blue light. She didn't see any other light source in the room, but the blue light was sufficient illumination to navigate anywhere.

She saw one small circular floor light in front of each cylinder and Stanley's space displayed the number 357. She figured the light must come on as part of the cylinder activation as none of the other cylinders had such a light shining now. She looked at the floor of an adjacent cylinder and could see that it also had such a light, but it was not lit now. She also noticed the spot immediately next to Stanley's cylinder, spot number 358, was empty but had a small plaque which read: "Reserved." She shuddered as she read the sign. *So that is my 50K spot. What a waste, stupid waste,* she thought.

Initially, she had no real interest in seeing Stanley. She had just wanted an excuse to look around, but then she thought to herself: *Why Not? I could at least stay a moment.*

She wasn't sure she wanted to light up the cylinder, and almost started to leave, but then changed her mind, turned back, and stood directly in front of it. She only stared at it for a while. Finally, after summoning all her courage, she raised her right hand toward the upper blue lit portion of the cylinder. She almost touched it, but quickly pulled her hand back. Her emotions were starting to get the best of her. *I need to do this,* she told herself. So, taking a deep breath, she raised her right hand again, and this time touched the upper part of the cylinder.

Immediately, the top portion of the cylinder illuminated, revealing Stanley's serene face frozen in time. His eyes were open and he appeared to be staring directly at her. It was such a shock, she lost her footing and fell back against another cylinder, then tumbled to the floor where she remained motionless, unable to move.

After a few moments, she was able to sit up and slowly began to cry. Her crying intensified and she started to shake. She tried wrapping her arms around herself, then bent over in grief, sobbing for several minutes. As she sat on the floor surrounded by all the cylinders that were each emitting the strange blue light, she was at long last experiencing the grief she had somehow kept bottled up inside herself since Stanley's passing.

The light in Stanley's cylinder had long since turned itself off as promised. Martha had not planned, nor had expected any of this to happen. Now she found herself desperately trying to regain control of her emotions. She began gathering the contents of her purse which had spilled when it hit the floor. She grabbed her cell phone and USB adapter she kept with it and was putting things back when she spotted her small compact case. The compact lit up as she opened it. She looked at herself in the cracked mirror and began to cry again. She buried her face in her hands and sat back on the cold lonely floor.

Finally, she stopped crying long enough to locate and take out a small pack of tissues and once more tried to regain her composure. It took several minutes, but she slowly made it to her feet being extra careful not to touch Stanley's cylinder again. She looked around in an effort to orient herself so she could find her way out.

Retracing her prior steps, she eventually exited the door back into the lighted hallway. She felt a complete sense of relief. Looking down the hall, she decided it was time to visit the chapel.

Chapter 35

Martha was sitting in the chapel when she heard the announcement. At first, she was relieved her visit was over since everyone was being asked to leave the building, but then she had another idea. Quickly gathering her things, she proceeded out into the hall when she heard someone coming up the stairwell. Quickly she crossed the hall and slipped into another room, surprised to find it housed the ancient patients.

She listened to voices of people passing by the door, then, looked around, and noted the first stainless steel vault was completely open with no body inside. It looked as though someone had just cleaned it, leaving it open to air dry.

Wonder what happened to old Number One, she thought. Taking out her cell phone, she took a quick snapshot. Approaching the second cylinder, she tried to open it but found it locked. She stepped back and took a picture of the entire row of vaults. Seeing nothing more to do, she returned to the door and slowly opened it to peek out. Satisfied no one was present, she quietly started down the hall but saw several people waiting by the elevator. Seeing a stairwell door almost next to her, she quickly disappeared into its recess to take the stairs down. Exiting on the first floor, she saw a line of people signing out and turning in their badges. Now being last in line, she tapped the shoulder of a young female student immediately in front of her.

"I know they want us to leave as soon as possible," she told the young woman, but I really need to use the bathroom. Would you mind holding my badge until I get back, so I don't lose my place in line? If you get there before me, can you just put it in the box when you turn yours in?"

"Sure," the student said. Martha gave her the badge and walked toward the bathroom where she entered a stall to wait. After some fifteen minutes, she heard Palidore on the PA system announce:

"Attention please: Our electronic monitoring system indicates all visitors and student badges have been accounted for, and the building is now vacant of nonemployees. Everyone, please proceed to the third-floor conference room. Remember to have your cell phones, tablets, and other electronics checked at the door. The building has now been locked down and you will need to use the employee exit in the back of the building when you leave."

Martha waited a few more minutes to be certain everyone had a chance to make it to the third floor before she exited the restroom. Then she made her way over to the main office where the diplomas were displayed on the wall. She entered. After a moment, she began taking multiple pictures with her cell phone. Spotting the vintage picture on the desk, she went over to examine it closer. She picked it up, put in flat down on the desk, and took a close-up photo of it. After replacing it on the desk, she went around to the other side, sat in the leather seat, and looked at the drawers. Opening each one, she found nothing unusual except in the top right drawer where a handgun was nestled. It caused her to pause for a moment.

Then continuing her search, she found a handle on the bottom left. Thinking it was a file drawer, she tried pulling it out, but instead, it swung open revealing a safe. The safe's handle was at a slight angle. She pushed it down and the safe opened.

Someone was in a hurry, she thought. Quickly rifling through the papers, nothing stood out. Then she noticed a small drawer inside the safe which she opened, revealing a thumb drive labeled "1V." She glanced up to see if anyone was coming, then grabbed the thumb drive. At first, she was going to take it, but then remembered her USB adapter was in her purse and wondered if she could copy its contents. She inserted one end of the adapter into her phone and the other end into the thumb drive. Within two seconds, the cell phone displayed a message: "Do you want to import this video?" She hit the "Import Video" button and watched as the file quickly uploaded to her phone. Disconnecting it, she put the thumb drive back into the drawer inside the safe.

Should I leave the handle as I had found it?

Ultimately, she decided that whoever had attempted to lock the safe probably was unaware the door had not fully latched. *It will raise fewer questions if I leave it like the owner thought he had left it,* she reasoned. Slowly, she moved the handle into the locked position until she heard it latch.

Now, she exited the room and started to head toward the back of the building. Not exactly sure where the back exit was, she headed in the general direction she had seen a few directors go through to the outside parking lot. Entering a hallway, she heard the elevator begin to move and voices coming down the stairs. Hurrying to the end of the hall, she saw a steel door with a crash bar. Pushing down on it, she left and closed the door as quietly as possible behind her. Now sweating profusely, she nearly jumped the final steps to the ground and proceeded to her car. There was no sentry at the exit, and the automatic gate arm lifted as her Audi drew near. She drove off, went around the block before pulling into her garage and closing its door.

Still high on adrenalin, she sat in her Audi with her head resting on her hands still holding the steering wheel. *Am I getting too old for this kind of intrigue?* she wondered. Finally, she looked up and exited the Audi, proceeding up the elevator and into her flat.

Inside, she put her purse on the counter, retrieved her cell phone and connected it to her laptop. Once she located the new video file, she copied it to the computer. Trying to open it, a message asked for a password. *Oh, well, this is beyond me,* she thought. *I'll have to get Jeff to try and crack it.* Physically and mentally drained, she made her way to the refrigerator and reached for her bottle of Chardonnay. Pausing with the bottle still in hand, she changed her mind and put the wine back, shut the door, and stood leaning against the refrigerator while looking down at the floor.

Her emotional day had caught up with her, and now her body ached; she could hardly move. Drawing a breath, she headed for the bathroom and turned on the shower. Then she undressed right where she stood leaving all her garments in a pile at her feet. She reached in and checked the water temperature, turning it up as hot as she could possibly stand before stepping in.

For more than thirty minutes, hot water pulsated over her body, soothing her tense muscles. Steam poured out of the shower as she exited. After a quick toweling off, she grabbed her white terrycloth robe and returned to search for her bottle of Chardonnay. Reaching the refrigerator she felt the temperature of her overheated skin which had become trapped by her heavy robe causing her to perspire. She let the robe drop to the floor. Feeling better, she retrieved her bottle, poured a full glass and crossed the room where she stood staring out the large window at the MCS building.

She didn't know, or care, if anyone could see her wearing nothing. She had shed more than her robe, for in that single moment, she finally felt free and liberated. She had rid herself of the grief and guilt bottled up inside for so long. The emotional stress finally released its grip on her tired aching muscles.

She took a sip of wine and thought how ironic it was that she and Stanley had each wound up being housed in old buildings across the street from one another in downtown D.C.

I must confess, I like my place better than his, she thought and settled into her leather stressless chair, drawing her knees up to her chest, leaning back, and staring at her ornate metal stamped ceiling.

"Alexa, play Kenny G."

Chapter 36

The Alpha team, consisting of Drs. Robinson, Beyer and Cotton, and the Beta team, consisting of Drs. Montgomery, Miles and O'Hara sat down for their monthly meeting. In practice they were distinctly separate medical teams that alternated weeks of being on call, but they met, studied, and planned together. In front of them was all the most recent information available from the testing of Kevin Washburn.

The teams were reviewing their plans in the event another ancient client became ready."It appears that both blood-thinners warfarin and heparin will work based on the small amount of blood we tested from Mr. Washburn's sample," Dr. Cotton said. "After dividing his blood sample into two parts, we tested each one separately. Both gave us an INR reading of 2.1 which is perfectly within the desired parameters. Now that we know what to expect, when another patient awakens, we will be able to prevent blood clots from forming in the future and having the patient die suddenly as happened to Mr. Washburn"

"So, the issue before us," Dr. Robinson spoke, "is whether we should abandon the use of Compound B and use one of our known blood thinners to prevent blood clots from forming." He looked around for any facial reactions but saw none.

"As head of the Alpha team. I don't think we have a choice," Robinson continued. "I suggest we use warfarin as a substitute for Compound B immediately. We know everything about warfarin, and nothing about this Compound B. If we had sufficient time to study it, I am sure Compound B would also work amazingly well. The problem is, however, that the blood in the patient has lain dormant in a gelatinous state and has not been circulating for so long that when we jump-started the heart, in Mr. Washburn's case, we couldn't circulate the compound fast enough. Therefore, blood clots start forming immediately before we knew what to expect, and that's what did him in within minutes, as we all saw. Because warfarin assimilates extremely fast, I believe we should use that method in the future."

Dr. Sarah Miles, spoke next. "I'm wondering if we could modify our procedure tables so when a patient is close to awakening, the table would undulate up and down, head to toe, causing the blood in the body to begin moving *prior* to injecting the blood thinner. Actually, we may want to place the patient on the table a day or two ahead of our scheduled attempt at revival. This would give the blood a chance to being circulating before we inject the warfarin. In fact, this may be the thing to do regardless of which blood thinner is used," Dr. Miles said. "I also agree with Dr. Robinson that we should substitute warfarin for Compound B.

"As you will recall, it was my idea to test the blood sample with warfarin and heparin. Now that we know each one works well, I believe it would be malpractice to continue using the ancient Compound B precisely *because* we know so little about it. Placing the body in motion certainly can't hurt, and it will likely help speed up the introduction of warfarin into the bloodstream."

"I like the idea of putting the body in motion," Dr. Beyer said, "but I think we are making a huge mistake if we discontinue using Compound B. You acknowledge that you do not know much about the compound and are assuming it is only a blood thinner. What if it is more? We only know that Compound B counteracts Compound A, which is another compound we know nothing about. What if warfarin only thins the blood, but does not counteract all the other lingering effects of Compound A? Where are we then? Maybe we don't know everything about Compound B, but we *do* know it neutralizes

Compound A *and* is a blood thinner. Warfarin is just a blood thinner. So, if Compound B does more than thin the blood, by substituting warfarin, then we may have a problem. I think we shortchange the early physicians who likely knew more about these compounds than we do now. Let us trust their judgment and stay with Compound B."

"With all due respect to Dr. Beyer," Dr. Miles said, "he is operating on an assumption that simply has no basis in fact. We need to stick to science and science tells us that we need to use the fastest acting, best blood-thinner we know."

"I think both of you have valid points," Palidore said. "and we could likely debate this for hours because we are debating the unknown. So, I think it is time to take a vote. All in favor of substituting warfarin for Compound B on our next subject, raise your hand."

Four hands went up.

"All those who think we should stay with Compound B and not use warfarin, raise your hands." Only Dr. Beyer and Palidore raised their hands.

"Then, it is decided: We will substitute warfarin for Compound B at our next opportunity. I will also see to having the procedure tables modified."

***

Six weeks later, Palidore came to look at the procedure tables that had been retrofitted with new undulating motion machines; he'd been anxious to get them in place. Now, he wanted to try them out and decided it wouldn't hurt if a subject or two was placed on the tables. He asked one of the interns to bring in clients number two and three and position them on the new motion tables in the procedure rooms for testing.

While waiting, he returned to his office and started going through his mail. Within minutes, his watch beeped with a message that read: "Please come to Procedure Room One. There is an issue." He jumped up and proceeded to the room. Upon arriving, he saw the client strapped on the table now moving slowly in undulating motions.

"What's the problem? Everything looks okay to me," he said.

"Well, there is nothing wrong with either *table*, they are both working fine; but, when we placed Client Two on this table, he felt extremely light compared to Client Three, or compared to anyone, for that matter. So, we examined him carefully and it appears that something has eaten away a portion of his backside coverings, which has allowed air and moisture to access the body for God only knows how long."

"Then I can't believe you bothered to strap him on and started this thing going," Palidore said gruffly. "Shut it off at once, and let's take a look." The intern hit the switch and the table returned to a normal, horizontal position.

Palidore unstrapped the body, and with the help of the intern, turned the body over. A small hole about three inches in diameter was clearly visible on the lower portion of the bandages previously covering his right buttocks. Putting on a pair of latex gloves, Palidore inserted his index finger into the opening and felt around, then removed it and lifted it to his nose. There was no odor, but nothing would have shocked him, if there had been. "What in hell . . . how did this happen?" he uttered. "*When* did this happen? Clearly, this body has been compromised. We have lost this subject. He is simply irretrievable. Contact Dr. Cotton at once to do an autopsy on the subject. There is little to no odor, so he has probably been like this for decades."

Clearly agitated, Palidore went into the second procedure room and hit the button to stop the table so he could check on Client Three. Everything appeared to be fine with this one.

"Thomas," he called to the intern. "Please check all remaining ancient subjects to be certain there are no issues with any of them." Then, as if an afterthought, he said: "When you talk to Dr. Cotton tell him I think we should take x-rays of all remaining subjects and log results into their charts."

"Consider it done, Doctor," Thomas said. "Actually Dr. Cotton is due here in a couple of hours. Should I tell him then, or do you want me to contact him now?"

"Actually, there's no rush," Palidore said much calmer now. "It was just kind of a shock to find client Three in that condition. Just let him know as soon as he arrives, Thomas. Thank you."

Chapter 37

D r. Cotton knocked lightly on the open door to Palidore's office and stood waiting to be acknowledged. Palidore looked up and smiled. "Richard. Come in, I've been anxious to hear what you found out about client Number Two."

"Well, frankly nothing we didn't expect," Richard Cotton said. "The body was basically gone except for skin and bones. There was no muscle remaining. Most of the skin was well-preserved, however, which was a bit of a surprise. I'm of the opinion this breach must have happened almost immediately following his preservation. As you know, the first ancient bodies were transferred to this building by your ancestor more than two hundred years ago. So, it may even have happened prior to them moving the body to this building."

"Really," Palidore responded in a surprised tone. "Why do you say that?"

"Well, if it had happened here, I think there would have been more evidence of body fluids on the bandages or a noticeable odor; but that's just a guess on my part."

"Seems reasonable," Palidore said.

"But the x-rays are something else," Dr. Cotton said. Palidore's eyes looked at him in anticipation of something more. "Well, as you recall with client Number One, we found a bottle containing a note that was attached to his body." "Yes, I remember."

"Well, we checked the others and there *is* a bottle attached to each body, except that client Number Five has *two* bottles attached to him. It appears that our ancient physicians had much more to say about that subject than the others. Now that we have x-rays, it appears the bodies were completely wrapped and treated *prior* to the bottles being added. So, I believe we can carefully remove the bottles *before* the time a revival would be attempted. At the very least, this would give us more time and information about what these patients were afflicted with at the time of their demise. That would allow us to be more prepared. What do you think?"

"Oh, I don't believe there is much 'thinking' to do," Palidore said. "Let's do it! This could be unimaginable. I would like to jump right to Client Five, but perhaps, we should do them in order. Let's start with Client Three and work our way to Client Five. That way, if he is someone special, we will know more about the revival process."

Both doctors headed off to procedure room Two like kids in a play yard. They found Client Three still lying on the undulating table. Dr. Cotton stopped the table's movement and put the side views of the x-rays up on the light board. The exact location of the bottle was clearly visible in the film. Palidore opened a cabinet and took out a wrapped surgical kit. He broke the seal and removed a scalpel, put on a pair of latex gloves, then carefully made an incision directly over the area where the bottle was located.

Dr. Cotton held the two sides of the separated cloth apart as Palidore removed the bottle. They carefully checked the bottom of the now vacant pouch in the chest of client Three to be sure it was still air-tight, then put both sides together and applied strong medical tape to keep it shut.

"Well, that was far easier than I thought it would be," Dr. Cotton said. "Let's see what this note says." He cut the wax off the bottle top revealing the cork. Then took a corkscrew out of a drawer and removed the cork to retrieve the note. Reaching inside his vest pocket, he slipped on reading glasses and read out loud: *"This is Richard Brockwell, age 68. He was suffering from a cardiac issue at the time of his death. (Signed) Dr. Marshall Robinson, June 15, 1798."*

"Okay then, not much information on this patient. Let's fetch client Four." They went to the room housing the ancient inventory and carefully placed client Four on a gurney, moving him into procedure room One and transferring him to the table. Following the same procedure as with client Three, they removed the bottle without issue.

Palidore uncorked the bottle this time and retrieved the small note to read out loud: *"This is Frank, a Negro aged 71, who was complaining of severe abdominal pain at the time of his death. October 24, 1798. Dr. Palidore H. Montgomery."* The doctors stared in shock at what had just been read.

Palidore, was the first to speak.

"He has no last name, and he is a negro. Back then, there were few, if any, wealthy negroes so you have to wonder how *he* was chosen to be treated or who paid for the treatment."

"And if he was a *wealthy* negro, he would certainly have had a last name which most everyone would know. So you have to wonder if he was a slave. To my limited knowledge, slaves were primarily known only by their first names even if they had a last name. Which leads me to the conclusion that some wealthy person was very fond of Frank, so they wanted him preserved."

"Let's put him back and fetch client Five," Palidore said.

They put client Four, now known as "Frank," back on the gurney and proceeded to the inventory room. They had just settled Frank back into position and were starting toward client Five when Palidore's watch beeped a warning.

"Another subject needs our attention," he said looking at Dr. Cotton. "Richard, I'm not sure if placing client Three in motion has hastened matters, but it appears he is now ready to be revived."

"Well, his blood sample is not attached to his body so the undulating table would not have set off the sensor," Dr. Cotton said. "In any case, I guess it's just his time, so we need to move."

As they made their way to Procedure Room Two, Palidore took out his cell phone and made sure the same message had gone out to the rest of Beta team on call, and to Lynn. As head of the Beta Team, Palidore began to scrub in preparation for the effort. Dr. Cotton headed toward the observation room.

A short time later, several cars sped into the parking lot, each member hitting a button in their cars to control the gate. One at a time they parked and headed for the back door. Lynn also arrived and made her way inside to join Dr. Cotton in the observation room. The Beta team members quickly scrubbed in and assembled around Client Three. Palidore informed them that he had already removed the client's bottle.

"The note inside said this man suffered from a cardiac issue at the time of his death," Palidore said briefing the team. "Therefore, my immediate concern is whether we *can* reactivate his heart."

The button was hit placing the table back to a stable, horizontal position, and the team proceeded to unwrap and clean him with antibacterial soap. "I know the note says Mr. Brockwell here is sixty-eight," Dr. Miles said, "But, again, this subject's body appears to belong to someone no older than forty, if that."

No one responded as they continued preparing. An EEG machine to measure brain activity, and a ventilator to help with respirations were put in place and ready for use the instant a heartbeat could be detected. Two intravenous lines were inserted, one in each forearm so the warfarin could be administered to the body from both sites. Palidore slowly administered the warfarin into saline bags attached to poles on either side of the table and adjusted both lines for a small drip of the dosages through the IVs. Then he started the table moving again.

Some thirty minutes passed before Palidore stopped the table, took the paddles from the cart nearby holding an automated external defibrillator (AED) machine. He placed the paddles on the patient's chest, waited for the machine to rev up to the advised number of joules, asked everyone to stand clear, then administered a shock to the patient. The body bounced upward once, but no heartbeat started.

Increasing the voltage, Palidore advised everyone to stand back again and administered a second shock. Still nothing. He grabbed a syringe of epinephrin and plunged a full dose through the chest and directly into the patient's heart. Client Three lay still.

Not one to give up easily, Palidore again advised everyone to stand back and once again shocked the body. This time, after the patient bounced, a heartbeat was detected on the monitors and a cheer went up from the staff. Hands flew in all directions as the ventilator was put on the patient to help respirations, and an ECG machine began monitoring the heart. The virtual reality visor was also put on him after which Palidore stepped back and set the table back in motion.

No one spoke as they all waited for something more to happen. Everyone appeared to be holding their collective breaths. In the observation room, Lynn had tears slowly tracing down the curve of her cheek as she wiped them with the cuff of her sleeve.

"And there it is," Dr. Miles spoke. "We have brain activity."

No sooner had she gotten the words out of her mouth than the patient's body went into shivering spasms, despite the copper-infused blankets now covering him. He seemed to shake his head rapidly back and forth as if objecting to something. Palidore placed his hands on the patient's head attempting to halt its motion which seemed to help, and he lay still again.

"If this patient had a cardiac issue at the time of his death," Palidore spoke, "he will need additional attention very soon, but for now the blood thinner seems to be working. I think he is too fragile to begin any sort of treatment at this time. My advice is that we keep him right here and continue to monitor him. However, all of us do not need to be here, so maybe one of us can stay, and the rest can move to the observation room where it's more comfortable. Then we can take turns spelling the person in the procedure room."

"I'll stay," Dr. Miles said. "Actually, I want to stay, if that's okay?" Palidore nodded as he and Dr. O'Hara left the room. He removed his surgical garb and went upstairs. Entering the observation room, he was greeted by Lynn who hugged him as Richard gave him a high five.

"You did it!" Lynn exclaimed. "I can't believe it, but you did it!"

"Yes, we did!" he said.

"But I have to say, the patient again looked like he was shaking his head, 'no,'" Lynn said. "And that concerns me since it has now happened with two different people. You stopped him from shaking his head, Palidore, but clearly, he was trying to send a message."

A long sigh escaped Palidore. "I knew you were going to focus on that, Lynn. I stopped him because I believed it to be an involuntary twitch, nothing more. His whole body at one point shook. It was just a final manifestation of whatever caused his body to shake. I suspect the sudden onset of blood and oxygen rushing through his body once again reinvigorated his muscles. Certainly it would cause some involuntary muscular actions. He is going to be fine; and you, Dr. Radford, had better be ready to go to work!" The words were no sooner out of his mouth then he heard Dr. Miles call out.

"Palidore, come back here! We have a problem!" Palidore and Dr. O'Hara quickly made it back to the procedure room.

"What is it?" Palidore said coming in the door.

"See for yourself. He's having small convulsions, and there's a gurgling sound emanating from his throat." Palidore removed the ventilator mask from his face and witnessed a white foam seeping out Client Three's mouth. Then, he began convulsing more violently.

Lynn, watching from the observation room and closed her eyes to begin praying. *"Please God, put your healing hands on this man and do your will with him."* Palidore was attempting to suction the patient who was moving violently from side to side. Suddenly, he collapsed into a non-responsive state.

Using the medical crash cart and equipment, Palidore tried again to start the heart with the AED unit, but nothing happened. The patient's color began changing to an ashen gray, his eyes were now bloodshot, glossed over, and began rolling back in his head.

However, a small, visible smile was on his face. It was obvious to all that it was over. Palidore finally stopped his efforts and placed both hands on the side of the table, bending forward, sweat pouring from his forehead. He couldn't move. Only the beeps of the machines could be heard. Finally, Dr. Miles put her arm around his shoulder.

"Palidore, you've done all you could. It's not your fault . . . come on now. Let's go." He didn't move at first, but then slowly rose up and allowed her to escort him back to the observation room where he collapsed in a chair, totally exhausted.

Chapter 38

Palidore had no choice but to schedule another Directors' meeting which he was now calling to order. Again, he asked the secretary to leave so they could have a discussion off record. After everyone viewed the video recording of their unsuccessful attempt to revive Client Three, Palidore called on Dr. Cotton to reveal his autopsy findings.

"As you can see from the video, once again, we were able to revive one of our ancient clients but were met with another unsuccessful outcome," Dr. Cotton began. "The takeaway lesson is that it is *possible* to bring one of these people back to life after they have been treated with the ancient compounds. The problem is that after two attempts, we have failed to maintain their lives but for a brief period of time.

"My autopsy revealed that client Three's blood turned bad within minutes after his revival and that he succumbed to its poisonous nature. So, to summarize: client One died from blood clots, client Two's body was not useable, and client Three's blood turned toxic. As you know, with client Three, we substituted warfarin for Compound B which cured the blood clot issue, but may also have been a factor in allowing the blood to turn toxic.

"I then took a sample of Client Three's blood which had *not* been treated with warfarin and treated it with Compound B. That blood sample did *not* turn toxic. So, either warfarin reacted with something in the client's blood causing it to turn toxic, or the client's blood is destined to turn toxic *unless* it is first treated with the mysterious Compound B.

"Therefore, it seems that going forward we have two choices: We can substitute another blood thinner for Compound B, or we can just use Compound B again. Both present risks. I will open the floor now for questions or comments." Dr. Cotton recognized Dr. Beyer to speak next.

"This is exactly what I feared when I opposed using warfarin instead of continuing with Compound B at our team meeting," Dr. Beyer said. "It is clear that Compound B is an antidote for Compound A. Therefore, I believe it is essential that we follow the medicine our ancient physicians have prescribed. They knew both compounds better than we do, and successfully used Compound A to preserve bodies. They did leave us in a unique position. But *whether* to use Compound B should *never* be the question. There is only one question and that it is *how* and *when* to administer compound B."

Dr. Miles did not wait to be recognized. "I will concede now that Compound B is necessary," she said, "but it seems to me that it doesn't act fast enough to prevent the formation of blood clots. Therefore, it seems logical to administer our next client with both warfarin *and* Compound B. This will ensure that blood clots do not form while allowing

Compound B to treat Compound A and prevent the blood from turning poisonous." "You can't be serious!" Dr. Beyer immediately responded. "For all we know, it was the interaction of warfarin with compound A that caused the toxin in the first place. We have learned a lot and now have the rotating table to help speed the circulation. I believe administering compound B is just a timing issue. We may also want to increase the administration of it by having more IVs in different locations, but under no circumstances do I believe we should re-introduce warfarin." His voice was strident and his face was getting red from emotion.

"Okay, okay," Palidore jumped into the conversation. "The problem does not seem to be in reviving an ancient client, but in *keeping* him alive. We can experiment with several options hoping to select the correct one, but my fear is that we will run out of subjects before we exhaust the number of options available to us.

"On the other hand, we can rely on the advice of our medical ancestors who were clearly successful in preserving the bodies in the first place. None of these ancient patients would be here if it wasn't for the expertise and care of those doctors who treated them. The team members will recall, I voted to stay with Compound B when we decided to try warfarin. We are in uncharted territory. I need to be open-minded enough to accept the combined wisdom of my fellow doctors, and I am still willing to do so, but I must say that I, again, concur with Dr. Beyer. The doctors who so carefully preserved these patients are in the best position to advise us. The problem being those doctors are no longer with us. However, their research is well-preserved, and it is replete with suggestions that we administer Compound B as quickly as possible.

"Given the dates associated with our ancient patient inventory, there are only two more patients who are candidates for revival any time soon. After that, it will likely be another decade at the earliest. In my opinion, we just cannot experiment with these two patients. We need to use the medicine that is known to counteract any lingering effects of Compound A and that is Compound B.

"Now, despite my personal feelings I am willing to abide by the collective ruling of my fellow physicians. So, there are two options available to us: We can use Compound B *along* with another blood thinner, or we can use *just* Compound B. Does anyone else have anything to say before we vote?"

Palidore's tone of voice coupled with his stern conviction was meant to put a damper on any further discussion. "All right, then, let's vote. You see the two options on your screens.

Please cast your ballots now."

The vote was an instant 20 to 0. Apparently Palidore had even convinced Dr. Miles to change her mind. "Very well, we will treat the next available ancient patient with just Compound B. Is there anything else we need to discuss?"

"Once again, it appeared that our last patient looked very young for his age," Dr. O'Hara spoke. "Do we have any more information concerning this phenomenon?"

"Dr. Cotton?" Palidore said. "Do you have an opinion?"

"We don't know much more than we did with the first subject. It appears the treatment these individuals were subjected to had the effect of slightly. . . " he paused trying to search for the right word before continuing. ". . . bloating . . . for want of a better word. It seems the body's tissues engorge, something like receiving a Botox treatment. There is also evidence that any unhealthy cells are not affected by the treatment of Compound A which seems to result in unhealthy cells dying off in favor of healthy cells. Another way of looking at it would be to say the healthy cells crowded out the unhealthy cells. So, if one of our patients had a severe infection at his time of passing, it is likely that upon revival, the infection will be gone. There also seems to be some sort of tightening of the muscular tissues which may be due in part to the 'bloating effect', but we can't be sure. We have had just two subjects to study, and not for a very long period of time. Of course, we are interested in this phenomenon and will continue our research."

"Any other comments," Palidore asked.

"I know there are two surgical revival teams, and they are called into action when a client appears ready," Dr. Tillar said. "but I am wondering why all of us are not notified. Obviously, this is a significant event, and even if we are not participating in the revival effort, many of us would like to be here. We understand the observation room can only hold so many, but we could meet in one of the classrooms and watch a video feed."

"I see," Palidore said, somewhat taken aback. "Well, we have certainly tried to provide information as soon as possible to keep everyone in the loop, but I guess we have felt less confusion at the time is better for all. That is not to say that we shouldn't consider your request. On the other hand, the intensity of the moment requires our surgical teams to be totally focused on the patient. I should also confess that legal counsel has advised that unless, and until, there is a medical success, we should keep access to the event at a minimum. Notwithstanding that, let me have the staff look at how a larger group wanting to witness a procedure could be accommodated. I am pleased you have brought this to our attention. Can we get back to you?"

There was no response to his question, so Palidore informed the directors that the video of the unsuccessful attempt at reviving Client Three would be destroyed as was done with Client One. Then he thanked everyone for their attendance and summoned the secretary back in as he formally closed the meeting.

As everyone was leaving, Palidore called out. "Dr. Cotton. . . would you kindly stay a moment. I would like to have a word with you."

Chapter 39

Nearly everyone was gone from the conference room, leaving Palidore and Richard Cotton the last to leave. "Richard," Palidore said. "Do you want to take a look at the notes on our fifth ancient client? As you will recall, he had two bottles attached to him."

"I find that curious," Dr. Cotton responded.

"Absolutely! I've been dying to get back to those notes. Care to have a look now?"

"Yes, let's do it," Dr. Cotton said. The two men went to the inventory room and removed client number five from his location. They rolled the cart back to the procedure room where they carefully removed both bottles without affecting the airtight casing surrounding his body.

Each bottle had a number etched on it. They were labeled "1" and "2" respectively. Palidore opened one bottle and Cotton opened the other. Palidore found a letter of several pages in bottle one from P. Hugh Montgomery, M.D. A lesser number of pages was in bottle two. Rather than read them quickly, the men decided to take the notes back to the study after returning client Five to inventory. Securing him in his location, they proceeded to the study where they turned on lights and Palidore poured a snifter of brandy for each of them. Then they settled themselves comfortably in lounge chairs before opening the notes to study them. "Why don't you go first, Palidore?" Dr. Richard Cotton suggested.

"All right," Palidore said, putting on his glasses and opening the note. He began reading aloud:

"I have done so many drafts of this note that I have grown tired of trying to find the correct words. I can only hope the person or persons who someday receive this communication will know what they are about to read is the truth and not a hoax. So, this is it. My final attempt to explain what I assume you will find unbelievable despite my best efforts. Here goes:

Twenty years ago, my father, Dr. Palidore H. Montgomery, treated the body to which this note is attached. I was aware of this person and that his preservation was going to occur, but like my father, I was powerless to prevent it. At the time of this note, there are six subjects in our inventory, and this note is attached to subject number five. He was the last subject my father agreed to treat. I pray there will be no others added to our inventory, but sometimes it seems unavoidable.

Originally, each body had a name properly displayed. My father felt it was the correct thing to do as they had no headstones. When I took over after him, however, I decided that names should no longer be displayed. My primary reason was that if the name of patient number five was to be found out, there could be serious repercussions from all levels of people. And though we have proper documentation to protect us, there would still be unimaginable consequences that I am unwilling to let myself, or my family, be put through.

So here it is: Client number five is George Washington, the first president of our country. I feel certain that your eyes can hardly believe what you have just read, but it is true."

Palidore abruptly stopped reading. His mouth and eyes opened wide in disbelief, and his hand holding the paper was shaking. He put the paper down on his desk, stood up, and began walking around the room, saying nothing, but with a puzzled blank stare on his face. He stopped in front of his ancestor's diploma, placed both hands on the glass, then looked down at his shoes before saying: "How *could* you?"

Dr. Cotton came up behind him and put an arm over his shoulder leading Palidore back to his chair and forcing him to sit down.

"Come on – let's think this through." Palidore took out a handkerchief and dabbed at his brow. It was cool in the room, but he was overcome with nervous heat. Soon, his breathing slowed and returned to normal.

"This can't *possibly* be true; you know that, right?" Palidore said, looking for support.

"No, Palidore, I don't know it at all," Richard responded, "but it could be some sort of sick joke."

"I don't think so. It's starting to make sense to me now. The ancient photo on my desk proves my ancestor and George Washington knew each other well enough to be seen together. We are standing in the very building that was transferred from George Washington to my forefather and Dr. Marshall Robinson. Why would President Washington do that if there wasn't something afoot?" Palidore thought for another moment. "And I don't think anyone would joke about such a thing, if they weren't going to be around to see the reaction. No, as unbelievable as it may seem, this revelation could very well be *true*."

Silence prevailed before Richard spoke again. "Well, it could all be true, and, perhaps, *not* true." Palidore gave him a look like he had lost his mind. Richard read this expression and continued. "Now don't look at me that way, hear me out. Suppose it was true, and they had an agreement, just as Hugh said, but whoever was supposed to deliver the president's body to your ancestor could not acquire it, so he just brought him a body and *claimed* it was the president, a reasonable look alike. I mean, isn't that possible?"

Palidore thought for a moment. "Well, that *could* have happened. All right, let's finish reading the note." Richard fetched the letter and tried handing it to Palidore. But instead, Palidore held up the palm of his hand, refusing to take it.

"No, this time *you* read it. I'm not up to it." Richard took the letter and skimmed down to where they left off and continued reading:

"President Washington found out about the first couple of patients who had been treated by my father and became fascinated with his work. They quickly became friends and, ultimately, it was President Washington who wanted his body preserved. He hoped that God would bifurcate his life so that he could actually see the future of this great country in which he was so instrumental in helping to form. My father resisted, and I objected, but the president could not be dissuaded. In the end, we could not refuse him.

"We never thought it would actually happen because we could not see how his body would ever be delivered to us without anyone knowing. However, one day, Major Ronald Hudson did, indeed, deliver the body just as the president said he would. We have no idea who is really buried at Mount Vernon, but it is not George Washington.

"My father, feeling every patient should be treated exactly the same, attached a brief note to his body as he had done with the others. I have felt over the years that a greater explanation should be provided concerning this subject, as he most certainly would present a more delicate situation for the physicians attempting to revive him in the future. Accordingly, I have taken the liberty of removing the original note and replacing it with this more detailed explanation. I am hopeful that you agree with what I have done.

"In the second bottle, you will find documents signed by the president and given to my father, certifying that the treatment of his body was done at his own, sincere direction. In addition, since we have continued our experiments with this process, I have chosen to enclose our most recent clinical findings and observations. I wish you well in this endeavor and would truly like to know the outcome. But I know that will occur well beyond my own lifetime.

"Dated: October 24, 1819 (signed) P. Hugh Montgomery, M.D.."

"Should we tell the board about this?" Dr. Cotton asked.

Palidore put his head in his hands for a long moment clearly trying to come up with the right answer. Then slowly, he began to shake his head from side to side. "I really don't know, and since I don't know, I think the answer has to be 'no' for the time being. I have never kept anything of importance from the board before and this is too important to keep from them for long; but I need time to think through the implications before I let them in on it.

"Right now, maybe we can see if there is a signature on the documents that came from bottle two along with their research. If so, we can have it compared to known copies of President Washington's actual signature. If there is a match, then, unless the wrong body was delivered, it is likely we actually have George Washington in inventory."

Richard held up the rolled documents taken from bottle number two showing it to Palidore with a questioning look on his face.

"Yes, let's do it," Palidore said. Richard slowly unrolled the papers and placed them on the table. For moment, he set the research paper aside and turned the others face up. Palidore put his finger on the signature. "There it is."

Silently, they both read the message to themselves. It was short and to the point, but pretty much exactly as Hugh Montgomery had promised. Both Palidore and Richard continued to look at it and finally exhaled, almost in unison. "I don't think you'll need to send it off - look, there's his presidential Seal," Richard said. "I agree, it seems we have George Washington in a preserved state. Now what? I mean, can we get into trouble? Will the government want the body? Will protesters or religious groups try to prevent us from proceeding if word gets out?"

"Well, to answer your questions, we just found out that we *had* him, and we have this paper to prove it was his desire to be preserved, so I don't think we can get into any real *legal* trouble," Richard said. "It's likely the government will declare his body a national treasure and seek to get it back. But then, the other document appears to be a standard contract. We could argue that we are contractually obligated to try and revive him. Lastly, I am certain there will be protests from weirdos and religious groups."

Palidore stood up and took a small walk around the room. "Richard, I've changed my mind. We need to inform the board and convince them that our prior decision *not* to disclose a patient's history should stand. Just because we now have a famous person should not belie the logic behind our prior decision. Yes, that is precisely what we should do, but let's sleep on it for a day or two giving us time to plan for the meeting."

"Would you like to review the research paper that was enclosed?" Richard asked.

"Why not," Palidore said. Richard spread it open. It consisted of five pages explaining the research with dogs, a couple of diagrams and a summary. Richard picked up the summary and began reading it out loud.

"As can be seen from our diagrams and experiments, we believe that as the effects of Compound A wear off, there may be a problem with blood clots forming. It is interesting to note that when you have a large quantity of blood treated with Compound A, it can easily be reversed to its prior state with the addition of Compound B. However, when the same amount of blood treated with Compound A cannot be reached all at once with Compound B, such as when circulation has stopped, then it becomes problematic and that is when clots can form.

We believe to successfully revive a patient, it will be necessary to circulate the blood outside the body somehow and treat it all at once with Compound B. We do not know how that can be done at this time, nor how the blood could be put back into the body. Hopefully, future physicians will find a way and will succeed.

Lastly, great care must be taken not to allow the blood to become too thin as this will cause the remnants of Compound A to become extremely toxic which would most certainly be fatal to the patient."

Palidore could hardly believe it. Here were all the answers they had needed with clients One and Three. "Well, damn, how stupid we are! There is a good chance we could have saved the other two patients if we had just read this first. Dr. Beyer was right all along: 'Just trust the first physicians,' he told us."

"Well, certainly with this knowledge," Cotton answered, "we never would have introduced warfarin, but how could we know about the procedure to introduce Compound B?"

"But now we do. We can proceed just like a heart bypass procedure," Palidore said. "Or perhaps, we can use a modification of a dialysis treatment where all the blood is cleaned through a machine outside the body and reinfused into the body again. In any event we need to figure this out before our next patient starts coming around."

Chapter 40

Martha sat in her living room staring at the electronic whiteboard displayed on her large screen TV. Early in her years of investigative work, she would cover a wall with paper and diagrams to get a visual look at all evidence. Now she was doing the same thing but using her computer to show the images. She could move photos, documents, and notes around on the screen and study them more closely. She could draw lines and post questions with a few strokes of the keyboard. This way was much easier to change things around and not clutter the house.

Once she got things displayed the way she wanted, she would take a screenshot and save it to a file with a special name. Then she would rearrange and start over again, giving herself an opportunity to look at things from a different perspective. It was an investigation in a modern age.

I'm certain that Palidore Montgomery is engaged in something fraudulent, she thought. *I think he's taking advantage of vulnerable people, offering them hope when there is none and charging them a fortune,* she thought.

It had been no financial burden for Stanley, but Martha was certain there was someone out there who had given up everything to acquire his services.

I'm going to figure it out and bring him to justice!

She had hired the best people to try getting a patient list, but obviously, it was somehow under tight lock and key. There were several obituaries in the papers referring to MCS, but that was it. She had already contacted those families. Only three had agreed to talk to her, and they seemed to feel the service was expensive but admitted they had not been coerced or misled into paying the money.

One elderly lady, Molly Sturgis, however, had said she really believed they would revive her husband any day now, and was so looking forward to having him back. "I call them daily to check on his progress, but so far, they say he's just not ready yet."

I'll just bet they do, Martha thought. *And he probably never will be!*

"His name is Arthur, and he's been there for eight years," Mrs. Sturgis told her. Martha felt strongly that Molly had been damaged by MCS in living her golden years of life hoping for something that was never going to happen.

She had already reviewed this particular situation with her legal team, but they said the case was very doubtful at best, and impossible at worst, unless Molly was willing to pursue a claim, which she wasn't willing to do. She loved MCS and Dr. Palidore Montgomery, in particular.

"They're going to bring Arthur back to me," she said.

How sad, Martha thought. *This is wrong, so very wrong!*

Her cell phone rang. She saw it was from Jeff, her IT guy, and quickly answered

"Were you able to crack the password code?"

"Yes," he said, "I sure did. I'm sending you the file back along with the new password I set. You should have it in a couple of seconds." She heard a beep as Jeff was saying, "Hey, you aren't getting in over your head now, are you?"

"I might be, but don't worry, I'm a big girl. Thanks, Jeff." She hung up and cleared the whiteboard from the screen, opening Jeff's file in its place. It was a video file. She hit the arrow to start playing it.

A man, wrapped in white cloths, was on an operating table surrounded by three doctors. One of them said: "The sample of blood has fully resumed its prior liquid state; and therefore, we must assume the client's blood has done the same. We will begin by removing the body wrap from the patient."

As she watched, the men found a note which they read aloud. She made note of the name 'Palidore H. Montgomery' with no 'Jr.,' or Roman numerals following it. Could this be the one whose name was on the diploma located in the special case in the office? She hit the pause button and pulled up the photo of the diploma she had taken, pasting it on the whiteboard. Then sitting still for a moment, she tried to comprehend what was going on and remembered the room had contained twelve vaults. *Maybe this is the one that was rolled out.* She popped another picture up on the screen next to the video.

Okay, that explains the one vault being opened. They are trying to revive one of the supposed ancient patients, she thought. Hitting the 'play' button again, she watched intently as they removed the remainder of the cloths from the man and scrubbed him down.

She found it interesting the man had no hair anywhere on his body and looked younger than the age they had stated was in the note. Like people in the observation room, she was holding her breath and was excited when they got his heart to beat. Upon hearing 'there's brain activity,' she smiled with a feeling of elation. *That is pretty exciting*, she thought.Then, shockingly, the man cried out, 'No!' before collapsing back onto the table. Tears whelmed in her eyes as she watched everyone working so hard to revive him and found herself secretly pulling for the team to succeed. Then she heard Palidore's voice on the intercom say: "Great job today . . . we had him back, even if it didn't hold. We had him back, and that is truly historic!" She could hardly believe what she had just seen. She played the clip back two more times before sitting back and trying to process her emotions.

Am I wrong about MCS and Dr. Montgomery? she wondered *Could they be on the up and up, even . . . honorable?*

After reflection, she decided what she had viewed on the video clip changed nothing. *The whole thing is still a scam, and vulnerable people are still being taken advantage of,* she thought. *So they tried to revive a guy. He was not even one of MCS' clients, but some lost soul from long ago. And in the end, they still failed! But it was right,* she thought, *that when the situation presented itself, they at least tried.*

Nevertheless, Palidore and his pals were getting rich and people like Molly were being hurt and deceived.

Even if they were successful and actually revived one of their patients, what then? she thought, *would life insurance companies want their money back? How about all the stuff distributed pursuant to the patient's estate? What if the spouse has remarried? Has anyone thought of those implications? I'll bet they haven't,* she thought.

She had to keep trying to expose this operation for what it was, even if she had only reached dead ends for now.

Chapter 41

The directors sat silently in the conference room staring at the documents Palidore had sent to their embedded monitors. They were each intently reading the letter from Client Five's bottle and reacting with versions of startled facial expressions. Some were fidgeting in their seats. One director pushed back from the table and put his head in his hands. Another looked up and appeared as though he desperately wanted to say something while looking straight at Palidore who put a finger to his lips and shook his head as if to say: 'Not yet.'Palidore had opted to let the directors learn the news the same way he had, so he could get their individual untethered reactions. He had warned them the information would be startling, and they would need to review all documents multiple times before coming to any firm conclusions.

He had allowed an hour for their review and provided a typed version next to each original to speed up comprehension. When the timer went off, everyone remained silent for a few seconds, then almost at once, everyone was talking to their neighbors. Palidore interrupted the chatter.

"May I have your attention, please!" He looked around the room. "We have now all seen the documents, but before we react too much, I want to provide you with some additional information." On the electronic board behind him, and on their monitors, the following information was displayed:

- This building was once owned by George Washington.
- This photo depicts my ancestor with George Washington
- My grandfather once told me that one of the ancient bodies was someone very special.

"So, when you answer the questions I am going to send to your monitors, please keep these additional facts in mind. I will now send you the questions one at a time. When you see the question please answer immediately." He pushed the buttons at 15-second intervals.

Q. Do we really have George Washington in our inventory?

     A. 19 yes   1 no

Q. If we have the body of George Washington should we announce it publicly?

     A. 2 yes   18 no

Q. If we have the body of George Washington should we inform the government?

     A. 4 yes   16 no

Q. At the appropriate time should we attempt to revive him?

     A. 20 yes   0 no

He looked at all results before addressing the directors.

"Thank you for your candid answers. I would like to hear from the one person who answered 'no' to the first question."

Dr. Miles rose from her seat. "You may keep your seat Sarah," Palidore said, "just tell us your thoughts, please."

Sarah Miles sat down and took a deep breath. "I know the evidence seems overwhelming, but I just can't believe it; maybe I don't want to believe it. It seems impossible to me that the body of *George Washington* could have been secretly removed from his grave so soon after his death without *anyone* knowing.

"Surely, there would have been guards surrounding the mausoleum. We also know at one point in history, someone actually broke into the mausoleum and tried to take his head. So, it's clear that *someone* is still in the mausoleum. To have pulled off this body exchange means not only would someone have gotten to the president without being seen and secretly removed his body but would also have had to deliver a replacement body. It just seems highly unlikely all that could have happened.

"It's not that I *disbelieve* the notes, or feel that Dr. Hugh Montgomery was lying, it just seems more likely they were scammed, and the person who was supposed to deliver the body just delivered 'a body,'" she said, looking around for someone to agree with her. But she was only met with blank stares. "I just can't believe we have the genuine body of our first president. That's all."

"Thank you, Sarah," Palidore said. "So, may I assume that since you do not believe we have the correct body that you also feel it is unnecessary to notify anyone?"

"Well, that would *not* be correct," she said. "I think the documents are real, and that Dr. Hugh Montgomery felt he had the correct body, so that is historical in and of itself. Therefore, we should turn the documents over to the government."

"Wouldn't that cause the government to also want the body to conduct DNA testing?" Palidore asked.

"I suppose so," Sarah responded.

"The vote to attempt a revival at the correct time was 20-0, so that means you all voted to try and revive, which we could not do, if we do not have the body, does it not?"

"Well, I did not say *when* we should turn over the documents," Dr. Miles said, which made Palidore smile.

"All right, fine. Now there were four of you who said we *should* inform the government that we believe we have George Washington's body, but based on your answers to the last question I must assume that you agree with Sarah's approach, that is, any such notice would necessarily have to come *after* a revival attempt? If anyone disagrees with that assumption, please speak up now." No one spoke.

"I know this is a lot to absorb and I am grateful for your responses. Now, let me please share *my* thoughts with you: It is clear we have a body that in all probability is that of George Washington. We also have other bodies of less renowned individuals. We have previously decided the correct course of action would be to attempt the revival of these individuals and, if successful, let them decide whether they want the world to know what has had happened to them.

"After careful consideration, I feel strongly that we are correct in that decision. The fact that one individual was famous should not change our view. If it was right before we knew the individual's identity, then the mere fact we now know who we are dealing with should not, in and of itself, negate our prior judgment.

"We do not know if we will be successful in the revival of any of these ancient bodies, but we should operate under the assumption that we will succeed at some point, therefore, take every step necessary to prepare for a successful outcome.

"I have not informed Lynn Radford, our psychologist, about these recent developments, as she is not a member of our board. But feel we must bring her up to date now to help her prepare. To my knowledge, she should be the only non-board member with whom this knowledge is shared. I hope you agree. If not please let me know now."

The room remained silent while all eyes stayed on Palidore. Then Dr. Judith Doyle stood up at her seat.

"No need to stand, Judy, if you're more comfortable sitting," Palidore advised her. But she remained standing. "Everyone here knows how much I cherish and value each of you as a colleague and as a personal friend. It is precisely *because* of our strong personal and professional relationship that I find it so difficult to inform you that after considering everything I have learned here today, I have no choice but to resign my seat on the board. Please understand that I feel everything Palidore has said to be correct. I feel he has outlined the only moral and proper course of action to take, and I a hopeful that he and MCS succeed. . . I really am.

"Nevertheless, I have to look at this in terms of how it will impact me, my emotions, and my family . . . and I just don't feel I can deal with it, regardless of whether we succeed or fail. I just think it would be best for me to resign, so that I am not part of whatever happens going forward. I am absolutely confident I will not be able to handle the emotional fallout from all this, let alone the public scrutiny that may result from an eventual public disclosure.

"I will continue to refer patients here, and I want you to succeed, but this is simply more than I signed on for." She sat down looking serious and slightly shaken. Palidore was almost lost for words. Every face was focused on his.

Finally, he broke the awkward moment. "Well, I must confess, I didn't see that coming. Still, I understand what you are saying, and won't try to change your mind; except to say that, if at any point, you do change your mind, you would be welcomed back with open arms." Judy wiped tears away with the back of her hand. "Is there anyone else who feels the same?" he asked.

Three more people stood. "Are each of you resigning for the same reasons?" Palidore asked. Each nodded affirmatively, then sat down again. "I want to thank each of you for all you have given to this effort. The resignations will be recorded in the minutes but will not be able to state your reasons for leaving. Please leave your access cards here as you leave today; feel free to contact me at any time should you have questions or concerns. Oh, and as much as I hate to bring this up at this time, I am compelled to remind you that your non-disclosure agreements are still binding. As to what happens to your interests in MCS, I believe our bylaws properly cover what happens under these circumstances. If no one has any further questions, I think it is proper to adjourn now. However, I would ask the Alpha and Beta teams to remain. We are adjourned."

***

After the goodbyes and hugs for those resigning, the Alpha and Beta team members returned to their individual seats at the conference table. Palidore returned to the lecturn."I have previously sent you a synopsis of the information we've gained from the ancient research papers of Dr. Hugh Montgomery. As you know, he said something we did not know: Due to having an adequate supply of compound A, he continued to experiment. His study confirmed two important results: 1.) that compound B *was necessary* to counteract compound A to avoid a residual poisoning effect, and 2.) That compound B was most effective if it could be introduced into the blood rapidly and suggested we somehow route the blood outside the body, treat it with compound B, then reintroduce the treated blood back into the body. He also cautioned *against* thinning the blood too much to prevent blood clots.

"He did not know how to suggest we manage the blood treatment outside the body since it was not possible during his time. However, it is now. As you know, we routinely do this in dialysis treatments, and during cardiac bypass surgeries. The question before us now is to determine how we wish to proceed with our next two patients. Since Dr. Cotton and I have discovered the research, we've had a little more time to consider a proper approach.

"Richard, would you please explain the approach and make your comments?"

Dr. Cotton looked at the group remaining, cleared his throat and began speaking."Well, in a normal situation, the less invasive and safer procedure would be to modify what we do in a dialysis setting. Obviously, we would not be *dialyzing* the blood, but rather treating it by injecting compound B as it passes through a modified dialyzer on its way to returning into the body.

"However, after much consideration, I believe a cardiac bypass procedure would be more effective. As you know, such patients' hearts are not beating at the moment we seek to revive them. And now we can actually accomplish this without cracking open the chest as we are not going to be working on the heart.

"We can start blood circulating through the bypass machine, begin treating it with compound B, reintroduce it into the body again and once we feel the treated blood has successfully circulated inside the body, we can then take the patient off the bypass machine and restart his heart.

In this manner, we can treat a greater quantity of blood much faster and relieve some of the strain on the patient's own heart in the process. At that point, we think placing the patient into an induced coma for a time, perhaps, a few weeks, would give us time to assess the patient's other physical needs and give his body a chance to heal. I will now take your questions."

"Richard, I think you are spot-on, I like it," Dr. Robinson said. "Do we have any idea how long we can leave the patient on the bypass machine prior to transferring him back to his own heart?" Dr. O'Hara asked. "I mean the longer we are able to circulate the treated blood, the better, I think. So, why take him off too quickly?"

"Good thought, Bill, I agree with you," Palidore said. "However, we would not want to leave his own heart exposed too long. That said, it is not uncommon for us to have a patient on bypass for several hours while we repair a heart, so my guess is that we could safely leave him on bypass for three to four hours. Any other thoughts or comments?"

"Yes," Dr. Miles spoke. "Once the patient is stabilized and we are certain that compound B has had a chance to do its job, would we consider putting him on a blood thinner at *that* time?"

"Probably not, Sarah," Palidore said. "As we know, compound A can immediately become toxic when combined with a blood thinner other than compound B, which apparently is a blood thinner of some sort. I know your concerns, and share them, but we would certainly want to wait long enough to be certain there is no residual amount of compound A remaining in the body.

"Obviously, we want to avoid blood clots, but also want to avoid the poisoning effect of compound A. In this respect, I caution us to adhere to the prescribed instructions of Dr. Hugh Montgomery." Palidore then recognized Dr. O'Hara who had raised his hand. "Yes, Bob?"

"I think your suggestions are the right approach," Bob Marsh said. "and we should follow it. Perhaps each team could spend some time developing a more precise procedure. We could also discuss this for hours but seems clear to me that we are headed in the right direction.

"This has certainly been a stressful, yet exciting day, however, at this time I just feel we need to sleep on it. The teams can start working on an implementation plan for our next meeting."

"I'll take that as a motion to adjourn," Palidore said. "Are there any objections?" Seeing none, he declared the meeting adjourned and signaled the secretary to come into the room from her cubicle. The day had been an exhausting one for all.

Chapter 42

Looking through her high-powered telescope, Martha noticed workmen removing names from four of the parking spots at MCS. *What's up with that?* she wondered, taking another sip of coffee. *Four directors leaving at the same time? Something's wrong."*

She began moving the telescope around, checking the whole building. But there was no other activity; nothing else to watch. During the day, she couldn't see inside the building because the windows were tinted against the harsh sunlight. Only occasional shadows of people moving around inside were visible; she had been checking daily. Today, however, there weren't even shadows. *Maybe I'll have better luck later when the lights are on,* she thought. A soft beep sounded. Her computer . . . she had a hit. A constant Google search was set up to check for anything related to 'Montgomery Cryogenic Services,' 'MCS' or "Dr. Palidore Montgomery." Anytime someone posted something containing any of those words, she would be notified. Many notices had come across her screen, but most were unimportant or of little help.

What have you found today? Something to do with the four departing directors? she wondered walking over to check. The hit was a newspaper article concerning jobs in the D.C. area. One such hit said: "Montgomery Cryogenic Services (MCS) has an opening for a communications director." Martha wasn't sure to whom they were attempting to communicate. *But it would certainly be a different kind of experience,* she thought perusing the article.

Sitting back, she thought about what she had just read. Her Google search wasn't set for databases of various employment agencies, but if this article had not been written, she wouldn't have known about the job opening because she wasn't looking for a job. *However, maybe I should think about this one.* Her friend, Jeff, was an internet tech. *He could look into this for me. If he finds it's still unfilled, maybe I'll apply.* After all, she had a degree in journalism from Wayne State University in Detroit, was proficient in all kinds of software, and had a vast history of experience. *And there is the fact that my beloved Stanley is a client.* She copied the hit and forwarded it to Jeff with a note asking him to check it out.

Meanwhile, she would look at her old resume. It was out of date, but formed a good framework in developing a new one. *First let me go online and see what people are saying should be in a resume these days.*

***

It didn't take Jeff long - a couple of days - to get the actual job posting to her. MCS had posted it with an agency specializing in finding personnel for hospitals and places devoted to the practice of medicine in some way or other. She checked the agency's web site and found they sought employees for medical institutions, and for people desiring work in the field of medicine. She couldn't tell how many people had listed their resumes, but felt very few journalists would think to list with this type of agency. It didn't mean, however, that the agency wouldn't search other sites to find MCS a qualified employee. *But if I list myself with them, maybe it would give me a leg up. This could be great,* she thought, *rather than just applying for the job, I will list my resume with the agency and, perhaps, just perhaps, they will refer me to MCS. Of course, I will need to add a note or two in my resume about an interest in cryogenics to be certain their computer will find my resume and associate it with the job at MCS. Then I can fain 'surprise' if I get an actual interview. It's perfect.*

It took her over an hour to work through the various fields required to list herself with the agency. She paid the $250 fee with her credit card, attached her revised resume, and hit the enter key on the keyboard. An immediate canned response appeared saying how much the agency appreciated her listing with them; they would verify her credentials and try and find her a suitable place of employment in the very near future.

Three days later, she received a call from Mary at MedStaff who advised her they had a possible job opportunity for her.

"Are you available for an in-person interview at the agency next Friday?" Mary asked. "Of course, I cannot say who the prospective employer is at this time until we speak to you in person," Martha agreed to meet at the agency at 1:00 p.m. She planned to turn down an offer from anyone other than MCS.

That Friday, she woke early and after a shower, found herself staring at her clothes in her small, but adequate closet. She preferred pants with a blouse to a dress or skirt any day. As she flipped through the blouses one by one, she noticed how many still had the tags on from her favorite shop, "Just Tops by Sherry". She settled on a light gray pant suit with lavender blouse, and a pair of gray open-toed flats. For jewelry, she chose a simple herringbone silver necklace and a pair of small silver hoop earrings. She wanted to look professional, but not overstated.

Calling an Uber ride would make sure no one would recognize her car, besides she wasn't exactly sure of the best way to MedStaff. She arrived a fashionable fifteen minutes early and entered the tall, fourteen-story building. A lobby directory indicated that MedStaff was on the eleventh floor, so she hit the elevator button and rode up. The door opened to a reception area which seemed generic in appearance. She approached the desk and gave the receptionist her name.

"Please have a seat, Mrs. Vaughn. Someone will be with you shortly." She was directed to an alcove with a water cooler, love seat, four matching dark green chairs, and a coffee table adorned with an assortment of magazines. *I wonder if anyone looking for a job ever really reads them,* she thought. Precisely at 1:00 p.m. a door opened, and a handsome man with slightly graying hair, came over to her."Mrs. Vaughan, my name is Jim Bottoms. I'm with Med Staff. Before your interview I would like to go over a couple of items with you, if that's all right."

"Certainly," Martha replied. He showed her to a small office just large enough to house a small desk, credenza, desk, executive chair, and two comfortable guest chairs. As he was moving around the desk headed for his chair he said,

"Please have a seat. This won't take long." Martha sat and Jim continued. "Your resume is impressive. I see you attended Wayne State University in Detroit. How did you wind up in the DC area?"

"My husband and I were both raised in Detroit and attended Wayne State University, where we met. He developed a career in securities and became a hedge fund manager. The company he initially worked for, transferred him to the DC area, and as a dutiful wife, I followed him here."

"Your last place of full-time employment was the Washington Post, but it appears you have not had a full-time job in several years. Why is that?

"Well, Stanley wanted me to stop working, so I would be more available for the activities surrounding his career and lifestyle."

"And now you want to go back to work?" Jim asked.

"Though Stanley left me financially secure, I nevertheless feel the need to restart my career, I am not content just playing the role of widow," She replied.

"I see," he said, realizing she had revealed her position in life. Federal law had not allowed him to ask directly. "Well then, please view this as a practice session. The questions I have asked are the threshold questions you will likely get in your interview with the company seeking a communications director. I must say, your answers seem reasonable and sincere. Your next interview should start in a few minutes. Do you have any questions for me?

"Yes, I do. Naturally, I'm curious to know why the name of the potential employer has been kept such a secret," Martha asked.

"A very good question. We do that because too many applicants do a lot of Internet research concerning prospective employers and, ultimately, come off a little too practiced, therefore, . . .how shall I say . . . a little disingenuous. So, it is better for you to come in a little less prepared but sounding sincere. I hope that answers your question. Having said that, I am now at liberty to tell you it is a company called Montgomery Cryogenic Services, LLC, who is the prospective employer. MCS is the abbreviated version of its name. While not considered a large employer, MCS has some eighty employees and a stellar reputation. You will be interviewed by Renee Janson who wears many hats for MCS, one of which is Human Resources. If you're ready, I will take you to meet her now."

Martha smiled and nodded her head.

"Good. Please follow me."

As they walked down the hallway, Jim Bottoms continued talking. "Your resume stated that you have an interest in cryogenic services. I think that caught Renee's eye. She's the one who asked to interview you. We probably would have suggested the interview, but they beat us to the punch," Jim said. "I know they're eager to hire as soon as possible."

He stopped at another office door. "Here we are." As he opened the door, Martha saw a small conference room adorned with an oval table, six chairs, a cadenza, a recording device, and a computer. There were pink and lavender flowers on the credenza along with a tray with ice water, tea and lemonade. "Renee, please meet Martha Vaughn," Jim said as a middle-aged, well-dressed woman with a short, professional haircut stood to greet her. He quickly left, closing the door behind him.

Jim had been right on with his initial questions which helped put Martha at ease. Then Renee asked:

"Martha, a note from our records indicates that your name

appears as a person who has paid a fairly substantial fee to reserve a place at MCS, is that correct?"

The question took Martha a bit by surprise, but she handled it seamlessly. "That's correct. My husband, Stanley Vaughan, is a patient there."

"Clients," Renee interrupted. "We refer to them as 'clients.'"

"Yes, of course, I apologize," Martha said, picking up right where she left off. "Stanley was very ill and had done some research concerning cryogenics. He talked to Dr. Beyer about it who referred him to MCS. Stanley and I read everything we could get our hands on concerning the process, hence my interest in cryogenics. It was Stanley's desire to purchase a spot for me, an impulsive move on his part, but it seemed to make him feel better, so I did not object at the time. When I listed my resume with MedStaff, I never actually dreamed there might be a possibility I could work for MCS, or any cryogenic company. In fact, I just learned a few minutes ago that I was interviewing with you. Does this somehow create a conflict and disqualify me for the job?"

"No, not at all, to the contrary, it may be helpful. A communications director who knows personally how difficult it is to make such a decision could be the best person to spread the word," Renee said. They discussed salary and benefits, which were of little interest to Martha, but she put on a good show.

"Should this position be offered to you, it wouldn't be a true journalistic job in the sense of the word. You would not be at liberty to write or communicate what you see or learn about MCS without our approval. In fact, your sole purpose would be to put MCS in the best possible light in any written or electronic news item such as social media. I suppose it's more accurate to say you would be acting more as an advocate, than a journalist. Every piece of your work, at least for the near future, would have to be read and approved by me. Do you understand what I am saying?"

"I do understand," Martha said, "And I completely agree."

Renee then stood and extended her hand. "Well, this has been pleasant. I cannot say definitively at this time that you have the job, but I can say it looks favorable. I will let you know something in a week or two. Thank you for your time." They shook hands and Martha gathered her purse and sunglasses.

"Thank you for affording me the opportunity to interview. I will look forward to hearing from you." *You have no idea how much I will be looking forward to hearing from you*, she thought as she found her way outside, again.

Chapter 43

Both the Alpha and Beta teams were involved with the bypass procedure on Client Four when his time to be revived had come. It was a resounding success. By following instructions from Dr. Hugh Montgomery's letter, they had successfully revived Frank and had performed surgery to investigate and repair his abdomen at that time before placing him in a medically induced coma for rest and healing.

Now Lynn Radford sat at a computer monitor outside the room housing Frank. *I still can't believe this is real. We did it, he's back!* she kept saying to herself. *He's alive!*. She knew he would be in a coma for at least two weeks, maybe longer, but couldn't help herself from looking at the monitor trained on the patient to watch his progress. Her emotions fluctuated between anxiousness and deep concern now that she needed to report, again, to the observation room. Both teams were assembled around Client Five. His time had come.

For the second time in less than a month, both the Alpha and Beta teams were on their feet for over three hours in Procedure Room One. So far, everything had gone well. Having done it once on Client Four only recently, introducing Compound B into the client's blood supply outside his body had been easier this time. Now the machine was reintroducing Client Five's treated blood back into his body. It would soon be time to take him off the by-pass machine.

Despite a cool temperature in the room, sweat was running

down Palidore's back as they applied the paddles to the heart to restart it. He called the "clear" signal. Hands came off the body, the electric shock was given . . . and there it was . . . a heartbeat showing on the monitor. The ventilator began supplying much-needed oxygen to the lungs, and the EEG monitor began displaying signs of brain activity. Still, everyone remained silent, waiting for something new to go wrong. Miraculously, nothing did.

Palidore administered a cocktail of medications through the IV line to place Client Five into an induced coma. "Dr. Cotton, you may finish him up, and let's do something with his teeth before we wake him."

The pent-up tension in the room finally let loose and there were high-five hand claps all around.

In the observation room, Lynn stood motionless and alone as if she were in a trance. She was staring at the client's face, wondering how someone who looked so young could be so old. The paintings and photos she had seen of the former president looked nothing like the man on the table. It was hard to believe this man could possibly be George Washington. But then, the other ancient clients had also looked younger than their true ages. Lynn was suddenly seized by a sense of sheer fear as she contemplated the job that lay ahead for her. *I feel so over my head in this responsibility, and I'm not allowed to seek any outside advice. God, if this is truly Your will, please guide and direct me,* she prayed.

***

For the next several days, MCS was a beehive of activity. Client Five was moved to the special bedroom on the third floor that had been prepared for him, decorated in a 1790s theme some time ago. He was breathing on his own now, and all signs remained positive as he lay asleep in his induced coma. The staff tending to him had been carefully vetted; regardless of their assigned duties, they were either all physicians or registered nurses.

So far, only the directors and Lynn were aware of the

suspected identity of Client Five. Everyone involved had signed a strict confidentiality agreement containing severe damage clauses for any breach of unauthorized information.

As time passed, both clients Four and Five began healing from the surgeries and dental work. Bandages were changed on both the abdominal and chest areas for Client Four and the chest area and dental work on Client Five. Both men had endured quite a lot but were healing well. There was also a noticeable amount of hair growth on Client Five, which puzzled Lynn. The patient looked so young, yet the emerging hair on his head was nevertheless gray, almost white. Apparently, whatever the ancient preservatives did to cause the youthful appearance had no effect on hair color. In any event, she was not a fan of stubble and felt he should have a shave prior to his ultimate awakening. She would have to inquire about having it done.

Palidore was at his desk when Renee came in with Martha Vaughn. Because of Palidore's open-door policy, he was accustomed to staff entering unannounced. The sound of Renee and Martha entering the room caused him to look up from the papers he was reading. He knew Renee, and recognized Martha at once, but couldn't quite place her in his mind. "Palidore, I'd like you to meet our new communications director, Martha Vaughan." As soon as he heard her name, everything came back, and he knew exactly who she was. The realization caught him a bit by surprise as he shuffled to his feet and held out a hand to greet her. He asked Renee to close the office door and invited both women to sit around the table.

"Mrs. Vaughan, I must confess, I'm a bit surprised by Renee's announcement. For some reason, I had the distinct feeling you were not totally supportive of MCS or cryogenics in general." Martha smiled, appearing at ease and in total control.

"Well, unfortunately, that's probably the impression I left for which I must apologize. You and your staff have treated Stanley and me most professionally. It was just such an emotional time, and given our religious beliefs, there were times when both Stanley and I were conflicted. However, I have now spent considerable time researching your work, and have been able to resolve the conflict surrounding Stanley's decision."

Palidore sat emotionless before responding.

"What prompted your decision to seek employment? I was under the impression you didn't necessarily need to work." Again, Martha smiled as though she had anticipated this question.

"You're correct, again. Fortunately, Stanley left me financially well-off, so it's not a question of finances. I suppose my motivation to seek employment can best be described as an attempt to fill a void. With Stanley gone, I suddenly find myself with plenty of time on my hands, and a desire to do something meaningful. Prior to marrying Stanley, I was an investigative journalist so, I decided to find a job that could benefit from my experience and education.

"Having gone through the decision-making process with Stanley concerning cryogenics, I listed that as one of my interests on my resume. I never dreamed I might actually wind up working for MCS, but then, here I am."

Still displaying a poker face, Palidore looked at her before his next question. "Do you see any conflict here? I mean, working for MCS and having your husband as one of our clients?"

"Not at all. To the contrary, I feel it's an asset. While you may view cryogenics as simply the last in a long line of medical decisions a person might make throughout their lives, I see the emotions, fears, and endless questions your clients must answer before making a decision like this.

"I'm hopeful that because of my personal experience with MCS, I'm in a unique position as your communications director to address those concerns. Forgive me for saying this . . . but quite frankly, the people who seek your services, need more than a clinical reason to pull the trigger on going forward with this process. They need to feel the warmth and compassion that comes from knowing the preservation of one's personal body is just as natural as the burial of that body.

"Lastly, I feel strongly that they must see it as final. They must be able to move on with their lives, and not sit around waiting for their loved ones to return. Just as I am doing now. I have finally accepted the fact that Stanley is gone, whether he be in a casket, or in a tube. To me, he is no longer here, and while he may still have a life in the future, I must move on with my life now. So, for all those reasons, I think I can uniquely deal with these issues in the information we develop and present to others." She took a deep breath. *Did he believe her?* "So, have I said too much? I sincerely hope I haven't offended you by showing you all my cards today."

Palidore looked over at Renee, then back at Martha. "Not at all. I find your motivation very compelling and your insight refreshing. I think I understand why Renee chose you for this post, and look forward to working with you, Martha. Welcome to MCS." They rose and shook hands again.

As Renee escorted Martha out the door Martha had her own thoughts swirling inside her head. *Yes! Now I'm on the inside and in a position to finally learn what's really going on at MCS.* Yet, an uneasy feeling she couldn't quite figure out was suppressing her happiness.

Could I actually have some admiration for what Dr. Montgomery is doing? She quickly dismissed it. *Surely not,* she told herself, *But I must say, he was smoother about my hire than I imagined he would be. No, he's just good at his con game and now I'm in a position to expose it.*

Chapter 44

Lynn tapped on Renee's open door and gave a little wave with her hand when the human resource director looked up.

"Lynn, come in. So good to see you," Renee put down a file she had been going through.Lynn entered and closed the door behind her, a complete opposite response to the expected "open-door" policy of the company. She took a seat in one of the chairs in front of the older woman.

"You look a bit preoccupied, Lynn," Renee said. "What's on your mind?"

"You can see, huh? I *have* been 'preoccupied' with a potential problem that may or may not have actually occurred. As you know, we have two subjects currently in comas, and if and when they wake up, it will be my job to introduce them to the world as it exists now. Perhaps the weight of this responsibility has begun playing tricks on my mind. But I'm trying to assess the multitude of things that could go wrong in order to prepare to handle them. I can plan for most of these potential issues, but not without advance guidance."

Renee nodded as if she knew what Lynn meant, before deciding to simply ask. "Well, now you have me intrigued; what is it you need guidance on?"

"We're all under strict instructions not to reveal the existence of our two notable clients or the miracle of their revivals to anyone," Lynn said. Renee nodded in agreement. "So exactly *who* will have to deal with the repercussions if news of this gets out? I don't know how to address this. I mean, what will be the company line? When and how will other clients be informed, and what will they be advised to do? I can't begin to prepare for this until I know answers to these questions."

"And why are you concerned this will get out?" Renee asked. "It's obvious that too many people know, too much is going on, too much data is being recorded," Lynn said, her eyes growing wide as if she were listening to herself. "I know, and the remaining sixteen directors know the suspected identities of our special clients. Even if the nurses and doctors tending to them do not know their names, eventually they will suspect something special is going on here. I mean, look at how they must dress in early eighteenth-century clothing. Not to mention the decor of the rooms. So, I fear it's only a matter of time before something gets out. Then what? Who will handle the onslaught?"

Renee twisted a bit in her seat as if uncomfortable with the direction of the conversation. "Lynn, you know the reason for all the secrecy. It will be your responsibility to explain to our special clients about the implication of disclosing their revival to the world. Then, it will be *their* decision to make, not ours. In fact, I think this was precisely how you felt it should be handled, isn't it?"

"Yes, I know, I know, I know," she said in a somewhat anguished way. "And I *still* feel that way. I believe we should do all within our power to keep it secret until they can become the decision-makers. Please don't misunderstand what I'm saying. I'm just worried that we're not *prepared* for the possibility, that despite our best efforts, the significance of this might get out and catch us all off guard. I think we should be more prepared for that eventuality. That's what I mean. I would feel better if I knew how we would handle such a breach of trust.

"Would we deny it? Would we be forced to lie? Or would we tell the truth? And if we do tell the truth, would we tell the *whole* truth? That's what's bothering me because in the end, if there is a breach, and our clients are being assailed, then I will be the person trying to explain it to them."

Realizing she had never fully considered this completely, Renee sat back in her chair and pivoted toward the window, considering what her response should be. Then she turned and made eye contact with Lynn again. She picked up a pencil and without realizing her tension, began drawing circles on her desk calendar.

"I'm not sure I have an answer for you, but you seem to have given this careful consideration. Why don't you go ahead, and tell me what *you* think we should do?"

That was the question Lynn was prepared to answer. It might have been the opening she was looking for when entering the room. Now, taking a breath, she paused, then answered."Well, unless there's some reason she can't be trusted, or there's someone else who should handle this, I think we need to bring in our new communications director and let her develop a series of possible responses. One for every conceivable way we could address such a breach."

Unconsciously, Renee had begun applying more pressure on her doodling. Now the lead broke with a discernable 'pop,' forcing her to refocus quickly on Lynn's suggestion.

"Um . . . well . . . thank you for bringing this to my attention. It's something that should be considered, but I'll have to discuss it with Palidore. Why don't I get back to you with his answer?"

Lynn rose from her chair feeling lighter, as if a burden had somehow been lifted from her shoulders, and started toward the door. "I didn't mean to create a problem for you, I am actually trying to prevent one," she said. "But thank you for hearing me out."

"No Lynn, I'm glad you felt comfortable enough to bring this to my attention," Renee said, taking a more conciliatory tone. "But for now, let's just keep this issue between us. Okay?"

"Sure," Lynn said before leaving. Intentionally, she left the door open.

Chapter 45

Palidore, Renee, and Lynn were waiting for Martha to arrive. They were seated around the small conference table in Palidore's office, when she finally entered the room. "Martha, good morning, please come in and have a seat. Can I get anyone something to drink before we get started?" Everyone declined, and Palidore closed the door before returning to the table. He took a seat and cleared his throat before beginning to speak.

"Martha, I think you've met everyone with the possible exception of Lynn."

"Actually, Renee has previously introduced me to Lynn," Martha said, returning his smile.

"Great, then we can proceed." He picked up a small stack of papers, tapping on their short edge as if straightening them, before looking up again.

"Lynn has expressed concern regarding our information security which Renee has brought to my attention." For a brief moment, Martha's eyes grew wide in surprise. But no one else seemed to notice.

"As you know, everyone has signed a strict confidentiality agreement with a substantial liquidated damages provision should they make such a breach. We have also taken steps to secure what data we have accumulated to date and limited its access. However, up to this moment, we have failed to develop a plan for *how* we would, or should, proceed in the event an actual breach of information should occur.

"Lynn believes we should plan for unauthorized disclosure of protected information and has suggested that *you,* Martha, be brought up to date on some information and be asked to prepare possible ways for us to deal with any breach of that information. Therefore, I have decided to follow her advice. We've called this meeting to ensure you receive the most current information you need to do your job. With that in mind, please know that what you are about to learn is *highly* confidential. Absolutely no portion of it may be revealed without my personal permission."

Martha sat in silence and nodded her agreement; only the tapping of her foot against the table leg showed her curiosity had reached a fevered pitch. No one could see her blood pressure rising nor the skin on her hands become clammy. Her outward appearance failed to reveal her inner turmoil as she appeared in total control to everyone in the room.

"Do you recall when you and Stanley first visited here?" Palidore continued. "We took a brief tour and I showed you the room where we housed twelve ancient bodies?"

"Yes, of course, I recall that." Martha said.

"Well, as I indicated to you then, we have never tried to keep it a secret that we had these individuals in our inventory. In fact, I even wrote a paper concerning them, but it never generated any interest. At least, not in the medical community. To the contrary, at best, there has been a 'so what' reaction. In any event, I believe I told you and Stanley that they had been treated with Egyptian chemicals which had perfectly preserved the bodies; and we were monitoring them, as at some point in time the chemicals would eventually wear off which would open an opportunity for us to try and revive them."

"I remember," Martha said. "Well, a couple of months ago, the oldest of our ancient subjects reached the point where we needed to attempt a revival.

We actually were able to revive him for a short while, but

he developed multiple blood clots and despite our best efforts, he did not survive. "Not long after, we tried to revive a second patient, this time trying to use a trusted modern-day blood thinner instead of the ancient blood thinner we had used on the first patient. Again, we were able to revive the patient for only a short time, but the residual toxins still in his body poisoned him and he, also, did not survive."

Martha looked startled at this news as she tried keeping her composure, now looking somewhat uneasy in her seat. Palidore noticed. "Are you alright? Is this too much for you to take in?"

"No, not at all," she said, hiding her trembling hand and remembering the video she had stolen from Palidore's office. "It's extremely interesting. Please continue," she said to him.

"For various other reasons, we decided to x-ray the remaining subjects. During that process we found information on the bodies of clients Four and Five which was of vital importance. It was the detailed notes from Dr. Hugh Montgomery, son of the original Dr. Palidore Montgomery. At the time of his notes, Hugh had assumed responsibility for the ancient inventory. Because of his notes, and by us following his detailed instructions, we were able to successfully revive both clients Four and Five who are now in induced comas but very much alive at this very moment."

"Oh, my God!" Martha cried out, no longer able to cover her genuinely emotional state. "Oh, I'm sorry . . . so sorry, it's just so incredible! she said, trying to divert attention from her true feelings. Palidore reached over and put his hand on her shoulder.

"Don't apologize, your reaction is normal. What we have accomplished is unbelievable, and beyond exciting; it's truly a miracle. However, neither client is awake yet, and we are uncertain whether they will be able to communicate, or even capable of intelligent thought upon wakening. There are signs of brain activity, but at present, it may just be that portion of the brain which controls the body's involuntary functions such has breathing and heart beating.

"However, we decided some time ago, that in the event intelligent communication became possible, we should plan for the next step which is where Lynn comes in. She has been preparing information modules covering a large variety of subjects. And since we now have *two* clients to educate, she is also training her assistant, Susan Trott, who will be working with Client Four while Lynn concentrates on Client Five. The goal is to allow each client to determine what and how much information they wish to receive, so we are preparing for almost anything. It has been a daunting and time-consuming task. But I believe we are now as prepared as we can be.

"We have also decided to allow each client to determine if he wants the world to know about his revival. You can imagine if the world learns of this, that our clients would be besieged by the media without mercy. On the other hand, if they are brought up-to-date on how to survive in our present-day society, they just might want to go out on their own and continue their reactivated lives free from such intense scrutiny."

"Excuse me," Martha said, "but how are *you* going to profit from this tremendous accomplishment without the world finding out?" This was the answer she needed; it was the entire reason she was here.

"If our clients want to keep their lives private, then of course, our 'profit' will simply be the satisfaction we have knowing we helped these individuals restart their lives. Of course, it would be wonderful to study and follow their progress," Palidore acknowledged.

Martha had a difficult time processing what she had just heard. She had believed MCS was all about the money, scamming people out of their life savings in exchange for a hopeless promise to one day resume their lives. But this new information had stopped her cold. "So, if we are to afford these clients this choice,"

Palidore continued, "we must protect the information and data that we have, hence, the confidentially agreements, and document security.

"However, as has Lynn pointed out, in today's age of electronic media, despite our best efforts, it's always possible some information may leak out. Now you can see what a devastating effect that could have on our clients. It would deprive them of ever having a *choice* in the future direction of their lives.

"We need *you*, as our communications director, to develop a series of responses for possible information leaks. That means you must develop a series of possible leaks, then develop an appropriate response should any one of them arise. Our responses could vary depending on the information that is leaked. If possible, we want to avoid an outright lie, but, if necessary, we may need for you to prepare such a denial. Ultimately, we will have to decide whether or not to use it. So, we know this may be a most difficult task. I suggest that in each scenario, you develop a truthful answer, an answer that *may* be truthful but does not relate all we know, and then an outright denial. Do you understand the assignment?"

"Yes, but to be honest, as a journalist, I'm not sure I can tell an outright lie," Martha said.

"No, *you* would not actually lie to anyone. Any response leaving this company would come from *me*. Any outright denial would be on me, not you. Please understand, if there is no leak, then there is no problem; but if news of our accomplishment comes out, then we must do what is in the best interest of our clients. I am hopeful this will not be necessary.

"Now, on the other hand, it may develop that one of our clients may *want* to reveal the truth about his past. If that should occur, we will be looking to you at that point for input on how best to present this news to the media."

Martha smiled, nodded, and tried to give the impression she would welcome the opportunity.

"Lynn will help develop a series of possible leaks, some true, some false. She will then give them to you, so you can develop possible responses. Can you do that?"

"Certainly," Martha responded, looking at Palidore with steady eyes and a poker face ."I will look forward to working with Lynn on this."

Palidore paused and looked over at Lynn and Renee with a questioning look. They each gave him a slight nod. He took a deep breath and continued.

"Now that we're all on the same page, I want to tell you more about our two clients. What I am going to tell you is going to make your job much more difficult." Palidore then took Martha's hands from the table into his own and looked directly into her eyes. She looked back with a bit of apprehension.

"We believe client Five is none other than George Washington, our first president." Martha immediately drew back her hands and put them over her face. She shook her head back and forth. There was silence. Then she took her hands down and looked at the three of them.

"You're joking, right?" But no one was laughing. They were focused intently on her, waiting for her to absorb the news. She looked at each person then focused on Palidore. "You're serious, aren't you? You really believe this, don't you?"

"No Martha, we don't just suspect it . . . we have substantial evidence in our possession that leads us to believe client Five may very well be our first president" He picked up his small pack of papers and held them up for her to see.

"This is only part of the evidence. These are the notes from Doctor Hugh Montgomery which were stored on client Five's body. They explain how the president's body came to be part of our inventory and the problems it presented him. You're encouraged to review this later. In addition, you should note this very building was deeded to my ancestor by George Washington and the photograph you've admired in my office clearly shows my ancestor was a friend of the president. So, absent an elaborate hoax perpetrated on my ancestor, there is little doubt that George Washington is here, and he is alive. However, we are not sure if he or client Four will ever be capable of genuine intellectual thought when they awaken from their induced comas. They may remain in a vegetative state --- we just don't know, but we are about to find out."

Martha sat there without speaking. "Ok, then," she finally uttered. "Who is client Four . . . Jesus?"

Palidore smiled at the sarcasm. "Actually client Four was a slave," He paused for a brief moment to take in Martha's reaction. The look on her face was priceless.

"Client Four was a slave who acted more like a personal butler to President Washington. We know very little about him other than that he pre-deceased the president who beseeched my ancestor to treat him. He was actually our first successful revival, and if the world ever finds out about it, he will own that trophy in history. Had things been normal, he would have already been awakened, but during his revival, his body scan revealed an abdominal mass which we removed. Follow-up tests showed it was benign, but his recovery will now take a bit longer. We only know his name is 'Frank' and are unaware of a last name.

"Actually, we think having both of them is a bit of good luck, assuming their mental capabilities can be fully restored. Now, they each have someone alive from their own era to confide in as they discover the future. Certainly, they will be able to lean on each other as they adjust to their new environment."

"Honestly, this just gets more incredible by the minute!" Martha said.

"Doesn't it though," Palidore responded. "But once you absorb it all, you'll see your job just got more difficult. So . . . once again, I need to know if you are fully on board with this now that you know the magnitude of what we're dealing with here."

Martha said looking directly at Palidore. "I am, and truly honored to be part of the team,"

"Good!Then I think we can adjourn this meeting and let Martha mull over the implications of the information she's just received." Palidore looked pleased. He glanced at each woman seated around the table. "I believe that's all for now."

Chapter 46

Later that evening, sitting in front of her window, Martha was relaxing with a glass of Chardonney, reliving her moments during the time Palidore was describing their first revival efforts, Martha had seen in her mind's eye, the visual images of the video she had stolen, replayed in her head. She had known the fate of Client One and had suddenly felt a pang of guilt trying to fain "surprise" while Palidore was talking.

That's when I thought my real motives were found out, she thought. *What a relief he kept talking.* Learning that the two most recent revival efforts had actually worked nearly undid her cover. But understanding they weren't looking to profit from this incredible event unnerved her completely.

Could it be that MCS really is above board?

Now, she would be a party to helping disguise exactly what she had sought to uncover! *How cruel is fate?* she wondered. Now, she would become accessory to helping Dr. Palidore Montgomery and MCS retain their sterling reputations, while knowing they *were* hiding groundbreaking results.

Can I really do this? She took a sip of wine. *How far can I go before I sell my soul?*

She began calling up various versions of her whiteboards on the television. Tilting her head one way, then another she began looking at the information as if hunting for something.

Not seeing what she was looking for, she flipped to the next document.

Actually, she wasn't exactly sure what she was searching for. She had been so certain that Palidore was the mastermind of a huge scam, certain that he was selling hope to the hopeless for outrageous sums of money. She had been so convinced this man and his buddies were nothing more than a bunch of unethical doctors who deserved to be exposed and receive the ridicule and wrath of the public. But now, tonight, after all she had learned today, for the first time, she had doubts.

Could I possibly be wrong? Have I wasted all this time and money chasing a fantasy? Is it just possible that Palidore really is trying to help these people; could he really believe in his science? She didn't know anymore. She just wasn't sure.

Pulling up the video clip she had stolen, she watched it again, intently this time, focusing on the faces of each physician. They seemed sincere, really wanting to succeed. *But then, of course they would! Reviving someone who had died a couple hundred years ago would make one instantly famous and wealthy beyond belief.* Her emotions waffled. But they all seemed willing to keep their accomplishment a secret, so the patient could   decide whether to tell the world of their return -- or forever keep it a secret. How could they benefit from that?

What a turn of events, she thought. *Now, I'm in a position to get it all firsthand, and the last thing I want is for the world to know. By revealing what I find, it would make Palidore and his buddies famous and rich. . . and I won't be a party to that! So, for now, I guess we're on the same team. How ironic!*

The one thing she could do was help keep their tremendous accomplishment a secret. At least until she knew more. *If they've kept this secret from the public so far, who knows what other secrets they still hold. Oh, no, Dr. Palidore*

Montgomery. You're not off the hook yet. I'm not done with my research, but I must say you have surprised me She was becoming extremely excited about being in the inner circle. *The easier it will be for me to find out what else you're not telling me.*

Chapter 47

It was over two months since the directors had last met. Now they were milling around the conference room moving toward their places at the large glass conference table, anxious to be brought up to date on the latest developments. The floor under their chairs was lit with a bright Kelly green color today. The color of success – or money.

In front of each director, embedded in the glass on their individual monitors, was the agenda which was headlined: "Good News!"When Palidore entered the room in all smiles and a bounce in his step, everyone stood up and gave him a round of applause. He motioned with his hands for everyone to sit down as he stepped to the tabletop lectern."Well, thank you, everyone, and you don't even know what the good news is yet! Now, before I officially call this meeting to order, I need to make a brief statement - off the record. Oh, you can stay this time," he told the secretary as she prepared to leave. "Even though several of our previous meetings have been off the record due to the sensitive nature of the subject matter, this one is different." She took her seat again.

"According to our legal counsel, the absence of an official record relating to significant events could be interpreted as if something was wrong, therefore, upon her advice, I have called this particular meeting not only to bring you up-to-date, but to be certain our corporate minutes properly reflect what is now going at MCS." He adjusted his coat and took a drink of water from the glass on the table.

"Before I officially begin, I would like to ask you to hold your comments or questions until I have finished - and I'm sure you will have a lot of them – but by then, we will once again be off the record. It is still my opinion that a certain amount of information must stay protected and off-the-record." He gestured to the secretary to begin recording. "Well, it looks like we have a quorum present, so I will officially call this meeting to order. First, let me welcome our four new board members, Drs., Ronnie Pierce, Peggy Slate, Jeffery Pace and Thomas Stovall. It is certainly nice to be back at full strength again. I know everyone has had a chance to meet them at our reception last month, and many of you have known them professionally for some time. But since this is their first meeting, I wanted to extend an official welcome.

"I can advise you all that I have privately brought each of our new directors up-to-speed on what we have been doing, or trying to do here, this past year. What they, as well as some of you, do *not* know is the exciting developments of this past month. So, here is the 'Good News.'" Pausing a moment, he looked out at the assembled directors knowing they would be excited."I am pleased to officially announce that we have *successfully* revived *both* clients Four and Five! They are presently in medically-induced comas and recuperating in the suites specially prepared for them here in this facility." There was a shock of silence before the room erupted in an outburst of chatter and joyous high fives. Palidore used a louder voice to bring the room back to order.

"First – first, let me apologize to those of you who have been, more or less, kept in the dark, but considering the identities of these two clients, we felt compelled to keep access to information regarding them at a minimum, at least until we have a better read on their ultimate outcomes. For the same reason, we did *not* videotape the procedures and have reduced our record-keeping to paper only to be kept under lock and key except when new entries need to be made in their charts, or if something has to be reviewed.

"Having said that . . . we now feel the remainder of our trusted board members need to be updated so they can share in this momentous accomplishment." Chatter broke out again and Palidore had to bring the room to order once more.

"That does *not* mean we can let our guard down! To the contrary, we will be even more vigilant in protecting the information as you will hear, momentarily, from our new communications director.

"Now for details: As you recall some time ago, the board decided that *if* and *when* we were able to revive one of our ancient clients, it would ultimately be *their* decision, not ours, as to whether the rest of the world would learn the good news. Certainly, their lives would be forever changed upon the release of this information, even possibly their very futures. Since we have made that commitment, it is *imperative* that we do all within our power to prevent even an inadvertent disclosure of a minor detail which might lead to knowledge of our accomplishments leaking to the press."

Palidore pushed a button for a document to appear on the screen behind him. It also came up on the individual monitors in front of each director. "What you are looking at is a list of those who have some knowledge versus another list of those with full knowledge of recent events. Those with partial knowledge are four nurses and four former directors, our secretary, and our attorney. Those with full knowledge – except for our clients' names - include each one of you, Renee, Lynn, Susan, me, and now Martha Vaughn, our new communications director who will help us speak to the outside world should that become necessary.

"I suppose there should be another category of those who actually know nothing, but suspect something. People on that list might include our cleaning crew, some delivery personnel and, maybe, some of our interns. However, at this time, the people in this group can only speculate about what they have seen or heard.

To address this, we've recently changed our cleaning service and have rotated our interns to new patients, thereby redirecting their attention elsewhere. We have also begun ordering more supplies online. In addition to these actions, we've turned off our monitoring on this floor so no electronic records can be leaked. Even the minutes of this meeting will be under seal. In short, we have tried to anticipate and plan for as much as we possibly can.

"Notwithstanding all these efforts, Lynn met with Renee recently and made a case for developing potential responses in the event of a leak. That brings me to Martha Vaughan who you see seated here next to me. I would like to call on her now to address what she is doing to prepare for something we hope will *never* happen. So please welcome our new Communications Director, Martha Vaughan." There was polite applause throughout the room as she stood to speak.

"Thank you for your welcome and your attention. First, let me say how grateful I am to have the trust of Dr. Montgomery, and of course, the board. In the spirit of full disclosure, I want to reveal that my first contact with MCS was not in a professional capacity, but rather as the spouse of Client Number 357, Stanley Vaughan. He did a great deal of research concerning cryogenics before making the final decision to become a client here. In all honesty, I was not in favor of his decision, but when I saw how much it meant to Stanley, I relented and supported him . . ." *That's not true and you know it,* she thought. *Call me a liar then.* " . . . and know it brought him great comfort in his final days.

"That being said, I must confess when I was told of this latest accomplishment, I, too, was truly taken aback. What has been accomplished here is unbelievable. It took me time to grasp the magnitude of what has occurred here at MCS.

"That's when I decided that if *I* had difficulty believing this . . . even with evidence right in front of me . . . that very fact may ultimately be our best defense against an unauthorized or unintentional release of information. Simply stated, most people do not believe in cryogenics and would certainly find it difficult to believe it possible for patients to be revived who died *before* the current advancement of cryogenics as we know it today.

"So, when given the task of preparing responses for various types of potential breaches of information, I became convinced that any answer we give, should include a question in return asking whether the person inquiring believes cryogenics is a true science, or are they looking for evidence to disrupt our work here.

"It is extremely unlikely that complete disclosure of MCS' work will ever occur. It is more likely that some small, peculiar piece of information will cause someone to ask questions leading to other questions, and so on. That is how things of this nature unravel. Lynn and I have been going over the only available records and attempting to come up with a list of items that would raise eyebrows should it get out. It is a bit like trying to find a needle in a haystack without having the haystack.

"I do not want to bore you with our analysis of each potential breach. Let it suffice to say that, if possible, we will provide a response that avoids any outright untruth, while at the same time protect the rights and identities of our clients until such time as they may decide for themselves what should, or should not, be disclosed about them.

"I could not help but observe your excitement and joy over the news Palidore shared with you. We are all excited, and quite frankly, *that* is my biggest concern. It is human nature to want to share news of great achievement. Can you imagine getting a hole in one on a difficult hole with no one around, or *not* telling anyone about it? Or catching a record-setting tuna and *not* letting everyone know? Of course not. You would do your best to shout it to anyone who would listen.

"Yet what has been achieved here, without doubt, is the single greatest achievement in the history of mankind. And we are asking you to keep it a secret! Wow! Well, if you succeed, then *that* will be the second greatest achievement in history. Yet this is what we all must do for the future success of this company, and your own involvement here.

"Timing is important. For your own selves, we find it imperative that our work continue without fanfare for now. Please understand, this is for *your* own benefit as well as for the future of this company and more importantly our clients.

"Now, let me give you a couple of examples of what *not* to say:
1. 'I'm not at liberty to say anything more than MCS is doing some great work.' - or -
2. 'Mark my words, you're going to be hearing a lot more about MCS in the future'

"You see, if you work for a cryogenics company and suggest, in any way, that there has been a tremendous accomplishment or breakthrough, then what will people think? How does a cryogenics company measure success? People will quickly put two and two together. Oh, they won't guess, necessarily, that we have revived an ancient *ancestor*, but they will assume we have revived *someone* and that will get enough attention to raise a thousand questions. The media will be camped out here in droves! Our every move will be scrutinized.

"Please remember it's not just the casual friend to whom you make a flip comment, but anyone who might overhear you. Ears are listening everywhere; or your friend's curiosity may be more than you imagined. People repeat comments. One Google search and a hard-nosed investigative reporter can be all over it. People will start talking to relatives of our clients, our doctors, our interns, and/or anyone else who will listen. You get the picture. A non-statement is a statement, and you must be on guard against making *any* type of comment that will raise eyebrows.

"In short, you must put this out of your minds, and continue as if nothing has occurred. The best comment may be to simply say: 'Well, work is work." The room was silent now, and everyone was focused on Martha's words. She had made her point clear.

"I'm not sure what else I can say at this time. As your communications director, I am responsible for all our outgoing information on a variety of subjects. Should any of you have concerns or suggestions, please know, my door is always open. Feel free to contact me at any time."

Chapter 48

A fter the meeting, Martha asked Lynn if she would like to stop for a drink together. "That sounds like a good idea, but we're a bit off the beaten path for someplace decent, aren't we?" Lynn replied.

"Actually, I know of a place nearby that I think you'll enjoy," Martha said, knowing at some point word would get out about her flat across the way. She thought it best to reveal her secret first, so it didn't look like she was hiding something.

"You do? Well, okay, then. Let's do it."

Martha led Lynn across the street, into her elevator, and up to her flat. As they entered Lynn took a slow look around. "Wow! This is great. Who knew you lived so close by? When did you get this place?" Martha was busy fetching the Chardonnay from her fridge and didn't immediately answer. She poured two ample glasses of the wine, before answering the question. "Hope Chardonnay is okay."

"Perfect; actually my favorite," Lynn said.

"Have a seat while I get us some cheese and crackers," Martha said, not hearing Lynn respond, nor realizing she was looking out the window at the MCS building. There was a new plant next to the window where the telescope had once stood. Martha carried the snacks out of the kitchen and set them down on the coffee table before taking a seat on the couch. Lynn turned and took a seat in the stressless chair, first swinging it around and away from the window so she was now facing towards Martha. Then reaching for a piece of cheese she asked again.

"So, when did you say you got this place?"

"I didn't actually say. It was a difficult time for me. I got it when Stanley was alive and struggling with his health. Initially, Stanley and I were not in total agreement about his being treated at MCS. We're both Catholics and the whole cryogenics thing just seemed to fly in the face of our religion. Stanley however became more and more committed, and actually, somewhat obsessed about it. He wanted to investigate it more. He liked the idea of being close by so he could 'study it' - so to speak. Knowing that he was going to pass on, we decided to put the place in just my name. I had no intention of keeping it after he was treated, but there was so much to do with the estate, I just put it off. And then, when I got this job, I decided to keep it. So that's my story." Martha felt she had covered all bases with her story, even though giving Stanley credit for the decision wasn't exactly truthful. In fact, Stanley never even knew about the place but, obviously, *he* wasn't going to tell anyone.

"Interesting," Lynn said. "How about a tour?"

"Sure. It's really pretty simple. As you can see, it's a corner unit, so the outside walls are reclaimed brick. The interior walls are sheetrock, but the dark forest green paint helps keep it rustic. The kitchen counter is large enough to serve as both a table and a bar. It was supposed to be two levels, but we decided on keeping the entire countertop area one height, creating this large surface," Martha studied Lynn's facial expression. It was relaxed. She was simply listening. "In case you're wondering, the surface is made of white concrete with crushed bits of blue glass in it polished to a high gloss."

They walked toward the master suite where Martha continued talking points of décor.

"So, it's not too large, but comfortable, and the en-suite is a little larger as we were able to steal a few feet from the back bedroom which now doubles as my office and spare bedroom. That's pretty much it." They moved back to the living area.

"Nice, very nice."

"I like it. Actually, I prefer it to my home in Georgetown."

They sat for a while, sipping wine and nibbling on the cheese and crackers before Martha felt comfortable enough to continue the conversation.

"Lynn, I was wondering if I could see him."

"Who?" Responded Lynn

"Client Five," Martha said, pausing, then quickly adding, "Well, actually, I would like to see *both* clients Four and Five."

"Oh, I don't know about that. Access has been really strict, but tell me: Is there a professional reason for your request?" Martha quickly picked up on the opening,

"Yes, actually there is. I think that as communications director, I should be vested with as much knowledge as possible, and actually seeing them in person would help me get my head around what's happening. Sometimes you just need to experience something to fully understand it, let alone try and write about it."

Lynn was silent, thinking about Martha's request.

"Who makes this Chardonnay," she said, breaking their line of conversation, stalling her answer. "I love it."

Martha had just taken a mouthful of wine and nearly spit it out laughing."Well, you won't believe it because it's really inexpensive! On sale, I can get it for five bucks a bottle. I could purchase more expensive wine but, quite frankly, this brand is very satisfying. It's Berringer's Main Street. A nice name and a nice price." Now Martha knew Lynn was stalling. She hadn't answered her question. *I better not push it,* she thought.

Lynn raised her glass for a toast and Martha responded by raising her own.

"To Berringer's great wine then!" They clinked glasses and each took another sip before setting their glasses down. "You know clients Four and Five are still in their comas. We're not exactly sure when they'll come around. We're being careful to monitor their vital signs and taking every precaution to ensure their health and safety. So, if you see them, you won't be able to do anything but look. They aren't responsive . . . so . . . I guess I don't see any harm in letting you in for a peek.

"Actually, Susan Trott is handling Client Four and I'm handling Client Five, so the only one I can let you see is my client. You would have to ask Susan about seeing Client Four. But, if you do, don't let on that you've talked to me about this. She needs to make her own decision without being influenced by my actions."

Lynn saw the sparkle in Martha's eyes. She could see the joy her response had given her. "So, come by maybe tomorrow, around 3:00 p.m. There won't be anyone but myself attending him at that time. Final checks won't be made again until the evening shift comes on. Just tap on the door after three; I'll be in the first suite where we're watching Five."

"Oh, thank you so much," Martha said. "I will certainly be there, and on time! This calls for another toast." They raised their glasses again, this time saying nothing, just smiling as the glasses clinked together.

Chapter 49

After Lynn left, Martha decided to have another glass of wine to celebrate and plan. She would work in the morning, as usual, and try to act as if nothing special was going on that day. She could take a late lunch, return to her flat, and change into fresh clothes for the meeting. Not sure what to expect, or how she would react, Martha was enormously curious. She knew she would be looking at a male patient who would appear to be sleeping, so that wouldn't be anything remarkable.

Still, just the thought that this person was over two hundred years old, and now alive again, made her feel uneasy.

Will he look more like a ghost than a human?

It seemed she had just fallen to sleep when the alarm sounded. Out of habit, she jumped up and headed for the shower, needing it to wake herself. She had laid out an outfit the night before so she could save decision-making time. Nothing special for the morning: A pair of black slacks and a lightweight, v-necked, gray sweater. She added a silver necklace Stanley had given her years ago to complete her look. Slipping into a pair of black flats, she grabbed her jacket and handbag as she headed for the elevator.

At work, Martha was grateful nothing much was going on. She didn't want to talk to anyone. She ran into Susan Trott in the ladies' room and thought about asking her if she could see client Four, but thought it better to wait. At her desk, she had difficulty staying focused, spending most of her time checking social media to see if anyone was talking about them. When she grew tired of that, she looked over the proofs for the latest MCS brochure.

Checking her watch, time seemed to be crawling. Deciding she needed something as a pickup, she opened a desk drawer and popped the top on a can her favorate energy drink and downed it. Finally, at 1:00 pm she headed for the door and made her way back to her flat across the street.

Once inside, she took another quick shower and donned the outfit she had picked out for the afternoon. Same sweater, but a short black skirt instead of slacks. She wasn't hungry but decided she needed something, so ate a candy bar. She checked her makeup and hair, then headed back out the door.

At MCS, she checked to see if any messages had come in on her computer. She took time to respond to a couple of emails before leaving the office and heading to the top floor. Knowing exactly where the two suites were and, in particular, where Lynn would be, she started down the hall but froze for a moment wondering why she was so uptight. Standing in front of the suite door, she made herself take a couple of deep breaths to calm down before tapping twice on the door.

Within a minute, Lynn opened the door, and they both looked shocked and stared at each other. Almost in unison they both cried out: "What are you wearing?"

Lynn recovered first and realizing what was happening, came out into the hallway and quietly closed the door behind her. Clearly, Martha had not been brought up to speed or had forgotten entirely, about the dress code required for being in the suite, so she explained again.

"I'm wearing clothes similar to those worn when client Five was alive. The suite is also decorated to resemble furnishings of the late eighteenth century – 1790 – to be exact. Just in the off- chance Five should awaken while we're in the room and so he will feel more comfortable. I thought you knew this."

Martha was dumbfounded and looked down at her own outfit, then back up. "I'm sorry, but I didn't know the dress code was in place now. I don't think I have anything in my wardrobe that will fit the bill. Does that mean I can't go in?"

"It's my fault for not reminding you. I hope you understand."

Martha's disappointment played on her face. Moisture was building at the corners of her eyes. As she started to turn and walk away, Lynn took her arm while focusing on the length of Martha's skirt.

"You know, he's not awake, and it's doubtful he'll awaken any time soon. At least, we better hope not, or you might give him a heart attack," Lynn said as she pulled Martha into the suite.

It was like going back in time. Martha looked around the dimly lit room with candles strategically placed. Most of the bare wooden floor was covered with an old carpet. There were fake windows and curtains covering them from floor to ceiling. The details were amazing from pictures on the wall down to small items adorning the dresser all in the era of the eighteenth century. A couple of side chairs were placed near the bed and separated by a small circular table that provided a home for a tray containing a pitcher of water and two glasses. An old pipe stood guard in its pipe stand. A large bookcase held vintage volumes that looked well-worn.

Client Five lay on the bed covered in a soft blanket. Since the room was large, he was too far away for Martha to get a good look at his face. Lynn took Martha's hand and made a motion toward the bed. Martha froze in place.

"Just give me a minute, Lynn."

"He's not asleep, Martha, he's in a coma; you don't have to whisper."

"I know, but he looks like he's sleeping." Martha said, looking at the monitors overhead which were checking his vital signs. Two poles were placed on either side of the bed. One held a clear bag with plastic tubes traveling down to an IV dripping fluid into his arm. "Is that for hydration?" she asked.

"Yes," Lynn answered. Another pole held a soft yellow substance with a tube traveling downward and disappearing under the covers.

"He's also being given nutrition through a feeding tube into his stomach. It's going very slowly to allow his system to adjust," Lynn said. She pulled again on Martha's hand, and they started across the floor toward the bed, Lynn leading, and Martha following with a little resistance.

Reaching the bedside, Lynn saw that Martha's eyes were shut. "You can look now," she said softly.

Martha slowly opened them and gazed at the man in front of her. He looked to be in a state of peace. Lying on his back, both arms were at his sides. *He looks like a statue, a living one,* Martha thought.

If it wasn't for his shallow-breathing he would have appeared lifeless, yet, somehow, she felt a connection to him. He was clean-shaven, and his youthful appearance made him look fit and strong.

"He's attractive, don't you think?" Martha said,   It surprised her a little that his white hair didn't diminish his youthful appearance in her eyes and that she couldn't take her eyes off him. "Even though his hair is white, why does the rest of him looks so young?" she asked.

"Good observation, Martha." Lynn said in a quiet voice. "When he was unwrapped, he had no hair at all. Clearly, all hair was removed from his body as part of the treatment process. The hair that has grown back is white which would indicate the treatment process did not seem to affect it. So, you have a young man with hair of an elder statesman. There are theories about why this occurred, but we really can't explain it."

Lynn took Martha's hand again, this time trying to move her away, but unlike before, Martha didn't seem ready to leave the bedside. Turning away, Lynn tried a little more pressure to pull her away when Martha actually jumped, bumping into Lynn and causing them both to tumble onto the floor together. Lynn gave Martha a "what-the-hell-happened" look.

"Oh, I am so sorry, Lynn, I didn't mean for that to happen, but I think . . . I think he tried to grab my butt."

"Oh, please!" Lynn said as they both slowly stood up.

"No, he *did*, I swear, or at least he touched the back of my leg!"

They both looked over at the man on the bed. Nothing looked different except that one arm was now dangling down off the bed. Lynn walked over to him and put his arm back at his side. She pointed her forefinger at him. "Naughty, naughty," she said with a funny smile on her face. Then she led Martha out of the room.

Once outside, Martha asked, "Do you think he tried to grab me? I mean his arm was clearly moved."

Lynn thought a second before answering. "His arm did move, and you felt something, but I think at best, it was an unintentional, involuntary movement. There couldn't have been anything intentional since he's not capable of that, at least not now."

Martha was quiet as they walked down the hallway. "Obviously, he hasn't heard about the 'me-too movement' yet." They both laughed and walked toward Lynn's office.

Once inside and seated, Martha became serious. "Do you honestly believe the man lying in that bed is President George Washington? I mean he doesn't resemble any portraits I've ever seen of him, or even in the antique picture on Paladore's desk."

"You've heard the same evidence I have about the ancients being some two hundred years old and how this building was once owned by the actual George Washington before being given to Dr. Palidore Montgomery," Lynn replied. "I can't run a DNA sample to verify anything because we don't have an original sample to compare it with, but I want to believe it. There is, at least, one doctor who believes the body initially transferred for treatment was a past president. However, when you think about it, in a very real sense it doesn't matter. The fact remains that we have revived two individuals who lived more than two hundred years ago. If client Five truly is one and the same as the founder of this country, that would be incredible. Right now, all we know is that client Five has been revived. We still don't know if the brain activity we're monitoring is anything more than the brain controlling involuntary functions of his body like heart and lungs.

"But soon enough, we'll know more when he comes out of his coma. Then we'll see if he is capable of communicating with us. I guess we can ask him his name at that time. Then we'll know for sure."

Chapter 50

The two women were back in Lynn's office having just come from the recovery suite where they had been observing client Five. Lynn had changed from her eighteenth-century hoop dress into her regular clothes in the adjoining bathroom of her office. Now she moved to sit in her comfortable black leather desk chair while Martha took a seat in a smaller visitor's chair at the front of her desk.

"Lynn, do you mind if I ask a few questions about what will happen if and when Five wakes up?"

"Depends on the questions, but sure, go ahead."

"Well, I mean, *who* will be present when he wakes up?"

"Hopefully, just me, unless there is some medical reason for someone else to be present. At least that's the plan right now. I'm on call 24/7 for that very reason. We want that event to be a quiet one . . . no cameras, no lights, no crowd of people. Just someone quietly attending him when he awakes. Palidore is watching all the time from a hidden monitor. Sort of like the ones used to monitor babies; no recording, just monitoring him. We're always cautiously watching.

Once they remove his feeding tube, I think his awakening will be imminent."

"Have you thought about what you'll say?"

"Sure, but I also think a lot will depend on the moment.

I've also thought about what I *don't* want to say. For example, I'm not going to use his name or title. I would prefer to get him to offer that up which will help me verify if he is who we think he is. Of course, I'll try to answer his questions. But it seems logical that the first thing he'll want to know is where he's at, and who I am. After that, I'm guessing he might want to know what year it is. I don't know if he'll remember what happened to him, or have any last memories. I'm not even sure if he'll be rational and in his right mind. There are many questions still to be answered.

"In any event, I have rehearsed so many possible situations, I'm afraid if I keep it up I may just overthink it all and what I actually say will come off as too rehearsed. But I feel pretty comfortable now with the planning for the moment. I've seen him so much that the whole thing doesn't feel so strange to me anymore. At least that's how I feel now, but who knows how I'll feel when the time actually comes." She looked at Martha, giving her a moment to consider everything she had just said. "Any more questions?"

Martha looked at her and relaxed with a smile. "No. As you've said, we'll know when the time comes. Even though I'm looking forward to it as much as you are."

"Good. Why don't we both take a break and get some rest while we can."

They both rose and moved toward the door. "Thank you so much for allowing me to join you today," Martha said. "It was really exciting and your confidence in me means a lot."

"We're a team," Lynn said. "I'm glad you're on board."

***

Two days later, Palidore buzzed Lynn, asking her to meet him in his office. She was there almost before he finished talking. "Please have a seat," he said, motioning to a chair. "Well, are you ready?"

"More than ready; what's happening?" she replied

"We took his feeding tube out this morning. Tomorrow we are going to administer the drugs to help him come around. We've decided that there's no reason to wait any longer. So it should only take a few hours after receiving the treatment before he begins to stir."

Lynn took the news in stride. She knew this day was coming and had planned well for it over the past few months. Yet an uneasy silence enveloped the room. Both knew the significance of the event about to take place. Still, anything could happen no matter how hard they had planned. A natural sense of anxiety was building, anticipation, maybe. Lynn recognized it, had even studied it.

It's something athletes experience minutes before their championship game; or soldiers feel before the beginning of their biggest battle, she thought *Yet this seems far greater, more significant. Maybe because it's history-making and happening to us.* She broke the awkward silence

"Palidore, what do you really think the chances are he'll be truly coherent?"

"Lynn, do you remember Kevin Washburn, our first revival?"

"How could I forget! It was so emotional."

"Exactly," Palidore said. "So, what made that so memorable? I'll answer for you," he said without hesitation. "He spoke. He uttered just one word. He said, 'no,' and that really got to everyone. But that one brief utterance told us *volumes* about his mental state. It told us that he was experiencing something, and he appeared to voice a dissent. Or to put it another way, he thought about something, and then said something. In short, he exhibited a coherent thought, processed it, and reacted to it. Kevin was preserved in the exact same fashion as client Five, so there is every reason to believe that Five will also be coherent and capable of communicating with us."

"But at the time, you told me it was probably just an excited utterance, or that he was just repeating the last word he spoke when he died."

"Yes, I did, and that may very well be the case, but the fact remains that even under those circumstances to will oneself to speak verbally is good evidence of coherent thought. "

"So, you're not worried at all about this?"

"I wouldn't quite put it that way, Lynn. I worry about everything. The human mind is still pretty much a mystery to us. The drugs may have adversely affected him; he may have other issues that may prevent him from communicating with us, or may render him unable to process the information we are presenting to him. No, there is much that could go wrong, but at this moment, I guess I would say that we can proceed with guarded optimism."

"I'm still amazed that you don't want to attempt to record this. Surely there must be a way to secretly record his awakening without him knowing it."

Palidore looked directly into Lynn's eyes. "We've had this conversation before, haven't we? Such evidence would have tremendous value in and of itself. Should anyone lay their hands on it, they could duplicate it, or disseminate it, and become instantly wealthy.

"Furthermore, should we be asked during some future investigation whether there exists any form of evidence of this remarkable event, we need to be able to *honestly* answer in the negative. We have decided that *this* will be his decision, and should he decide to remain anonymous, we should not have evidence laying around that could destroy him. So, we will not be recording this event even though every bone in my body wants to.

"As you know, you have been equipped with a silent emergency button that you can push at any time, should you need me to come in. Hopefully, that will not be necessary. I will also be watching the monitor. The only other piece of technology is the tracker chip we have placed in his left leg. That is for his future protection. We will want to know where he is at all times. Because if all goes well, he will someday leave us. It was far easier to implant the device now, than seek his permission later on. That's because we live in a very different time than when he did. He won't be able to understand the world of today, and its dangers, for some time. That's why we must protect him for now. Beyond that, there should not exist any other proof of our connection to him going forward.

"Now, my having said all that, please understand, I will expect to be read in on every detail of your encounter as soon as possible. Now, do you have any other questions?"

"Actually, I do. When any person, let alone *this* person, comes out of a chemically-induced coma, will they be confused or disoriented.?"

"Perhaps so, but that should not interfere with their thought process. For example, they may be confused, not know where they are, or not recognize people or their surroundings, but if you asked them what the sum of 2+2 is - they should be able to give the correct answer."

"So, how long will he likely remain alert?"

"We're not sure, but the norm is for one to be awake for intervening periods of time with each period of time becoming longer in duration, much like a newborn as it begins to grow."

"One last question: How much should I push him initially?"

"Well, he may just look around at first, then dose off. The environment we have established will look familiar to him and help put him at ease, thanks to your direction. Having a person in the room is something we know from experience will be reassuring and give him a good since of security. So, to answer your question a little more precisely, you will have to play it by ear. My gut tells me you will know whether an attempt at communication is warranted. Just trust your intuition. You have the training and education to know what to do and when to do it.

"I have the utmost confidence in you. Now, if there are no more questions, please try to get some rest. Take a sleep aid if necessary. Tomorrow will be a long and stressful day, and we need you as well rested as possible." Palidore rose from his chair, came around his desk, and gave Lynn a pat of reassurance on the shoulder.

"Thank you for your time and dedication to this Lynn. All your hard work and efforts are about to pay off."

Lynn appreciated his vote of confidence and, while unable to speak, she mouthed the words: "Thank you."

Chapter 51

July 4, 2025

The day was dark and cloudy. No rain was in the forecast, but the sun was staying hidden behind an overcast, brooding sky.

How ironic, Lynn thought as she showered, *that the second half of George Washington's life should begin on the fourth of July.* "That is, if it really is him," she said aloud, "I guess we'll eventually find out."

Somehow, she felt the coincidental date was no accident. Palidore must surely have arranged for it to happen this way, she thought, continuing her soliloquy. Once it looked like the timing might work out, he must have decided to play God and make it happen. That was okay with her; it seemed appropriate. In any event, one way or another, it was going to be the most memorable July fourth of her life. She had followed Palidore's advice and taken a sleep aid before going to bed which had helped her doze off. Now wide awake, she had plenty of time to get ready since it was still early. She was focused and anxious to get to work at MCS and begin the exciting day ahead.

Traffic was no problem as she arrived and entered the building by 7:00 am. She and Palidore planned to meet in his office at eight. He was going to allow her to read over the updated medical records for client Five that he usually kept in his safe.

The lights were on in Palidore's office, so she popped her head in. Palidore looked up from his reading and motioned for her to come in; he pointed to a file folder lying on his small conference table. She took one of the seats, slipped off her jacket, put down her purse, and picked up the file which she began reading from the beginning. Not knowing exactly what to look for, she still felt something might jump out at her.

Having studied the life of George Washington in detail, she had absorbed as much as possible about the history during his lifetime. The medical records, however, were something else, and seemed to be the only thing left for her to double down on. For the next hour, she studied the file, but nothing seemed out of the ordinary. Finally, she closed the cover and proceeded to stretch out in all directions before rising from the chair.

"I've administered the drugs to bring him out of his coma about an hour and a half ago," said, . "We've removed the IVs, monitors, and feeding tube so there's nothing to alarm him. You should probably change into your costume and take up your position in the suite before ten. By then, he could begin coming around and start making sounds. There may be some slight arm or leg movements, but he won't fully wake before noon at the earliest."

"Thanks, I'll do that."

"God speed, Lynn"

"Thanks, again," she said over her shoulder while leaving the room. Reaching her office, she turned on the overhead light and proceeded to change into her eighteenth-century costume. She already had her hair pulled back into a bun today, and had applied only a minimum of makeup, not needing much anyway. Then, she slipped into the special pair of shoes she'd had made for herself several months ago. They looked the vintage part required to compliment her costume but were actually comfortable tennis shoes.

Once ready, she went to the guest area and stretched out on the sofa. Closing her eyes, she didn't expect to sleep, but rather hoped to simply rest. It didn't work. Not being able to get comfortable, she got up and proceeded to pop a single k-cup into the machine to make coffee. It tasted rich, and the steam emanating from the hot liquid felt good on her dry eyes.

With coffee in hand, she wandered over to the window and looked out to the warehouse condo building across the pathway. Gazing upward, she spotted a woman in a window on an upper floor looking down at her. She couldn't quite make out an identity, but it soon dawned on her: It was Martha. It felt kind of creepy seeing her staring out the window, but Lynn could tell Martha had spotted her, so she waved, and Martha waved back.

It's time, she thought, heading for the suite housing client Five. Destiny awaits, ran through her mind.

Reaching the door to the area, she stopped and stood motionless outside, almost frozen in place, contemplating what was about to happen. Then, summoning all her courage, she opened the door, stepped inside to look around.

Every time she entered the tranquil suite, it was like stepping back in time. The subdued colors of the room with its ornate gold-framed portraits, the antique furniture, even the books and hand-made doilies decorating the tables, lent themselves to a relaxed atmosphere.

It must have been a peaceful time to live in, she reflected.

Aside from the candle next to the bed, there were two strategically-placed hurricane lanterns responsible for lighting the entire room. It was a task they were struggling to accomplish as they barely gave off enough light to make objects in the room visible. Her special patient was lying in bed. He was in a comfortable state of repose. Lynn smiled to herself.

Well sir, you should be well-rested when you wake up. You've had one hell of a nap.

There was a vase filled with water and two glasses

305

positioned on the bedside table next to the candle. Lynn took her seat next to the bed positioned near his waist at an angle where she could clearly see his face. There was a bible on the table which Lynn had taken to reading over the last couple of weeks while monitoring her patient. She studied his face a little more intently, thinking somehow it should look a bit different today. Maybe just a little more alive, she thought. but then concluded, for now at least, he looks as lifeless as ever. Picking up the bible, she began reading, looking up every now and then, to see if any change had happened to her patient, before resuming her reading.

An hour later, Lynn realized she wasn't comprehending anything, and was about to put the bible down when she noticed his head move ever so slightly. She froze; eyes glued to his face. His nose twitched, and eyebrows raised a bit. Her heart quickened as he turned his head ever so slightly and opened his eyes.

Oh my God, this is really happening!

She watched as his eyes began opening ever so slowly. No head movement, just eye movement. Then slowly, deliberately, he moved his head to the side and appeared to be intently staring, not at her, but at something across the room. It was as if he had not even noticed her. His face looked colorless, cold, and void of expression. Lynn wondered what he was looking at, thinking of, or if he was even capable of intelligent thought.

After what seemed like an endless moment, she slowly turned her head to try and determine what he was so intently focusing on.

She scanned the far side of the room, attempting to spot the object of his attention. Then she felt a hand on her shoulder. She froze in place, not knowing what to do, almost overcome with a profound sense of fear. Turning back, she found herself looking directly into the eyes of her patient who was now wide awake . His left hand resting on her forearm , eyes clearly focused on hers. Her heart was pounding and she tried to regain her composure.

Calm down, she told herself, *don't show your fear or anxiety.* She managed a fake smile. Then without thinking, almost as a defensive move, she slowly removed his hand and placed it in his lap.

At that moment, his expression changed ever so slightly as if his soul had somehow returned to his body. His face took on a softer, warmer look, and the expression in his eyes changed from ice cold indifference to one of bewilderment, causing Lynn to feel a tenderness toward him. After placing his hand back in his lap, she thought how overwhelming everything must be for him. After all, he was just coming back from the afterlife.

"Well, good morning. Would you like some water?"

He didn't answer. With her eyes still on him, she slowly began to stand from her chair. The movement had the effect of releasing some of the stiffness that had seized her. She paused, took a breath, and poured a small amount of water into a glass before presenting it to him. He did not reach for it, so she put it to his lips, and he took a small sip. When it became clear he wasn't going to take another sip, she put the glass down.

"Maybe you should lay back down for now." She carefully laid him back on the pillow which he didn't resist. She straightened his covers and with her fear subsiding, began to talk again. "How do you feel?" There was no immediate response, but just as she was going to ask again, he spoke in a slow, deliberate manner.

"I . . . am . . . fine. How . . . are . . . you, Lynn?"

At the mention of her name, Lynn was shocked. Her mind filled with questions. *Oh, my God! He knows my name. How could he possibly know my name? Why didn't I see this coming? I'm not ready . . . this isn't even close to what I planned for. What should I do now?*

While trying to wrestle with the developing situation, it suddenly struck her like a bolt of lightning: This person, this man, her patient, whoever he was, was fully back and capable of reasoned thinking. Her mind was moving at hyper speed, trying to simultaneously comprehend the ramifications of the miracle she was witnessing against the need to respond to the question just posed to her. A few seconds that passed seemed like an eternity.

"I am fine," she finally said. "But if you don't mind my asking, how is it that you know my name?" Her patient took on a bit more expression in his face and a tiny bit of perspiration appeared at his hairline.

"I . . . have . . . been . . . listening . . . for a long . . . time . . . and your voice is always the one . . . that responds to the name of . . . 'Lynn'."

Oh, my gawd, he's been listening while in his coma. For how long? What has he heard? What has he learned? Of course! Since dying patients are able to hear long after they lose their ability to communicate, it's obviously the sense that lasts longest. Clearly patients who come back will regain their hearing first. Why haven't we thought of this? she wondered.

His eyes appeared to be getting droopy, but she had one question she desperately needed to ask before he nodded off again.

"Since you've figured out my name, I think it would be nice if I knew yours. Can you tell me your name, please?"

He blinked his eyes a couple times and continued to struggle with keeping them open. Then, he tilted his head toward Lynn, gazing directly into her eyes. His facial expression appeared more tranquil, friendlier, and with a warmer glow now.

Just prior to nodding off again, he whispered, "My . . . name . . . is . . . George . . . George . . . Washington."

Sneak Peak into Book 2

TRANSFORMING
POTUS 1

Chapter 1

Washington DC, July 5, 2025

Palidore Montgomery and Lynn Radford sat at the end of the huge glass conference room table on the third floor of the Montgomery Cryogenic Services (MCS) building. Lynn glanced at the computer monitor displaying their sleeping patient in the next room, then looked at her boss.

"Okay, Palidore, you said it was urgent, so let's hear it."

He looked at Lynn. "I know we had a plan to handle client Five and his careful re-introduction back into society, and I know we agreed you would be his sole contact early on concerning the new world he will be experiencing. I helped develop the plan and signed off on it."

"So, now you're having second thoughts?" Lynn said, raising one eyebrow.

"Oh, no, no . . . well, not really. I'm basically totally happy with the plan, but it occurred to me that maybe we could tweak it just a bit."

"I'm listening."

"Well, I must confess I could be more helpful, at least initially." Noting the curious look on Lynn's face, he quickly added: "But I need you to hear me out, and perhaps you will agree with my reasoning."

"You're the boss, Palidore, you don't need my permission to step in."

"I know, I know . . . but you know I don't operate that way,"

Palidore said, holding his left hand out as if trying to hold back her comment. "I really hope my involvement could be something we would both agree upon." Lynn gave him a "go ahead" look.

"I think our patient is going to expect to be seen by a physician. He certainly is going to assume he is receiving medical care and would wonder what's up if a doctor doesn't show up. I also believe he may feel a bit more comfortable if he had a male figure to relate to. So, it seems logical that you could introduce me as his doctor, and we could proceed from there. I would, of course. follow the original plan and let you take the lead. What do you think?"

Lynn put her coffee down and let her professional, serious expression give way to a reassuring smile. "I'm not surprised at all that you want to be involved, and quite frankly, I would welcome your participation. At least if something goes wrong, all eyes won't be focused just on me. However, I do feel strongly that we should stick to the plan. It seems complex, but the short version is that our interactions must be focused on what the client wants and needs, and not on what we want to learn from him. We should just answer his questions and avoid asking him our questions. Are we clear on that?"

Palidore threw up both hands, surrendering the point. "Absolutely, I agree a hundred percent."

Lynn glanced over again at the monitor and noticed her patient moving slightly. "We'll soon find out about this; it looks like I need to get ready. Do you have a costume?"

"It's in my office."

Lynn smiled. "So, you anticipated my response?"

"I prefer to say that I chose to be prepared," Palidore said, grinning sheepishly.

"Ok then, get changed and meet me back here in five."

***

A short time later, Lynn said: "I'll go in first and you watch the monitor. When you hear me mention 'the doctor will be coming to see you soon,' that's your cue to come in."

"Got it," Palidore said.

Lynn entered the room and took her position in the chair next to the bed to wait for her patient's awakening. His color and complexion looked good; his breathing appeared normal, but somehow his face seemed to have a more mature, confident look today.

Maybe it's the white hair, she thought. Still, just looking at him gave her chills as she wrestled with what seemed to be the impossible: Just inches away from her lay the nation's first president alive after over 200 years in a preserved state. She knew each day her patient would be awake longer, and become more lucid, as effects of the coma drugs in his system began wearing off. She saw her patient begin to stir, then watched him drift back to sleep.

Thirty minutes later, George Washington opened his eyes and looked up at the ornate ceiling. Nothing looked different from the ceiling at home where he lived with Martha. The year, as he remembered, was 1799. His last memory was of being ill, but he felt much better now. Stretching his arms out, he was surprised to see a young woman seated next to his bed. She smiled at him.

"Good morning Mr. Washington." She had intentionally not addressed him as 'Mr. President,' since she did not want to let on that she knew.

"Good morning, Lynn," he responded. Her name had automatically come to him.

"I trust you slept well last night."

But Washington did not respond. He kept looking around the room. Something was different. Something had changed. "Where am I? I've been sick, haven't I?"

Lynn carefully weighed her words. "Well, you've been receiving medical care for quite some time, but I think you are doing very well now. In fact, your doctor, Palidore Montgomery, should be coming in soon." In the monitor room, Palidore recognized his cue and jumped to join them.

"Palidore . . . yes Palidore and I are friends, but I don't believe he is actually my *doctor.* I will, however, be pleased to see him,"

312

His comment caught Lynn by surprise. *How could he know Palidore?*

At that moment, Palidore entered the room and approached the bed. Washington sat up and studied his face.

"Good morning, Mr. Washington, I am Dr. Palidore Montgomery." He offered a hand to shake, but Washington did not take it. Instead, he looked directly into Palidore's eyes and tilted his head.

"*You* are not Doctor Palidore Montgomery. You favor him, but I know the *real* Palidore Montgomery, and you are certainly not him!"

Palidore suddenly realized that Washington was expecting to see his ancestor and quickly responded, "Of course, you are correct. I am not the *same* Palidore Montgomery whom you have known. I just have the same name as he did."

"'Palidore' is not a common name, so forgive me if I have trouble believing you," Washington responded.

Palidore held up one finger as if to say, 'give me a moment,' then bent down, opened his bag, and produced the ancient photograph he had taken from his desk at the last moment while changing his clothes to the 18th-century garb he now wore. He showed the engraving to the man who had just survived a 200-year leap into the future.

"Is this the 'Palidore' you were expecting to see?"

Washington took the photo, studied it, and looked up. "Yes, that is Palidore and his wife, Anabel." He continued to point, "and that is Doctor Marshall Robinson with his wife, Sara; and, of course, that is my wife, Martha." He slowly lowered the engraving to his lap before turning to Lynn. "I'd like to see my wife. Can you please fetch Martha for me?"

Palidore was caught off guard by the request; he had not anticipated this at all. Glancing over at Lynn, he saw her calm response. She was clearly prepared for this request.

"I am sorry, but Mrs. Washington is not here."

Washington handed the framed photograph back to Palidore who was anxious to change the subject.

"So, if you don't mind, sir, I would like to give you a quick checkup." Without waiting for an answer, he took Washington's wrist and began taking a pulse reading. Then he took out a stethoscope and held it in one hand to show the man. "This is a new instrument we use to listen to your lungs. I am going to place it on your chest and your back. If you don't mind, would you please take a deep breath each time I move it?"

The ancient man, newly revived to life, said nothing but followed the routine as Palidore carefully placed the scope in different locations on his chest.

"I am going to place something on your forehead for a moment," Palidore continued. Without showing the item to his patient, he placed a tape thermometer on Washington's forehead and waited for a number to appear before removing it. He made a note on his clipboard. "One more small thing," he said, taking a small object from his pocket which had a small rubber tube attached to it. Placing it on his finger, he kept the battery-powered device in his pocket. He was expecting to be questioned about it, but Washington remained silent, his mind seemed to be elsewhere.

The whole purpose of what Palidore had done so far was more to establish a patient-doctor relationship than actually learn anything he did not already know.

"Well, it looks like you are doing fine."

Lynn was pleased with how things were going until she heard Palidore ask something she didn't want to hear.

"So, how did you come to know my relative, the 'Palidore' in the picture?" the doctor asked.

Lynn shot him a look to kill, *That question is "off-script;" not part of the plan*, she thought. But Palidore was focused on Washington's response.

"I am not sure, but I needed to find something out. Wait a moment . . . I am sure I can remember, just give me a moment." He squinted, trying somehow to force the memory out. Then his eyes lit up.

"It had something to do with Richard . . . Richard Brockwell. Yes, it definitely had to do with him. Yes, his funeral - there was something wrong with his funeral - and he was Dr. Montgomery's patient or wait a minute - maybe he was Dr. Robinson's patient. I am not sure, but something was wrong with his funeral, and I needed information from both doctors."

Lynn noticed perspiration on Washington's face. It had changed color, and she was immediately concerned. She poured a glass of water and placed it into his hand.

"Please take a drink, and don't be too concerned if you experience some difficulty with your memory. That's why we are here - to help you." Washington took a drink and seemed to calm down. Lynn took the glass from him and placed both of his hands in hers. She positioned herself directly in front of him, cutting off his view of Palidore.

"You are doing really well today, but perhaps we should rest a while." The sound of her voice and the touch of her hands seemed to have a calming effect on him, and he laid back down as Lynn continued talking.

"Dr. Montgomery has to leave now, but I will remain here with you for a while longer. Can I get you anything? Are you hungry?"

There was no response. Washington was already asleep.

Chapter 2

"OK, I know, I blew it!" Palidore said as Lynn walked into his office.

"Big time!" she responded. "The plan was not to satisfy *our* curiosity, but to address his."

Palidore waited before responding. "Well, I guess I wanted to get his mind off of wanting to see his wife, and the picture was right there, so it just popped out. I'm sorry, it won't happen again."

"That's right, it won't," Lynn said. "What on earth prompted you to put that photo into your medical bag in the first place?"

"Really, I don't know, I was getting dressed, excited about seeing the president and there was his photo sitting next to my bag. I just instinctively grabbed it and put it in. I don't know why or what I was thinking; it was just a spontaneous act. Then when he accused me of not being the Palidore he knew, I thought the photo would help explain."

Lynn accepted the explanation. "Ok then, but why ask him about how he came to know your ancestor? We agreed to answer *his* questions, not ask ours."

"As soon as I asked the question, I knew I screwed up. You are obviously better at maintaining protocol than I am, but I was just putting the photo away and the question popped out. I was making small talk. I can see we can't put pressure on him. I will try to do better going forward." There was a prolonged silence.

"He wasn't awake long, when do you think he'll be awake again?

Lynn knew Palidore could answer his own question. She audibly sighed. "If he gets excited, or becomes stressed, he'll tire fast. I thought you knew that. In any event, I expect he will sleep a couple of hours at most. He should remain awake longer this time, especially if we don't stress him out or put pressure on him. So, if you don't mind, I'll take the next session with him alone."

"I think that would be good. Yes, yes . . . just you this time." Palidore rose to leave. "I am going to my office now. Please buzz me when he's awake so I can return to the monitor."

***

In less than an hour, he received a buzz on his watch and read the green and white message: "He's awake again, I'm going in." Palidore flew up the stairs to his seat in front of the monitor in time to hear Lynn greet the president.

"Well, I see you're awake again, can I get something for you?" Washington ignored her question choosing to ask one of his own.

"Where am I?"

Lynn calmly responded: "You are in Washington, D.C."

"Good, that's good. What is the date?"

"It's actually July 5th," Lynn replied.

"Oh, did I miss the July 4th celebration?

"I'm afraid you did," Lynn said.

Washington went silent a few moments before saying: "You said it was July 5th, but you didn't mention the year, and that seems to be an intentional omission."

Lynn marveled at his intellect and ability to read between the lines.

"So, what year *is* it?" he persisted.

Lynn knew the moment had arrived. She had prepared for it and was hoping her response would not appear too rehearsed.

"Mr. Washington, before I answer your question, I must tell

317

you that you have been asleep for a very long time and what I am going to tell you is going to be very difficult for you to believe, but we want to be truthful with you at all times. So, to answer your question . . . the year is 2025. That is 226 years since you went into a suspended trance."

Lynn offered nothing more but watched his face for clues as he processed the information. Washington seemed frozen in a moment of time. He moved only his eyes around the room. Then, he sat up and slowly got out of bed. He walked around the room, picking up various objects, appearing to study them before putting each one back down. He then turned and walked back toward Lynn.

Palidore, watched on the monitor and didn't know what to think. He wanted to burst into the room, but knew better, particularly after his last performance. His skin felt clammy although the humidity and air temperature were carefully regulated.

Washington returned to his bed and sat on the edge looking directly into Lynn's eyes.

"So, when you told me that Martha was not here, what you meant was that she is no longer *alive*, didn't you?"

Lynn felt like a witness being grilled by an attorney on a witness stand. Nevertheless, she was able to calmly reply.

"Yes sir, that is correct." She studied Washington's face, watching for any visible reaction to her answer. She found it interesting that Washington did not seem to display outward signs of grief. In fact, his face seemed to lack any discernable expression at all. The only thing Lynn could detect was a forlorn look of resignation. She was certain he had already deduced that it was not just his beloved wife, Martha, who was no longer here, but anyone he had ever known . . . that all were gone.

She wanted to tell him about his faithful servant, Frank, but thought it was too soon as Frank was not out of the woods yet. If something happened to him, she didn't want her patient to have to deal with another sadness right now.

Lynn remained quiet, waiting for him to deal with the reality of all she had told him. She didn't want to hurry the conversation or even change the subject just yet.

Finally, Washington spoke again. "But I clearly heard you say her name. Someone was with you, and you called her, 'Martha', I remember. I couldn't see as I wasn't awake, but I clearly remember what I heard. You were near me and someone else was with you, and you called her 'Martha.' "I tried so hard to speak, to wake up, to reach out. I tried so hard .... and ... my hand, I finally willed it to move . . . I touched her. I'm sure I did."

Lynn remembered the incident well. She and Martha Vaughan were in the room together and after his hand touched her leg, Martha had jumped in surprise. She had bumped into Lynn causing them both to fall on the floor. Later they had even laughed about the incident. Lynn thought it had been just an involuntary movement. She had no idea he had tried to reach out, that it had been intentional.

"What you recall is correct. There was another woman in the room with me, and her name *is* Martha, but she is a different 'Martha.' Her name is Martha Vaughan, and she works here."
Washington absorbed the information without changing his blank, expressionless stare.

"Oh," he said.

Lynn wasn't sure what was next. At the outset of the conversation, she had thought he might try and question the veracity of information she had given him. However, he appeared to accept it all. Now, wanting to reassure him, and move the conversation in a slightly different direction, she spoke again.

"Mr. Washington, we want to help you work through any emotions or doubts you may be experiencing."

Washington turned his head toward her and focused, once again, on her face. "You cannot know the emotions I am experiencing right now, or how to deal with them. Of that I am certain, it is something only I can deal with. However, you can be assured that I no longer have any doubts . . . it is all starting to make sense to me now."

Lynn briefly allowed a questioning look on her normally placid face. Washington saw it.

"I have been telling you, while asleep or 'in a trace' as you say, I have been listening to you for quite some time. Nothing I've heard made sense to me then . . . but now . . . it's all coming into focus, so don't look at me that way." He appeared to be more energized and spoke in a somewhat demanding voice. "I want to see that Dr. Montgomery who was here earlier."

Lynn was surprised by the request, nevertheless, responded calmly. "Actually, he should be here any time now."

Palidore, glued to the monitor, heard his cue from Lynn. Now, he jumped up and bounded into the room to greet his patient, again.

"Mr. Washington, pleased to see you up again."

"Pull up that chair, Doctor, we need to talk," Washington said, gaining his composure. Palidore did as instructed and when he was seated, Washington continued. "I feel I owe you an apology." Palidore gestured that none was necessary, but Washington continued without interruption. "I now realize the photograph you produced likely shows a distant relative of yours. I am beginning to remember things rather vividly now, and I want you to hear this. I think it will be most fascinating to you."

Both Palidore and Lynn were riveted in anticipation of what President George Washington was about to say. . .

***

IF YOU'VE ENJOYED THIS SNEAK PEAK INTO

BOOK 2 OF THE POTUS 1 SERIES

TRANSFORMING POTUS 1

by GIL HUDSON

PRE-ORDER IT NOW ON AMAZON.COM.

About the Author

Gil Hudson

Gil Hudson is a retired attorney from Virginia who now resides in The Villages, Florida with his wife of 52 years, Aletha Hudson. They have two sons and five grandchildren.

Having followed politics for most of his life and being a delegate to the 1980 Republican Party Convention that nominated Ronald Reagan, he often wondered how our forefathers might view the present state of affairs in our country today.

This query inspired him to consider writing an historical fiction depicting how it would be if George Washington could be revived. He ran the idea for the book by his niece, Jenny Hale, a nationally known best-selling author, and she encouraged him to write it. With her encouragement, he was persuaded to undertake the work.

After spending countless hours researching the first president, he tapped his legal writing skills and vivid imagination. The work has now become a planned series of books. Underlying subplots, combined with the intrigue of seeing how our historic forefather would react to present-day problems and challenges, makes the story a compelling read.

Made in the USA
Columbia, SC
17 December 2021

51888799R00183